Readers everyw...
the Danforths of Lancashire.

Praise for *Ashton Park*...

"The first installment of Pura's The Danforths of Lancashire series intro-
duces the inhabitants of Ashton Park, a centuries-old manor near the shores
of northwest England. Tensions of the early 20th century, including WWI
and unrest in Ireland and Palestine, create a backdrop for a tale rife with sus-
pense and emotional twists as the large, extended Danforth family encoun-
ters its share of romance, human tragedy, and skullduggery. Sir William
and Lady Elizabeth and their brood of independent-minded daughters and
gallant sons have their honor tested, the bonds of family strained, and the
goodness of God questioned. Amid trials and treachery, Pura draws poi-
gnant exhibitions of integrity, staunch lessons in forgiveness, and tender
pictures of love and devotion...a most enjoyable introduction to an intrigu-
ing family saga."

Publisher's Weekly

"Reading *Ashton Park*. Oh my. Your best writing ever! I like the way you tie
in history with it in a clear way...Is there another one after Downton, I mean
Ashton?"

Karen Anna Vogel, author of The Amish Knitting Circle series

"Just finished reading Ashton Park...LOVED IT!!!!!!!!!!!! Can't wait for the
next installment of the series."

Carolea from Nova Scotia, Canada

"This was an amazing book! I could not put it down. It had well-developed
characters, interesting storylines, and a host of well-described landscapes. The
relationships between characters was complex and real not namby-pamby.
I wanted to 'see' the castle and the ash trees. I could feel the breeze through
them. This author is on the order of Jane Austen but for our time...I would
highly recommend this book and hope to see it in a mini-series or movie."

Reviewer on CBD.com

THE DANFORTHS OF LANCASHIRE

BENEATH THE DOVER SKY

MURRAY PURA

HARVEST HOUSE PUBLISHERS
EUGENE, OREGON

Cover photos © Chris Garborg; Bigstock/elenathewise, Waynehowes

Cover by Garborg Design Works, Savage, Minnesota

BENEATH THE DOVER SKY
Book 2 of The Danforths of Lancashire series
Copyright © 2013 by Murray Pura
Published by Harvest House Publishers
Eugene, Oregon 97402
www.harvesthousepublishers.com

Library of Congress Cataloging-in-Publication Data
Pura, Murray
Beneath the Dover sky / Murray Pura.
    p. cm. — (The Danforths of Lancashire ; bk. 2)
ISBN 978-0-7369-5288-0 (pbk.)
ISBN 978-0-7369-5289-7 (eBook)
1. Aristocracy (social classes)—England—History—20th century—Fiction. 2. Social classes—England—History—20th century—Fiction. 3. Lancashire (England)—Fiction. 4. Domestic fiction. I. Title.
PR9199.4.P87B46 2013
813'.6—dc23
                                                                            2013001581

Printed in the United States of America

13 14 15 16 17 18 19 20 / LB-JH / 10 9 8 7 6 5 4 3 2 1

*For Debbie and Brian
and Larry and Karen.
Family through the blessing of marriage
Family through the blessing of Christ.*

ACKNOWLEDGMENTS

My biggest thanks go to Nick Harrison, who not only worked on this project with me but really inspired it with his love of the genre and of England. Thanks as always to the Harvest House crew who worked on the editing, marketing, book cover, etc. People like Barb Gordon, Kim Moore, Shane White, Katie Lane, and Laura Knudson. Thanks to my family who put up with the long hours of typing and word processing and creating. And thanks to my great dog Alaska, who stuck by my side when I wrote this book in our backyard last summer and fall. He was always there and made sure I never wrote alone.

MAP OF DOVER SKY

THE McPHAILS

DRY STONE FENCE

N
W   E
S

THE KNIGHTS

PATH

SWAN POND

PATH

PATH

STREAM

DOVER SKY

MAIN ROAD

WILLOW TREES

APPLE TREES

OAK TREES

LANE

CAVE

DRY WELL

DRY STONE FENCE

THE GILLANS

THE CHARACTERS

William Danforth—Lord Preston, Marquess of Preston; husband to Lady Elizabeth; father; Member of Parliament (MP); head of Ashton Park, the family estate in Lancashire, as well as Dover Sky, the family summer home in the south of England
Elizabeth Danforth—Lady Preston; William's wife; mother

Sir Arthur—Lady Elizabeth's father
Lady Grace—Lord William's mother

Edward Danforth—William and Elizabeth's eldest son
Charlotte Danforth—Edward's wife; former employee at Dover Sky
Owen—their eldest son; **Colm**—their youngest son

Kipp Danforth—William and Elizabeth's middle son; pilot
Christelle Danforth—Kipp's wife; French
Matthew—their son

Robbie Danforth—William and Elizabeth's youngest son; serves in British Army
Shannon Danforth—Robbie's wife; Irish
Patricia Claire—their daughter

Jeremiah (Jeremy) Sweet—Anglican clergyman, married to Emma
Emma Danforth Sweet—William and Elizabeth's daughter; married to Jeremy
Peter and James—their fraternal twins; **Billy**—their youngest son

Catherine Danforth Moore—William and Elizabeth's daughter; widow of Albert
Sean–her son

Michael Woodhaven IV—American; pilot; married to Libby

Libby Danforth Woodhaven—daughter of William and Elizabeth; married to Michael

Jane—their daughter

Montgomery—Libby's maid; American

Ben Whitecross—pilot; Victoria Cross recipient (WWI); former employee at Ashton Park; married to Victoria

Victoria Danforth Whitecross—youngest daughter of William and Elizabeth; married to Ben

Ramsay—their eldest son; **Tim**—their youngest son

Calvert Harrison—groundskeeper at Dover Sky; married to Holly

Holly Danforth Harrison—William's sister; married to Harrison

Lady Caroline Scarborough—daughter of Danforth family friends Lord Francis and Lady Madeleine Scarborough; longtime friend of Kipp Danforth

Charles—her son

Tavy—butler

Skitt—butler and groundskeeper at Dover Sky

Norah Cole, Sally, Harriet, Nancy, Bev—servants at Dover Sky

Mrs Longstaff—head cook

Fairburn—groundskeeper

Baron Gerard von Isenburg—Danforth family friend; German

Albrecht Hartmann—theologian and professor; German

Terrence Fordyce—Royal Navy officer; serves on *HMS Hood*

Tanner Buchanan—nemesis of Danforth family; MP

June, 1924
Dover Sky estate, Southern England

"All right, Father, you can open your eyes now."

"Are you sure?"

"Quite sure."

"Very well then."

The older man in the back cockpit of the biplane took a look, adjusted his goggles, looked a second time, and laughed. "I've never even seen them by boat!" he shouted. "Never mind by air!"

The pilot turned his head and leaned back. "The gulls see this every day, Father. Not so bad a life, is it? Soar, glide, dive for fish—the white cliffs of Dover for your world."

"The white cliffs and the blue sea and sky. Thank you, my boy, thank you. This is quite the view."

"An early birthday present."

"Is that what this is? It's very early then. The date's over a month away."

The pilot grinned. "I didn't want to miss this chance. My plan was to do something special for you. It's not every day a man turns sixty."

The older man snorted. "I thank God it isn't or I'd have been a relic by the time I was twenty, Kipp."

"You look terrific, Dad."

"Thank you, my boy. For sixty I suppose I'm not so bad off. I can keep up with the grandchildren, and my eyes are still like a hawk's."

The plane swooped over the high, chalk cliffs and the wheeling white gulls. Late June sunlight made the whitecaps in the English Channel beneath the aircraft leap with a brightness the older man never saw on land. The blue sky and sea seemed that much deeper by contrast. He took it all in, white on white on blue, thanked God, and suddenly put his hands outside the cockpit, letting his fingers trail through the swift flow of air as if he were dangling them in a stream of water.

"There's Dover Sky, Father!"

The plane banked over long, green fields and the town of Dover, with its miniature buildings and streets and cars. Further out in the countryside, set solidly on a hill, was a house of windows and verandas and pillars that seemed whiter than the whitecaps and the white cliffs, taking the day's light into its walls and sending it back twice as strong so that the two men in the biplane had to squint.

The older man reached forward and tapped his son on the shoulder of his leather flight jacket. "I've never seen it look so lovely."

"It's a diamond from up here, an absolute gem."

"Whose car is that by the house? Ours is not half so long."

"I don't know, but let's take a closer look."

Kipp put the plane into a dive.

"My boy, my boy, you are not going to buzz the house?"

"Mum doesn't mind."

"But we must have guests if that strange car is there."

"Well, now we'll find out who they are."

They roared over the house. The older man recognized his wife, Elizabeth, his daughter Catherine and her son, Sean, and Norah Cole, their maid. There was also a tall, narrow figure with a sweeping moustache and a ramrod straight back.

"No one ran for cover, Dad. That's a good sign."

"I did not expect my family to run…or my servants. They are used to airplanes. And now that I see who our guest is, I wouldn't expect him to run either."

"Who is it? The car is a Mercedes Benz 400K, by the way. This year's model. Not cheap."

"Yes, the baron would drive a vehicle like that. Or rather, like me, have it driven for him."

"Baron? Which baron?"

"Von Isenburg. Gerard von Isenburg. A good chap. He gave us our German shepherds before the war."

"Has he come to bring us new ones?"

"I pray not. Gladstone and Wellington have years in them yet."

"Right. Here we go. Coming in for a landing. Hang on."

"Your son still loves the flying, doesn't he, Lady Preston?"

"Please, baron. I'm Elizabeth to you. It's a relief to hear someone call me by my Christian name now and then."

Baron von Isenburg inclined his head slightly. "As you wish. But then I must insist in return that you use my Christian name."

"I'm happy to do so, Gerard. Yes, our Kipp has never lost his love for airplanes and the sky."

The two of them watched the biplane land in a field beyond the house.

"William will be surprised to see you," Lady Preston said as the plane came to a stop, propeller whirling. "Surprised and pleased. It has been altogether too long. The war's been over for years. We really ought to have had you up to Ashton Park before this."

"Now is soon enough. I have much to share. And to tell you the truth, I prefer visiting at Dover Sky." He reached down and scratched behind the ears of the two blonde German shepherds who sat on their haunches beside him, tails slowly swishing as soon as he touched their heads.

"Should I be insulted at that remark, Gerard? What on earth is the matter with Ashton Park?"

"There's nothing wrong with it. I simply find it too, well, baronial. I see so much of that in Germany. Dover Sky is quite different—clean, white, shining like jasper. I much prefer it to your Lancashire estate."

"I see. So did you time your visit so it would coincide with our summer escape to Kent?"

The baron laughed and leaned on a cane with a silver pommel. "I am not so much of a schemer. I had a person to visit at Westminster, and a friend asked me to accompany him to England."

"I only see your chauffeur with you."

"No, Albrecht is not with us today. He hopes to come by later in the week, if you can spare a room."

"Spare a room?" Lady Preston glanced back at the manor. "What room can't we spare? Only Catherine came down for the summer with her boy. The others are too busy up north with their work and their families."

"A shame."

"We'll see them all for William's sixtieth birthday celebration at the end of July. Until then it shall be rather quiet...too quiet. We shall be glad to have a visit from your friend."

"I'll wire him. He'll be most grateful. He's wanted to meet your husband for some time."

"Really? Is he in politics?"

"Not at all. Albrecht is a theologian. He admires William's Christian convictions."

"Ah." Lady Preston waved as the biplane took off without her husband in it. "There goes Kipp. I'm sorry you two couldn't meet. He was just a boy when you last saw him. He has the Royal Mail for Liverpool and Manchester to deliver today."

The baron watched the plane grow smaller and more distant. "Another time. I am sure of it."

"Ah, Gerard! I spotted you when we flew over the house," William said before kissing his wife on the cheek. "We circled the cliffs, Elizabeth. It was marvelous."

"The way you came at us here on the ground, I'm glad you didn't fly into them."

"Ha!" William said with a smile.

"Lord Preston." The baron clicked his heels together. "It's wonderful to see you again after so many years. Yes, I thought you meant to pluck the hat off my head, your plane dove in so low."

"I very nearly could have done it."

The two men smiled and shook hands vigorously.

"What brings you to England, Gerard?"

"As I was telling your wife, Lord Preston, I had a person to see in—"

"William," interrupted Lord Preston. "You know I wish you to continue to call me William...or *Vilhelm,* if you prefer. I hear Lord Preston quite enough."

The baron bowed. "As you wish. I congratulate you on your new title Marquess of Preston."

Lord Preston nodded. "Thank you. Your cable of last summer was much appreciated. But now tell us why you are here. And how did you get that long, black Mercedes across the Channel?"

"Well, I have my own boat—a barge, really—and it could probably carry three of these. As for my visit, I had a man to see in Westminster."

"Westminster? Someone in the government?"

The baron held up a hand. "Over brandy and cigars?"

Lord Preston snorted. "You and your brandy and cigars. I'll have my tea while you make smoke." He smiled and knelt to pet his dogs. "So, just a man in Westminster to see, is that it? A mystery man?"

"Well, as I was telling your wife, I accompanied a friend here by the name of Albrecht Hartmann. He is a professor at Tubingen...a theologian."

"Is he? Wonderful, wonderful! Has he written anything I may have read?"

"He has written several books that have been well received. Alas, only one of them has been translated into English—and American English at that."

"I can tolerate American English. We now have a Yank in the family, you know. Married my daughter Libby. Do you remember little ginger-haired Libby? The pair are in the United States right now, though we hope to see them back here this fall or winter."

"Splendid. If you wish I can give you a copy of the book and you might be able to read some of the chapters before Albrecht arrives."

Lord Preston stood up. "He is coming to Dover Sky?"

Lady Preston put her arm through his. "I assured Gerard we had plenty of room."

"Plenty of room? I should say we have since our children and their spouses have abandoned us...but for Catherine." Lord Preston glanced about. "Have you seen her yet, Gerard? She was so young in 1911."

"He's only just arrived, William," said Lady Preston. "Catherine's off on a walk with Sean. She can meet Gerard at the evening meal."

"Why, I saw her from the plane. She was close by."

"I expect she was, but she's probably drifted since then. You know her moods."

"Yes, of course."

The baron's face behind his moustache grew somber, his eyes darkening. "My condolences once again. Her husband's death was a shock. Civil wars are always the worst for shedding blood."

Lady Elizabeth put a hand on his arm. "The flowers you sent were beautiful, Gerard. Quite the largest arrangement we received. Even the king noticed them."

"A small thing. One always wishes one could do more."

"Catherine will be glad to see you. I have no doubt of it. But she is a bit lost these days. She left Belfast to live at Ashton Park, but she doesn't seem content with us there either. Perhaps it's too lively for her with so many of her siblings having houses nearby. We are hoping a peaceful summer at Dover Sky will help."

"I pray so." The baron stared at the apple trees at the side of the manor. "You never stop worrying about your children. No, never. So much can happen in a lifetime."

"I know, Gerard." She gently squeezed his arm. "I'm sorry for what you've been through."

"Now, mind you attend, young Master Skitt. Next summer you'll be handling matters on your own."

Skitt looked at the map Fairburn was sketching. "I thought the estate here was just the land on the hill."

"A common misconception." The stocky man with a ginger-colored beard, moustache, and sideburns continued to draw, the pencil clutched in his red, stubby fingers. "Of course it's nothing like Ashton Park, but we have a hundred acres running east, west, north, and south. The swans are here—you must pay attention, Master Skitt. There have been poachers, and the police'll not mind if you nab 'em."

Skitt was glancing all about him as the two men sat on a boulder near a narrow stream. "I've not been here before, Mister Fairburn."

"We'll have a long walk today and get you acquainted with the lie of the land. But you must memorize this map. See—" Fairburn made several sharp strokes with a piece of charcoal he yanked from the pocket of his tweed coat. "I've been working on a dry stone fence for years to mark off our boundaries. The Gillans are to the south—good people, salt of the earth. To the east is the main road into Dover. Those fences are done. Of course I'm connecting 'em all together so Dover Sky's in an enclosure, like. So those two have met up. And the east fence is linked with the north fence and the McPhails—rogues, that lot, every last one of them. I've toyed with pointing cannon in their direction, I tell ye. I wouldn't be surprised if they're the ones poaching the swans and geese and deer. I've built that fence a foot or two higher on account of their general nastiness. Now to the west are the Knights—fine people, handsome daughters, no sons. That's the fence we need to complete before the leaves turn in September or October."

Skitt pointed to a spot on the map. "What's that?"

"Grove of oak trees. None near as old as any in Lancashire."

"And that?"

"An old well. We've boarded over the top so's a child won't fall in. The well's dry."

"And this here?"

"A cave. The Lord only knows how long that's been there. Found an ancient yew bow in it fifteen years back. The sinew was gone—y'know, the bowstring—but the wood was sturdy enough. I have it in me

groundskeeper's hut if you'd like to see it. Now, by the Gillans' property
—Lad, lad, where's your head at this time?"

"It's Cathy—I mean Lady Catherine."

Fairburn craned his neck. "Where?"

"Coming up the slope from the swans."

Fairburn saw her. "Tall and dark. I remember her. How is she then?"

"Why, for long stretches she's right as rain. Then a black mood just
takes over, and she's down in the dumps for a good spell."

"A cruel fate, no mistake. So young and a widow with a young boy
to raise. How old is he now?"

"About fourteen months."

"Has she shown any interest in, well, meeting another man who can
be a father to the lad and a good husband to her?"

"They bring lords and dukes and whatnots 'round to Ashton Park
on a regular basis to meet her. She's taken no interest in any of them.
Polite enough to 'em, she's all of that, still a lady, but never encourages
any of the men to call again."

They watched Catherine make her way towards them. Sean was
asleep in her arms.

Fairburn smoothed down his moustache quickly. "I don't recall her
being so comely."

"She's lost a good deal of weight since her husband's death. And she's
let her hair grow as long as the Thames. That's what you notice."

"It's glossy-black as a raven's wing."

Skitt nodded. "Aye."

Catherine glanced up and saw them on the boulder. She flashed a
smile. "Gentlemen, excuse me. I didn't notice you there."

Skitt and Fairburn got to their feet and whipped the flat tweed caps
from their heads.

"Ma'am," Fairburn greeted.

"Lady Catherine," said Skitt.

"Oh Skitt, Lady Catherine—that's too much for down here, isn't it?
We're hundreds of miles from Ashton Park."

"It comes to you with your father's title. It's a question of respect.
Imagine if your mother caught me calling you just plain Catherine."

"*Just plain Catherine?* Now that does sound drab, doesn't it?" She smiled at Fairburn. "Mum tells me this is your last summer with us."

Fairburn clutched at his cap in his hand. "That's so, m'lady. I'll be serving an English family in the south of France. Old friends of your father and mother, y'see, and in a bit of a bind for a competent grounds-keeper."

"Well, you'll certainly fit the bill. When do you take up your new post?"

"In November, Lady Catherine. After I've set everything to rights at Dover Sky, and young Master Skitt here's fairly squared away."

"I'm so glad we have you for a final summer."

"Thank you, m'lady. I'm grateful as well."

Catherine lifted Sean higher on her shoulder. "I'll see you gentlemen later then. I'm just going to get my boy here to his bed."

Skitt reached out with his hands. "I can help you with him."

"Thank you, Skitt, but I can manage. Ta."

The two men watched her carry on up the slope towards the house. "How long do you reckon she'll remain unwed?" asked Fairburn.

"Not long," responded Skitt. "You see she's pleasant enough despite everything. Ah, to be a lord and win her hand…"

Fairburn erupted in a laugh that sounded like coal rumbling down a chute. He planted his cap back firmly on his head. "We really are day-dreamin' today, aren't we, lad? Enough with this map for now. Y'need something to get the steam out of your system. Ever built a dry stone fence? No mortar a'tall?"

"No, I haven't."

"Today's the day then. Right. Let's head over to our property line with the Knights to the west."

Why do men look at me now? I'm so used to them staring at Victoria. Or my brothers' wives Charlotte and Christelle. What has happened? Do they feel sorry for me? Does my being a widow make them feel like they want to take care of me? Well away from Skitt and Fairburn and still distant from the house, Catherine spoke out loud. She glanced down at young Sean cradled in her arms. "It takes all the energy I have to put up a cheerful front. God, You know I can't do any more than that. When I think of loving another man I simply get weary. I don't have it in me. Maybe five years from now…or ten…but not now. Not yet." *Thank goodness the baron is an old man. He will not gape at me and pester me like the sons of lords do at Ashton Park.*

"There. Steak and kidney pie. They've all turned out perfect. Lord Preston will be happy with that." The short, round woman with curly hair the color of rust glanced about her. "Norah Cole? Sally? Where have you got to?"

Norah rushed into the kitchen. "Just setting out the bread and butter, Mrs. Longstaff."

"And the crystal? You've laid out the crystal as I asked? He's a baron, you know."

"And a German."

Mrs. Longstaff clicked her tongue. "Never you mind about that. The war's over and done with years ago. He's paid a price himself, you know. Two sons killed fighting the Russians. His wife dead of a cancer. Only the one daughter left. Have some Christian charity."

Norah tilted up her chin. "All right."

"In any case, he is an old friend of the Danforth family, and so was his father and his father's father. That's reason enough to treat him with a good measure of grace and respect."

"Yes, Mrs. Longstaff."

"And he gave Lord Preston those beautiful dogs."

"Yes, ma'am."

"Where's Sally got to?"

"In the wine cellar with Tavy. He's choosing a red, and she's choosing a white."

"Well, run and tell them to make up their minds and be done with it. I'm calling the Danforths to tea in five minutes. Help me with the pies, love. One to a plate. Mind you, Sir William—Lord Preston, I should say—be sure he gets two."

"Yes, ma'am."

Each of them picked up a wooden tray of the steaming pies and headed up a ramp to the dining room. Mrs. Longstaff's eyes took in everything as she placed pies at each place setting.

"You've remembered the high chair for Sean? Good. And you've got Lord Preston's knives and forks and spoons arranged for his left hand. Now did you know the baron is left-handed, as well?"

"I didn't."

"I thought I'd mentioned it. No matter. Only takes a moment." She moved the baron's cutlery around. "There. And we have spare pies in the oven just in case."

"You have some for our men?"

"For Tavy and Fairburn? 'Course I do."

"And young Skitt? He's a growing boy."

Mrs. Longstaff chuckled. "Boy? I daresay he's a man now, Norah Cole. You watch out for him this summer."

Norah sniffed. "I'm old enough to be his mother."

"His mother?" Mrs. Longstaff raised her eyebrows.

"Well, an older sister then. There'll be no to-do between the pair of us, I assure you."

The dining hall shimmered with light from a crystal chandelier that made all the crystal goblets, glasses, and side plates dance. The baron got to his feet after grace and raised his wineglass in a toast. "To my hosts! May nothing ever separate our families. Not war, not peace. God bless you all."

"Hear, hear!" Lord Preston rose. "May I return the blessing? In my best German? *Gott erhalte unsere Familien in der Einheit—für immer!* I think I have that right, Baron."

The baron bowed. "Excellent. Unity forever. I shall drink to that." He sipped from his glass of red wine and sat down. "Good English food, *ja?*"

"Indeed. Steak and kidney pie. Mushy peas. Fried potatoes and tomatoes. All a man needs, Gerard."

"I think so." He placed a white napkin in his lap and smiled at

Catherine and her toddler. "You look wonderful, Lady Catherine. How is your health?"

Catherine returned the smile as she broke open her piecrust with a fork. "I am very well, Baron. Thank you for asking."

"Your boy is coming along well."

She smiled at Sean, who was stuffing mushy peas in his mouth with his hand. "He is, isn't he?"

"His looks seem to favor you."

"People say that. But in some of his mannerisms he reminds me of his father. Such as now."

Her father and mother and the baron laughed.

Catherine drank from her glass of water. "I suppose we will find out who he really takes after by the time he is eleven or twelve."

The baron chewed and swallowed while shaking his head. "Oh, much before that, my dear. Believe me, much before that."

The household staff sat in the kitchen and ate together.

"This is right good, Mrs. Longstaff," said Skitt with his mouth full. "Is there much more of it?"

She watched him eat. "If the baron doesn't want seconds and Lord Preston is content with two, there should be plenty left over."

"That's good news."

"And there's plenty of bread and butter and yesterday's coney stew if the pies are gone."

"The rabbit stew? It wasn't all eaten?"

"Not a'tall."

"We were building a fence you see—dry stone—no mortar. Had to fit them tight together just so. Fairburn wanted to get it all done today—"

Fairburn bit into a heel of dark bread. "I haven't had decent help in years. I didn't want to waste the opportunity."

"Which fence is that?" asked Sally.

"We're bounding the property. East, south, and north are done. So this is to the west."

Tavy wiped the corners of his mouth clear of gravy. "What family is that? To the west?"

"The Knights."

"Short chap? Striking daughters twice his height?"

"That's the one."

"Have they been to Dover Sky for tea? Lady Preston wants me to put together a guest list. She finds the manor altogether too quiet without the other family members."

Fairburn dug into his pie. "Hmm. Years ago they've been, but not recently. It wouldn't be a bad idea. And the Gillans should be invited over as well. It pays to cultivate good neighbors in the country."

"Will there be a ball?" asked Norah. "I've never been to one here."

Fairburn grunted. "There are balls and balls. Servants can't attend all of them. But if they have a servants' ball, well then you're in."

"Certainly. It's the same up north."

Sally grinned and swayed back and forth in her seat. "I'd love that."

"Can I suggest it to his lord?" asked Norah.

"Oh no." Tavy shook his head. "It wouldn't be proper."

"Isn't anyone allowed to put a bug in his ear?"

Mrs. Longstaff got up and fetched another pie to the table, putting it down in front of Skitt. "There you go." She wiped her hands on her apron. "I'll drop a hint, if you like, to her ladyship. She's so lonely down here this summer I'm sure she'll agree to it."

Norah's face gleamed. "Now wouldn't that be something, Sally? A grand ball and us dolled up in the latest fashions from London and Paris."

Sally cocked her head to one side and fluttered her eyelids, striking a pose. "Rahlly, my dahling, I should find that enchanting."

Norah had forgotten her food. "Neighbors from north, south, east, and west. *Men* from north, south, east, and west."

"Never from the north," rumbled Fairburn. "Never any men from the north, my dear."

"Why not?"

"The McPhails are ugly as rubbish bins. Brute beasts. And they cannot dance." He looked at Norah, who was staring at him in surprise. "Depend upon it, Miss Cole. They would trample you into marmalade with their monstrous great feet."

"So do you honestly want brandy, Gerard?"

"I do."

Lord Preston placed a short, fat bottle on the table in the library with a thump. "There you are."

"Excellent." The baron brought out a cigar from the inside pocket of his suit jacket. "I know you don't indulge, Vilhelm, but may I?"

Lord Preston waved his hand and took a seat in a white wicker chair. "Be my guest. I opened all four windows in preparation."

"*Danke.*" Gerard slipped a cutter out of his pocket, snipped off the end of his cigar, placed the cigar in his mouth, and lit it. He sat near a window and across the room from Lord Preston. "Let me say that your daughter looks wonderful, Vilhelm. It is good to see her recovering so well."

Lord Preston nodded. "It will be two years this December. Her mother and I are anxious she begin to develop a new life for herself. Physically she seems to be doing better, but in her spirit? She covers up well, but she has a long way to go. We pray without ceasing for her, of course. If only one decent man would catch her interest…but we have yet to see it." He drummed his fingers on the arm of his chair. "Do you have that book for me? The one written by your friend?"

"It is in my room. I will drop it off at your door at bedtime."

"Very good. What is his theme?"

"The suffering Savior. He relates how Christ's sufferings establish a unique bond between the human race and God. That He has embodied the pain of His creation, not only of men and women, but of everything God has made. Because of this, He can never be distant or aloof to our struggles because they are in Him too."

"I should very much like to read that. When will your friend be joining us?"

"I wired him to join us Friday night or Saturday. He has his own car, and I'm confident he'll be able to find the estate."

"How did you get the telegram out?"

The baron turned his head and blew a stream of smoke out the window. "My chauffeur took it into Dover."

"Has your man eaten?"

"Your cook put a plate together for him, and he ate in his room. He's a bit of a loner, so he was quite happy with that." He got up. "I've forgotten my brandy." He went to the table, turned a brandy snifter right side up, and poured several ounces from the bottle into the glass. "Albrecht is at Oxford today. He's already been to Cambridge. He has guest lectures at Manchester and Liverpool as well." The baron took his glass to his seat. "I think I mentioned he teaches at Tubingen?"

"Yes."

"Professor of Protestant Theology."

"And you a good Catholic, Gerard."

"Appearances and history to the contrary, the two are not mutually exclusive."

"Hmm. How are things in Germany?"

The baron shrugged. "Not as bad as 1919 or last year. Inflation has been high. So has unemployment. We see some signs of improvement now, but the terms of the treaty were too harsh, Vilhelm."

"I know it. You've read my speeches in *Hansard*. I felt the same way about Ireland in 1916. I argued for magnanimity then, and I argued it for Germany after the armistice. Each time I was ignored."

"The reparation payments are absurd. When we asked for a reprieve, the French refused and sent their troops to occupy the Ruhr in '22. The German workers went on strike so that Paris could not make money off them. Berlin supported the workers while they were on strike. You remember?"

"Yes."

"The new chancellor of Germany came into power last summer. He agreed to resume the reparation payments to France and ordered the workers in the Ruhr to end their strike. There was a great deal of anger at this. He had to declare a state of emergency. Bavaria in particular refused to obey his orders."

Lord Preston nodded. "Certainly we were preoccupied with our own family matters in 1923, but I read the newspapers."

The baron leaned forward in his chair, brandy in one hand, cigar in the other. "When a situation becomes black as night—a night that has little or no hope of dawn—people become desperate for a savior. One they can see in front of them with their own eyes. They look for a man who will take control and fix everything. They don't care how. They just want light at the end of the tunnel regardless of how it is provided."

Lord Preston drummed his fingers again. "Like Mussolini marching on Rome and taking over in '22?"

The baron lifted his glass. "Exactly like that. You've heard of this Hitler fellow?"

"No."

"He tried to take over the government last fall. He and a group of thugs now called the Nazi Party. There was a great deal of furor over ending the Ruhr strike and resuming payments to France, and Adolph Hitler took advantage of that. He attempted to kidnap the rulers in Bavaria because he felt they were weakening in their opposition to the French and to the German chancellor. He stormed into a beer hall where they were meeting, waved a gun, and demanded they join his revolution to overthrow the chancellor, defy France, and march on Berlin as Mussolini had marched on Rome."

"What happened to him?"

"He was arrested and sentenced to prison for five years. We should not see him out again until 1928. But I don't think Germany will be much better off in five years. That worries me because I'm sure he'll try to take advantage of a black situation in '28 just as he did in '23."

"He may change, Gerard. Men change in prison."

"Or become even more fanatical and hard-hearted. I have discovered he is dictating a book while he is behind bars. The first volume is due to be published early next year."

"What is it about?"

The German inhaled on his cigar. "His ideology, his beliefs, his politics. I'm afraid he will gain a great following if the book touches on any of Germany's raw nerves. Others dismiss him, but I don't. A few of your people in Westminster don't either."

"Who are you seeing in London?"

"I'm not at liberty to say."

Lord Preston nodded. "What do you want of me?"

"I am hoping you will become directly involved in keeping Herr Hitler in prison. Or directly involved in preventing him from trying to seize power again. We must have your help."

"There is little I can do about the internal affairs of another country."

"We must figure out together what we can or cannot do."

"Baron—"

"Lord Preston." The baron's eyes were an icy-gray that cut through the haze of cigar smoke. "Are you willing to risk another war if this man gains control of Berlin just as Mussolini has gained control over Rome?"

June, 1924

Catherine noticed that the sporty red car had come up the drive to their house a second time, stopped, and was sitting there. The wide brim of her sunbonnet shielded her eyes from the afternoon sun so she could see the driver clearly since he had the top of the car down. He was young and clean-shaven. He had light-brown hair, a red woolen scarf about his neck, and brown leather gloves on his hands. He was wearing a brown leather jacket and dark sunglasses. The man gazed in her direction. Then he turned the car around and headed back to the main road. It was easy to spot him speeding south to Dover because all the other cars were dark in color.

I wonder what he's looking for? Catherine thought as she bent down and continued to pinch dead roses off their stalks. The manor was surrounded by white roses of different varieties. While Sean had his nap, she'd decided to pull on gloves and get rid of the brown-edged blossoms that detracted from the overall appearance of the bushes. She placed the dead ones in a basket that hung off her arm. The basket was almost full.

In what seemed like only moments later, she heard the roar of an engine. She turned quickly when a man's voice called out, "Hello? Hello?"

The red car was almost at the house again, and the driver was waving to her and calling as the car slowed to a stop by the rosebush she was working on.

"I'm terribly sorry."

His English was accented in a similar fashion to the baron's—not exactly, she noticed, but very close.

"You must think it odd to see me approach your house and then drive away again. I apologize for that. It appears I'm lost. Can you help?"

Catherine set down her basket and pulled off her white cotton gardening gloves. "I'll certainly try." She walked up to the car, tugging at the bow that held her sunbonnet in place. "What or who are you looking for?" Her bonnet finally came off, and her long, black hair, unpinned, came tumbling down over her shoulders as she shook her head to free it.

The driver stared at her and stumbled over his words. "I'm…well… I'm not sure…"

She was puzzled. "You're not sure what or who you're looking for?"

"I–I didn't think—I didn't think a young woman like yourself—I– I didn't know you were young, you see…"

"What?"

He took off his sunglasses. His brown eyes were almost golden in the sunlight. "Excuse me. I'm babbling. I thought you were an older woman, that's all."

Catherine felt a sudden rush of heat as his eyes remained on her. It astonished her. "Oh. Is the person you're looking for older?"

"An older woman? Not at all. I'm much happier to have found you." He put up his gloved hands. "Forgive me. I'm sure I'm making little sense. If you could direct me to Dover Sky, I'll be on my way and leave you to your rosebushes. They're lovely, by the way."

"You're looking for Dover Sky?"

"Have I got the name right? Isn't there a summer estate roundabouts that goes by that? It belongs to the Danforth family. You must have heard of the Danforth family. Lord and Lady Preston?"

Catherine stared at him and began to laugh. "Why, this is Dover Sky. This is the Danforth summer home."

"It is? You mean this is the right place and you're part of it?"

She felt a blush coming up from her neck at his burst of enthusiasm. "I expect I am. I'm Lord and Lady Preston's daughter Catherine."

"Catherine. What a wonderful name. So you're not the wife? You're not Lady Preston?"

"I am not."

"What a relief."

"Really?"

She saw his eyes glance at her left hand.

"I'm Albrecht. Albrecht Hartmann. Please call me by my first name—Albrecht."

"Ah, the baron's friend. The theologian."

"Has he been talking about me?" He turned off the engine. "Somehow I had the idea in my head the house would be blue. You know, a summer blue like the sky over Dover in fair weather."

"No." She smiled. "White like the cliffs."

"I see that." He opened the car door and stepped out. "Pardon me. How do I address you? You are the daughter of an English marquess?"

"Believe me, I'm quite happy with Catherine."

"But if this were a formal occasion?"

"A formal occasion?"

"A ball. A concert. An affair at Westminster. How would I be expected to address you?"

"Lady Catherine, I suppose."

He reached out his hand. Without thinking, she put hers in it and he raised it to his lips. "Then Lady Catherine it is. I'm so pleased to make your acquaintance."

"Thank you. Do you...do you have any title I should address you by?"

"Well, professor, I suppose. But I'd rather you didn't. This is the summer holiday, after all, and you are not one of my students."

"Doctor then?"

He shook his head. "Not yet. I have master's degrees in divinity and theology. Those will have to suffice for now."

"So I may call you Master Hartmann?"

"Oh no! Please don't. I much prefer hearing Albrecht roll off your—excuse me, but I must say it—your perfect lips."

The blush expanded from her neck into her cheeks and around her eyes. "My goodness, thank you, Albrecht. *Danke schön.* That's very kind. But it doesn't seem fair that I am free to call you Albrecht while you must go about putting *lady* in front of my name every time you wish to use it."

"I wouldn't want anyone to think I was treating you with any sort of disrespect. What if I call you Catherine when it is just the two of us and Lady Catherine if other people are around?"

"I'm fine with that." She dropped her eyes suddenly. "You must be eager to see the baron. Shall I show you to the back porch where he and my father are chatting?"

"I'd rather not."

Her gaze came up. "You'd rather not?"

"I've seen a lot of the baron, and I'll see a lot more. But I haven't seen Lady Catherine before. May I not spend more time with her?"

"I—I'm doing the roses." She hesitated, her mind whirling. "But... but if you wish."

"Perhaps you're free to show me around the estate?"

"My son is napping..."

Albrecht's face went white. His arms went to his sides and he bowed stiffly. "My apologies, Lady Catherine. I didn't know you were married. Here I am offering gallantries and pleasantries, and all the while thinking you were an eligible young woman. Please show me the way to the baron, and you shall quickly be rid of me. You must think me quite the brute. Never mind, Lady Catherine. I'm sure I can find my way to the back of the manor myself..."

"Albrecht!" interrupted Catherine. "I am not in the least bit insulted. Quite the contrary." She took a deep breath. "You have not been crass or rude. Forward, yes, but I, well, I find you charming in a very continental way. I was going to say my son is napping and he usually likes a three-hour rest. I'm certain that will give me plenty of time to give you a short tour of the estate. If you are still interested."

"But your husband?"

"Please walk with me, Albrecht. I'm going to show you the apple trees first." She started forward. When he didn't follow, she looked back at him. "Join me. Honestly, it's so rare that I meet new people I actually like."

He continued to hesitate. "It would not do for us—"

"My husband was killed, Albrecht. Almost two years ago now."

"I see. I'm very sorry, Lady Catherine. He cannot have been very old."

"He was an Irishman killed in Belfast. Gunmen targeted him because he wanted Northern Ireland to remain attached to Britain. He didn't want to be part of an independent Irish state. That's all it took."

Albrecht was silent a moment. "Often it takes much less."

"Now that is out of the way, shall we walk? I find you refreshing. You were drawn to me simply because I was a young woman out among the rosebushes. I find that appealing. So many people have been introduced to me in the hopes of making a match. But you didn't know me when you drove up. Nothing was prearranged. You are not Lord So-and-So's heir or Lady Push-and-Pull's youngest son coming to meet me at one of the balls I've attended lately. The whole business seems rather flat to me. But you? You just pulled up in your natty red convertible and asked for directions. You didn't know me from an acorn. As I said, I find that very refreshing. So would my late husband, to tell you the truth. He hated all the stuffed shirts."

"Well, if you insist." Albrecht relaxed. "How do you know I'm not one of those stuffed shirts?"

"I should hardly think so. Not the way you've been acting for the past ten or fifteen minutes." She smiled, her black hair shining in the warm sun. "Mum and Dad would be overjoyed to look out a window and see me strolling with a refined-looking man like yourself. So please don't be worried about how this will look. The staff will whisper, of course, but they always whisper. Just so long as you understand I am not agreeing to anything beyond a stroll on the grounds. I have made a new friend, the friend is a man, and I am enjoying that friend's company. Are you satisfied with this?"

He lifted an eyebrow. "You mean if I ask you to visit me at my castle on the Rhine and stay over for a month, you will refuse?"

"Most certainly."

"Then I will not ask." He joined her, and they walked into the apple orchard at the side of the house.

"You don't actually have a castle on the Rhine, do you, Albrecht?" she asked, the play of light and shade under the trees dappling her face.

His hands went behind his back as they walked. "In fact I do. Or rather my father does. But I'm afraid my older brother Walter will get it."

"And what will you inherit?"

"The old mountain chateau in Pura, Switzerland, with its sweeping views of the mountains and Lake Lugano and Italy."

"Now you're teasing me."

"I'm not actually. We really do have the chateau. Would you like to see it?"

"This estate will have to suffice for the both of us for now. Come, let me show you the swans."

"She said yes!"

"She didn't!"

"Aye, she did!" Norah grinned. "Lady Preston promised Mrs. Long-staff we'll have a dance in a fortnight—a servants' ball, though we'll not call it that. Can you imagine? The regular families from all around will be invited."

"What about the bluebloods?" asked Sally.

"No, no, they'll have their moment later in July when we celebrate Lord Preston's birthday. This is just for us common folk and the Dan-forths." She chewed on her thumb. "You can be sure Skitt will ask Lady Catherine for a waltz."

"A waltz? He don't know how to waltz."

"Neither do you. Neither do I. We'll have to learn before July twelfth. Such a time we'll have. They say the Gillans have two strapping sons, though I've never met them all the years I've summered here with the lord and lady."

"What makes you think the Gillan boys will look at the likes of us?"

"Oh, they'll look all right. We'll dress in such a way as'll turn their heads right 'round. You'll see."

"What are the pair of you up to?" Mrs. Longstaff came bustling into the kitchen. "We have to serve in fifteen minutes. How is the schnitzel?"

"Perfect." Norah opened the warming door of one of the large ovens. "You see?"

Mrs. Longstaff bent over and looked in. "Lovely." She straightened. "What about the roast potatoes? What about the cabbage soup?"

"The potatoes are done to perfection as well. The soup needed more salt, so Sally tended to that."

"Let me see!" Mrs. Longstaff took a large spoonful of the soup that was bubbling on the stove. "Mmm...well done, Sally."

"Thank you, ma'am."

"I'm not sure which you're better at—cleaning the rooms or helping me cook." She glanced about her. "Tavy has the table set in the dining hall. We have another mouth to feed tonight."

Norah groaned. "Have we?"

"Oh, you'll not groan once you've set eyes on him. The baron's friend he is. Handsome young man. Handsome as a prince, I'd say. A theologian from Germany."

"A theologian?" Norah rolled her eyes. "Why, he'd be a little shriveled man with spectacles."

"He isn't a shriveled old anything. He looks like one of the actors in *The Covered Wagon.*"

"I've not seen that film."

"Norah Cole, how is it an old woman like myself has seen it four times and you've never seen it once?"

"We're ready, ma'arm." Tavy stood in the doorway. "Not a minute to waste."

"Right! Norah, you run along with Tavy to the dining hall and see the shriveled-up theologian for yourself. Sally and I will send the soup up by the dumbwaiter."

"Are you sure?"

"Of course I'm sure. On your way now."

"I've not had better schnitzel in Munich or Berlin." Albrecht tucked into a second helping. "Who's your chef?"

"Mrs. Longstaff." Lord Preston lifted a forkful to his mouth. "She's an absolute wizard."

"Longstaff? She's not even European?"

"Not a hint of it. Good Lancashire stock, though there may be a touch of Viking."

"The soup was exceptional as well." The baron leaned back in his seat and sipped his red wine. "Tomorrow's Sunday. Where do you go for services when you're down here, Vilhelm?"

"St. Mary's. It's been in Dover since just after the Norman Conquest."

"Do you mind if Albrecht and I join you?"

"Of course not. It's Church of England, mind you."

The baron waved a hand. "A change of scenery is good for the soul." He smiled at Catherine who was helping Sean with his soup. "Lady Catherine, will you attend the morning service with our crowd?"

"Certainly, Baron. It's a beautiful stone church, and the choir and messages are inspiring."

"How does young Sean do?"

"Very well, sir. He—whoops!" Sean spat up some soup and laughed. She dabbed at his face with a napkin. "He seems awed by the interior—all the light and stained glass—so he's generally quiet."

"Good for him. Perhaps he'll make a fine theologian, eh, Albrecht?"

Norah appeared over Albrecht's right shoulder. "Coffee, sir?"

"We can always use fine theologians, Baron. The Lord knows we have few enough of them." Albrecht smiled up at Norah. "Nice to see you back here with your pot."

"Thank you, sir."

"A half cup would be just right."

"Very good, sir."

Lady Preston interlaced her fingers on the tabletop. "Tell me, Professor Hartmann, how would you sum up the role of the theologian in this age of skepticism?"

Albrecht put cream in his coffee. "What it has always been. To bring the supernatural into the natural world so that it is just as real as anything we perceive with our five senses."

"Bring it in? But isn't the supernatural always here? Isn't it all around us? Angels and devils and God and His Holy Spirit?"

Albrecht drank his coffee. "You're right. When I speak of bringing it in, I mean to say I wish to make it obvious and credible to the human race. That it is as present as water and air, which are vital to us, and that faith in God is equally as vital. Indeed, without it, we are lifeless and without a proper path so we do not attain to our destinies."

"Do you distinguish between orthodoxy—right teaching—and orthopraxis—right living?"

"I don't, Lady Preston. To me it is a false distinction. You cannot have a Christian faith that is all in your head or all in your intellect. That is meaningless. It must be lived out in your actions. By the same token, a body without a head is a monstrosity—your actions must be guided by your thoughts and prayers and beliefs. So there is only the one thing, orthodoxy. And orthodoxy is right belief. And right belief is lived-out and thought-out faith in Christ."

"Is it the wine or is my head spinning?" Lady Preston asked.

The baron smiled. "Perhaps we should remain at the breakfast table tomorrow morning and have our message here. I vote for a passage from the Gospel of Mark."

Albrecht shook his head. "I've gone too far. Forgive me. I return my lecture notes to my briefcase. Let us have our coffee and dessert in peace."

Peaceful silence permeated the room as everyone sat back in comfort.

"And here is our dessert now," Lord Preston announced.

"Really, Vilhelm!" protested the baron. "I am stuffed, as you English say."

"Pass on it if you wish. Mrs. Longstaff swears it's a traditional recipe from southwestern Germany."

Sally carried in a large cake on a tray and set it in the middle of the table. It was covered in whipped cream and cherries. Both Albrecht and the baron looked at it in astonishment, their mouths open but no words coming out.

Finally the baron sputtered, "Black Forest cake! Surely not with the cherry liquor *Kirschwasser*?"

"She swears it's traditional, Gerard."

"There is one way to find out!" Albrecht held out his side plate. "May I have a generous piece, Sally?"

"Of course, sir."

"I think Sean will have a wonderful time with this German delicacy, Lady Catherine."

Catherine bit her lip. "I hate to give him any, Professor Hartmann. He will just waste it. It will be all over his eyes and ears and mouth. And all through my hair."

"Believe me, Lady Catherine, that is not wasting it."

"You raised a few eyebrows with that remark," Catherine commented.

Albrecht was leaning on the railing of the front veranda and looking out over the fields barely discernible in the dark. He stood up straight as Catherine approached. "What remark was that?"

"About Black Forest cake in my hair."

"Well, it was true, although I did not mean to start a rumor with it."

Catherine put her hand on one of the thick, white posts. "Never mind...I'm just teasing. Gallant remarks seem to pop out of you naturally."

"Do they? That makes me sound insincere."

"No, I think you're very sincere. I guess it's a gift you have."

Albrecht went back to leaning on the railing. "Is your son asleep?"

"Yes."

"Are you...would you...take a stroll with me along the drive?"

"Perhaps not."

"I'm sorry. I didn't mean to make you feel uncomfortable."

"I love hearing your table talk, Albrecht. And I enjoyed our walk across the estate this afternoon. But I...well, I want to slow down a bit. I feel like my head is spinning, and I didn't have a drop of wine."

"I see." He laughed. "You're right, of course. I go too fast. Like a racing car driver." He cleared his throat. "I apologize. It is because the baron informed me a few minutes ago we would be leaving immediately after lunch Sunday."

"I thought you'd be with us until after breakfast Monday morning."

"So did I. Something's up in Munich, and both of us need to be there as soon as possible."

"But you teach at Tubingen."

"Yes, but there is no more teaching until the fall. This has nothing to do with being a professor of Protestant theology." A smile came to his face in the dark. "By the way, I caught that *Professor Hartmann* title you used at the table." He wagged his finger. "Never again."

"You called me Lady Catherine."

"We agreed on that."

"I like calling you professor."

"Do you?"

"I do, yes." She gazed over the fields just as he was doing. "I should not say I wish you were staying on. After all, I haven't known you but twelve hours. It's madness. But there you have it. I wish you were with us till Monday or Tuesday. It's like a huge roller has washed over me. I'm a bit stunned, I think. I suppose you'd better go. I need to sleep on what I've been feeling. Maybe I'll feel nothing after a few nights' sleep… or maybe I'll feel more of everything."

He didn't respond for several minutes. "Do you wonder why we must up and go just like that?"

"Of course I wonder. But it's really none of my business, is it?" She glanced at him. "It's a very hard life in Germany right now, I think."

Albrecht shrugged. "We see improvement every month. Inflation is on the decrease; employment is on the rise."

"Well then, that's good."

"So it seems. But that is why we must return. Foolish decisions are made in times of change, especially change for the good. There is a man who was imprisoned for trying to seize control of the government a year ago when times were much worse. Now that matters have improved, some of us are worried he will be released early. He is like a stick of dynamite rolling around that no one can quite get his hands on to throw away. Yet the wick is beginning to smoke." Albrecht's lips were in a straight line. "As it is, he is afforded special treatment in prison. It's almost as if he is on holiday at the castle prison in Munich."

"Who is this man? Are you worried he has a following?"

"His name is Adolph Hitler. He has a following, certainly. I am worried that he seems to be able to appeal to a broad spectrum of the German people. The man is a revolutionary when Germany doesn't need a revolutionary. We need peace and stability and growth. So we are working against him, Catherine, even though others say he is nothing and that the uproar he caused is over."

"Who is this *we?*"

"There are a number of us. We call ourselves 'The Brotherhood of the Oak,' *die Bruderschaft der Eiche.* The oak is one of Germany's national emblems. You English use the oak as well." His eyes looked impossibly deep to her when he looked up. "I tell you this in secret, Catherine. Please do not share what I have told you. I'm not sure why I've spoken about it. Am I trying to impress you? I hope not. Perhaps I wonder if you might understand. You seem like a woman who would understand and come alongside people in a time of struggle."

Catherine felt heat in her face. "Albrecht, I—"

"Lady Catherine, excuse me."

"Yes?" Catherine turned away from Albrecht and faced Norah. "What is it?"

"Young Master Sean is awake and crying for you. We're having difficulty settling him."

"I see. Thank you, Norah. I'll be right there."

Norah went back into the house.

Once Norah had gone, Catherine put her hand briefly on Albrecht's arm. "I would like you to tell me more about this. May we speak alone after breakfast before we drive into Dover for church?"

"Of course!" He gave her a smile. "I hope Sean is all right."

"I'm sure it was just a bad dream. Thank you for asking. Ta, Albrecht."

"*Auf Wiedersehen.*"

"Good morning, Papa."

Lord Preston put down his newspaper. "Ah, there you are, Catherine. How did you and Sean sleep?"

"Not well at all. Sean is still in his crib. Where's Mum and our guests?"

"Your mother is under the weather. It'll just be you and me heading to St. Mary's this morning. And Mrs. Longstaff." He picked up a bell by his elbow and rang it. "Sally will bring you some coffee and scones."

"But the baron was to be joining us. And Professor Hartmann…"

"Yes. They had to leave earlier than expected. Urgent business in Munich. You know how Germany is these days, my dear."

"I see." Catherine sat down at the breakfast table that was in an alcove off the dining hall. Rain tapped against the tall windows. "Is there any chance we'll see the pair of them again this summer?"

Lord Preston had his newspaper up to his face again. "Mmm? This summer? I wouldn't think so. Next summer is a good possibility however. Would you like that? Did you enjoy the baron's company?"

"W—was there a note left…or anything?"

"A note? Why on earth would the baron leave a note? The telegram came for them at four this morning, and I saw them off at four-thirty. Ah, here's Sally with your coffee, scones, and jam."

June
Berlin, Germany

"I expected you two much earlier."

"We were in England. I met with the man in Westminster you asked me to contact. And I recruited Lord Preston. This was as quickly as we could reach Landsberg Castle by car and rail."

"You're here now. Let's get down to business."

Baron von Isenburg, Albrecht Hartmann, and a third man were seated in the baron's Mercedes. A half mile ahead of them the turrets of a castle poked through a dense growth of trees.

"It seems impossible to keep Hitler in Landsberg Castle the full five years," the third man began, eyeing the battlements. "He has too many well-wishers. We have worked through the channels available to us to insist he serve out his full term. It's no use. He will be released before the end of the year, perhaps as early as this fall, though we are fighting that."

"Their argument?" asked the baron.

"Oh, you know. The Germany of 1924 is a different Germany from the Germany of '22 or '23. Berlin is getting a grip on inflation, the workforce is increasing, wages are improving—all of that. So Hitler will not have the base to draw from anymore; therefore, he does not need to be in detention. Apparently he will renounce violence and his former political beliefs."

"He won't change!" responded Albrecht.

"Of course not. But that is what officials want to believe, and he is only too happy to appear to give them what they want." The man pulled a large envelope from a briefcase at his feet. "We should not stay here much longer. Take this. One of our men inside the castle was able to get his hands on drafts of the book Hitler is writing. He made copies. It will be published in 1925."

The baron examined the envelope. "You have read his manuscript?"

"Most of it."

"Well?"

"It's the same sort of thing we have heard at his street rallies since 1920. Germany for Germans. Purebloods only. No immigration. Death to the Jews. Secure boundaries against the Russians. Down with communism. Open the east for German settlement. It's all there, just more polished and refined. A friend is editing it for him."

"We can't stop the publication?"

"No, Baron. We can only prepare ourselves to argue against his arguments in print." The man turned to Albrecht. "Which is where you come in, Herr Professor. We need a book from you to coincide with the release of Hitler's propaganda."

"I am a theologian," protested Albrecht, "not a politician."

"And Germany remains very religious with its mix of Lutherans and Catholics and Evangelicals. I am not asking you to pen rubbish. Counter Hitler's ideology from the Bible, from your own personal convictions, from the history of the Christian faith, whatever you wish, but write as well and as deeply as you have ever done."

"I have a full course load this coming term."

"Will you or won't you help us? The baron was sure you could be relied upon."

"It's a question of time."

The man leaned towards Albrecht. "Hitler has an uncanny ability to draw the German people into his sphere. You saw that at his street rallies. Forty thousand people at one."

"I remember."

"So now his ideas will go from one end of Germany to the other with this book. Suppose instead of 40,000 he rallies 40 million to his beliefs? Can you not try to rally those same 40 million to the Christian point of view instead? Is there any possibility you can bring Germany closer to the teachings of Jesus Christ than Herr Hitler's book brings them to the teachings of the Nazi Party?"

June
Dover Sky

"Lady Catherine! Lady Catherine!"

Catherine stood up. She looked beautiful in her white summer dress. "Yes? Sean and I are down here with the swans. Whatever is the matter, Skitt?"

Skitt came running down to the pond, and the swans quickly sailed away from shore.

"A letter just came for you by special post. I didn't want it to sit by your place setting until tea."

"A letter? Who is it from?"

Skitt handed it to her, yanking his cap from his head, his face scarlet from his run. "Doesn't say. It's not from England, that's all I know."

"Oh!" Her face turned as white as her dress when she glanced at the envelope. "Germany!"

"Is everything all right?"

"I hope so. Yes, yes, I expect so. Thank you, Skitt. I shall see you up at the manor."

"May I be of further help, m'lady?"

"Oh no. You're a dear for running it down to me. Bless you."

Skitt turned and headed back as Catherine sat down on the grass by Sean. He was playing with a long, white swan feather that had been shed near a tree. She held the letter in her hand, debated about opening it now or waiting. She decided to open it. With one hand on Sean's small back, she read Albrecht's note:

> Dear Lady Catherine,
>
> My sincere apologies. The baron and I had every intention of attending services with you and your family until the telegram arrived early Sunday morning. It was rude of me not to leave you with some sort of message, but it was all I could do to get packed, grab a bite to eat from the kitchen, and jump into my car. Will you forgive me? I very much wanted to speak with you further.
>
> There is something about you. I must say it—I think of you constantly. Here I am at this fancy hotel in Munich, and the baron is snoring like a trumpet in the other room. At any rate, I can't sleep. On the one hand there is the mystery of Lady Catherine to ponder. Why am I caught up with you? On the other hand there is Adolph Hitler to ponder. Why is Germany caught up with him?
>
> I have been asked to write a book to counter Hitler's book that is due out next year. His will be a memoir, and a political rant against the Treaty of Versailles that ended the war, and an attack on the Jews, the communists, and the socialists. Mine will be a volume of theology—but what I call "embodied theology"—a true orthodoxy that is a "lived out" orthodoxy. And it must be alive. The last thing I need to produce right now is a dry, academic treatise on the existence of God.
>
> I've read some of Hitler's book. The Brotherhood I'm involved with has obtained some early drafts. Hitler writes with passion

about something he believes in. People will pick up on this. I must write with equal passion about what I believe in. Good must have as much fire and heat as hate because it's to a better end.

I share this in strictest confidence. I wish I could share it with you in person. I fear it will be a long time before we see each other. Am I content with the time I've had with you? No. But I thank God for it just the same.

The blessings of Christ on your lovely head.

Your servant,
Albrecht

Catherine read it through twice. The color returned to her face—more color than had been in it all day. She gazed at the swans as they floated slowly back and forth on the green and silver water. "What is going on, God?" she whispered. "What are You doing in my life now? I have no idea how I feel about Albrecht Hartmann or what he's involved in. How am I supposed to respond to this?"

July, 1924
Dover Sky

"You needn't be so ceremonial, William. This isn't the Magna Carta. Open the letter. It's already sat for a week after Skitt put it in your hand and you misplaced it."

"I merely set it aside, Elizabeth. I was quite conscious of its whereabouts the entire time."

"Yes, yes, dear. Save your speeches for Parliament, please. Just read me Robbie and Shannon's letter."

"Will do." Lord Preston carefully slit the thin envelope with a letter opener that bore the Danforth coat of arms. Setting the opener down, he brought out a sheet of paper thinner than the envelope. "There are no photographs, Elizabeth."

"Well, I didn't think there would be. Oh, read it to me! Is Shannon with child?"

He unfolded the letter and cleared his throat as if he were about to say, "Mr. Speaker…"

> Dear Mum & Dad,
>
> Cheers! I'm sending this as quickly as I can. Shannon and I were planning to surprise the two of you by showing up for Dad's sixtieth birthday celebration. We were promised a month's leave from my post here so we were busy packing. On

47

the last day of June I was waiting to speak with an important member of the Jewish community. My adjutant burst into my office with the news the man had just been assassinated. I went to the scene immediately. It was a grim sight. At first we thought Arabs were the assassins, but further investigation made it clear it was one of the Jewish militant groups—the Haganah. Why did they kill one of their own? Simply put, Jacob Israel de Haan wanted a state that included secular and religious Jews in the government, as well as Arab Muslims and Arab Christians, but the Haganah want a Jewish state, period.

I'm used to the Arabs and Jews being at each other's throats. Yet I knew this region had shades of Ireland to it, where Jew might turn on Jew or Arab on Arab just as Irishman had turned on Irishman. However I confess I did not expect the cold-blooded murder of a Jew by other Jews. It has given me a bit of a jolt. Not least because I knew de Haan personally and he was one of my brightest hopes for Palestine's future. Really, the only way we can keep Jerusalem from spiraling down into a cycle of constant violence is to establish a nation that is inclusive of Muslims and Jews and Christians. That is the spirit de Haan epitomized, and he was having successful talks with Arab leaders. Obviously too successful in the eyes of the Haganah and the Zionists.

Well, it could just as easily have been the Arabs who had done it. They too have their hotheads who don't want a Palestinian state that includes Jews in its government. How will the moderates prevail when there are so many with their fingers on the trigger on both sides? And here we British are in the middle. How can I possibly sort all this out when the leaders I have most counted on to bring peace to this region are cut down in their prime?

I'll get this in the mailbag for England straightaway. I am so very sorry we can't make it up for your birthday, Dad, but you see how things are. Perhaps we'll be able to get away next year.

Meanwhile, despite all this, Shannon and I enjoy good health and relish this wonderful climate. God bless you and please pray for us here.

Love to all,
Robbie

Lady Preston was fingering her necklace and staring out the parlor window at the apple trees. "I should like to live to see peace in Jerusalem."

"It has been this way from time immemorial, Elizabeth. One group fighting another. Several Danforths went on Crusades, you know."

"I just don't want them turning on our British troops for lack of something else to do. There's a viciousness in Palestine I had not counted on. I fear Robbie is in harm's way again."

"Nonsense." Lord Preston folded the letter and tucked it back in its envelope. "They have no reason to go after our army. We're there to help."

"Now you settle in here behind this bush," ordered Fairburn.

"I'm not *behind* the bush," complained Skitt, "I'm in it."

"All the better. The poachers won't be able to tell you from a thatch of brambles."

The sun had gone down, but there was still enough twilight to see clearly when Skitt crouched down in the brush. Fairburn handed him a cricket bat.

"Now if you spot 'em, holler like the dickens and I shall come running from my hut. Whack them about a bit with the bat and soften 'em up for the constables. Remember, the poachers are on our land so they're trespassing. And if they've come for the swans, they're poaching as well. And they're not just taking anyone's swans."

"I know, I know. They're poaching the swans of the Marquess of Preston."

Fairburn made a sour face. "They're not just the Marquess of Preston's swans, lad. They're the king's birds."

"What do you mean?"

"Have I not told you? The swans of this estate have been under royal protection by edict since 1789. Twenty years back, they were Queen Victoria's swans. Today they're King George the Fifth's. All the more reason to knock the poachers about a bit and give them what for."

"I'll do my best."

"We'll spell each other. You have tonight and tomorrow night. Then it's my go. Have you got your flask of tea?"

"Aye. Mrs. Longstaff fixed me two great ham sandwiches as well."

"Good enough. We'll see you at dawn then, unless you catch 'em. Don't forget to make a great racket that will bring me on the run. Cheers."

"Cheers."

Skitt hunkered down further into the bush, opened his leather flask, sipped some tea, screwed the cap back on, and began to hum "Abide with Me" while he watched the swans glide around the pond. *They look like vessels with all sails set, so they do*, he thought. The great birds settled down as it became fully dark, tucking their bills back under their wings, some remaining in the water, others coming up on land. The July night was warm so Skitt felt no discomfort. He gripped his cricket bat firmly and flicked his eyes from one side of the pond to the other. He thought about the summer ball that was only three nights away. The great hall at Dover Sky was already decorated with white lights and streamers. He almost closed his eyes as he imagined that night...

Lady Catherine.

Ah, Master Skitt. To what do I owe this pleasure?

I brought you a glass of lemonade. You look a bit pink.

Why, that's so kind of you. Indeed, I was feeling the heat. How may I thank you?

Well, I was wondering if I might have this dance?

My goodness, you're asking me? A girl should be so lucky. I'd be honored. Please take my hand and let's go onto the floor. Do you know how to waltz?

Indeed I do, Lady Catherine.

Really? You are a man of many talents, Master Skitt. I do hope one dance will not be enough for you.

With a lady as fair as you, I doubt it.

How charming you are. Let us stay partners as long as we possibly can.

"It's not working! I knew it." Sally stood in front of the mirror, lifted up a handful of her hair, and then let it drop. Her eyes were narrowed and her lips tight. "I'm a fright. I can't go upstairs to the ball. I shall spend my night in bed reading a romance."

"Don't be ridiculous!" Norah swished up behind Sally wearing a red gown that flared out from her hips. She began poking pins into her friend's straw-blonde hair. "A few hairpins and you will be absolutely devastating."

"I will not. The night's a disaster."

"The night will be a triumph. Blue eyes, blonde hair, the tiniest freckles I've ever seen—the men will trip over themselves to dance with you. And there are quite a few of them."

"What? Have you gone and peeked?"

"I have. And they all look smashing. There are some soldiers and naval officers too, and their uniforms are lovely."

Sally bounced up and down on her toes. "Oh, I can't wait. Hurry!"

Norah put several pins in her mouth so she could move her fingers about more freely. "Mmm."

"Has anyone danced yet? I can hear the violins."

Norah plucked the pins from her mouth and plunged them carefully into Sally's upswept hair. "Lord Preston led off with Mrs. Longstaff, if you can believe it."

"Mrs. Longstaff! She said she wouldn't be caught within a hundred miles of here the night of the ball."

"I don't know who or what changed her mind, but she's done up in rose-and-pink ribbons and doesn't even look like our cook anymore. Honestly, she's a woman at least fifteen years younger."

Sally bounced on her toes again. "That's enough. We must get upstairs."

"One minute." Norah jabbed and stabbed. "Skitt's on the floor with Lady Catherine."

Sally whipped her head around and several pins fell out. "No!"

"Now look, we've got to do the right side again," grumbled Norah, bending down for the pins.

"I never thought he'd have the nerve."

"He was fortifying himself at the punch bowl before he asked her."

"But the punch doesn't have any alcohol in it."

"Of course not. Lord Preston's a good religious man. But Skitt didn't think of that. So he finally marched off thinking he was well fueled for his Waterloo with Lady Catherine."

"Well, if it was his Waterloo, he must have been Wellington if she let him take her out onto the floor."

"Twice that I saw. And you'll also be surprised to know he did us proud."

"What d'ya mean?"

"He glided about like one of those swans of his. Can you imagine?"

Sally almost whipped her head around a second time, but Norah's hands held it firmly this time.

"He did not!"

"You see," Norah said, "all those lessons you gave him made a difference."

"Me? You danced with him more than I did."

"I didn't."

"Three lessons for every one of mine."

Norah snorted. "I can't float like a swan over the dance floor. How could I have taught him how to do it, Sal?"

"Oh, I want to see!" Sally reached up and pulled Norah's hands away from her hair. "Enough. I don't care. Let's go upstairs."

"Sal," Norah said as she peered at herself in the mirror and brushed an eyelash from her cheek, "the ball isn't going anywhere."

" 'Course it is. It's going out the door at midnight. Hurry."

The great hall at Dover Sky was half the size of the one at Ashton Park, but it still held two hundred people comfortably. The walls had sea paintings—some of naval battles in the Channel and others of fishing boats, the background always including images of Dover's white cliffs. A string quartet sat at one end of the hall on a platform erected for the occasion. Tables groaning with meats and cheeses stood at the other end. White lights glowed, strung from one corner of the ceiling to the other, and colored streamers of crepe paper dangled down, stopping eight feet from the floor.

Norah and Sally had helped decorate the hall. Taking it all in at once—the lights in the semidarkness of the room, the string players bent to their task, the red coats of the army officers and the blue coats of the naval officers, the women in their gowns and the men in their morning suits, crystal glasses glittering in people's hands—gave the two young women a sense of being in a different mansion. It didn't seem like their well-known Dover Sky at all.

Sally seized Norah's hand. "There are two men of Nelson's Navy approaching us."

"Nelson's Navy? What in heaven's name are you talking about? It's 1924 not 1805."

"I like to think of the navy that way. I always have since I was a little girl." Sally stood as straight as she could. "I'll take the tall, dark, handsome one. You can have the other."

"The other one's shorter than me!"

"Shh! Do make the best of it." Sally curtsied as the officers bowed. She made eye contact with the tall one. "Good evening, sirs. May we have the pleasure of your acquaintance?"

"Seven dances! My goodness!" Lady Catherine laughed and fanned her face with her hand. "Who would have thought you had wings on your feet, Master Skitt?"

"I hope you enjoyed yourself, m'lady."

"Enjoyed myself? I don't think I've ever flown about a dance floor like that."

Skitt bowed, his morning suit tight on his slender frame. "My pleasure. And now I'm afraid I must go."

"What? The night's still young. I'd love to have another go 'round with you."

Skitt beamed, his eyes bright amid the shine of the lights hanging overhead. "It would be an honor, Lady Catherine, but it's my turn to be down at the pond. We're trying to nab the poachers, you see."

"Fairburn?"

"He's lending Tavy a hand there by the tables. This would be just the sort of night the rascals would choose to go after our swans, Lady Catherine, what with everyone in here at the party. I do hope I may have the pleasure of dancing with you again one day."

"Oh, of course, Skitt. I'll sneak you into my father's birthday ball in a fortnight."

"But I'm not gentry."

She patted him on the cheek with a gloved hand. "Never mind. We'll have our dance, I promise. Please be careful tonight."

"I will. Thank you." Skitt turned and marched through the great hall doorway.

Catherine snatched a drink of punch from a tray Tavy was carrying as he wandered through the crowd. "I need a drink or I'm going to faint," she announced.

"Are you well, ma'arm?" asked Tavy in his gravelly voice.

"Certainly I'm well, but Master Skitt is so much younger than I am. He would have danced on for another five hours if he didn't have his pond assignment."

"I'm sure you've made his night, ma'arm. Probably his year. Perhaps his life."

"Oh heavens, Tavy. Don't exaggerate. Hardly his life. The year will be done in December, so that might be closer to the mark if he feels anything for me like you're describing."

"Lady Catherine, he dotes on you, he does. Were it a thousand years ago he'd happily mount a horse and joust to win your hand."

"Now I don't know if I'm blushing from the heat or your description of Skitt's adoration. Thank you, Tavy. I'll have another." She returned the empty glass to the tray and picked up a full one. Tavy disappeared among the gowns, suits, and uniforms. Catherine stood and sipped as she gazed over the room.

"A beautiful woman left without an escort? What is England coming to?"

A tall, broad-shouldered officer in a dark-blue uniform was smiling at her, his eyes a brilliant blue and his face tanned like a golden sunrise. He bowed slightly. "Terrence Fordyce. I hope I'm addressing Lady Catherine Moore."

"You are, Leftenant Commander."

"Ah, you recognize the insignia."

"My brother Edward was Royal Navy during the war." She offered him a smile. "Did you come by your tan on Channel duty?"

He laughed. "That's not likely, is it? I was on the world tour with the *HMS Hood*. Australian sun blessed us, not to mention the Californian sun and the Jamaican sun. I had to leave the *Hood* in Canada and come across to Devonport on another ship. Naval business to attend to."

"When will the *Hood* be back in England?"

"I'd say September." He reached out for her empty glass. "May I take that for you?"

"Thank you."

"Would you like another?"

"I'm quite all right, thank you."

Fordyce went to the tables and returned. "Now your hands are free."

"So they are."

"May I have the honor of this dance?"

"Certainly, Leftenant Commander." Catherine was immediately conscious of the cologne Fordyce was using—a spicy scent she enjoyed. She caught whiffs of it as they moved about the dance floor. His hand on her back was firm but gentle, his footsteps sure and smooth, his grip on her hand warm. He didn't move as spiritedly as Skitt had because he didn't have the younger man's energy, but there was grace and dignity in his large circles over the dance floor that she liked. When the dance was done and he asked her for another, she said yes. This went on for several dances until her father showed up at Fordyce's shoulder.

"May I cut in?" he asked.

"Of course, Lord Preston." Fordyce stepped back. "Enjoy your waltz, sir."

"I shall indeed. Fordyce, isn't it? Family in Dover?"

"Yes, m'lord."

"Your father and mother have been good friends to the Danforths over the years. I'm very glad to see you here tonight."

"Thank you, m'lord."

"I shan't hold on to her long."

Lord Preston swept his daughter wildly into the middle of the room, several couples having to dodge as they swung near.

"What's this about, Father?" she asked. "I was enjoying myself."

"Believe me, the last thing I want to do is spoil your evening. It's a breath of fresh air to your mother and me to see you out on the dance floor."

"Then why did you steal me away?"

"So I could tell you who he is."

Catherine groaned. "I suppose he's a rake."

"Quite the opposite. I know what's going on with his career from my naval connections. He's bound for big things, so my advice is that if you like him even a bit, hang on to him."

"Hang on to him? I've just met him. I don't even know him."

"I am just…"

"Thank you so much, Father, but I'm twenty-five. I'll let you know how I feel about him in the morning." She kissed her father on the cheek. "Stop worrying about me."

"Well, your mother and I—"

"And I love you both for it. Now just waltz over and return me to the Royal Navy."

"Where is he?"

"Off by that horrid potted plant. Poor man looks like a boat adrift."

Lord Preston carved a path through the dancers, leaving dresses and suits and uniforms in disarray in his wake. He released Catherine in front of Fordyce with a flourish that embarrassed her and brought red to her face.

"There you are, sir." Lord Preston smiled. "None the worse for wear."

"Oh, m'lord," protested Fordyce, "you didn't even finish the dance."

"I leave that up to you. I must find Elizabeth…Lady Preston. I haven't had a go on the dance floor with her all night."

Fordyce shrugged as Lord Preston left. He extended his hand to Catherine. "May I complete this dance for you?"

"Please."

As she placed her arm on his shoulder she said, "Tell me about your cruise, would you?"

"Of course. Well, let's see. We darted down to Sierra Leone right from the start. We left from Devonport on November twenty-seventh last year, so I expect the captain wanted to get as warm as possible as quickly as possible."

She laughed. "A sensible British captain."

"Right. John Thurm is his name. We made it to Cape Town, South Africa, for Christmas, had a break, headed on for Zanzibar, Tanzania, and then anchored at Singapore in February. I remember the dates and times because I keep a journal. After that it was Australia and New Zealand—Adelaide, Melbourne, Sydney, Brisbane, and Auckland. Then full-steam ahead for Fiji and Hawaii."

"You terrible man!" Catherine felt free enough to tease him. "No wonder you have such a golden tan. We're suffering through our English weather, and there you are in Hawaii of all places."

"Defending Britain, Lady Catherine."

"Indeed. And where did the trade winds take you next, Leftenant Commander?"

"All sails set for Canada's West Coast. Beautiful great trees on Vancouver Island, the cities of Victoria and Vancouver are gems, then down the coast to California and San Francisco—"

"Still defending England?" she interrupted.

"Every morning and every night. And your ladyship, of course."

"Of course."

"So it was necessary to get to Panama and Jamaica to defend you and the flag. Then we went on to South America to do more of the same—Valparaiso, Buenos Aires, Rio de Janeiro—"

"Oh stop!" She was laughing. "I hardly know you and I feel like slapping you. I'd love to see all those places even if it took a lifetime. And you saw them all in a few months."

"We hope to do the tour again next year."

"You do not."

"The Mediterranean, in any case. Why winter here when you can winter in Malta?"

"You're not a man; you're a beast."

He stopped dancing. "There's the song done."

"And that's it?"

"Why, would you like another go 'round?"

"I don't know why, but I do. I want to hear about Victoria and San Francisco and Jamaica, for starters. I may want to hear about more after that."

The music began again, and Fordyce swirled her about the floor. "I don't think I can figure you out."

"What a dreary woman I would be if you could. We've been together less than an hour."

"Well, isn't Lady Catherine having the time of her life," Sally commented as she stood watching the naval officer whisk Catherine about the floor under the strings of electric lights.

"Thank the Lord, that's all I can say." Norah gulped at her punch. "She moped around Ashton Park for nigh on two years till I thought she'd joined the ghosts in the attic. A few weeks here, and her spirits have gone from night to day. It's wonderful."

"I thought she liked that German fellow…the teacher."

"So we all liked him."

"And she clearly likes this naval officer."

"Why shouldn't she? Look at him."

"One minute she's a nun, and the next she's the life of the party."

"Stop fussing, Sally. I'd hardly call her the life of the party. Just a lonely widow who decided it was time to unwrap the mourning band from her soul. I'm sure the lord and lady are thrilled." Norah put a glass of punch in Sally's hand. "Drink up. You're all hot and bothered."

"I am not hot and bothered," Sally retorted, but she drained the glass in a few seconds.

"We've had a fine night, and it's not over yet!"

Sally made a sour face. "We neither of us got two dances in a row from the same man. It's been first this one, and then the other one. I can't remember all their names, and they'll never remember mine. They all want to dance with the Knight girls. Those are the ones what will have the lads coming to call."

Norah watched one of the Knight sisters flash past on the arm of a scarlet-uniformed army officer. "Don't be so sure. They're too tall and thin so far as I can see. Men don't like that."

"They've not been off the dance floor all night, Norah."

"But it's the same few blokes over and over again, d'ya see? A lot of men like sturdier stuff."

"For heaven's sakes, is that what you and I are? You make us sound like Holsteins."

"Didn't I tell you?" Norah suddenly crowed. "Wasn't I right?"

Sally pushed back strands of damp blonde hair that had fallen into her eyes. "What are you going on about now?"

Two army officers in scarlet greeted them with short bows.

"Ladies," said the one, "we've had our eyes on the pair of you all night and have finally drummed up the nerve to approach."

"Please don't refuse us," pleaded the other man with a warm smile.

"Why, we would never do that." Sally returned the smile and slipped her arm through that of the taller of the two men. "If you've been waiting all night, we must make up for lost time. How will three dances do you, sir?"

"Only three, m'lady?"

"Why, I'm sure there should be more if we find we don't tread all over each other's feet."

Sally and the officer went onto the floor, leaving Norah with the shorter and stockier one who, nevertheless, continued to offer her one of the brightest smiles she had ever seen. He extended his arm. "I'd be honored, ma'am," he said. "You're lovely."

"You don't mean that."

"I do. I truly have waited all night. I've not had a single dance."

Norah put her arm through his. "Not a single dance? I don't know if I believe that, leftenant."

"I swear. I just kept thinking, *What would it be like to spin you about the room?*"

"You're not interested in my friend?"

"Ah, no. Not my type at all. But Squinty, that is, Leftenant Park, he's happy as a clam, isn't he?"

"What about the Knight girls?"

"I don't know them. I just wanted to meet you. Shall we dance?" He took her onto the floor. Whatever awkwardness had existed when he first spoke to her was gone once they moved about. He never stumbled or bumped into others. While he was not what Norah considered a smooth dancer, he was steady and sure-footed. After a few minutes she trusted him enough to let him take her wherever he wanted on the floor.

"What's your name?" he asked.

"Norah Cole, sir."

"And I'm Leftenant Bruce Milne. I'm pleased to make your acquaintance, Miss Cole."

"As I am pleased to make yours, Leftenant Milne."

"Bruce."

She smiled. "Bruce it is."

Fairburn strode down to the pond as dawn swept over the fields. He found Skitt huddled in his bush gripping his cricket bat. "No luck then?"

"Not with the poachers." Skitt's eyes and face were bright. "My night on the dance floor was another matter."

Fairburn squatted by him. "Ah, your grand moment with Lady Catherine. Well, not to burst your bubble, but she didn't exactly pine away after you left."

"What d'ya mean?"

"Others asked her to dance. She couldn't very well turn them all away."

"Who? Who did she dance with?" Skitt's eyes narrowed. "Did she dance with you?"

"Me? I didn't set a boot on the dance floor all night. Oh, it was a host of army officers and navy men."

"Who in particular?"

"Why, what are you planning to do with him? Pistols at dawn?"

Skitt's eyes grew darker. "What's his name?"

"Steady as she goes, lad. A naval officer named Terrence Fordyce. He serves on *HMS Hood*."

"Does she like him?"

"Well now, you know I didn't think to march up and demand that information from her, Master Skitt. But you can if you like."

Skitt suddenly stood up clutching his bat, a blanket, and his leather flask. "It doesn't matter. I shall continue on. We had a wonderful time together last night. We'll have a wonderful time at her father's birthday party as well."

"How do you, a groundskeeper, intend to get into a party for the nobility?"

"Lady Catherine said she'd slip me in."

"Slip you in? Under the door? Down the chimney? They'll all see you, Skitt. They'll know who you are and who you aren't. D'ya want to risk getting thrown out on your ear or even sacked?"

Skitt tilted up his chin. "Faint heart never won fair lady."

Catherine sat up in bed, sheets at her neck, arms wrapped about her bent knees, and glanced out the window. Two weeks had passed since the servants' ball, and a change had come over her. Last night, after her second official date with Terrence Fordyce, she'd collapsed into bed without drawing the curtains. Now she noticed the first streaks of sunlight winking off the dew on the grass. Her room was on the third floor and faced south so she could just make out the sparkle of the Channel at Dover. It was a perfect summer morning, and she felt like a perfect summer morning inside. It was the most light and joy she'd experienced since her husband's death.

You'd like him, Albert.

Well, Cat, he seemed like a good sort, right enough. You know I've wanted you to get past your grieving and find a man who'll be a good father to Sean. Fordyce might fit the bill.

It's too soon to say anything about that. Albert, I do so miss you still.

But you must have a life, Cat. That's what I want for you.

Would it be Fordyce then?

Mind, I liked the other chap too. Hartmann seems a solid type. If only he wasn't German. That spoils things.

Albert, what does it matter? The war's over. The Germans were our allies once against the French. You do remember Waterloo, don't you?

Albert's voice grew silent in her head. Continuing to gaze out the window, Catherine prayed, thought a bit, remembered Terrence's tanned face as he told her about Vancouver Island, and saw Albrecht's face, white and strong in the dark of the front porch. She closed her eyes. "Life is happening far too fast," she said softly. "One week I'm the grieving widow, and the next week I'm single and flattered by the attention of beautiful men sweeping me in a beautiful silk gown over the dance floor.

"People seem to like the change. Mother and Father certainly do. I don't know how I feel about it all though. Yes, it's spring and summer in my soul. It's spectacular. But marriage in half a year or a year? A father for Sean? I can't see it. I'm not quite sure who Catherine Moore is at the moment, and it's going to take a while to sort her out—never mind choosing between men as lovely as Terrence Fordyce and Albrecht Hartmann." She lay back on the bed, eyes still closed, and murmured, "Quite honestly, I really don't know what they see in me. Maybe I should take my vows—become a nun. That would solve everything, would it not?"

4

"Look, I'd like to win, but the truth is I'm happy if either of us wins."

"Yeah?"

"Yeah. I just don't want that buzzard Wolfgang Zeltner to win."

Kipp Danforth and Ben Whitecross stood by Kipp's SPAD. All around them ground crew darted back and forth between aircraft checking wing struts, wheels, ailerons, and everything else. Now and then an engine would cough to life, run for a minute, and then be shut down.

Kipp checked his watch. "Fifteen minutes to go. Zeltner got the first takeoff slot with two of the French pilots."

"It doesn't matter." Ben stared past the SPAD at the other planes nearby. "The officials time everyone from liftoff. Zeltner could land at Dover Sky five minutes ahead of you or me and it wouldn't make a difference—not if he'd set off ten minutes before us. We'd win." Ben pointed with his chin. "There he is."

They both stared under the wing at Zeltner, who stood tall, blond, and slender in his three-quarter-length black leather jacket.

"He's dressed like it's the Great War," grumbled Kipp.

"Perhaps it still is for him. You know he always regretted not besting Richthofen's record of eighty kills."

Zeltner appeared to feel their eyes on him for he turned and looked directly at the two of them. He lifted the hand holding his leather helmet in half salute.

They each raised a hand in response.

"It's Baron von Zeltner now, you know," said Ben.

"I saw that in the paper. When did that happen?"

"In '22. Your brother Edward said the Weimar Republic was looking for heroes. He was one of the ones they chose to put on the pedestal. Permitted him to add the "von" to his name. Yet a few weeks later von Zeltner joined a right-wing party the Weimar leadership detests."

"Edward is always up on the politics," grunted Kipp. "He fancies himself the first man in the kingdom in ten years."

"What was the name of the party Zeltner joined? The National Socialist…hang on…the National Socialist German Workers' Party, that's it. Big name, isn't it? Your dad and Edward call them the Nazis. Heard of them?"

"I'm too busy flying mail."

"Well," Ben went on, "they're a pretty violent lot. They go around and beat up people they don't like. Their leader's in prison right now."

"Hmm…so von Zeltner's part of that?"

"Right."

"I know he has a cruel streak." Kipp slapped his leather flying helmet against his pant leg. "Never pictured him as a thug though. Not his style, is it?"

"I'm sure he appoints others to do the street work while he sits in an office."

"That doesn't sound like his style either."

Ben shrugged. "He looks the same as when we met him in London in 1920." He leaned on the lower wing and stared at von Zeltner. "Remember that social event for pilots of all sides? He took an interest in your wife, if I recall."

"And to yours. Do you think he knows who we are?"

"Oh he knows."

"Then you can be sure he wants to beat you," said Kipp.

"And you, the son of the man hosting the race."

"But especially you, Ben. He'll never forget how you tore up his squadron and won the Victoria Cross in the bargain."

"Never forget...or forgive." Ben thrust his hands into his pockets. "This race needs to be won by an Englishman!"

"Gentlemen! Aviators!" A heavy man in tweed coat and cap stood in the middle of the parked airplanes. "We are about to begin. Your names will be shouted out in groups of three. Those three will take off side by side. Then another three will be called and so on until all twenty of you are up. The winner cannot be announced until time of arrival at the finish line is compared with time of takeoff and the exact amount of flying time is calculated. Obviously the pilot with the shortest flying time shall find himself the winner of the Lord Preston Cup and two thousand pounds sterling."

He consulted a sheet of paper. "Remember your destination is the estate of Dover Sky in Kent. Each of you has been furnished with a map. There are large markings chalked out on the airfield there. In addition red, white, and blue balloons surround the landing strip. Do not go below one thousand feet unless you have engine trouble and must touch down. Pray choose an unpopulated area if that is the case. Any questions?" He paused. "No?" He brought out his pocket watch. "Gentlemen, to your planes. The air race from Liverpool to Dover is about to begin. May the best man win!"

Kipp climbed into his cockpit. Ben ran fifty yards to his SPAD and swung himself up.

Contact! Contact! The words were shouted from one end of the meadow to the other as pilots started their engines. Roars and rumbles and exhaust filled the July air. Suddenly a flare gun was fired, and a red ball of fire arched over the field. The heavy man in tweed shouted through a megaphone above the growl of engines: "Von Zeltner! St. Laurent! Hugo! You are cleared for takeoff!"

Kipp watched the three SPADs taxi, lift off, streak south, and then head east as they gained altitude. Von Zeltner's plane had a distinctive paint scheme of black and yellow. Kipp muttered, "The same colors your squadron used. The same colors you plastered all over your Fokker triplane. It's not 1918, Wolfgang. I suppose if there hadn't been a rule that you had to use a SPAD you'd have a D.VII or an Albatros up there."

Three or four minutes later a second set of names was called, and three more SPADs took to the air. Kipp opened and closed his hand on the stick and gritted his teeth. A third set of names rang out, and another three aircraft took off. He squeezed his eyes shut and counted to sixty. Nine planes were already up and zooming through the sky for Dover.

"Whitecross! Dickens! Danforth! You are cleared for takeoff!"

Kipp waved his hand in the air and gunned the engine. His ground crew whipped the chocks away from his wheels and the SPAD rolled forward. Ben was on his left; Dickens on his right. They left the ground in unison, as if they'd been practicing the maneuver for weeks. Kipp adjusted his goggles and tightened the white silk scarf around his neck. It was the scarf he'd worn in France during the war. He nudged the SPAD higher and higher, leaving Dickens and Ben quickly behind. Then he aimed his plane towards the English Channel.

"All right, Wolfgang," he hissed through clenched teeth, "where are you?"

Dover Sky

Lord Preston stood by dozens of red, blue, and white balloons—the same colors as the Union Jack that flew from a pole next to a brand-new Quonset hut. He slapped a rolled-up newspaper against the side of his leg as he kept an eye on the northern horizon and glanced occasionally at the crowd of people spilling over onto the airfield.

"Shouldn't they be here by now?" he asked out loud. "Eh?"

Victoria laughed. "Oh, Papa! You haven't got anywhere to go. It's your birthday. Relax and enjoy it."

"I'd relax a lot more if this race were over and done with and no one was injured. Your mother feels the same way."

"Well, you put up the cup and the two-thousand-pound purse, Dad," Victoria reminded.

"In a moment of weakness, I assure you." He glanced about him. "Where have the children disappeared to?"

"You can't expect an empty sky to hold their attention. Only grown-ups are keen on that sort of thing. Aunt Holly and Harrison have the lot of them down to feed bread crumbs to the swans."

"The swans! I hope Harrison keeps his wits about him. The pond is deeper than it looks and—"

"Father, I think Harrison knows a thing or two about ponds. And if he's forgotten anything, Aunt Holly will be quick to remind him. Catherine, Christelle, and Char are at the pond as well. Please don't fret about that along with the air race."

"Hmm…" Lord Preston turned to his son-in-law, who was at his left elbow. "Jeremy, you and Emma have news?"

Jeremy looked at him in surprise, sunlight glinting off his round eyeglasses. "Who told you that?"

Emma put a gloved hand on her husband's arm. "I did, Jeremy, dear. But I said we'd tell him at his party when everyone was present—not out here by the airstrip."

"You can tell the others at the party," said Lord Preston. He placed the arm with the newspaper around his wife. "Elizabeth and I prefer to hear about it now. It is good news, I presume?"

"Very good news, Papa," replied Emma. "Though I think reactions will be mixed. Jeremy has been given a pulpit in London—and a very good one."

"London!" Lord Preston was startled.

"Why, that's miles away from Ashton Park!" exclaimed Lady Preston.

"We hear that Jeremy's being considered for the post of bishop, and that if he does well in London he's got it."

"Em," Jeremy reacted quickly, "you didn't need to tell them that."

"I did. It's the only thing that would soften the blow of us packing up and leaving Lancashire."

"A bishop?" Lord and Lady Preston responded together.

Jeremy looked at the ground and shook his head. "I'm sorry, Mum and Dad. I don't have to take the London church."

Lord Preston stared at him. "What?"

Lady Preston put her hands on his shoulders and kissed his cheek. "My dear boy, of course you must take it. God moves in mysterious ways. We're so proud of you."

"Well done, Jeremy!" Edward came over and pumped the cleric's left hand, carefully avoiding Jeremy's prosthetic right arm and hand. "This is excellent news. I fear I must let my own cat out of the bag now."

"What is that?" asked Emma.

"Mother and Father know, but no one else in the family does. The Conservative Party has chosen me for one of its candidates. I'm to run for a seat in Parliament the next election. I'm to run for Dover!"

Emma laughed. "No! Is it true? You and Char only a stone's throw from us in London?"

"If I win, yes."

Victoria hugged him fiercely from behind. "Of course you'll win, old brother Edward. You've always wanted to rule the world, and now you've got your start."

"Ouch! Careful of the pocketbook. I still have to get by Labor and the Liberals."

"That's nothing."

"Well, Vic, Labor took power from the Conservatives and formed the government in January. I can't underestimate them."

"You'll be first past the post, never fear."

"Here they come!" a voice shouted.

The crowd made their way off the landing strip as the judges yelled into their megaphones. Five or six dots could be spotted rapidly approaching, darting underneath a white bank of cumulus clouds and dropping in altitude. As the shapes of the planes grew obvious, the colors of the SPAD in the lead became clear to the people on the ground: yellow and black. Close on the lead plan's tail was a SPAD with a white cross painted on the fuselage.

"Ben! It's Ben!" Victoria exclaimed as she pointed. "He has the cross. He's right behind the leader."

"And Kipp is right behind Ben." Edward grinned. "See the black K?"

Lord Preston struck his leg with the newspaper. "First past the flagstaff wins."

The roar of engines blotted out conversation. For a moment it looked as if both Ben and Kipp would overtake the black-and-yellow SPAD, but its pilot opened the throttle and surged ahead, streaking past the flagpole half a minute before anyone else. A groan swept through the crowd. Victoria closed her eyes and put the back of her hand to her mouth. Lord Preston unfolded his paper and glanced at a list of entrants that included descriptions of their aircraft.

"I see." He shook his head. "A German won. A Baron von Zeltner. I'd hoped to give the Lord Preston Cup to an Englishman first time around. Well, well, can't be helped."

Von Zeltner brought his plane about and touched down on the grass. Ben and Kipp came in for a landing minutes after him. The judges barked into their megaphones and reminded people more planes would be coming in over the next few minutes even as a cluster of men and women waving the black, red, and gold flag of Germany's Weimar Republic rushed von Zeltner's SPAD. He cut his engine quickly and the propeller whirred to a stop moments before the well-wishers reached his plane. Climbing out, he was swarmed by the flag bearers and lifted up onto their shoulders. Once his boots were on the ground again, a teenaged girl in a dress the colors of his plane kissed him on the cheek and presented him with a bouquet of roses. Smiling broadly, he lifted them to his face. Some were yellow, others scarlet, and still others such a bloodred they looked black.

"Shall I bring the trophy from the hut now, Lord Preston?"

Lord Preston nodded, his lips tight. "Yes, Skitt. They've set up a table for it on the other side of the Quonset. Not with red, black, and gold bunting, thank goodness."

"That's not all there is to say about it, surely?" Jeremy looked at Victoria. "Didn't you tell me the planes all took off at different intervals?"

"Yes."

"Then who won must depend on when Ben and Kipp actually left Liverpool."

"If it was the same time as the German, the race is over and done, Jeremy," Lord Preston said.

Edward cocked his eyebrows. "Yes, but they might have taken off long after him. Jeremy's right. The judges will have something to say about this once everyone's touched down."

The Germans moved their celebration to the edge of the field as SPAD after SPAD made its way in and landed. Lord Preston counted every one and was relieved when number twenty bounced over the grass and sputtered to a stop. The children boiled up from the pond, whistling and yelling and waving their arms, Harrison and Holly running after them to herd them away from the airplanes. The judges gathered the pilots into a group by the Quonset where Skitt had placed the award cup on a table decorated for the occasion. The trophy was two feet high with large handles on either side and fashioned out of silver. Von Zeltner finally broke away from the Germans and made his way to the hut, the roses still in his hand.

"Tough break, England," he said as he approached Ben and Kipp. "The wind was in my favor. Perhaps God as well."

Ben said nothing, but Kipp bent to smell one of the roses. "Great bouquet. A very pretty girl put them in your arms. Mind if I take the flowers home, Wolfgang?"

Von Zeltner gave a half laugh. "Take them home? Well, why not? There will be plenty more for me in Berlin. Here!" He handed the bouquet to Kipp. "And if your French wife doesn't mind, you can take the young woman home too. That would spice up your marriage, Danforth."

Ben saw Kipp's right hand ball into a fist, and he stepped in to take the bouquet. "*Danke, Wolfgang*," Ben said. "But I wouldn't get my hopes up about taking the cup back to the Fatherland. They timed the flights, remember? And we took off *after* you did."

Von Zeltner was quiet a moment. "Not so long after, Whitecross."

"At least ten minutes."

"We'll see."

Von Zeltner stalked away.

"Thank you for that." Kipp was rigid. "I'm sure my father would have been less than impressed at his son brawling with a German baron at the Danforth summer estate. Could touch off another war."

"Ah, but think how much better you would feel right now if you'd permanently hammered his face into the landing strip. You could have walked over that baronial snout of his every time you flew in and out of Dover Sky."

"There's a heartwarming Christian thought."

"Right."

One of the judges, thin as wire and sporting a top hat and tails, walked into the cluster of fliers with a clipboard. "I've just rung up

Liverpool and gotten the departure times for every plane. The judges and I have matched those with your arrival times, and I have the final results here." The pilots grew quiet as he flipped through a few sheets. Glancing up, he spotted von Zeltner at the back. "Baron von Zeltner, I congratulate you on being the first across the line. However you were also the first to leave Liverpool."

Von Zeltner's voice was tight. "I took off in a group of three."

"Yes." The judge consulted his clipboard. "With Hugo and St. Laurent." He looked back up and met von Zeltner's gaze. "You had nine minutes and seventeen seconds head start on the second person across the line, Benjamin Whitecross. And he was only thirty-seven seconds behind you. Which means he beat you by eight minutes and forty seconds. Ben Whitecross wins the Lord Preston Cup Air Race!"

Von Zeltner's face whitened. "I demand to see that page of arrival and departure times."

"Certainly. You will notice it is signed and authorized by all four judges."

Von Zeltner pushed his way through the fliers and snatched the clipboard from the judge's hand. The other pilots crowded in and looked over his shoulder as he scanned the page. He dropped the clipboard on the grass and headed towards his plane.

"Are you not staying for the festivities, Baron von Zeltner?" the judge called after him. "It is Lord Preston's sixtieth birthday and there will be fireworks at ten."

"I will have my festivities in Berlin," von Zeltner snapped over his shoulder. "They know who the hero of the hour is."

"I see. Well, don't forget to fill up with petrol on Lord Preston's shilling. We'd hate to have Germany's hero wind up at the bottom of the Channel for lack of fuel."

The rest of the pilots swarmed Ben, shaking his hand and slapping him on the back. "Well done, Whitecross! Well done!"

Another ball of light trailed sparks and then burst overhead, forming a blazing flower with seven golden petals. A great "ahhhhhh" erupted from the hundreds of people spread around Dover Sky.

"Mum?"

"That one was particularly lovely. Your Father didn't want to spend the money, but I asked him when he intended to turn sixty a second time. Now and then we have to kill the fatted calf and celebrate."

"Mum?"

"What is it, Catherine? Ohhhhhh, look at that—the colors of the Union Jack!"

"I want you to know that I intend to remain at Dover Sky through the winter."

An explosion of green and white lit up the night sky.

"What did you say?"

"I said I plan to make Dover Sky my home. I'm not going back with you and Papa in the fall."

Elizabeth turned to look at Catherine. Red flashed over her face from the next burst of fireworks. "Of course you are returning to Ashton Park with us. There's no one at Dover Sky in the winter but Fairburn and a few other servants, and Fairburn will be leaving in November."

"I want to be in the south."

"Nonsense."

Thump. Thump. Thump. Gold and silver streaks shot through the darkness.

"Mum, do you want me to rent a flat in Dover? I've lived on my own in Belfast when Albert was on buisness trips, for heaven's sake. Why can't I stay at the summer estate?"

"My dear, no one lives here but the groundskeeper, and as the groundskeeper will soon be Skitt, it's out of the question."

"Why? He won't be a bother."

"A bother? The young man's dotty about you. It simply can't be done."

"Dotty? You have such quaint expressions." Catherine looked up at a particularly vivid burst of yellow. "I will go to Dover then. Or Folkestone. Or perhaps as far south as Plymouth."

"Plymouth? What on earth is in Plymouth?" Lady Preston's mouth opened slightly as Roman candles were lit and pumped dozens of stars into the blackness. "Ah, it's Leftenant Commander Fordyce, isn't it? You want to be closer to him."

"I don't really."

"You've been out with him several times now."

"Just to dinner."

"Devonport is still a long ways from Dover Sky."

Catherine folded her arms across her chest as bang after bang interrupted their conversation. "I'm not going to argue with you, Mum. I'm twenty-five. Certainly I'm well within my bounds to choose where I wish to live."

"I don't understand why you want to stay here."

"It's not a great mystery. Ashton Park pulls me down; Dover Sky lifts me up."

"Why?"

"I can't write out all the reasons why, Mother. It's just that way."

Six or seven fireworks broke open one after another.

"Very well since you are so determined." Lady Preston gazed upward at the showers of colored sparks. "There must be more staff. You cannot have Tavy or Mrs. Longstaff, but Norah and Sally have been helping Mrs. Longstaff with the meals so they will be well suited to the kitchen. It's quite impossible to leave Skitt here with you in the vicinity. Harrison must take over as groundskeeper. He will be amenable to that, although he will certainly miss his castle. Holly will fulfill the role of manager of the household staff. Hmm, and we must have more of those. I'll send along Nancy and Harriet. They'll do nicely as chambermaids, but we require a couple of footmen as well. You do complicate matters, my dear. It's bad enough having Emma in London this fall and Edward and Charlotte taking up residence in Dover so he can start ringing doorbells."

"But there's no election scheduled."

"There will be. Ramsay MacDonald and Labor have a minority government. Something always happens with minority governments. It doesn't take long before they topple, and there's another election. You could always room with Edward and Charlotte, of course, and save me all this trouble."

"No, Mum, I need to be on my own. Alone as I can be in a house you're cramming with servants."

"You'll find you need all of them. People will visit if Dover Sky is occupied over the winter months. What am I thinking? You'll require a butler as well. Liscombe? Tarrington?"

"Put in Skitt, Mother."

"What? Skitt as butler? A young man who is a groundskeeper? Ridiculous."

"Let him have a go. Skitt can do the job. He loves it here."

"I'm sure he does with the queen of his heart in her bedchamber upstairs."

"Don't talk rot, Mum. And you'll have Harrison and two footmen at Dover Sky in any case if you're worried about appearances."

"No, no, I'm sorry, my dear. Skitt staying is out of the question."

"So now it's just family and close friends." Edward lifted a glass. "A toast to my father, Lord Preston! May he live to see another sixty years and another Conservative government before the year's out."

People clapped and cheered. Lord Preston disentangled himself from his grandchildren on the library's couch and got to his feet.

"It may be more likely I see one hundred and twenty summers than I see the Conservative Party in power before Christmas." Lord Preston waved his hand. "We've already had a full day and more than enough speeches. I've promised the children angel food cake and ice cream before their special birthday bedtime, their regular bedtime being long past. So pray, I say, let's say grace and get on with it."

"Father." Edward held up several telegrams. "I have cables to read from Michael and Libby in America, as well as Robbie and Shannon in Jerusalem."

"Do you? Bless them for remembering me. But those are easily read out loud while we're eating cake, I think."

After the family and guests had cake and Edward read the various birthday greetings, the majority of the guests left for home. When just close friends and family were left, Edward announced, "There is also a special gift from Lord and Lady Scarborough."

"Is there? Where is it?"

Lord Scarborough stood up. "Difficult to wrap, Lord Preston. But I'll gladly take you to it in the morning."

"Take me to it in the morning? Where is it? At your villa in Portugal?"

"Not quite, old boy. The gift is down at the Port of Dover—berthed."

"What?" Lord Preston stared at him.

Lord Scarborough smiled. "I have not had the opportunity of presenting you with a prize worthy of your attainment to marquess and lordship. Now you are sixty as well. So many milestones. Not to mention our friendship. Lady Scarborough and I picked this out on our own. It is not brand-new, mind you, but it's utterly seaworthy and comes with a glorious history."

"What have you done, sir? It's not a boat!"

"I would not call it that. It is a forty footer with a bow as keen as a saber."

"A yacht, sir?"

"Indeed, a yacht, sir. She is christened *Pluck*."

"I can't wait for morning!" Lord Preston glanced around him. "Do you all understand? I simply can't wait for morning!" He pointed at the couch. "All those six and above, come with me at once. Harrison?"

Harrison got to his feet. "M'lord?"

"You will drive. Bring around the larger Rolls, if you please. Lady Preston, you must join me. And Lord and Lady Scarborough, of course."

"The Silver Ghost with the long chassis then?" asked Harrison.

"Yes, yes. Anyone else want to come along? I know this is highly irregular and the hour is late, but Lord and Lady Scarborough have indulged in a bit of madness and I can only respond in kind. Why, I couldn't get a wink of sleep in any case without going down to the harbor to see this vessel for myself. I trust you are not pulling my leg, my Lord Scarborough?"

Lord Scarborough barked a laugh. "Never entered my head but once or twice."

Lord Preston propelled his wife through the door. "If any of you are joining us, come along, come along! A glance out the window will give you Harrison and the Silver Ghost at any moment so sharp's the word and nimble's the action."

"Lord Kipp, you're not going with the mob?"

Kipp, glass of punch in hand, was staring at a sea painting of an English frigate clashing with a French warship off Dover, circa 1815. The lady's voice was instantly recognizable. He turned quickly, as if he'd been struck from behind. "Lady Caroline!"

She smiled. "*Lord Kipp. Lady Caroline*. Why are we standing on social niceties when the library is empty, and you're the man who saved my life?"

Her beauty filled his eyes and made him stumble over his words. "Don't you—don't you think that's an exaggeration?"

"No, I don't. Who else would have rescued me from France and that ogre Tanner Buchanan?" She was dressed in a gown the color of sapphire that heightened the blue in her eyes. "It's been ages. Do you have a kiss for me?"

Kipp hesitated. Then he leaned forward and put his lips to her soft cheek and wisps of shining blonde hair. "You look extraordinary," he said when he straightened.

She kissed his cheek in return. "Thank you. And you're still my handsome young aviator. You flew well today."

"Not well enough."

"Oh yes, well enough." She traced a white-gloved finger along the side of his face. "You're the one I'd have chosen for the prize."

"Christelle is just downstairs."

"Chris left in the third car with Matthew and Charles. The younger ones put up such a fuss they took the lot of them to Dover." She brushed his cheek with the back of her gloved hand. "Besides, it was Chris who told me to hunt you down and pamper you, so I'm doing that."

"Really? She said that?"

"Yes, she did."

"Have you...have you heard anymore from Charles's father?"

Caroline wrinkled her nose. "You do bring up distasteful subjects.

Tanner Buchanan writes letters to Charles. He comes by to visit in the company of that Kate Hall lady of his. He doesn't want me and I don't want him, if that's what you're wondering. It's only about his son. He's maneuvering for custody of him and for a seat in the House of Commons."

"Where has he set up residence?"

"Scotland. South Ayrshire. Robbie Burns country."

"What's he doing there? I thought Buchanan fancied himself a highlander."

"So he does. But this is the seat Labor offered him if there's another election. The other chap will be stepping down. Tanner's staking out his political turf, much as your brother Edward is doing in Dover." Caroline pouted, bringing her full lips together. "Do we have to go on about such a dreary subject? The last time I saw you was at your Aunt Holly's wedding a whole year ago. I wish you and Chris would come down for a visit to the Scarborough estate."

Kipp swirled the ice cubes in his drink. "Chris thinks the world of you. Your boy and ours get along. It's me...I'm to blame. Too much flying. And now Ben and I are doing the racing as well. There's another one next month—Paris to Madrid."

"So no time for your wife or me?"

"There's time for my wife. You're something else again. Why haven't you picked up on another man by now? If it were possible, you're even more beautiful than you were during the war—and at that time your charm was considerable."

"Not considerable enough to keep you."

"Truly, Caroline, you are a marvel. You can't tell me, what with all the guests your parents bring home, there hasn't been an offer or two."

"I'm damaged goods, remember?"

"It's 1925 in a few months. Attitudes have changed."

"Not among us bluebloods." She took the glass from his hand. "Here...let's put that to one side, shall we?" Her eyes seemed to catch fire in the lamplight. "Chris and you always say the same thing about me—that I'm getting more beautiful as I push ahead into my late twenties. Is it true or is it just a French kindness on her part?"

"Christelle's honesty is her French kindness."

"I see." Her lips brushed over his. "Then be nice to me, Kipp. Be kind. Just a little."

"Caroline—"

"I'm not asking for the moon and sixpence, Lord Kipp. Just some charity. For a beautiful woman no one wants."

"I'm married to Christelle now."

Her arms went around him. The perfume of her hair and her skin filled his head.

"Oh, Kipp," she murmured, tangling her fingers in his hair. "I love you."

He turned away abruptly. "No, no."

Without looking at her he walked quickly from the room.

She smiled after him. "We'll try again, shall we?"

5

October, 1924
Port of Dover

"The government's fallen! Can you believe it? Ramsay and Labor lost a no-confidence vote, and we're to have an election." Edward swept Charlotte into his arms and kissed her again and again.

Her hair had been bound up in a scarf while she cleaned the flat, but his sudden swoop and the draft from the open door brought her long, black hair down swiftly.

"That's marvelous!" she laughed. "So when is your first speech?"

"Tomorrow night at the town hall. All the candidates will be having a go and introducing their families."

"Their families?" Charlotte pulled back. "You're joking."

"I'm not. The good people of Dover and district shall want to see I am a respectable family man with a wife and child. And where is our little man?"

"Napping."

"Good! I can kiss you some more, you ravishing beauty."

"Come, Edward, not in the middle of the afternoon!"

"What difference does the time of day make? You are spectacular."

"I'm not! I'm all set up for cleaning."

"Really?" He kissed the dark hair that had unraveled from its combs. "You look ready to go door-to-door with me."

"Oh!" She pushed against him fiercely. "You're not getting me out any door when I'm looking like a bucket of slops."

"A bucket of slops? I'd like to know when you've ever looked like a bucket of slops!" He picked her up off the floor and swung her about in his arms. "You're not afraid, are you, my Lady Charlotte?"

"Your *Lady* Charlotte? Of course I'm afraid. You're the one who wanted to be a public figure, not me. I didn't even want to be called *lady*, but marrying you fixed that."

"It wasn't marrying me. It was dad being made a marquess by the king."

"I don't care whose fault it is, I'm quite happy to stay at home, and mop floors, and raise my boy, and brew tea. I honestly am. Now I suppose you want to become the prime minister of Britain and getting elected member of parliament for Dover is the first step."

"It is. And the rocky road to success begins with tomorrow night's speech and the unveiling of the magical and magnificent Lady Charlotte Danforth and her equally magical and magnificent son."

"I shan't say anything. I'll just smile and nod."

"Hair up?" Edward asked.

"Yes, hair up."

"Our lad in his suit?"

She smiled. "He'll be out of it in a month, so the suit might as well go out with a splash. Yes, our boy will be all suited up like his father."

Edward swung her about a final time and planted her on the floor. "It will be the most exceptional month—the most splendid array of days since the reign of Queen Victoria!"

"Oh, will it? Fancy that."

"I need your love to keep me moving forward."

"You always have that."

"And your kisses."

"You and your kisses. You get more than your share. Most men don't get half so many from their wives in a lifetime."

"I haven't had any lately. Not today." Edward raised his eyebrows. "And today is such a special day."

Charlotte put her hands on her hips. "Not today? How can you say that! You've been kissing me nonstop since you walked through that door and took me away from my broom and dustpan."

"There it is! I've been kissing you, but *you* haven't been kissing me."

"Is that so, Lord Edward?"

"It is so, Lady Charlotte."

She gave him a peck on the cheek. "There you are."

"Lip kisses."

"Lip kisses now? We'll be at this all afternoon."

"Excellent! Once I'm properly inspired, I'll write my speech."

"Little Lord Fauntleroy will be up in half an hour."

Edward peeled off his suit jacket with a grin. "Then we'd best get to the lip kissing. What a capital day for it!"

Charlotte shook her head and gave him a sly smile that made her blue eyes flicker with light. "I've never seen such a man for the loving."

"No other man has had you to love."

"Ah, a charmer." She put her arms around his neck. "Lip kissing it is for the future prime minister of England. Ready…set…go!" She brought his head towards hers with a sharp tug and kissed him with relish.

She didn't pull away until Edward was sure he was going to drop like a stone to the floor.

He tried to break the kiss, but she wouldn't let him.

Finally she drew her lips away only long enough to smile at him darkly and murmur, "Oh no you don't, Mr. Prime Minister! In for a penny, in for a pound."

October
Dover Sky

"Skitt! Good to see you."

"Leftenant Commander." Skitt's reply was frosty.

"I've come to collect Lady Catherine."

"Is that right, sir?"

Rain pelted Terrence's officer's hat and trench coat. "Uh, may I step inside, Skitt?"

Skitt opened the manor door a bit more. "As you wish."

Fordyce squeezed into the hall, water running off his coat and forming a puddle on the floor.

Skitt glanced down at the puddle. His lip curled. "I'll have to fetch one of the maids and have her come with a mop," he said in a flat voice.

"Sorry about that. English weather, you know."

"One shouldn't be out in it, sir." Skitt walked away. "I'll get the maid."

"Will you please tell Lady Catherine I'm here?"

Skitt glanced back at him. "To be sure. After I find Harriet or Nancy and help them get the bucket and mop."

Skitt vanished down the hall. Neither Skitt nor the maid appeared as Fordyce stood impatiently by the door. After a good five minutes, he glimpsed Catherine upstairs, moving from one room to another.

"Hullo, Cathy!"

She appeared at the head of the staircase. Peering down, she said, "Terry! What on earth are you doing standing there? I didn't even know you'd arrived."

"I'm not surprised. I don't think your butler approves of me."

Catherine put her hand over her mouth as her eyes crinkled. "Skitt doesn't approve of anyone. I'll be down in a minute. I want to kiss Sean goodbye."

In just a few minutes Terrence watched Catherine float down the stairs toward him. He helped her with her coat as they discussed the atrocious storm.

Harriet showed up with mop and bucket just as the couple headed out the door.

"Just a bit of water like this?" she grumbled. "Skitt made it sound like I had to mop up Noah's flood."

"Thank you, Harriet," Catherine said just before Terrence closed the door.

As they drove through the rain and the dark, Catherine rested her right hand on Fordyce's arm. "Mum will try Skitt out till Christmas, she says. He's mostly the groundskeeper; however, he's done very well as a butler. It's only my suitors he has issues with."

"Your suitors? You have more than one?"

"Oh, millions, Terry!" She smiled and gave him a kiss on the cheek. "That's all you get for now. Keep your eyes on the road."

"So we'll have time together after the speech?"

"We shall. I'll want a hot coffee and a snack."

"Char is so hospitable."

"She is. But it will be late, they'll have their son with them, and Edward goes on the road again tomorrow with this election flap. So you don't need to worry about losing out on our time alone." She leaned her head against the window. "It's absolute madness—only three weeks for an election campaign. One week gone now, and I'm sure neither my father up in Lancashire nor Edward here in Dover have had a wink of sleep. I just hope it's a happy ending."

"Me too. I've had my fill of Labor and the Liberals both." Fordyce honked as he passed a car. "Listen, I know everything's moving rather quickly between us, Cathy. But—"

She lifted her head. "Oh no! You have that naval 'take charge' sound to your voice. You're not going to ask for my hand in marriage, are you?"

"Nothing so rash. I just want to make sure you will attend the Christmas Ball in Plymouth in December with me. I very much want to show you off."

"Haven't we already established that I'll be hanging off your arm in silks and pearls at that event?"

"Just double-checking, love."

"Why?"

Fordyce hesitated a moment as he concentrated on driving. "It's a dirty night, isn't it?" He honked at a truck. "Those army lorries always take over the entire road if they can get away with it." He glanced at her. "You look lovely, Cathy. Have I told you that tonight?"

She narrowed her eyes and took her hand from his arm. "Come, Terry, out with it. What's up?"

"We're setting off after Christmas. First to Lisbon to take part in the

Vasco de Gama celebration they're having. You know, Vasco de Gama the great explorer?"

"Yes, I know who Vasco de Gama was. Then what?"

"The Med."

"The Mediterranean? But the *Hood* just came back from a world-wide cruise last month."

"I know it. But the lads want to go down to the sun belt. It's good for morale, and the Royal Navy has exercises for us to run."

"I'm sure they do. Our fighting navy off to Gibraltar and Malta to save the Empire. I suppose you'll be gone till spring."

"Something like that."

"Something like that? Oh Terry, things between us were just getting onto surer footing." She plunged her head back against the seat and groaned. "Don't fall for a navy man, every young woman is told. It's something we are told never to do. Now look at the mess I'm in."

"It's hardly a mess, Cathy. I care for you very much and—"

"Of course it's a mess! Here I'm living at Dover Sky through a rainy, dreary winter, and the one good reason to be doing it is off to work on his suntan after Christmas."

"Cathy—"

"So I'm supposed to be like the dutiful wife and wait by the window as I look out toward the sea, darn your socks, and pray for your safe return?"

"I don't know about the wife, window, or socks part of it, but I do hope you'll pray for my safe return."

Catherine sighed, her eyes still shut. "I will. You know I will. But Terry, we're not married or engaged. And I'm not saying I want to be right now. It's far too soon for anything like that. But quite honestly I don't want to sit around all winter as if I were. I do want to get out of the house."

"So there is someone else?" he said sharply, giving her a quick glance.

"There is no one else as close to me as you are. I just want you to understand if I go to a concert in London with a gentleman or attend a worship service in Canterbury with another, that it doesn't mean I want to break off with you. I simply have to get out to get some air."

"I understand that, I guess."

"You do?"

"Yes. And what's his name?"

"Terry! There is no one man...just some acquaintances." She looked at his worried face. "Horatio Nelson. It's him. Are you satisfied?"

"Not very."

"Well, that will have to do."

They rode in silence for several miles. Catherine finally spoke. "Let's not spoil our evening together. I care for you, Terry. I'm just not ready to start pining away again. I've been pining for more than two years already."

"I know that."

She put her hand back on his arm and gave it a squeeze. "Good. So you understand why I can't go back to that dark hole, not even for you." She stared out through the rain sliding over the windshield and the swipes of the wipers. "In any case, it works both ways. I shan't mind if you see a woman or two when you're in port at Gibraltar."

"I'm not interested."

"Maybe one of them will change your mind." She glanced at him and noted his clenched jaw and tight lips. "Don't be a martyr, Terry. I count on your cheerfulness. Come back to me, but don't come back to me sour."

Port of Dover

"We cannot have a trade agreement with the communists in Moscow! Only Ramsay MacDonald could think that was a good idea. Ramsay MacDonald and his Labor Bolsheviks." Edward paused as people in the packed hall cheered. "If I am elected, I will help form a Conservative government with Stanley Baldwin once more at the helm. Then we will tear up that agreement. We will have no trade with those revolutionaries—those assassins whose hands were dipped in blood with the murder of Tsar Nicholas and his family, even his children! I say it again: No trade with the murderers and Bolsheviks!"

The audience erupted into applause again. Edward waited for the roar to subside. "But I don't want you to send me to Westminster just to deal with the Red Menace, important as that is for the future of Great Britain. I also want to do something for Dover. I want to do something for you—the workingman—and for your children and your grandchildren. More shipping, more across-the-Channel traffic. A bigger harbor—a deeper harbor and a more protected harbor."

Men jumped to their feet, clapping and waving their hats in the air. "I want a port second to none in Great Britain! I want a port that will bring prosperity to Dover! I call upon you to send me to Westminster so I may ensure a Conservative government puts money into you and into our harbor. I call upon you to send me to Westminster so I may ensure a Conservative government that will *pour* money into our harbor!"

Edward tried to continue but the applause drowned out his words. He smiled and lifted his hands. Finally he shouted, "A vote for me on October twenty-ninth is a vote for Britain and the British people! God save the king!"

Fordyce made his way through the crush of bodies and managed to shake Edward's hand and slap him on the back. "Well done, Lord Edward. A great speech."

Edward grinned. "Thanks, Fordyce. I have to give another seven or eight tomorrow, so keep me in your prayers."

"We'll pop by the flat after you're free of all this to say hullo, and then Lady Catherine and I are heading out."

Enthusiastic men and women jostled Edward and called out his name. He kept smiling and shaking hands as he spoke with Fordyce. "Actually, I'm not going back to the house. I'm taking the car to Deal. I have a meeting there in an hour and another at seven in the morning. I was going to ask if you wouldn't mind taking Charlotte and Owen to Dover Sky with you. I'll be gone a week, and I'd like them to be with family."

"Why of course! I'll collect them right away. Where are they?"

"Just at the back. I'll be over to say goodbye once I'm finished here. I won't be but five minutes."

Fordyce struggled through the well-wishers. He'd just broken clear when Catherine slipped up beside him and kissed him on the cheek.

"There, that's done. I'm ready for my coffee right after we say hullo to Char."

Fordyce gave her a cold look. His voice was clipped. "We're to ferry Char and Owen to Dover Sky straightaway. Your brother is driving over to Deal when he's done here, and he'll be gone a week. He wants his wife and child safe and sound at the estate."

"I see." She hesitated. "Well, that only makes sense, doesn't it?" She held his arm. "Cheer up. I'll have Norah fix us up a pot of coffee when we get home, and we'll squirrel away in the den. It'll be better than a coffee shop or restaurant. And you'll have me all to yourself."

"Will I? We can't leave Charlotte on her own, can we? How hospitable would that be?"

"I thought you liked her."

"I do. She's wonderful. Edward married a gem. But I'll not be able to get away for another month—not until Guy Fawkes—and I'd hoped you and I could have a good talk."

"Terry, we can. I—"

"Oh, there you two are! Cheers!" Charlotte stood in front of them wearing a red dress with a matching red hat and feather. "I hear you're my cab. I really don't want to put you two out. We'd be perfectly happy at our flat while Edward's gone. He gets terribly old-fashioned about things like this."

Fordyce found his best smile quickly. "Nonsense, Char. If it were me, I'd want the same thing for my wife and son. Where's your boy? Where's the luggage?"

"Owen's with the Conservative Party's secretary for this district and probably getting horseback rides on Mr. Tippin's back, I'm sure. Poor man." She smiled. "I'm afraid we'll have to drop by the flat for the luggage, Terry. It's all terribly inconvenient. Edward just came up with this plan before he got up to speak so there's nothing packed."

"That's all right. We'll wait while you get ready."

"I'm dreadfully sorry."

"Not at all." He glanced about. "I'll fetch Owen and give Edward a wave. That'll be his cue to make his way through the multitudes to the parking lot. Come along, you two."

Charlotte walked beside Catherine. "He's a lot more chipper than I'd be if someone had ruined my plans for the evening."

"Yes," Catherine replied. "Terry can reach deep down into his sea chest and usually find the right hat to wear."

"What do you mean by that?"

"I mean he rises to the occasion."

"Well, the very least I can do is leave you two to yourselves once we're at Dover Sky. I'll tuck Owen in and read to him. Then I'll—"

Catherine put her arm through Charlotte's. "I shouldn't bother hiding away on our account. I doubt Terry will stay very long after he's seen us safely home."

"Why not? It's only eight now."

Catherine shook her head. "He'll be on his way back to the fleet."

"Something up? I thought he'd move heaven and earth to be with you for a few hours."

"We had…um…we had a bit of a disagreement on the way here. The *Hood*'s going south to the Med after Christmas and won't be back till spring."

"What? Then all the more reason for the pair of you to spend all the time you can together."

"Yes, well, once Owen is settled in and Terry leaves, you and I can have tea together and I'll explain the winter and rough weather of taking a fancy to Lord Preston's daughter Catherine. At the most unfortunate times, I get my Danforth up."

When they arrived at Dover Sky, Terry pulled up to the front door. He escorted the women and boy to the front door, went back and brought Charlotte's bags in and left them with the poker-faced Skitt. Then he tipped his officer's hat to Charlotte and Catherine, and headed back into the sheets of rain. He got behind the steering wheel and drove away.

"You were right about that, weren't you?" Charlotte sat in a corner of the library ten minutes later, a model of the clipper ship *Cutty Sark* on the shelf above her head. "Terry didn't let any grass grow under his heels."

Catherine poured from a Royal Doulton teapot. "He's hurt."

"Will you explain?"

Skitt had started a small blaze in the fireplace, and a log snapped twice and hissed.

Catherine wrapped her hands around her teacup but didn't drink. "It's not hard, really. He wanted me to wait for him faithfully with a stiff upper lip while he's down at Gibraltar and Malta and who knows where. I told him I couldn't. And I can't, Char. We're not married. We're not even engaged. We've scarcely kissed."

"I—"

"One moment. I've been two years in the tomb waiting for Albert to resurrect. I walked out of that tomb with Sean in my arms this past summer when I realized I was the one who needed the resurrection. I can't go back into the tomb, Char. Not for Terry, not for anyone. It would kill me."

Charlotte didn't drink either. "I think I understand."

"Terry doesn't. But then he scarcely knows me. He thinks he does, but he doesn't. I'm more stubborn than he realizes. I'm not in a hurry to find a man, not even for Sean's sake. And I've got a fighter's streak running through me as thick as the cable that holds *HMS Hood* in place. I can't sit at Dover Sky all winter waiting for him to return from sea with Drake and Raleigh and Nelson. I want to go to the theater, eat at restaurants where crystal chimes and forks and knives make a great clatter because people are happy all around me. I want to go to concerts in London, get a glimpse of the king and queen in their royal box, and walk under the cliffs at Dover with someone other than Aunt Holly."

Charlotte slipped her a smile. "And other than your sister-in-law?"

"I adore you, Char. For that matter, I adore Holly too. But yes, I want to hear a man's footsteps beside me. I want to smell his cologne, have his hand take my arm if I stumble, take in that lovely man scent I've missed so much—the tweed, the pipe tobacco, the leather gloves and shoes. I miss manliness, Char. I'm starved for it, and I shan't be without just because the navy likes a Mediterranean sun more than four months of English rain."

Charlotte put her teacup to her lips. "Why didn't you stay at Ashton Park if you wanted people and men around you?"

"No, no, no!" Catherine put her teacup down. "Not brothers and sisters and aunts and uncles and lords and ladies. Different people… different men."

"What men?"

"I don't know. There's a couple of nice chaps who attend the church in Dover. Also an army officer or two. A sexton from Canterbury Cathedral I met seemed nice. I don't want anything serious or dramatic, Char. But I want to be treated like a lady by a man. Once a week would be just perfect…or twice."

"So you don't love Terry?"

Catherine was silent for a moment. "I love his easy ways and his big smile and his uniform, but I don't want a ring or a proposal from him anytime soon. I won't wait by the pier for his return. I'm no nineteenth-century painting with the title 'A Woman Longs for Her Sailor.'" She lifted her cup and drank. "Not much of a widow, am I?"

"You were a very good widow in '22 and '23 and most of '24."

"Was I? What am I now?"

"A very good lady."

"Hmm." Catherine glanced at the ship model as another log cracked and spat. "I suppose I've changed, but I can't help it. It was either change or turn to dust." She smiled at Charlotte. "What about you? You're an election widow. How does that feel?"

Charlotte rolled her eyes to the ceiling. "I'll be so glad when I don't have to be introduced to noisy crowds anymore." She glanced at Catherine. "Election night will be a fright, but I can't wait for it to arrive. What a relief to have the campaigning over and done."

"Will Edward win in Dover, do you think?"

"Don't I pray for that? I hope God doesn't mind, but an unelected Edward will drive me 'round the bend. He needs to be in the House making his speeches and arguing with whomever dares to cross swords with him. Please, Lord, not a mansion on the hill like Dover Sky or a yacht at the dock like Lord Preston. Just a plain, ordinary seat in the British Parliament is all I'm asking for Edward."

"Amen! Well, here's to election night and that God's will be done. Only two weeks left to go. More tea?"

"Please. Is it still hot?"

"Very. I parked it by Skitt's fire."

Election Night, 1924

"Hullo, Mum. It's Charlotte. I've been trying to reach you all night."

"The lines are jammed all over Britain with the election," Lady Preston replied. "Are you calling from Edward's office?"

"It's a complete madhouse in that headquarters of his. I finally fled an hour ago. The nanny's with us overnight, so at least Owen didn't have to endure all those cigars and cigarettes and pipes. My eyes are still red and puffy."

"I understand. For years I attended election night frenzies with William until I'd had enough and decided to stay home with the children. I'd advise you to remain at home until Edward finally wanders in at four in the morning. How are things looking for him?"

"I don't know. Edward's crew is happy one moment and worried the next. They keep changing numbers on the chalkboard. Newspapermen dash in and out as if they're delivering military communiqués that will determine the fate of the Great War. The battery of phones is always ringing off the hook. Clouds and clouds of smoke. Everything made me quite dizzy. I have no idea what's going on, but I'm sure we're holding our own against Labor. How about Dad? What's happening with him?"

"He thought he could manage things from Ashton Park with the one phone. Well, he kept losing the connection or else he couldn't get through to his people in the city. I finally shooed him out the door. Todd drove him into Liverpool to his campaign office. I've heard from him once since then. He said he thought things were a bit dicey. Then he got cut off."

"Oh, Mum, I don't know what we'll do if we lose. Edward has his heart set on joining his father at Westminster."

"Don't fret, my dear. Believe me, I've been through plenty of close elections in my time. The Lord has a way of working things out one way or the other. Even if Edward doesn't win, he'd still be his father's parliamentary assistant."

"That won't satisfy Edward anymore. He wants to debate, make speeches, cast a vote in the House, make policy."

"Yes, yes, just like William—down to the nose on his face. We can only wait and pray, Charlotte. The votes are being counted all over the kingdom. It will be the wee hours of the morning before anyone gets a good grasp of things. Call me the minute you know anything for certain."

"All right."

Election Night
Port of Dover

Charlotte Danforth lay on her back on the bed. The clock in the hall downstairs struck three. She punched her pillow, put it under her head, put it over her head, and then finally tossed it onto the floor. She cradled her head on her arms. She was able to drift off for a few minutes in this position, but the dream was unpleasant. Edward had lost and had taken to drink. She found him wandering by the Dover docks with a bottle of gin in his hand and tears rolling down his face.

"Ah, don't cry, my love," she pleaded, throwing her arms around him. *"We'll be all right. We'll get back on our feet."*

"We won't," he rasped.

"We will! I swear we will. How many elections have we had in the past few years? Three? Four? Another's bound to come along soon, and when it does you'll run again and win. You'll win, Edward!"

His watery eyes struggled to focus on her. "Are you...are you a...a lady of the evening?"

Charlotte sat up and put a hand to her face. "That was nasty," she mumbled. She got up and got dressed. *I'm not going to risk another dream like that, Lord. I'm going down there. And whatever's happened, we'll deal with it, that's all.*

The door to Owen's room was ajar, and she peeked in. The nanny was asleep in the bed by Owen's crib. The two-year-old was curled up under his quilt, eyes shut, breathing softly. She made her way quietly downstairs, took her woolen peacoat from the rack, tugged it on, added a black scarf, and headed outside.

"Brrrr." She brought black leather gloves out of the pocket of her coat and pulled them on. "What a time of year to have an election."

Her boots made a *snip-snap, snip-snap* sound on the cement as she walked. The streets were dark and deserted. She put up the high collar of her jacket against the cold. Finally she reached an avenue lit by lamps and slowed down, enjoying the amber glow in the cold blackness. She dreaded turning into the narrow side street that made its way to the waterfront and Edward's tiny office. She'd been there earlier in the evening, and but for the light from the office windows it felt like being in the coal mine she'd visited as a little girl. She could almost taste the coal dust. The empty shops looked like the shored up walls of the mine. It made her feel hemmed in.

"Ma'am? Mrs. Danforth? Lady Charlotte?"

She'd barely emerged into the open by Edward's office when a man barreled into her. His hat was crooked, his tie askew, his eyes wide and a huge, a wild smile creased his face.

"Mr. Gibbons!" She was startled by his appearance. "Are you all right? Is anything wrong?"

"Wrong? Wrong?" He gripped her shoulders and laughed, his breath almost knocking her over. "A landslide! Right across the country! More than four hundred seats. That's how it's shaping up, m'lady! Labor's out and the Liberals…why, the Liberals have lost three hundred seats and are down to forty! It's not settled yet, but that's what's shaping up. That's what the phones and the newspapermen are telling us!" He let out a whoop and hurled his hat into the night. "We have a Tory government!" Running past the silent shops he disappeared into an alley still hollering with joy.

"What about my husband?" she called after him, but he didn't turn around or offer an answer.

Edward's office was only a block away now. Light was spilling out of the open door into the street, and people were milling about, arms waving, voices loud, laughter and squeals and singing echoing off the buildings. She heard her husband speaking, his words ringing out. She pushed through the crowd to get inside.

"An amazing evening, an historic evening! Yes, a miraculous evening! Don't you think so? A miracle happened in Britain tonight!" Edward's voice was strong with certainty. The people's roar was so overwhelming Charlotte instantly thought of a rugby game or football match. The room was packed with bodies, and she could get no further than the doorway. She stood as tall as she could while the cheering went on, even going up on her toes hoping Edward would notice her. He didn't. He was reaching down to shake hands while women hugged him and newspapermen were shouting in his ear.

You look so handsome, so young, so alive, so ready to take on the world! Charlotte thought. She unwrapped the scarf from her neck and pulled the high collar of her peacoat down from her face. She drew her hair out from under her coat, shook her head, and let the blackness fall over her shoulders. *I'm here, my darling. I'm with you!* Looking up, she saw him staring over the crowd in her direction.

Stretching a hand out, Edward said, "My friends, ladies and gentlemen, the greatest support I have in my life—may I present my wife and the mother of my son, Lady Charlotte Danforth. Please make a way for her. Thank you! Please let her through."

A lane opened for her lined with people who smiled as they continued clapping. She'd hardly started forward before Edward came to her, took her in his strong arms, and kissed her. The clapping grew in intensity.

She broke the kiss and put a hand to his lips. "There are more than a hundred people here, Edward. Don't do anything rash."

He grinned. "I'm MP for Dover, love! I'll be as rash as I like tonight."
He kissed her again, lifting her off the floor.

She pushed against his arms for a few moments but finally laced her
arms around his neck and returned the kiss with as much passion and
abandon as she'd ever shown in public. The cheering shook the windows as her hair spread like a shining wing over her back.

November, 1924–April, 1925
Dover Sky

My dear Catherine,

I hope my note finds you well. I regret I will not be able to get to Dover Sky as planned for Guy Fawkes on November 5. I fear I will have to cancel on the Christmas Ball as well. A great deal must be done to prepare the *Hood* for another long voyage, and I am expected to do more than my share. I hope to stay in touch, and trust I may be able to call on you once we have returned in April or May.

With profound apologies,
Terrence

Terry,

I received your note this morning. I should have preferred a phone call. I'm sorry you are so busy we can't see each other even for a Christmas dance. Are you seriously going to be rushing about making everything shipshape right through the holiday season? I can't help but believe there are other reasons for this change in the weather.

Terry, I grieved as a widow for two years. You were one of the people who helped me get out from behind shuttered windows and into the light of day. I counted on you to understand

I cannot be a widow again while you go to sea, but I do not think you do.

I'm not trying to hurt you. I'm not asking for liberty to "play the field" while you are gone. I simply ask you to see things from my perspective. I must get out. I must get around. I will need escorts who are not brothers or uncles. I intend to be here when you return, and I very much want you to call.

I'm sorry Guy Fawkes and the Christmas season couldn't have been all the merrier for being spent in your company, my dear.

Catherine

"Ah, splendid! Splendid!" Lord Preston raised his hands over his head and clapped. "You've outdone yourself, Master Skitt! See what a fine butler he is turning into, Elizabeth."

Lady Preston squinted as flames leaped up. "If building and burning effigies of Guy Fawkes is what makes a fine butler these days, then yes, I expect Skitt is well on his way. It's a good thing he escorted Catherine home for this celebration."

The effigy was a man's figure in a tall black hat and beard. It stood about fifteen feet high and was mounted on a rough wooden sled. Skitt and Harrison were tugging it towards Lord and Lady Preston and their family. Yellow flames curled up the legs of the effigy. The men pulled it up to a high mound of dead brush and pruned branches right in front of the Danforths. It immediately ignited the wood and created a bonfire. Fire shot up to the effigy's nose and eyebrows, giving it a glowering, sinister look.

"Look at that wicked fellow!" exclaimed Lord Preston. "Just think, Edward, had he succeeded in blowing up the Parliament buildings—and he certainly had enough kegs of gunpowder to do it—you might be giving your maiden speech in a shack come the new year."

"Surely not, Father." Edward lifted up his son, Owen, so the boy could see the effigy's smoldering face better. "We'd have put up something wonderful by now to replace it, don't you think?"

"Well, well, I expect so." Lord Preston glanced at Victoria, who had her son snuggled against her shoulder. "How are you holding up, my dear? Would you like me to take young Ramsay?"

"He's half asleep, Dad, bonfire or no bonfire. Two-year-olds can only last so long. I'm all right so don't worry. I'm only three months into my pregnancy, and I'm from sturdy Lancashire stock."

"I see. I pray so. I'm only sorry Ben couldn't make it back from that race of his in France. Kipp is here, after all."

"Kipp didn't qualify, Dad. That's why he made it back for Guy Fawkes Night."

"He told me the race would be finished yesterday afternoon."

"It was. But, well, there was an accident, you see. Not Ben. He's fine. But a mate of his and Kipp's bought it…excuse me, he crashed and was killed. He hit power lines. It's dreadful, really. I didn't want to bring it up and trouble you and Mum."

Lady Preston was aghast, her face a mask of fright in the reflection of the flames and the shadows. "How terrible! The poor man and his family. But Ben is all right, you say?"

"Yes, yes, as fine as he can be seeing a friend flip over and blow up. Excuse me, I talk like a pilot all the time now. Ben is returning with the body tomorrow. The young widow lives in Canterbury. Kipp went to see her this afternoon."

Lady Preston placed her hand on her daughter's arm. "How did that go?"

"Kipp didn't say much about it. He took Jeremy with him, and he said Jeremy's presence helped a great deal. There was a lot of fuss—a lot of crying. They were the first people to tell the young woman about there being any accident, you see."

"That's awful. Is that why Jeremy and Emma didn't come down from London with the boys for Guy Fawkes?"

"Possibly. Kipp overnighted with the Scarboroughs at their estate before coming here to be with Christelle. I'm glad Mrs. Longstaff is nursing Chris back to health. That is a nasty bug she picked up."

"It really is." Lady Preston turned back to the blaze. "Well, we'll see Emma and Jeremy tomorrow when we get Edward and your father settled into the flat just down from the Parliament buildings. Fancy them living together when the House is sitting."

Victoria gave a sharp laugh. "The cooking and cleaning will be masterful, I'm sure."

"I expect they will eat out at Tollers a good deal and hire old Mrs. Brill to do the cleaning. She needs the money, in any case. She has five young ones to support since her husband was killed in the war. She gets along pretty well even though she has a bad eye."

Victoria looked into the soaring flames and thought about this. "I met her at Jeremy's church, didn't I? The very thin woman with the eye patch and the biggest smile?"

"That's Mrs. Brill."

"Was her husband Royal Navy?"

"He was, dear, yes."

The bonfire flared and plucked everyone out of the shadows, illuminating them as if they were statues on display. Victoria spotted Catherine, who had been standing further back.

"Hullo, Cath!" she called out. "We were speaking of the navy, and now I'm wondering where your naval officer is. Wasn't he supposed to be here for Guy Fawkes?"

Catherine folded her arms over her chest and kept gazing into the bonfire. "He couldn't make it. Something came up."

"I'm sorry to hear that. You'll see him before he ships out to the Mediterranean, won't you?"

"It looks like not. The *Hood* needs his attention before they weigh anchor for Gibraltar."

Victoria smiled. "Surely you need his attention too?"

Catherine didn't look away from the effigy of Guy Fawkes that suddenly popped and sparks erupted. "I don't, you know."

Dear Mum,

A quick note to let you know we'll not be driving up from Dover Sky as planned for Christmas. I'm so sorry, but Sean seems to have that on-again off-again bug Christelle has been fighting all fall. I really don't want to move him. You don't need to worry though.

We'll have a fabulous time here. Skitt and Harrison have finished winterizing the house up and down, and we're as cozy as hedgehogs in their burrows. Holly has promised a special dinner Christmas Day, and she's had Norah and Sally working away as if the king and queen are paying a visit. Best of all, we'll see Edward and Char on December 22 before they take the train to Liverpool. We'll also see Jeremy and Emma on December 23 before they head back to London for the church services.

I'll have presents for the boys, and Holly and I have bought gifts for all the servants here too so we'll be ready for everyone.

As for Sean, well, the men here are going to spoil him rotten. You know they are bringing down a pony for him? He's from Old Todd Turpin's mare. They'll hide him in the barn they put up in August. Sickbed or not, my Sean will be up on his feet and begging to ride him without so much as a hot biscuit in his tummy, I'm sure. Not quite two but going on twelve, that's him.

So you see, it will be quite wonderful here, Mama, though we will miss you and Dad and the crew at Ashton Park terribly. I'll ring you up on Christmas Eve before you attend the candlelight service at church.

I love you and Dad very much, and the two of you are always in my prayers.

Best wishes this Christmas season,
Catherine

P.S. Please let me know how Christelle is getting along. When Kipp was passing through on his way to see Lord Scarborough about some sort of investment in the airline he looked troubled. And Kipp seldom looks troubled. Please keep me up-to-date about absolutely everything, Mum. God bless and keep you.

Dover Sky

"How was your Christmas, sir?" asked the courier.

"Very well, thank you," replied Skitt. "What do you have for me?"

"Not for you exactly. It's a message for the lady of the manor—for Catherine Moore."

"She's not home at present."

"It's from Leftenant Commander Fordyce of the *HMS Hood.*"

"Ah."

The motorcycle courier lifted his goggles and held up the letter. "See here—see the stars? That means it's an important message—really important. I brought it up from Dover as fast as I could." He handed the note to the butler.

Skitt held the telegram. "If it's so important, why didn't the Leftenant Commander phone?"

"I don't know the contents of the cable, o'course, but I do know there was something about the phone lines out of Plymouth and Devonport acting up."

"I see."

"Lady Catherine Moore needs to see that right sharp, sir. Right sharp, I say."

"I know my business. Thank you for doing yours. Good day."

The courier tipped his hat and stepped back from the door. "I know my place just as you do."

"Good."

Skitt closed the door. He looked at both sides of the telegram, glanced about, and then quietly opened it with a pocketknife.

MY LOVE

PLEASE FORGIVE ME. I BEG OF YOU TO COME TO DEVONPORT BEFORE WE SAIL WHICH WILL BE IN 24 HOURS. I'VE BEEN A FOOL. I WILL MAKE IT UP TO YOU. I BEG OF YOU NOT TO IGNORE THIS PLEA DEAREST. IF YOU CAN SEND A CABLE AHEAD SO I WILL KNOW WHEN TO EXPECT YOU THAT WOULD BE GRAND. I DON'T WANT TO

SAIL WITHOUT SEEING YOUR BEAUTIFUL FACE
ONE MORE TIME.

WITH ALL MY HEART
TERRY

Skitt read it through twice. He glanced about again before walking to the peat fire flickering in the grate in the parlor. He tossed the telegram in, and a corner quickly took on a yellow edge and was engulfed in flames. In an instant it was charred paper and then ashes.

Parliament, Westminster, London

Edward Danforth paused after he rose. He glanced up at the visitors' gallery and saw his mother, his sister Emma, and her husband, Jeremy. Looking across at the Opposition benches, he saw only a blur of faces until his eyes focused on one—Tanner Buchanan. Staring over Buchanan's head, Edward began his speech.

> Mr. Speaker, as proud as we are of our nation and our Empire,
> I say we cannot afford to rest on our laurels.

Hear, hear! came from his fellow MPs in the Conservative government seats around him. He could distinctly make out his father's voice.

> While it is true that we have peace in our time, it is also true
> we have a Bolshevik menace to the east that some members
> of Parliament sought to bring into our bosom before this last
> election.

Members of the Labor Party across the aisle began to shout and point at him. Edward noticed Buchanan remained in his seat, his face calm and composed.

> The result should scarcely have been different to Great Britain than the effect achieved by Cleopatra when she coaxed the asps to fill her body with their poison.

The roar from Labor grew. Edward spoke over the cries.

> Shakespeare declared it: "With thy sharp teeth this knot
> intrinsicate of life at once untie: poor venomous fool be angry,
> and dispatch." Bolshevism would have been Britain's death.

Shouts of fury and defiance from the Labor Party swirled about
the chamber amid the yells of "Hear! Hear!" from the Conservatives.
Edward waited for the tumult to die down, but it didn't. He spoke as
loudly as he could.

> We must guard our freedom. We must remain vigilant. Not
> only against Moscow but with an eye always on Europe,
> which often as not boils over once or twice every century. We
> are grateful that borders are secure once more on the Con-
> tinent. We thank God Germany has crawled out of the ash
> heap of defeat and degradation the Kaiser abandoned it to. It
> now has a workforce that is employed and an economy that
> grows sounder each day. Nevertheless, I say the world requires
> a strong Britain, a free Britain, in order that the world itself
> may be free. To that end, we must maintain our navy. Britain
> must continue to rule the waves!

Men pounded their hands on wood for him, and other men
pounded their hands on wood against him. Edward used his stron-
gest voice to finish.

> Vigilance in time of peace so there may be victory in time of
> war. We should deepen our harbors and build at Portsmouth
> and Plymouth and Devonport; and build at Dover and Clyde
> and Scapa Flow.
>
> The navy has always been Britain's lifeline. We cannot neglect
> it. I say no to any treaties that would limit the construction
> of our warships. No, no, and a thousand times no shall the
> heirs of Nelson's legacy—the race who won at Trafalgar and
> the Nile—be left like beggars on the shore, cap in hand, hop-
> ing other navies will defend them! "Rule Britannia! Britan-
> nia rule the waves! Britons never, never, never shall be slaves!"

With tumult all around him, Edward sat back in his seat. In the pandemonium of *nays* and *yeas* his eyes locked onto those of Tanner Buchanan. He'd not opened his mouth, or thrown paper, or pounded his fist. In fact, he'd remained motionless. Nor did his eyes flinch from Edward's stare. Finally Edward glanced up at the gallery. Noticing his gaze, both Emma and his mother blew him kisses. Jeremy raised his hand and briefly nodded.

Dover Sky

Catherine looked out the window as the February sleet turned the ground white. It wouldn't last, but she found herself thinking about mountains—snowcapped mountains with sunlight flashing off the peaks. Then she found herself daydreaming about long stretches of ocean with curling whitecaps. *I thought you would at least write. Are you so angry you won't even drop me a line or wish me happy birthday? I know I hurt you, but I thought you were a bigger man than this. I honestly did, Terry.*

The Bible was open in Catherine's lap as she sat on the window seat in her room. She flipped a few pages and her eyes fell on Nahum 1:15: "*Behold upon the mountains the feet of him that bringeth good tidings, that publisheth peace!*" Catherine had scarcely read it before there was a knock on the door.

"Lady Catherine? There is a telephone call for you."

She frowned at the interruption but kept the annoyance out of her voice. "Very well, Skitt. I'll be right down. Who is it?"

"Baron von Isenburg, m'lady."

"Baron? Hullo?"

"Yes? Lady Catherine?"

"Yes, this is she. How are you keeping, Baron?"

"Ah, very well, thank you. This year has been good to Germany in terms of less inflation and much more employment."

"I'm so glad to hear it."

"Listen, Lady Catherine, Professor Hartmann has been given leave from the university to complete his book. Do you know about his book?"

"I remember him mentioning it."

"In any case, he asked specifically if you might join us in Switzerland to help him write it."

Catherine felt heat rush into her face. "What?"

"We are going to his family's chateau in Pura, Switzerland. It's quite lovely and peaceful. Cool in February with plenty of snow. The mountains—astonishing and magnificent! We truly wish you to join us and see them for yourself."

"That's…that's gracious of you, Baron. But I have my boy—"

"Naturally he will be most welcome as well."

"He just received a pony for Christmas. I don't think I can tear him away."

"Nonsense. The pony will be at Dover Sky when he returns. There is a stable by the chateau filled with beautiful horses your son will find fascinating, I'm sure. That will certainly take his mind off his pony. They have Lipizzans there. Do you know that breed?"

"No."

"Dark-colored at birth but milky white at maturity. They are strong, noble creatures who are great jumpers and often trained in dressage. I'm sure we can persuade Herr Salzgeber to let Sean ride a stallion or two under supervision."

"A stallion?"

"Under strictest supervision, I assure you."

"I don't know, Baron. How long of a trip are you planning?"

"Six to eight weeks. You could return in April or May. The chateau is fully staffed, and you would, of course, be assigned your own servants."

"I'm grateful you've thought of me, but I'm not sure why you or the professor would want me along on an occasion like that. I'm no writer or scholar."

"You are extremely intelligent and strong-minded. Herr Hartmann values that. He believes your opinions would ensure his book had adequate depth, was thorough, and was…*harten Gleichgesinnten…* how do I say this in English? Ah, tough-minded."

She didn't know how to respond.

After a moment, the baron added, "You appreciate how important this book will be to Germany?"

"Yes, yes."

"That subversive, that man Hitler, was released from prison just before Christmas. His autobiography will be published in July."

Catherine put a hand to her forehead. She felt warm and flushed. "Honestly, I don't know what to say. I'm flattered Professor Hartmann thinks so highly of me, but it is a lot to take in. I should like to think about it."

"Naturally. May I call this evening? We intend to set out tomorrow."

"This evening would be fine."

"We would, of course, come to Dover Sky and escort you and Sean to Pura."

"Thank you for the invitation, Baron. I'll consider it carefully."

"Okay, then. I'll phone you tonight. Good day."

"Good day, Baron." Catherine set the phone in its cradle and leaned a hand against the table it rested on. *What's the matter with me? It's a simple request. And the reply is also simple: No thank you.* She opened the door and left the parlor. Skitt was standing by the staircase.

"Everything all right, m'lady?" he asked.

She gave him a quick smile. "Fine, Skitt. I wonder if you could get Nancy to bring me up a spot of tea?"

"I'll take care of that personally, Lady Catherine."

"Thank you. How is Sean? Do you know?"

"Still with Harrison and Holly."

"Good. Very good."

In her room she sat and waited for the rap on the door. When it came she called, "Enter." Skitt came in and she nodded toward her writing table. He placed the tray with tea and biscuits there before leaving. Catherine set herself up at the table near the fireplace. She poured her tea and watched the rain slide along the windowpane. *Mountains. Sun on the snow. How lovely.* She'd scarcely thought of Albrecht

Hartmann since she'd met Terrence Fordyce. Now, at the mention of Albrecht, not only her mind but her entire body had reacted just as it had when she first met him in his red sports car the summer before. His golden-brown eyes, light-brown hair, and dark tan stormed her senses. She could almost smell the eau de cologne on his body. She drank her tea quickly and poured another.

The book. Yes, the book to offset this Hitler fellow's book. But was the invitation really about the book? Or was it about Albrecht and her? About them as a couple? She picked up a pen and opened the journal she'd named Cornelia.

> My dear Cornelia, my diary,
>
> I was just sitting here thinking how dreary the weather is in February. I was also thinking about Terry and wondering why he hasn't sent even a birthday card. At the back of my mind I was admitting a long line of escorts is all good and well, but that loses its charm after a while. What I want is a man I can really speak with and listen to and explore absolutely everything in heaven and earth with.
>
> I suppose that is why I was pining after Terry and moaning about the rain and sleet. By chance—chance?—my Bible opened to the book of Nahum, and I read about someone on the mountains bringing good news just when I had been longing to see sun on the snow of a tall peak. How amazing of God is that? Then to complete the string of unusual events, the phone rings and it's Baron von Isenburg asking me to spend two months in the mountains of Switzerland with him and Professor Hartmann. Mountains! Sunshine! And a stable of white stallions too!
>
> But here is the tricky part. The baron says the invitation is for me to help Albrecht write his book. My opinion is valued apparently. Rot or not? It may well be my opinion is valued. It may also be the professor values my womanhood just as much. After all, he came on very strong when we first met— saying how lovely I was, how sweet I was, how beautiful my eyes were. But we never saw each other again.
>
> Then it was all Terry, Terry, Terry.

Now, eight months later, the baron mentions Albrecht Hartmann in a phone call, and I blush like a schoolgirl. Either this
is all in my head or even over a phone line I'm picking up on
something between the handsome academic and myself. Do
such feelings cross land and sea and know no loss of force due
to time and distance?

I want to jump in one of their German Mercedes and go with
them to Switzerland! Sean would adore riding a white horse.
But another part of me just wants to stay squirreled up in my
room and wait on Terry Fordyce. Will he write, send a telegram, post a gift, show up at the door, come to call in April
or May?

Catherine put down the pen abruptly. *Why, I have become the sea
widow yearning for her sailor after all!* She stood up and pressed the
buzzer. Skitt was at the door in minutes.

"M'lady?"

"Skitt, please get Nancy and Harriet. I'd like them to help me get
packed. Sean and I are going to Switzerland for a few weeks, and we
will need the warmest clothing we have."

"Switzerland! Why Switzerland? Aren't you comfortable here,
m'lady?"

She patted him on the cheek and then quickly withdrew her hand.
"I'll be back, Skitt. I'm sure you'll keep Dover Sky clean and cozy against
my return."

Parliament, Westminster, London

"Ah, Lord Danforth, there you are." Tanner Buchanan approached
Edward on the busy street outside the Parliament buildings where pol-
iticians and automobiles and carriages were rushing back and forth.

Edward kept his hands behind his back and his top hat on his head.
"Mr. Buchanan."

"Lord Buchanan actually. My dear old papa's earldom finally made
it through the gates and chutes."

"Earldom?"

Buchanan tugged on his black leather gloves while he gripped his silver-headed walking cane under his arm. "Indeed. You never knew much about my father up in Scotland, did you? He has benefactors and allies who are now my benefactors and allies."

"Congratulations."

"Thank you. What did you think of my maiden speech today?"

"About the same as what you thought of mine the other week."

Buchanan barked a laugh in the chill gray air. "True! We are met on the field of battle and neither shall be the first to cry 'Hold! Enough!' How will it play out in the end, Lord Danforth?"

"Since you are fond of *Macbeth*, I expect with you yielding 'to kiss the ground before young Malcolm's feet and to be baited with the rabble's curse.'"

"Do you think so? And who will this young Malcolm be? You? Do you intend to be the ruler of the realm?"

"Here's my cab."

The driver got out and opened the door for Edward.

"Tell me, Lord Buchanan, do you really think you will bless England and these islands by scrapping our capital ships and securing relations with Moscow as a bulwark against a resurgent Germany? Or was your speech merely crafted to be in direct opposition to my own?"

"What does it matter?"

"It matters to me if you mean it. I'd rather you actually meant it, to tell you the truth, than to hear you were making speeches as part of an ongoing duel with me and my family. Governing Britain is no place for personal games."

Buchanan smiled and shook his head. "On the contrary, the House of Commons is the perfect place for games. It always has been. Fox and hound. I being the hound who shall rend you limb from limb."

Edward got into the hack, and the driver shut the door.

Buchanan stood tall and dark on the sidewalk, tapping the silver head of his cane in a gloved palm and nodding. "Limb from limb, Lord Danforth. How I enjoy blood sport."

Scarborough estate, Southern England

"Kipp." The warm hands came from behind and slipped under his arms and over his chest in the dark. "I didn't know where to find you! Dad said you'd gone walking in the rain, so I said I'd take a peek at the horses." He felt her lips press lightly against the back of his neck and closed his eyes. "So then I knew you'd be in our secret place—our little tack room beyond the stables that is warm, dry, and delicious with the scent of leather." Her mouth found his ear and her breath made his skin tingle. "Every time Dad tells us you've come on business, my heart leaps. I can't help myself. You do love me, don't you?"

"Caroline, the Lord knows how attracted I am to you. I don't even know all the reasons why. But I love Christelle. She's my wife."

"You love us both, Kipp."

"No I don't," he said as he swung around within her embrace to face her.

"You do." Her lips touched his ear, his neck, his cheek, and hovered near his mouth.

"No man can love two women."

"You can." Her lips brushed his. "Push me away if you don't want me."

"I do want you, but I love Christelle."

"You don't think you love me?"

"I shouldn't be caught up with you, but…"

She kissed him softly. "But here we are in each other's arms."

His hand reached up and stroked the long blonde hair that was loose about her shoulders. "I can't get you out of my blood."

"Good. That's where I want you to stay." She kissed him again.

"Two women. My life revolves around two women and a son."

"Only two women? Are you sure?"

"Believe me, Christelle and you are enough. A man can only handle so much beauty." He placed his lips against her hair. "I wish it were ancient times—ancient biblical times—when men had more than one wife. That would work for me."

"In a way you do have that."

"I know you genuinely care for Christelle and our son, Matthew."

"I adore them. Just as you do. And I know you love my son, Charles."

He leaned his head against hers. "This makes no sense, does it? I don't want to hurt Christelle. I don't want to hurt my family. And I don't want to hurt you. I've done that enough." He kissed her forehead.

"You're not hurting her." She smoothed back his blonde hair. "And I'm certainly not feeling hurt right now."

"Christelle is hurt; she must be hurt. She knows there is something between us. Chris is no fool. She's always told me I still care for you. Even when I object she shakes her head and says it doesn't bother her because she knows that you may have part of my heart, but she has all of it."

"Shh."

Their eyes had adjusted to the darkness of the tack room. For the first time, he noticed she was wearing a tweed jacket, and raindrops had beaded on its shoulders.

She took his hand and sat on one of the English saddles resting on a wooden stand. She gestured to the saddle on a stand next to her.

When he sat down, she turned away from him and shook her head, letting her hair fall over her shoulders to her waist.

"Will you brush it for me, Kipp?"

Kipp ran a hand over her hair's rich thickness. It was damp in some spots and wet in others. He took the brush she gave him and began to pull it gently through. The rain brought out the scent of her hair, and it came to him along with the leather of the saddles and traces, the wax and polish, the musk of horses and ponies, and the dryness of the wood on which the bridles and halters and lead ropes and saddles were hung. He sank his face into the softness and the richness. He placed his hands gently on her shoulders and guided her around until she was sitting up and facing him. Then he gathered her into his arms.

"I suppose I do love you. I love you both. There's nothing I can do about it. God help me, it is not the Christian thing. But Christelle and you are rubies and diamonds to me. You both are silver and gold. I can't walk away from either of you."

He fumbled in his pocket for matches. When he found them, he struck one and held the amber flame a foot from her face.

"What are you doing?" she whispered.

"I just had to see your eyes."

The flickering match filled her eyes with brightness and shadows. The blueness was a sky at early morning, and he could almost feel the cool breezes moving over him. Tears came from her eyes and spilled onto her cheeks, glistening from the light of the flame. Then the match went out.

"Don't light another."

"I want to see you."

"No…don't…please." Her hand folded over his in the dark.

"Your parents will worry."

"They were already turning in when I walked out into the rain." She brushed his nose with her hair. "You didn't get very far. It's still wet and matted from our April showers."

"I got as far as I could. Your beauty is overwhelming when I'm with you. I'm helpless, really. It's the same way with Chris. One can only do so many chores. Then one has to love."

"My goodness, is my hair a chore now?"

"It's your crowning glory. I love you. It's wrong; but I don't know what else to say. God forgive me."

She traced his mouth with her finger. "And I love you. And we both love Christelle and care for her very much."

"Yes."

"Hold me. I'm afraid."

"Of what?"

"How strong my feelings for you are. I don't know where they're going to take us, Kipp."

He brought Caroline into his chest. Once again the scent of her hair mixed with the straw and leather and wet and now he heard the tapping of the rain on the roof. The moment seemed to make everything fall into place. Caroline, Christelle, Charles, Matthew, God, love…

"I won't ever abandon you, Kipp," she said quietly. "I bind you to me tonight. You'll never be lost, never be alone as long as I have breath. I swear it. I'll care for your son just as I care for my own. My love for you won't stop…ever."

"That's a lot to promise."

"Kipp, I make this promise to you *and* to Chris."

"What do you mean?"

She reached into the pocket of the riding pants she was wearing. She pulled out a small envelope and placed it in Kipp's hand.

"Christelle sent this to me, and I need to share it with you. You'll need a light to read it."

"What is it? You want me to read this right now?"

"Yes."

She sat up and unhooked a lantern from the wall. "Perhaps you'd better use this."

"Why? Have you given me a book?"

"The ink is faint."

"What were you using to write with?"

"I didn't write it."

He flicked a match with his thumbnail. It caught and he pushed the match inside the lantern as she held it. The wick took the flame and lit up the shed.

Caroline hung the lantern back up. The glow revealed her tweed jacket and the pants and boots she wore. The tumble of her hair about her shoulders and the blue-and-gold of her eyes shone.

He stopped what he was doing and took in her beauty. Then he looked at the note in his hand. "I don't understand…"

She avoided his gaze and glanced at the tack hanging on the walls. "Read it, Kipp. It's from Chris."

He looked at the blank envelope. He pulled out the notecard that was covered with barely legible writing. He recognized his wife's hand. "Caroline, what's going on?"

She didn't look at him. "Read it, please. You'll understand."

My dear Caroline,

As we've discussed, you know I'm gravely ill. The doctors say I will probably not live long past April. I need your help…Kipp will need your help.

I know this may be awkward, but please let Kipp know you love him. Take him in your arms and kiss him. Tell him everything you feel. At first he will push you away. But keep trying.

I know what is in your heart for him. I know you've held back because of our marriage. But he still loves you, just as he still loves me, even if he will not admit he has feelings for you. I want you to help him find that love for you again. I don't care how hard it is. Reach out to him. Use all the words you have inside you. Be beautiful for him. Touch him. Let him discover what is in his heart for you.

Kipp loves me, and he will always love me. Long after I am gone, he will love me. But he has enough love in his heart for both of us. The last thing I want is for him to be alone in his grief. I don't want him to wander off to try to find solace in the arms of someone who will care nothing for his soul.

There is only one person I trust him—and our son, Matthew—to, and that's you.

Love him, Caroline. Love him forever. For me. For our son. For you. For him.

When the time is right, show him this letter. Thank you for this, Caroline. This is such a difficult time.

Your friend always,
Christelle

7

May, 1925
Ashton Park

CHRIS

I HAVE TOLD HIM.

CAROLINE

Christelle sat on the couch with the telegram in her hand. Todd Turpin had brought it, his collar turned up against the May Day rainstorm as he trudged through mud puddles to the cottage in the ash grove. He'd asked how she was feeling, and she'd told him she was much better. He had not been gone five minutes before pain cut into her stomach. She bent double as she tried to get her breath.

Her three-year-old looked up from where he was sitting on the floor playing with wooden blocks.

She forced a smile. "I'm fine, Matthew, my darling. Just a game, *oui*? A game mommy likes to play." She rested on the couch until her breath came smoothly and deeply. Then she put her son down for his nap, returning to the couch to think as she stared into the flames in the fireplace. She heard the front door of their cottage open. She turned, thinking it might be Victoria or Lady Preston.

Kipp caught her up in his arms, the wetness of his clothes pressing against her cotton dress as he kissed her. His blonde hair had been flattened and darkened by the wintry storm. The moisture was cool on her face, but she also felt the heat of his tears. She patted him on the back.

"Shh…" she soothed. "Shh, my love."

"I don't understand." He could hardly get the words out. His voice was rough and low, making it difficult to hear. "I don't understand any of this," he whispered.

"Sit with me." She took him to the couch and held him as she spoke, now and then kissing his head and face softly, moving her fingers over his cheeks and through his wet and tangled hair. "The doctor made the diagnosis in the fall. I asked him to keep it in strictest confidence because I wanted the winter to be happy. I wanted you flying, Victoria to be joyful about having her baby in May, and Lord Preston and Edward in London making their speeches. What good would all the moping and fussing have done if I'd announced it sooner, my love? It would not stop the cancer that is all through me. So as long as I could tell everyone it was a bad illness that was hard to treat during the cold weather, I decided to do that."

"We have to tell Mother and Father," Kipp choked out. "There may be places we can take you in Paris or Madrid…or in America." He stroked her hair in a clumsy fashion, his eyes dark. "I will cable Michael and Libby right away. In New York we can—"

"*Non, non*, Kipp. I told you. The cancer is everywhere. It cannot be cured. It's not in just one place where you can feel. It's inside me all over. I can feel it everywhere. It was this way when the doctors discovered it."

"Chris, I can't just watch you die in front of my eyes without trying something…without doing something."

"I want you to love me, and cherish me, and rock me. Trust me, that will be the best blessing."

"A blessing?" Kipp framed her small face with his damp hands. "How can you say that?"

"Christians say they wish to be with God, *oui*? But when it comes time to die, they do not want it to happen so soon. If I cannot stay here with a good mind and a strong body, I wish to be with God. It's better for you, and me, and Matthew."

"No! No, it's not."

"I will become less and less of me, so yes it is, my darling." She kissed each of his eyes. "That is why I asked Caroline to love you. You will need her after I am gone. You will need someone who loves you. She is someone I trust, and knowing she will be helping you makes this easier for me."

His body stiffened. "How can you expect me to turn to her, to betray my love for you?"

"You will not betray me. I want you to return her love, to love her. I asked her to let you know she still loves you and will love you when I'm gone."

"How could you ask her that?"

"I do not want you and Matthew to be alone. And I don't want you bringing home a woman I don't know to love you and Matthew. I think a great deal of Caroline. Matthew likes her and he likes Charles."

"I want nothing to do with Caroline. I feel as if she played with my heart, trying to draw me to her when I still have you."

"How can she play you if she loves you?" Christelle gripped his face with sudden strength. "Caroline did not want to approach you. She did not want to hurt me or hurt you. She didn't want to do this for me. I argued with her. I pleaded with her. I cried, yes, until she said she would try. She did not think you loved her anymore."

"I don't."

Christelle smiled softly. "We must be about the truth now, my love. There's no time for lies. Caroline is a good woman, and it is right for you to love her."

Kipp's face grew dark with anger as blood rushed to his cheeks. "No, I can't. Not now."

"Kipp, I *want* you to love her."

He shook his head. "I can't accept that."

"I prayed for you to understand you have this love in you, do you know that? God knew I would be taken early. He knew Matthew would have no mother around and you would have no wife, no lover. I do not want a stranger in my house. I do not want a stranger holding you and saying she loves you when she does not. I do not want a woman I don't know raising my son. I love Caroline, and you love her. She loves both of us, and she loves Matthew. I see that in her. I want you and Caroline to be with each other when I'm gone."

"No one in my family will accept such an arrangement, Chris. We don't have your French way of looking at things, your ability to accept one person loving two people at the same time. I can't lose you one day and take up with another woman the next. Certainly the Scarboroughs wouldn't approve either. This wild plan of yours will not work." He ran his hands through her now silver hair. "What I need is for you to live."

She put her hands on his arms. "My love, I will not live. Not here on this earth. I will be in a different place. Here, you will need another to hold you. I know you, and I know you need that. So let a year go by if you must, but let the love blossom while you must be apart. People and their foolish notions! Let Matthew play with Caroline's Charles often. Visit a lot. Make sure there are family gatherings where you can talk discreetly. A year after I am gone, marry her."

"I won't."

"You must! If you love me, you will marry her. I have told you—I trust her. I trust her with you and Matthew. I have said this again and again, and you do not want to hear me. If you love me as much as you say, you will do this for me. You will be honest with yourself and admit the love you've always had for Caroline even while you loved me with all your heart. You will put a ring on her finger, cherish her, make a home with her, and create a loving family. If you do this, you will make me the happiest woman in heaven." She ran her fingers down the side of his face.

She suddenly grimaced and doubled over. Kipp clutched her as well as he could, supporting her through the pain.

"How often is this happening?" he demanded. "Are you all right?"

"Just…just hold me," she said through gasps. Finally she caught her breath. "It doesn't happen…that often."

"You should be in a hospital."

"No! I do not want to die in a hospital room."

"They can control the pain much better than anything you or I can do here."

"I have medications here—opiates. It looks worse to you than it feels to me, I'm sure."

"So that's why."

"Why what?"

"Your calmness. The way your eyes are now and then. I didn't see it often, but when I did I didn't know what to think."

"I have not used large doses. And I have not used some every day. Only recently have I needed more." She rubbed his arm. "I'm sorry, Kipp. Perhaps I should have told you a long time ago. But *non*, I did not want you worked up for so many months. *Non...*"

He kissed her hair and closed his eyes. "You're so beautiful, love. This is not right. God knows this is not right."

"Jesus was crucified and died slowly after being whipped, yes? Paul was *décapité*. Andrew faced crucifixion. Peter a crucifixion also. We are not spared suffering, but it does not mean we are not loved by God."

"Your calmness confuses me. You're dealing with something terrible. We can't keep pretending it's a winter illness. This is a crisis! We must tell my family."

"No, it would change everything."

"You are already sick, and everyone is worried. Do you think letting my father and mother wake up one morning to find you dead is going to bless them or be any easier on them?"

She patted him on the back. "Shh...shh. Matthew needs another hour of sleep or he will be *un monstre—très difficile*. Hold me more tightly, my love. I like to listen to your heart beating." She snuggled into him. "Of course you are right. They are family. It is important there comes a day when they will be told. I turn thirty on the second of June. You could arrange a party—a grand party. Everyone will be happy. Everyone will act normally. A few days after that, I will tell the family. Oh, but I do not look forward to them moaning and groaning over me, but I see it must be done."

"What about your parents?"

"*S'il te plaît, amène-les ici pour moi.*"

"Would they let me fly them to your party?"

"Fly? No. Someone must help them get here on the train or by car."

"I will take care of that."

"I want you here with me."

"I will see to it. Harrison is at the estate in Dover. It's just a short hop from there. Someone can take him, and he can come back by car or train with your parents. I'll do anything that will please you."

"It will please me to have Caroline and Charles here for the birthday also."

"No."

She lifted her head. "You said *anything*."

"She made me feel like I was betraying our love."

She held his jaw in her hand. "She reached out to you as I asked her to do, as I prayed for her to do. Now I am asking you for this. Will you bring her and her son to my birthday party? *Oui?*"

"Chris, I can't do that—even for you."

"Will you bring her? *Oui?*"

May, Pura, Switzerland

Catherine glanced out the window as her son was led about on a tall, white Lipizzaner stallion. The baron kept his hand on the young boy's leg as he walked beside the horse while Herr Salzgeber, the stallion's owner and trainer, led the horse along the beach. Behind them Lake Lugano was a blaze of blue and white in the spring sun. She watched for a few moments, smiling. Then she turned and looked at the sheaf of papers on her desk.

> *Das Wesen des deutschen Geistes ist nicht Gewalt sondern Schöp-*
> *fung*...The essence of the German spirit is not violence but
> creation, it is not exclusion of the races but inclusion, not
> fear of the Jew but friendship with the Jew. It is not simply
> ensuring industrial capitalists have the liberty to generate
> wealth for themselves, but that those they employ also have
> the means to secure housing, food, clothing, knowledge, and
> the assistance of a physician when there is illness or injury.

What makes Germany great is a vast and generous involve-
ment with Europe and the human race—not a retreat from
the European nations or the peoples of the earth or a desire
to make war against them under misguided notions of Teutonic pride and identity.

A hand lightly touched her shoulder. Recognizing the touch, she
leaned her cheek against the hand and arm. "As usual, your writing is
eloquent," she said. "I see you took my advice to be more forthright."

Albrecht, red scarf around his neck even though the day was warm
and the house comfortable, sat down on the arm of a couch near her.
"*Ja, ja. Ich glaube, Sie haben recht.* I believe you are right." He ran a
hand through his messy hair and adjusted his reading glasses. "Are you
almost done do you think?"

"A few more pages. Why?"

"I have translated my next-to-last chapter for you. I hoped you
could read it before dinner."

"Next to last? Really? That's quite an accomplishment. Of course
I can. Sean only wants me around if he skins his knee." She laughed
as she watched him on the stallion again. "Even then he probably
wouldn't cry out. Instead he'd look to the baron or Herr Salzgeber to
help him. Or perhaps he'd simply bite his lip and tough it out."

Albrecht took a look over the top of his glasses. "It's true. The boy
acts like a ten-year-old who wears a saber at his waist. Your young cav-
alryman. How he has grown up since February!"

"His grandparents probably won't recognize him at the birthday
party for Christelle. And yet he's just two." She leaned back in her chair
and gave Albrecht her warmest smile. "I wish you would reconsider.
The family has included you and the baron in the invitation."

He was looking at the chapter in his hand and turning over the
pages. "I hope my grammar in the English is correct." He glanced
at both sides of one sheet. "Yes, your sister-in-law's thirtieth birthday,
hmm? She is French and from Amiens, isn't she? Or somewhere close
to Amiens? It is only seven years since the armistice, and France har-
bors a great deal of hatred towards Germany. I don't think she will want
to see me there."

"If you knew Chris, you wouldn't say that. What an amazing soul she is! She loves everyone—yes, even a nasty German such as you." She kicked him gently with her bare foot. "Please reconsider."

"We have much to do before my book can be published."

"A few days at Dover Sky—what will that cost you? Besides, I have two kings I have not played."

He continued to peer at the pages scrawled with handwriting. "Ah, a card playing reference…Liverpool Rummy or American poker?"

"She has read your book—the one on suffering."

"What?" Albrecht lifted his head sharply. "Christelle has?"

"Yes."

"She has not. How could she?" He took off his glasses and stared at her.

"The baron gave my father an English translation of it last year. Chris found it at Ashton Park and read it. She said she liked it very much. Her English is excellent, so she didn't have any problem understanding it."

"She read it?"

"Yes! I promise you. She'd be dazzled if her German theologian showed up at her party. Can you imagine?"

"Hmm…that is quite a card to play. What is your other one?"

"Well…me."

"You?"

She leaned forward and put a hand on his knee. "More than three months we have been together here. I have grown used to all your little habits and quirks, as well as your constant gallantries. And none of them irritate me. I have grown quite fond of them." She paused and then decided to say it. "And quite fond of you."

"You have never said a thing about this! I thought we agreed in February we would be good friends and working partners and nothing more during this time together."

"That's what we said in February. Now it's almost June. I've decided to change my mind."

Albrecht put the pages he was holding on the floor. "How much of a change are we talking about?"

"A great deal of change. A sharp change in the weather—and for the better. A distinct change of seasons."

"You are being as bold as I usually am."

"Bolder! I guess I have picked it up from living in this chalet with you. If you come to Dover Sky that will tell me I mean something to you too. That I am more than just a friend or working partner."

"*If* I come? This sounds very manipulative…almost Machiavellian."

"It *is* very manipulative and is bordering on the Machiavellian, I grant you that. But it's not a game of rummy, professor. The reader of your chapters and the editor of your book has taken a very deep interest in you."

"As a writer?"

"As a writer and theologian…and a man."

"We've never even kissed."

"Yes…well…come to Dover Sky with me, and I'll see what I can do about that."

Half of his mouth curved upwards. "That sounds like a third card."

"I suppose it is."

"An ace?"

"Certainly not a joker." She patted his knee again and sat back. "Have I thrown you off your game?"

"I admit it will take a great deal of concentration to get back to my final chapter, Catherine."

"So then it means something to you when I say these things?"

"Means something?"

"It matters to you that I care about you?"

Albrecht gazed at her. "Of course! I've always liked you…only there was this sadness in your eyes—you were like a dark moth. I did not know if it could be chased away or by what means a person could help cause it to vanish."

"So is it gone?"

He nodded. "For the most part. I'm not sure if it was the mountain air, or your son taking to the white horses, or the Swiss cooking and chocolate, or—"

She kicked him with her bare foot, a bit harder this time. "Stop it!" she commanded before laughing. "I'm serious."

"So am I. All those things bless a person and take one out of tunnels and caves. I'm at a loss to say what I may have done that I had not already done to encourage you to be intrigued with me. The same old flirting, the same old teasing, the old-world Prussian charm. Nothing was new here in Pura. In fact, there was less of it because I was so caught up in writing the book."

"Well, I suppose that was why. I was captured by your devotion to a cause. I was fascinated by what I read, chapter after chapter that you translated into English because you cared so much what I thought. Only an extraordinary man can write this well, this profoundly, this passionately. I have feelings for you because the book allowed me to read your heart."

"Is this another card you're playing?"

"It may be another card, but all my cards mean something, Herr Hartmann." She drew a circle on his pants-covered leg with her toe. "I feel quite like a young woman of twenty-one again when I'm here with you. I wanted to leave a dungeon behind and get out into the light of day, and I did! I thank God in my prayers every night for your invitation to come here. My late husband may be in heaven, but I haven't been anywhere remotely close—until this winter and spring." She pushed her toe against his leg. "It wasn't just the snow and the mountains and the sunshine and fresh air, Herr Hartmann. Or the cooking or the Lindt chocolate. It was *you*."

Her eyes took on a golden light Albrecht had never seen.

"I want you to come to Dover Sky, my theologian. I want you to come as my man as well as my writer and my professor. Will you do that? Or is Berlin more important? Is Tubingen more important?"

He breathed out noisily. "What a bomb you drop on my head! I can scarcely think."

"Good!"

"Good?"

"If I didn't matter to you one way or the other, what I've just said wouldn't have knocked you off your stride. Is that not true? I care about you, Albrecht. It matters a great deal to me that I see you also care about me. That I affect you." She stood up. "Come with me, please."

"Pardon me?"

"Can I make it any plainer? *Komme mit, bitte.*" She glanced out the window and saw that the white stallion with her son astride was far away, moving along the lakeshore. She held out her hand. "It will only take a moment, and then you can get back to your book."

"I wonder if I will be able to do that. Are you going to play another card?"

"I expect I might. Don't be afraid of me, Albrecht. I want you—I need you—at Dover Sky by my side, that's all. A very simple need, really."

Gripping his hand she led him down the hall towards the study where he worked. Books were stacked everywhere, and his desk was overflowing with paper. They'd hardly stepped through the doorway when she turned and pushed him up against the wall.

"This is my final card. Are you coming to Dover Sky?" She narrowed her eyes. "Why do you have those glasses on again? Did you think we were going to read a book?"

"I wasn't sure what we were going to do."

She removed the glasses, reached back her arm and placed them on the desk. "It won't take you long to understand my intention, professor. Believe me." She placed her hands on both sides of his face and ran her thumbs over his skin. "When was the last time you shaved?"

"Sunday…for church."

"Five days. I don't mind." She rubbed hard against his cheekbones. "This won't hurt, I promise." Her lips brushed his, and then she pressed against him with more force before pulling away. "You see?"

He caught his breath. "Is that all, Lady Catherine?"

"No, it's not, Professor Hartmann."

She tugged his head towards hers. This kiss was stronger, and she didn't release her grip on his face or stop pressing in with her thumbs. Breaking away a second time, she took the measure of him through his eyes.

"Do you understand me?" she asked him.

"I think so, *ja.*"

"Because this is my ace." She leaned forward and kissed him again. When she finished, she continued to grip his face in her hands.

Albrecht felt warm and tired and weak.

"I haven't felt this way about a man in a long time," she said.

"You surprise me, Lady Catherine."

"I hope I do." She smiled. "You do look a little flushed." She kissed him softly, letting her lips linger near his when she was finished. "Four of a kind," she whispered.

"Yes?"

"I'm alive again, and I'm not going to die if I can help it. No more sitting alone in the dark. Will you help me with that?"

"*Ja.*"

"Will you?"

"*Ja—ich helfe. Yes, I will.*"

"Then we're agreed. We will go to Dover Sky. And if there is more work to do on your book, we'll do it there." She kissed him gently. "And if there is more work to do on us, we will do it there also."

He finally raised his arms up and around her, pulling her in with a sudden burst of strength that made her inhale sharply.

"That is my prayer," he replied. "May God answer it!"

She caught her breath and ran her fingers over his lips. "Oh, He's answering it, *Herr Hartmann.*"

8

June, 1925
Dover Sky

A rap on the door was followed by a woman's voice calling, "Christelle? Are you all right?"

"I'll only be a minute, *Maman*."

"Please, dear, let us not stand on ceremony in a bedroom. I'm Mum to all my daughters-in-law and sons-in-law, especially when your own mother and father could not be here." She opened the door a crack. "May I help you? Everyone is wondering where the birthday girl has gotten to."

Christelle braced one hand against the bed and held the other over her stomach as she fought a wave of pain. "*Oui, oui, je suis désolée,* you needn't come in. I'll be right down."

Lady Preston stepped inside. "It's no trouble. Do you—" She saw Christelle bent over and rushed to her side. "What is it, dear? What's happening to you?"

"Just a stomachache, nothing more. I've been having severe cramps when my time of month comes since Easter—" She suddenly drew in her breath sharply. "*Oh, mon Dieu, aie miséricorde. J'ai besoin de ton aide et puissance…*" she prayed through a moan.

Lady Preston gripped Christelle's hands. "Squeeze mine. Go ahead. I'm years younger than my husband, and my bones are still strong."

"*Non, non.*"

"Go ahead! I am not fine china. I won't break." She winced slightly as Christelle tightened her grip. "That's fine. Go on. I'm fine," she encouraged.

"*Non, Maman.*"

"I'm fine. Let me help." Lady Preston shook her head as Christelle doubled up again. "It's not cramps, is it? And it's not this bug you say you've been fighting all winter and spring."

"Yes, of course it is—it's both. I only need another minute."

"No one in the family believes you. We don't know what it is, but it's certainly not the flu or an ordinary illness." Her eyes were sharp. "Back at Ashton Park I talked to the doctor about you."

"What?"

"He was tight-lipped. No amount of threatening or pleas could get him to speak. He cited physician–patient confidentiality and a lot of rubbish. I told him, "Listen, every month she is thinner—and she was thin enough to begin with. Something is making her waste away, something serious. What is it?"

"He didn't—he didn't tell you though?"

"No."

"Good."

"By his very evasiveness, the doctor has convinced William and me that whatever it is it must be very bad indeed—worse than we had feared. And seeing you like this makes me quite afraid. Is it your heart? Is it your stomach or intestines? Come, my dear, we love you. You are family. Please don't continue to leave us in the dark. Do you think you're sparing us some pain? Seeing you this way doubles and triples my anxiety. Please tell me what's happening to you."

"*Non, Maman.* I will, but not yet."

Lady Preston put her arms around the young woman until the spasms ceased. "Please, Christelle, listen to me. Kipp is saying nothing even though he looks like death with his worry over you. Ben has told us you must be using opiates. He saw a bottle at your house once. I chose to ignore him."

"*Non, non.*"

"I've been worried. I've seen the way you…well, the way you drift in your speech now and then, and even more over the past few months. Once or twice your eyes were different—your pupils were so small—when you spoke with me."

Christelle sank her head against Lady Preston's shoulder. "*Maman*, do not be mad at the doctor or Kipp. I did not want anyone to know. I didn't want to be placed in the hospital to die. I wished to be among all of you and for everything to be as normal as possible for as long as possible."

"To *die*? What is wrong with you? What has the doctor said? With the proper treatment and medicine, you will get better, will you not?"

"No, *Maman*. It is cancer."

Lady Preston's body stiffened. "How long have you known this?"

"Since the fall."

"Why…why on earth did you keep this a secret? It should have been operated on long ago. It should have been cut out."

"They could not, *Maman*. Even back then it was growing all through me. It would be—how do you say it? *Etriper un poisson,* like gutting a fish."

Lady Preston's eyebrows darted inward. "The doctor said that?"

"*Non*, he was very polite, but that is what he meant. He said the surgery would kill me. So I said, 'Tell no one. Keep this in strictest confidence. Let me live as ordinary a life as possible for as long as possible.' He reluctantly agreed and prescribed opiates for the pain. He has been most kind."

"He lied to us."

"*Non*, Doctor Pittmeadow did what I wished and what a physician must do, *Maman*. It was between him and me, correct? He had no choice. Please do not be angry."

"Still we can do something, check out more options and new treatments."

Christelle kissed her on the cheek right where she'd spotted a tear slowly making its way to her mother-in-law's chin. "You can pray, *Maman*. And you can go back out to the party with me. It is time for the children to have cake and ice cream. I want to hold Victoria and

Jeremy's baby boy, sweet Timothy. Please help me enjoy those I love. If we talk about the cancer now, it will ruin the day. Tomorrow or the day after I will tell the family. But not now. Not today. I want this day to be special and joyful."

"How long—how long do you have then?"

"The doctor said six to eight months last fall—if I am lucky…if I am blessed. So I am happy to still be here."

"When did you tell Kipp?"

"Last month."

"He is not doing well with what you told him."

Christelle bit her lip. "*Non.* He is angry with God and angry with life." She shrugged one shoulder. "And angry with Lady Caroline."

"With Caroline? Why?"

"Because of me again. I am doing all these things and making all these decisions for when I am no longer here, and he is not happy with them."

"What have you said to him?"

"That I adore Caroline. That our children get along so well. That there was a time he loved her, and I believe he still has love for her. I want him to marry her, *Maman.* I want them to become husband and wife and raise our children after I am gone."

"Marriage!"

She took Lady Preston's hands. "I trust her. I do not want Kipp to be with someone I've never met. I do not want Matthew to be raised by a stranger. Kipp is fighting me on this, but this is so much what I want for him. Can you help me?"

"Oh Christelle!"

"Will you help me, *Maman?*"

"Child, child, I don't think Kipp will listen to anyone if he is as angry and upset as he seems. He is long past the age when he will happily listen to his mother's counsel, especially when it goes against his will. I don't like to even think about him being wed to a woman other than you. This is much to take in so quickly…far too quickly. I see it matters to you though. If it will put you at some measure of ease, I will speak with him. Caroline is a wonderful girl and, yes, there was a time William and I were sure Caroline and Kipp would be husband and wife. I'm astonished you are the one who wants to bring the two of them together again."

"*Maman*, if I am not here I believe she will be the right woman for him and the right mother for our son."

Tears came more swiftly to the older woman's eyes. Lady Preston hugged Christelle. "You've always been one with such a large heart that few can understand. I confess I still don't understand. But if it pleases you, I will sit down and talk to him. Who knows? Perhaps he will change his mind. I will do this, but I don't even like to think of such things with you in front of me with your beautiful smile."

"*Merci, Maman.* I am sure Kipp will listen to what you have to say."

"I'm not as sure as you are, but I promise I will do what I can."

"Kipp?"

Kipp didn't turn around.

"Kipp? Are you going to go on avoiding me all day?"

"It's been working so far."

"Chris has asked to see us both."

"I'm busy." He sliced a lemon. "How did you find me?"

"Mrs. Longstaff said you'd be down in the kitchen making punch. She said you insisted on doing it." Caroline moved to within his line of vision. "It's Chris who is asking, not me."

Kipp glanced up at her, his gaze flat. "A request you put her up to, no doubt."

"Kipp, since when has anyone been able to put Chris up to anything? You know your wife better than anyone. She's a free spirit. She goes where she wants and does what she thinks is right."

"For the most part, yes. But the illness has affected her judgment."

"Meaning in regard to *me*?"

"Who else would I mean?"

"Kipp, stop treating me like a witch. I never wanted to do what your wife asked me to do. I never wanted to reach out to you like that and force the issue between us. But how could I say no to a dying woman when she pleaded with me over and over again?"

"You probably didn't need much convincing, right?"

Caroline folded her arms over the front of her summer dress. "The attraction seemed pretty mutual when we were last together."

Kipp chopped limes loudly and rapidly with a large knife. "Sometimes I lose my way. Big blue eyes do that to me. Unfortunately, I can be pretty weak."

"Is that what it was? You said you loved us both."

"I don't, Caroline. I only love Chris."

"So the wrong words just popped out of your mouth?"

"Like I said, it was a weak moment."

She brushed at her tears with a finger. "So I mean nothing to you?"

"That's right. Nothing."

"And Chris was mistaken to think I might be a good companion for you after her death and a good mother to Matthew?"

Kipp laughed bitterly. "A hooker from East London would be a better mother to my son than you."

Caroline's face whitened and tears shot down her cheeks. "I don't deserve that, Kipp! I can understand your pain and anger over your wife's cancer, but I won't forgive what you've just said to me. I love you, Kipp. Everything I've done has been out of love for you and for Christelle. You can't blame me for the fact she's dying, but you're going to anyway, I see. Just throw all the blame on Caroline, is that it?"

Kipp poured water into a large crystal bowl. "I don't blame you for Christelle's cancer."

"Are you sure? You seem to want to blame someone very badly. God isn't readily at hand, but I am."

Kipp said nothing as Caroline brought a white cotton handkerchief out of a pocket in her dress and dabbed at her eyes.

"Then it's come to this, Kipp. You've broken my heart enough times, but you won't get any other opportunities after this. I'll tell my parents I don't wish to overnight at Dover Sky. I don't care if we have to book a hotel room in Liverpool. I will leave you to your anger, Kipp. You'll never see me again. Do try to have a good life. If not for yourself, at least for Chris's sake…and for your son's." Caroline turned and walked swiftly towards the kitchen door.

Kipp laid down the knife and leaned on the tabletop with both hands. "Where are you going?"

She paused in the doorway. "I'm going to say goodbye to your wife. I'm going to spend a good while doing it because I won't be at Dover Sky or Ashton Park again. When I came into this kitchen there was still the possibility of a love between us. Now there is not. You are a cruel and hard man, Kipp Danforth. I feel very sorry for you, but not sorry enough to watch you destroy the remaining years of your life—and that of your son."

"So tell me, professor," Edward settled next to Albrecht on a couch in the library, "how are things in Germany these days?" He dug his fork into a piece of cake on a plate in his hand. "What about Herr Hitler? What's he up to?"

Albrecht sipped his coffee before replying. "The economy is much better, so fellows like him have a harder time stirring up the populace. He is out of prison now, and his autobiography is due to be published next month. Even though he has been out of the political picture for a while, his book is bound to make a few people sit up and take notice."

"How many seats does his Nazi Party have in the government?"

"Only fourteen."

"I see. What will be in his book?"

"He attacks the Jews and the Slavic people. He rails against the trade unions, the Communists, and the Socialists."

"Does he?" Edward reached for his own cup of coffee. "Then he can't be all that bad, can he? Perhaps we should bring him over to straighten out the Labor Party."

"His ways are very violent, Lord Edward."

"Yes? Well, we don't have the Bolsheviks as close to us as the Germans do. We have our wonderful moat—the English Channel. I can understand why Herr Hitler might resort to force."

Albrecht set down his coffee. "He will not unleash his street gangs against only the communists and socialists, Lord Edward. Anyone Hitler considers his opponent is fair game."

"Hmm." Edward set down his coffee, wiped his mouth with his

napkin, and put aside his plate. "My sister tells me you are working on your own book."

"Yes. It is meant to coincide with the release of Herr Hitler's. I challenge him on many of his political positions."

"Not on his stance against Bolshevism surely?"

"On the way he means to recreate Germany and the power he wishes to exert to achieve his vision. It is very much like Mussolini's fascism."

"Mussolini's not all bad, is he? He's brought a certain strength and honor back to Rome."

"He seized power, Lord Edward. He didn't form the government by means of a democratic election. I very much fear Hitler may one day look for an opportunity to do the same. Such people think alike."

"I cannot wholly blame them. Democracy can be a very tedious and toadying process where people ingratiate themselves to all manner of rank and file in the hopes of gaining votes. Imagine if Labor had gotten the majority, Herr Hartmann. Just on a whim of the dockworkers or hog farmers who turned out to vote. What then? We'd have Bolshevism in the House of Commons and trade between London and Moscow. That would be unacceptable! What could a person do if that happened? Wait another four or five years in the hopes of ousting the Reds by means of the democratic system? And what if my father and I and the Tories didn't grovel enough to suit the dockworkers and pig farmers and coal miners? Another five years of Bolshevism and Labor after that?"

Edward shook his head and reached for his coffee. "We would have to march on Westminster in the same way Mussolini marched on Rome. We'd have to seize power in the name of all that is holy and good. There would be no other choice if we wanted to save England." He chuckled. "Forgive me, Albrecht. I get too intense. Father is always warning me about that." He leaned back. "So my sister assisted you and the baron with your book?"

"Yes, she was quite valuable."

"I'm glad to hear it. Would you make use of her skills again?"

"Certainly."

"And it goes no further than that?"

Albrecht wrinkled his forehead. "Pardon me?"

"Come, Albrecht! We're grown men. Let's not play parlor games. We're perfectly alone and can say what we mean without fear of others repeating our words in the wrong places. I'm glad you offered Catherine an opportunity to get out of the house and do something that required her intelligence. She's mourned too long…far too long. Truly she had become rather sallow in appearance. The Swiss air and food obviously did her good. Her countenance is greatly improved. I am grateful to the baron and you for that."

"Thank you."

"You understand it must end there though. If she marries again, she must marry an Englishman."

Albrecht sat up straight. "Excuse me, Lord Edward?"

Edward smiled. "I've seen the way she looks at you. I thought she was going to take your hand when we were singing happy birthday to Christelle an hour ago. I'm glad Germany is getting back on her feet. I sense Germany can be our ally against Russia and the spread of communism. But a German—even a good German theologian—as part of the Danforth dynasty? Impossible. I think you understand that, don't you?"

"Yes, I think I do understand you."

Edward patted the arm of the couch. "Excellent. I didn't think there would be any trouble. Mind you, I don't intend to stand in the way of any working relationship between Catherine and you. That's just what Catherine needs. Let her help you with a thousand of your books. But no more than that. She has her castle, and you have yours. All right?"

Albrecht inclined his head. "This might be something you should raise with your sister, Lord Edward."

"I may do that." Edward got up. "Thank you for a stimulating insight on European politics, professor."

"It was interesting."

"How is Matthew?"

"He's all wound up from the big day, and he's disappointed Charles left so early with his mother."

Kipp buttoned his pajama top. "Couldn't be helped."

Christelle sat on the edge of the bed, the dark lines under her eyes and her tightly clasped hands revealing her tension. "He says he won't sleep until you kiss him good night."

"Are you all right then, Chris?"

"No, I am *not* all right. We'll talk when you come back." After Kipp left, Chris dragged herself under the covers and turned off the lamp by the bed. She looked out the window and in the moonlight she saw Skitt walking toward the pond carrying a paper bag, a cricket bat, and the thermos Catherine had brought him from Switzerland. She wondered what he was doing, but she soon drifted off. When a spasm jerked her awake, she clenched her fists against the pain and prayed.

> *Seigneur*, I took so much medication today to get through the celebration. Must I take more now just to sleep? *Dieu*, I love Kipp and my son. I love my English family. But I think it would be better if You take me now rather than after I become an opium eater. I have no wish to end my life as an addict. *Aie pitié, Seigneur.*

"Are you asleep?" Kipp asked in the semidarkness.

"*Non.*" She patted the bed beside her. "Come and lie beside me, my love. Are you afraid I am going to throw the clock at you?"

"I might be," he said as he climbed into bed.

"Well, I don't have the energy for that." She turned on her side to face him. "You will have to decide for yourself what you will do about Caroline Scarborough. I have said enough. In any case, I don't think what I wished for—and asked for—will ever happen. She did not tell me what you said to her, but whatever it was hurt her deeply. There was no need of you to do that, Kipp. That is not what you do to people. You have never been like that."

"I'm sorry. It was not a good day for me."

"I am not the one you need to apologize to. And perhaps she will not hear your apology anyway. I believe she and Charles are gone from your life for good. I hope this is not something you will regret a year from now."

"I don't know. When I think of a year from now, all I see is there will be no birthday party for you next year. There will be no balloons, no candles…and none of your smiles."

"Shh. Look! I am smiling for you in the dark."

He reached out and touched her face. "Yes, I can feel that."

She suddenly drew in her breath. "The pain is a little worse. I will have a restless night. You might wish to sleep in another room."

"I'm not going anywhere."

She took his hand. "Always the gallant one, my knight in shining armor."

"You looked very good today. You did very well. People remarked on your thinness, but you had so much enthusiasm and charm everyone was delighted. How beautiful you are, Chris! Even while you're fighting this monster, how much life you give to everyone. You're radiant."

"*Ah, merci.*"

"You don't really know, you know. You might overcome this cancer."

"*Non*, Kipp. Do not allow yourself to think that way. It is not going to happen. I don't feel that happening inside me."

"You can't be completely sure."

"I don't want you to believe I will recover. It will make it worse when I—when I—" She stopped. "Just pray. Will you pray? That will help. Hold me close and pray."

"I'm not good at that anymore."

"Try. I am asking you."

He kissed her on the lips. "Yes. For you, of course."

"Hush." Catherine put a finger to her lips. "Remember, Skitt is standing guard at the pond."

Albrecht looked. "Your butler? What is that all about?"

"Poachers go after the swans, so Harrison and Skitt take turns standing guard. They've never caught any though, and this is their second summer at it."

"It would be best if we moved away from the pond then, I think."

"I agree." She took his hand in the cozy darkness under the trees. "I thought you might have changed your mind, you took so long to join me."

"Me? No. Your brother would wish me to, however."

"My brother? Kipp?"

"Edward. He made it clear he didn't want German blood in the family. A working relationship with you is fine, he said."

"Don't take Edward personally, Albrecht."

"How should I take him?"

She caught the tone in his voice, stopped, and faced him, still holding his hand. "He fancies himself as the leader of the Conservative Party in ten years and then prime minister. After that, emperor of the world, I suppose. This has nothing to do with you. He's not comfortable with Chris either because she's French."

"So no wedding bells in our future?"

"Do you want wedding bells?"

"I don't know. The chat with him did give my train a bit of a lurch."

"The oddest thing is he had a huge row with Mum and Dad when it came to his marriage. Char was a commoner, you see, and they weren't happy about their eldest son marrying her. But he fought them until he got what he wanted. Now he turns up his nose at my interest in a German theologian? This is one of Edward's little hypocrisies. Perhaps he'll grow out of it."

Albrecht glanced up at the stars. "His political views seem a bit harsh. I hope he grows out of those first."

"What views?" asked Catherine.

"He's a little too approving of Adolph Hitler's ideas."

"Against the Jews?"

"I didn't get any sense of that. It was mostly being against the trade unions and communists where he found common ground with the Nazi Party."

"You have to bear in mind he's taken on the role of scourge of Bolshevism. That's all it is. He's no fascist, believe me. Too much of an Englishman for that." She led Albrecht under an old apple tree. "But we didn't come out here to discuss my brother Edward's idiosyncrasies, did we?"

"No."

"Or marriage. We don't want to make a hash of things when we're just getting started, do we?"

"I agree with you. Talk of marriage is *verboten*."

"Good. Let's keep our relationship uncluttered, shall we?" She kissed him gently on the lips. "Did you get a chance to speak with Chris?"

"Very briefly. The children were playing out on the lawn while she told me my book on suffering meant a great deal to her. She said it made her able to accept her ongoing illness in a better spirit—even to contemplate death in a less fearful manner."

"Death? I hope that's not on her mind."

"Now and then it's on everybody's mind, Catherine. Even if it's only for a few moments. She hoped we could talk more tomorrow after breakfast."

"I'm sure you can. Didn't you say you were staying over another night? At least?"

"At least? Where did that idea come from?"

"I thought I might persuade you with my English charms." She kissed him on the lips a second time, much more slowly, hands on his chest. "We were allies at Waterloo, remember?"

"Oh? Were you there for the entire battle?"

"Yes. Right next to you."

"Did we kiss?"

"Before and after, yes, quite a bit."

"Remind me."

She put her arms around his neck and kissed him a long time before stopping to brush her lips over his cheek and whisper in his ear. "Remember now?"

"It's coming back to me. I can see Blucher and Wellington. Maybe even a glimpse of Napoleon."

"Then I'm not doing this right. Let's try this." She kissed him with more force and then released him.

He looked at her in kind of a daze.

"Well?" She cocked her head and smiled. "What do you see now?"

"Why, I must admit, not much. Just you."

"Ah, now we have the chemistry just right, Professor Hartmann. What shall we do with it?"

He ran his hands through her long, dark hair. "Carry on I hope, Lady Catherine. *Die Nacht ist jung.*"

"It is young. But still not a star or the moon or a kiss should be lost. We must use them up."

"Once again I agree with you wholeheartedly."

Kipp woke in the dark. At first he lay still as he listened. Matthew wasn't crying. There was no noise from inside the house or outside on the grounds. He reached over to touch Christelle's arm. It was cold and rigid.

"Chris! Christelle!" he cried.

He threw back the covers. Moonlight revealed her open eyes were lifeless. Her lips were parted in a small smile. Her hair was spread over the pillow like silver feathers.

"Christelle!" he shouted.

He moved to her side of the bed. Sitting down, he pulled her into his arms and looked for any sign of life. He clamped his hand over her heart and then grabbed her wrist. He kissed her and cried out again. Her arms remained stiff as stone. Her entire body seemed as smooth and hard as marble.

"Oh no! Oh no! God, my God…no please. Not this…no…no… no!"

He heard the sound of running feet. Switches must have been clicked on because light blazed all around him. Hands gripped his shoulders. He turned his head and recognized Ben. Victoria was slightly behind him, her hand over her mouth as she took in the scene.

"I'm sorry. I'm so sorry, Kipp." Ben's face was wet with tears. "God, please help us."

Then Kip noticed his father and mother looking pale and old. There was Catherine, tears cutting across her face. Emma was clutching Victoria. Edward rushed in with Charlotte, whose hair looked like

Christelle's—wild and shining, except it was moving as she moved and Christelle's hair only moved because he was rocking her and weeping into the thousands of soft strands.

"Our Father," Jeremy touched his shoulder and knelt beside the bed, "who art in heaven." Jeremy's round glasses had smeared. He took them off. Grasping his prosthetic right hand with his left hand, he dropped his head onto his hands. "*Que ton règne vienne, que ta volonté soit faite sur la terre comme au ciel. Donne-nous aujourd'hui notre pain de ce jour.*" He stopped. His voice became a whisper. "Forgive us our sins. As we forgive those who have sinned against us. Lead us not into temptation. But deliver us from evil. For thine is the kingdom. And the power. And the glory. Forever. Amen."

Matthew stood looking at his mother. Kipp saw that he was very slender and very young and that his eyes were as dark as his mother's eyes had been.

9

July, 1925–October, 1926
Dover Sky

Dear Cornelia, my diary,

How many times have I intended to sit down and write? More than a year has gone by, and it's July again. But I am determined to tell you everything this evening.

I must start with our loss of Christelle last summer. None of us knew how sick she was. She kept the truth about her cancer from everyone except Kipp until the day she died. Kipp was absolutely shattered. We all were. It was a tremendous shock.

Then the funeral was scarcely over—we laid her to rest at the family cemetery at Ashton Park—before Kipp was gone. He made arrangements with Mother and Father to take care of Matthew. Then he flew off in his SPAD to enter an air race from the Orkneys to South Africa. The first leg he landed at London a half hour behind that horrid von Zeltner fellow. The next day was a short hop to Paris, and the day after that the contestants overnighted at Madrid. Kipp was still behind, but by the time he reached Cape Town in South Africa he was more than an hour ahead of von Zeltner! He won the race and the purse was five thousand pounds! He sent the money to Mother and Father to use for anything Matthew might need.

The next thing we knew, Kipp was missing. He'd taken off for the return flight. Somewhere over the Sahara he just disap-peared. Even von Zeltner looked for him. We were frantic for weeks as people searched. If Victoria's husband, Ben, hadn't been so concerned about Vic and their new baby boy being sick, he would have flown down and hunted for Kipp himself.

Finally we heard that Kipp had been rescued by French For-eign Legion troops after his plane ran out of fuel and crash-landed in the desert. Father rounded up everyone from Ashton Park and Dover Sky, and we attended a special ser-vice of praise and thanksgiving at Jeremy's church in London even though Kipp wasn't back yet. It was a wonderful time of rejoicing.

But for all that, we still haven't seen Kipp since he left for the Orkneys last July. He joined the Legion and remained in Africa. He writes his son often, and the letters are read to Matthew. Kipp sends photographs that we frame and hang in Matthew's room. My brother looks fit enough in his funny French hat and desert uniform. We think he's been doing some flying for the French, but he's very vague about his duties.

The news tells us France is siding with Spain in the war in Morocco against the Berbers of the Rif region. The Legion has been sent in. We haven't heard from Kipp in at least a month, and Mum is fretting that he's caught up in the fight-ing. We know it was very fierce in May. All we can do is pray. Between you and me, Kipp's behavior since his wife's death seems suicidal.

It was fierce enough in England in May too. We had a dread-ful general strike that lasted a week and just about brought everyone to blows. Edward was ranting about communists and Bolshevists, and I suppose he wasn't far off the mark. The workers walked out by the millions—especially the coal min-ers. There was indeed a strong revolutionary element stirring the pot. Prime Minister Baldwin maintained his calm and didn't send the army in with rifles firing. Eventually the awful strike was over and done. Dad says the time of the strike will come back to haunt us in the next election. He thinks voters will punish the Conservative Party for turning a deaf ear to the workingman's plea for better wages and working conditions.

Then there is my life. What do I do about men? How nice if I could just traipse off and marry my man as our servant Sally did with her soldier (and leaving us a maid short). I've come to an understanding of sorts with Albrecht Hartmann. We adore one another but won't speak of marriage. I helped him with his book that came out in August last year. We've remained close ever since, and we grow closer all the time. He writes constantly and has asked me to join him on his sabbatical from the university that begins this fall and carries over into 1927. I don't see how I can join him, at least not for all of it, without causing a scandal. Edward is working hand in glove with the prime minister's office, and he would have me strung up from the yardarm if anything I did cast our family in a poor light right now. I really can't say what will happen, but I have until September to sort it out.

Speaking of yardarms and the navy, guess who popped back into my life? Terrence Fordyce! He came calling a few weeks ago. I hadn't seen him in at least a year and a half. I was taken aback. He is more handsome and tanned than ever and keen on picking up where we left off. We've gone out for dinner a few times and to a naval ball.

Yes, I did tell him about Albrecht. It doesn't seem to faze him. I expect he figures that since I am not engaged or married, I am still on the market, which is true enough, I suppose. I don't know how to solve the marriage riddle when it comes to Albrecht Hartmann and Terrence Fordyce. Edward would have an absolute fit over my marrying Albrecht, whereas Terry would graft nicely into the Danforth family tree.

I confess my affection was all for Albrecht until Terry came to call again when the *Hood* was back from the Mediterranean. I am so fickle and feel I am playing the coquette. This is all rather difficult. It would help if either man grew ugly or boorish or witless but alas, the truth is they are both lovely in all respects. My head spins like a weathercock, and I fear my heart does the same. "Frailty, thy name is woman!" Do shut up, Hamlet!

What else to write about, hmm? My sister Libby and her American husband, Michael, are at long last returning to England. They've been gone far longer than anyone expected, so Mum and Dad are ecstatic. The pair are supposed to show up in Dover this fall. That's very convenient for me because now I can tell Albrecht I can't possibly commit to anything until the new year. After all, I must welcome Michael and Libby back and see them settled. It also permits me to spend more time with Terry and see him off to the Med in January. That will give me ample opportunity to decide what to do about Albrecht and his yearlong sabbatical.

One other thing, Cornelia, before I forget. Dover Sky is about to become something of a hive. First, we have Lady Caroline Scarborough planning to move here for a while. She had a falling out with her father over something. What, I can't even begin to imagine. She asked if she could room here temporarily. Mum, Dad, and I were quick to say yes. We love her and want to do anything we can to help. Lord Scarborough made it clear to Dad that while he remained at an impasse with his daughter, he was grateful we had opened our door to her.

Then, as soon as Matthew found out Charles was going to be living at Dover Sky, he wanted to come and live here too. No amount of cajoling from his grandparents or his Aunt Victoria could convince him otherwise. After all, it brings him closer to Owen in Dover as well as to Emma's boys in London. So he's leaving Ashton Park. Poor Ramsay! Vic's older boy will feel quite left out stuck up there at the Lancashire estate all by himself, I'm sure. Perhaps we can convince Victoria to let him board here at Dover Sky with the others.

For whatever reason, Michael and Libby want to lodge at Dover Sky this coming winter after they arrive. Mother and Father are a bit put out by this, but Libby is quite settled on the matter. She says in her letters that she feels it would be best for her and Michael, but she doesn't explain why. What's up there, I wonder. All things will be made clear in due time.

Until then, first things first. Caroline and Charles arrive in the morning, and I want to be up early and be ready for them. Terry is dining with us in the evening so it will be a full day. Things will probably never be the same at Dover Sky, Cornelia.

"I love July. It really is my favorite month."

Catherine glanced at Caroline as they walked to the swan pond in the sunset. "It suits you."

"Thank you. Not much has suited me lately, so I'm glad summer does." She bent over and picked a yellow dandelion that was vivid against her blue cotton dress. "I know they're a weed, but the scent is wonderful." As they walked she continued to hold it under her nose. "I enjoyed meeting your Leftenant Commander Fordyce. He's a nice man."

"Yes, that he is."

"Do you see him often?"

"No. He doesn't get away from the *Hood* all that much. And, as you noticed, he has to head back to port while the night's still young."

"Charles loves uniforms just as we ladies do."

Catherine laughed as she played with the string of pearls at her neck. "Terry's quite a friend of the family."

"I see that. Do you mind my asking if the two of you have future plans?"

"Plans?" Catherine stopped and pointed at a large white swan that had just unfolded its wings. "Isn't it spectacular?"

"What a beauty!" Caroline said as she pulled several pins out of her hair. They continued on their walk as she pushed the hairpins back in. "I don't want to intrude, so forgive me if you think I'm being too forward."

"Not really. Terry and I haven't talked much about it."

"I suppose you're wondering what my being here is all about—my leaving Mum and Dad and coming to live with you?"

"Yes, I was wondering but didn't want to ask. I knew you'd share when you were ready."

"It has to do with men. Well, one man in particular. That's why I was asking about your future plans. I hope they are going along better than mine."

They'd reached the benches by the pond. The water and reflections were emerald and scarlet in the last burst of sunlight. Catherine had a paper bag of bread crumbs, and she tossed them a few at a time into the water. Swans and ducks arrowed towards her from all directions.

"To tell you the truth, I wouldn't mind being married again." Catherine handed the bag to Caroline and said, "Have a go." She wiped her hands on her white summer dress. "There are two men who fascinate me right now. One the family would embrace if we were to wed. The other—well, a marriage to him could cause some problems."

Caroline finished tossing out the big pieces and then upended the bag into the pond. Bills snapped and water splashed. "That's how it is with me. Papa threatened to cut me off. I don't care really."

"What upsets your parents about him?"

"They just don't like him. He has a history with the family." She smiled at several ducklings who had fought their way in to grab up some soggy morsels. "I hope you'll let him visit me here at Dover Sky."

"He's not Jack the Ripper surely? Of course he can call."

"I should tell you who he is first. Then you can give me your answer." She tossed the dandelion into the pond. The birds stormed it. One swan took the dandelion up in its bill and quickly spat it out.

"If you wish. I'm certain it won't affect anything."

"No?" Caroline turned her blue eyes on Catherine. "The man is Tanner Buchanan."

"Buchanan? The man who—who took advantage of you?"

"Yes."

"Kipp rescued you from him."

"Sir Kipp of the Round Table and his mighty deeds." Caroline picked another dandelion and plucked its yellow flower to bits as she stared at the birds. "Now you understand why my parents have problems with him and me. And why the Danforths might."

Catherine looked at the ground. "Yes, quite."

Two days later Ben Whitecross landed at Dover Sky with Kipp's son, Matthew, and his luggage. Matthew immediately ran off with Charles, who was waiting at the edge of the airstrip. Ben saw to the plane and eventually made his way to the manor where coffee and Danishes were waiting. Sitting back in his chair in the parlor, he immediately drank off half his cup of coffee. "Ah, splendid! Thank you, Holly. So where are Matt and Charles?"

"At the pond with Harrison," Holly replied as she patted Ben on the knee. "How was he on the flight down?"

"Fine. I told Vic he'd be a flier, but she isn't keen on any of the children getting into it. The planes are getting too sleek and fast for her."

"I'll bet you can't wait for Michael to show up," chimed in Catherine.

"I can't. He's been gone forever it seems. And with Kipp out of the picture, I've had to take on two new pilots to handle the work. None too soon because we'll have our first monoplanes delivered in '27. Business is booming all right, and I need help to keep up."

Holly poured tea into her cup. Her black hair was loose and hung past her shoulders. "What news do you have of Kipp?"

"There was a letter just the other day for Matthew. Kipp can't go into detail, of course, but there's no doubt he's in the thick of the fighting in Morocco. The problem is the letters are always months old."

Caroline sipped from her teacup and glanced through the lace-curtained window.

"I don't understand how the French got into it," Catherine said as she leaned forward and clasped both hands in her lap. "The papers always said it was Spain and the Berbers who were mixing it up."

"The Berbers made the mistake of attacking a chain of French forts they felt were on their side of the mountains back in April of 1925. They killed over 1000 French troops. So France sided with Spain and sent in almost 300,000 men, including Kipp's unit in the Legion. So he's been fighting for over a year in the Rif, the mountain region the Berbers claim is theirs."

"Poor Mum. She has both Kipp and Robbie to worry about. And you too, Ben, with all your wild air racing."

"I've always wanted to be a Methodist missionary and go to Africa. Perhaps she'll be pleased with that."

"You're joking."

"I have, really. There's a bit of Jeremy Sweet in me, along with a dash of jungle pilot."

"I doubt that will calm Mother's nerves very much."

"If it's any consolation, I think the fighting is coming to an end in Morocco. The Berbers will lay down their arms. Some guerrilla warfare is bound to continue though because not all the Berbers will surrender. Kipp will have to keep his head down."

Holly frowned. "I can't see Kipp crawling along the desert with a rifle, can you? Don't you think the French would have him in the air?"

Ben bit into a Danish. "The Legion doesn't have an air force, but who knows? These are good. Did Norah bake them?"

"A new girl actually," replied Catherine.

"Amazing. You're running quite a little show down here now, aren't you?" He smiled at Caroline. "You're looking well, my lady."

She turned her eyes from the window. "Thank you. It's good of your family to take me in."

"I'm sure you'll bless us as much as we bless you." Ben finished his coffee and stood up. "Have to be on my way. I need to stop in at our air base by London before I scoot back to Lancashire."

Catherine got to her feet and hugged him. "Tell Mum and Dad I miss them. I'm sorry they won't be dropping down to Dover this summer."

"They thought it best to stay with Vic and me this year. But they'll be here for a visit once Libby and Michael show up, you can count on that."

"How are Lady Grace and Sir Arthur?"

"They're holding their own. Sir Arthur falls asleep at the dinner table now, but he always has something exceptional to say once he wakes up. And Lady Grace hums hymns to herself and wanders about the rooms speaking with the dukes and duchesses who lived at Ashton Park centuries ago. Actually, it's your father's dogs I'm worried about. They're both failing."

"Oh no! That would kill Dad to lose them."

"I hope they'll live out the year, but I think not. Vic is trying to persuade him to pick up of a couple of puppies, but he won't hear of it." Ben kissed Holly on the cheek. "Cheers!" He took Caroline by the hand. "I hope you have a wonderful time here, Lady Caroline, and that everything falls into place for you. I can tell you that at every family devotional at Ashton Park Lord Preston prays for you and your parents."

"Thank you, Ben. Tell Lord and Lady Preston how very much I appreciate their hospitality. I will ring them up myself in a few days."

Just over an hour after Ben took off in his SPAD S.XX for London, a black Rolls Royce Silver Ghost pulled up in front of the manor. Skitt met the car in the drive and opened the door. Tanner Buchanan, Member of Parliament, stepped out. His chauffeur got out and grabbed two large suitcases from the boot before following the two men into the manor.

Harrison tucked a cricket bat under his arm and led the way down the slope in the last of the evening light. "Every summer we lose one or two, Lord Tanner. We find the feathers where they pluck 'em and that's it, except a boot print now and then."

Buchanan strode beside him, silver-topped walking stick in one hand. "If you've been trying to catch them at night and been unsuccessful why not hide out during the day?"

"Nowhere to hide. Unless I used a drinking straw and crawled under the water. Never fear, we'll catch 'em one day. Eventually they'll slip up." Harrison cleared his throat. "You're welcome to the manor and no mistake, Lord Buchanan. You can stay the weekend, if you like. But it'll have to be the first and last for you. If ever Lord Edward dropped in and found you here, I expect there'd be a brawl."

"We're both gentlemen, Mr. Harrison. Gentlemen don't brawl."

"They have disagreements."

"Something like that."

"Well, whatever you wish to call it, I think you'll agree with me your presence here is a bit of a sticky wicket for the Danforth family."

"I most certainly agree with that, yes. I despise your employers, so I can understand how my visit to their Dover Sky estate could be viewed as an impertinence."

Harrison stopped walking. "They were your employers once. They treated you well enough."

Buchanan's eyes hardened into a cold gray color. "Until I was accused of taking advantage of Lady Caroline. Did anyone stop to ask if she might have been the one who approached me?"

"What d'ya mean?"

"Did anyone ever wonder who had seduced who?"

"Is that what you're saying? That *she* led you astray? A strapping big bloke like you?"

Buchanan grimaced as if he'd swallowed hot tea too quickly. "Strapping or not, her Medusa charms laid me low. And no one asked for my point of view, did they?"

"Medusa charms? Is that how you see her? A woman with a hundred snakes writhing on her head who turned men to stone?"

"I do see her that way, Harrison. Didn't she seduce your Lord Kipp as well?"

"What nonsense is this!"

"Didn't Caroline entice him into an…um…shall I say an indiscretion while his wife was dying? That's the word going the rounds."

"It's a lie!" Harrison's face was bloodred. "Not another word on those lines or lord or no lord, I'll lay you flat."

"Will you?" Buchanan smiled slowly. "I'd like to see you try."

Harrison stopped, laid down his cricket bat, and turned to face Lord Buchanan. "Why do you talk this way about Lady Caroline when

I've heard you have every intention of marrying her? And isn't that why you've come to Dover Sky? To call on her?"

"Why, it's a marriage of convenience, Harrison. I'm hoping my wicked little Medusa will destroy Lord Kipp for his great insult against her. And she allows me closer access to the Danforths."

"That's despicable."

"I despise Kipp Danforth for striking me during a dispute in France. I despise the Danforths for sacking me without permitting me to speak a word in my defense. I despise Edward simply for being a Danforth and being in the wrong political party. So Lady Caroline and I shall get back at you all. I will destroy both father and son in the House of Commons and make them look the proper fools they are. And my wicked little Medusa shall destroy Lord Kipp. She'll turn him to stone."

"You are a madman. He doesn't care for her anymore."

"Ah, but he does, he does. She's convinced of it. And equally convinced the day will dawn when he gets over his grief at his wife's death—such a pity, so beautiful a woman—and his guilt at betraying her by seeking solace in Caroline's arms and kisses—"

"Lord Buchanan! I swear by all that's holy you'd better quit now!"

Buchanan grinned but his eyes remained hard and flat. "He'll come to her again. He'll plead with her to hold him, to love him. She'll toy with him a while, get him well into her lair. Then she'll have at him and make sure all of England knows it—the newspapers, the aristocracy, the king, the church, members of Parliament, everyone. The scandal will break the Danforth clan, absolutely break it."

Tanner laughed harshly as he imagined it. "The Conservative Party will be done with them, the Church of England will be done with them, Buckingham Palace and the nobles will be done with them. There will be photographs of the seduction, as many as anyone could like. And to top it all off, Lady Caroline will claim rape. Why, it will ruin Lord Preston's business contracts as well…and I hope bankrupt the airline. The Danforths will become paupers, swilling gin by the Liverpool docks and begging for bread in East London. How I'll gloat!"

Buchanan expected the punch Harrison threw and easily blocked it with his hand. The second one he stopped with his arm. Then he struck Harrison in the stomach and hit him with his walking stick. Tanner lifted Harrison's chin off the grass with the toe of his boot and tapped Harrison's head none too softly with the silver top of his cane. "You're lucky I'm not going to report your impertinence to your employers, Harrison. Next time I won't go so easy on you, old man.

"I don't mind telling you all of it. Who are you going to go to? How are you going to stop me? I'll make my speeches in the House and tear Lord Preston and Lord Edward to pieces. Caroline will marry me and wait in her room for Kipp to come back from his war in the Rif and look for her. *Be a mother to my son,* he'll plead. *Be a wife for my manor.* She'll laugh and turn her Medusa head on him and that, old man, will be that. *Finis,* as the late Christelle Danforth might have said, God rest her soul."

Harrison grit his teeth. "You're mad."

"Not at all. It's merely politics, Mr. Harrison. Politics and pleasure." He turned and walked back toward the manor as the sun disappeared.

"Cathy? Are you up?"

"I'm just brushing out my hair. What is it?"

Holly stepped inside Catherine's bedroom and closed the door, leaning her back against it. She was in a maroon dressing gown. "My husband came up from the pond this morning with a huge bruise on his stomach, a cut on his face, and a lump on his head. His knuckles are bruised too. He said it was poachers, but they got away. I don't believe him."

Catherine put down her brush. "That's terrible! Is he going to be all right?"

"Physically he'll be sore a few days and probably just shake it off. But behind his eyes I see something more. I don't know what's going on, but I am certain Lord Buchanan is part of it."

"What do you mean?"

"I know Buchanan went down to the pond last night with Harrison. I think they had words that led to blows exchanged. Harrison won't budge on his story, so I thought I'd engage Tanner Buchanan in conversation to see if I can discern the truth. He's a brute, but I'm a sly wildcat who might just get the better of him."

"Holly—"

"Don't worry. I won't bring a scandal down on Dover Sky. But my intuition tells me he might try."

"How can you be so sure it wasn't poachers?"

"Because I went down there this morning. There were no boot prints in the muck at the edge of the pond or in the bushes. There were no signs of the fight Harrison claimed took place on the shore. No tracks leading away, no feathers, no dead swans. And no missing birds either. I counted to make sure. But a ways up from the pond there was some blood on the grass. And a handkerchief Harrison always carries in the pocket of his corduroy jacket was on the ground, also bloodstained. He used it to wipe the cut above his right eye, he says. And the welt on his face is narrow—just about the width of a walking stick."

Catherine put a hand to her face. "This is dreadful."

"I want to speak with Caroline about this first. Do you want to come? After all, don't you think it's strange she should want to walk the aisle with the man who dishonored her so many years ago?"

"I asked her that when she told me about him. She said, 'He's my son's father, and he's never been unkind to me.'"

"What!"

"That's what she said...and that's all she said." Catherine got up from her vanity. "I feel very bad about this. Buchanan being here is just asking for trouble. I asked Harrison to speak with Lord Buchanan about his visit here. I asked him to reinforce that it could be this once, but only this once. Can you imagine what Edward will say when he discovers Buchanan slept under our roof? Can you imagine what Mum or Dad will say? Or what Kipp might do when he finds out? Perhaps talking to Caroline and then approaching Lord Buchanan is the best thing to do."

"Harrison can give a good account of himself in a fight, but he doesn't carry heavy walking sticks he can knock people about the head with." Holly opened the bedroom door. "The household's barely stirring. Skitt, the cooks, and the maids are just starting their duties. Will you come to Caroline's room with me?"

Catherine threw on a white housecoat. "She might be still sleeping, Holly."

"Then we'll have to wake her, won't we?"

Caroline was up and dressed in a light-yellow gown the same color as her hair. Her bedroom door was already open, and she was standing by her window, one hand on the white curtain as she drew it aside to peer outside.

"Good morning!" she said, turning very slightly—just enough to glance at the two women before looking back out the window again. "Do you know there was a heavy dew last night? The grass is simply blazing with the reflected sunlight from the dawn."

"I hadn't noticed," Catherine said. "We're sorry to disturb you so early, but we need to talk with you."

"Not at all. Is this about Tanner?"

"Yes, it is."

"I'm sure it's uncomfortable for you to have him here. I hope he hasn't caused any trouble. You must understand the demands that are being made on him by the Labor Party and his constituents in Ayrshire South. He's not had a moment's peace since the new year. Even with the House in summer recess, his phone keeps ringing. He thought a short holiday and visit with me here in Kent would relieve some of the strain. And naturally I wanted to see him as well."

Holly closed the door. "Why should there be trouble?"

Caroline continued to stare out the window. "Oh, you know. Edward hates him. Kipp hates him. The Danforths in general hate him. And here I am at the Danforth estate in Kent, so he has to come here if he wants to visit me. He's bound to be a bit wound up about the situation. Wouldn't that be understandable?" She paused, still not turning towards them. "Has something happened?"

Holly clasped her hands in front of her. "I believe my husband and your fiancé—"

"Not yet. We're not engaged yet," interrupted Caroline turning her head just enough to see them before staring out the window again.

"Whatever the case might be, I believe Lord Buchanan and my husband had an altercation by the pond last night. Harrison was quite bruised up this morning, and his face was cut. It looks like he was hit with a walking stick."

"Did he accuse Tanner?"

"No. He said it was poachers. But down by the pond there are no signs of poachers or a scuffle. And I know Lord Buchanan and Harrison went to the pond together last night."

"And did you talk to Tanner?"

"No. I haven't gone to see him yet."

"So what would you like from me?"

"I did find blood and grass on the toe of one of Lord Buchanan's boots. He took them off and left them in the front hall by the door."

"Not much proof, Holly. Sherlock Holmes could have done better."

Holly raised her eyebrows. "Could he?"

"Yes. There are clues you missed. Have you examined Tanner's walking stick for marks or blood? The cane is resting against the wall on your right, just inside my door."

Catherine and Holly looked, and then Holly walked over, picked it up, and examined it.

"There are no blood or marks on it," Holly said.

"But it is quite polished, is it not?"

"Yes."

"Especially the silver top—almost like a mirror."

"Yes."

"I wonder why?"

Holly stared at Caroline's back as understanding dawned. She closed the bedroom door before turning back to Caroline. "Did he ask you to clean it for him?"

"He did."

"Where is the rag you used to clean it with?"

Sunlight streamed into the room around Caroline as she gazed out on the lawn. "The trash would make it too easy to find, don't you think? I'm sure Scotland Yard would check that and under my bed and under my pillow."

"Where is it then?"

"Why, it's where even Sherlock Holmes wouldn't look if he were a gentleman." Caroline tugged a soiled rag from the bosom of her dress and held it over her shoulder. "I had no opportunity to discard it. Your butler seems to prowl around all night. Doesn't he ever sleep?"

"Perhaps he was concerned for our guests?" Catherine offered.

"Or perhaps he heard an altercation…" Caroline responded.

Holly and Catherine looked at each other and then back at Caroline.

Caroline suddenly turned from the window to face them. One side of her face was purple and black.

"My word!" exclaimed Holly as she rushed to Caroline's side. "Did Tanner Buchanan do this?"

"Have you put ice on this yet?" Holly asked.

"How could I do that without your butler or the cooks noticing and having a fit?"

Catherine came forward and grasped Caroline's hand. "Why did he hit you?"

"I noticed the blood on the cane and refused to clean up the mess. I told him I wanted to know what had happened. He told me he'd beaten off a mad dog. I said I'd ask the household staff about it…and they would clean and polish his cane for him. He told me to do what he'd asked. When I refused again, he slapped me. I fought back, and he used the cane." She gave the rag to Holly. "Your husband's blood and my blood should be ample evidence."

Holly's face was drawn and white. "I shall ring the police in Dover."

"He's Lord Tanner Buchanan, MP. The authorities won't believe my word against his."

"They'll take my word," Catherine said.

"But you saw nothing."

"Once Harrison hears about Buchanan beating you, he'll speak up," Holly said.

"He won't."

"He's no coward!"

"Even if the police believe us, Tanner is still a member of Parliament. The authorities won't do anything. You know how they are. Tanner told Harrison that he means to destroy the Danforth family and included my part in it. If Harrison tells that, the police will think he's raving mad. Tanner knows that, so he thinks his plans are safe."

"What plans?" Catherine squeezed Caroline's hand.

"Never mind that right now." Holly crammed the bloodstained rag into a pocket in her dressing gown. "Catherine, I'm going down to fetch water and ice for Caroline. You two had better—"

There was rapid knocking on the door.

Caroline's eyes went dark. "Yes?"

"Lady Caroline?"

"Yes, Skitt?"

"Lady Caroline, are Lady Holly and Lady Catherine in there with you, by chance?"

"Indeed they are. We're just having a quick chat."

"I thought your ladyships would like to know that a car has just pulled up at the front."

The women looked at one another.

"I see," replied Caroline. "And who would that be at this early hour, Skitt?"

"It's Lord Edward, my lady. Lord Buchanan has already opened the door to him."

"What are you doing here?" Edward asked, trying to keep from shouting.

Buchanan stood on the porch, his chauffeur and suitcases beside him. "Enjoying your family estate."

"You have no business at Dover Sky."

"I do, Danforth. My fiancée is here, so I swung by to see how she was."

"Fiancée? And who is that?"

"Lady Caroline, of course."

"Caroline? You're joking! Why would she wed the cad who ruined her life?"

"Perhaps she decided your brother Kipp was the bigger cad."

"I want you off our property right now!"

Buchanan smiled and pulled on white cotton gloves. "I'm leaving. And don't worry, I'll have plenty to say about your family in a speech I'll be giving in the House this fall."

Catherine suddenly showed up in the doorway out of breath, with Skitt following closely behind.

"What's this about, Cathy?" demanded Edward. "Is it true what he says about Caroline being engaged to him?"

She hesitated, and then she straightened as she stepped forward. "No. No, it is not."

Buchanan whipped around. "She is my fiancée!"

Skitt stepped between Catherine and Buchanan. "Steady on, Lord Buchanan."

"She knows very well Lady Caroline is engaged to me."

"That may have been true until you beat her!" snapped Catherine. "It certainly isn't now. Get your bags and leave Dover Sky immediately."

"I never beat Caroline. Is that what she's telling you? She tripped on the stairs during the night. Let me speak to her."

Catherine blocked the doorway. "No, you will not. Lady Holly is tending to the wounds you inflicted."

"I've done nothing, I tell you." Buchanan picked up his cane from where it leaned against his baggage. "I think it best Lady Caroline leave with me."

"I'm afraid not, Lord Buchanan. She is under our roof and our protection."

He barked a laugh. "Your protection? Do you imagine this the Middle Ages? In any case, who is going to protect her? You? Whelps like your skinny little butler?"

Skitt put his hand up. He looked at the chauffeur. "Please load the luggage in the car at once." He looked at Buchanan. "That will do, sir. You've been asked to go. Please leave at once."

Buchanan seethed and swung his cane. There was a crack, and Skitt clutched his wrist as he fell against the wall of the house. "Don't meddle with me, boy." Buchanan pulled on the silver top of his cane and a sword emerged, glittering in the light. "All of you stay back. I'm going to fetch Lady Caroline and her bags, and then we're leaving this wretched estate. Stay back, Lord Edward, I say. Stay back, Lady Catherine. I am a dangerous man when crossed."

"Aye, you may be dangerous, but I am even more of a threat, Lord Buchanan." The words were followed by several sharp metallic clicks.

Buchanan turned and saw Harrison walking toward the porch holding a double-barreled shotgun.

Buchanan snorted. "You wouldn't dare. I shall contact Scotland Yard."

"If there's anything left of you to make the call, you'll be welcome to do so on our shilling," Harrison replied. He came closer and pointed the shotgun directly at Buchanan's stomach. "Now be off."

"Not without my fiancée."

"She's not your property."

"Oh, but she is. And she comes with me or I'll tear this godforsaken excuse for a manor down around your ears. Who do you think you are?"

"We're all you'll never be, Lord Buchanan." Harrison jabbed the shotgun at him. "Clear off. I'll not say it again."

"Lady Caroline is my woman, and she comes with me."

"I am not, Tanner." Caroline stood in the doorway, her yellow dress a stark contrast to the side of her face that was dark red and swollen.

"Caroline…" Buchanan said softly. "Bear up and back me up. Remember our plans. Remember what I can help you do." He sheathed his sword and extended a gloved hand. "Come. We'll have a physician in London tend to the bruises from your fall. Then I'll have you as my bride before the day's out."

Caroline remained in the doorway. "Tanner, I loathe you. You're a spider I wish I could squash under my boot. You may thank whatever god you worship that Harrison holds the shotgun and not me. I would have already pulled the trigger."

"Caroline, don't lose sight of what we want to accomplish together."

"You mean what *you* want to accomplish. All I wanted was a peaceful life, an honorable husband, and a good father to help me raise Charles."

"Don't be a fool."

Harrison stepped forward and cut in. "Goodbye, Lord Buchanan. Your car's ready. You and your chauffeur can take off. Now would be a good time."

Buchanan slowly came down the steps of the porch. "You are a brave man when there's a gun in your hands, Harrison. One day it will not be there, but I will."

"And you're a brave man with a sword in your hand."

"I won't need a sword or a walking stick to deal with the likes of you."

"May God speed the day of our next meeting, Lord Buchanan. Until then, be off."

Buchanan looked up at Caroline. "You'll regret this."

"I doubt it. I haven't felt this good in months."

Buchanan and his chauffeur walked to the car. The chauffeur set the luggage by the boot, opened the door for Tanner, closed it, and then loaded the luggage. He climbed into the driver's seat, and a few seconds later the black Silver Ghost headed down the drive toward the main road. Buchanan turned for one last stare. His face was like granite.

"All's well that ends well." Edward smiled at Harrison. "Thank you for your help. Is the gun loaded?"

"It is, my lord."

"Ah. Then, as Wellington said, that was a 'near run' thing." He glanced up at Skitt who was getting to his feet with Catherine and Norah's assistance. "That was well done, Skitt. I'll have more to say to you later, but that was well done indeed."

Skitt was still gripping his wrist. "I would die rather than let a beast like that lay a hand on Lady Catherine, my lord."

"I believe it." Edward nodded at Caroline. "I came by for an early breakfast before heading up to London, but breakfast and London will have to wait. Lady Caroline, we must get you into Dover for medical attention. That goes for you as well, young Skitt. We'll take my car. My driver will have us at the doctor's in half an hour."

Caroline shook her head. "I've been trouble enough. My face will heal in time."

"There could be broken bones. That's true of you as well, Skitt."

"But, sir," Skitt protested, "who will man the door? And what if Lord Buchanan comes back?"

Holly came through the door. "Thank you, Skitt, but Harrison and I shall take care of that. You defend Lady Caroline in case that wretch Buchanan is lying in wait on the roadway. We'll defend Dover Sky."

A gleam came into Skitt's eye. "D'ya think he might try to waylay us, Lady Holly?"

"I shouldn't be at all surprised."

"May I—may I take the shotgun then?"

"Ah." Holly patted his cheek. "Our young lion. No, we shall have it here, I think. But you have one good hand, Skitt. And Lord Edward will be by your side. I fear for Buchanan if he should attempt to stop the car and carry Lady Caroline off. I truly do."

Dear Cornelia, my diary,

Well, the summer has swept past. After that dreadful business with Lord Tanner Buchanan the rest of July and August were delightful. Caroline's bruised face healed up nicely, and Charles and Matthew are getting along famously. The twins came up from London twice with Emma and Jeremy, along with their little brother Billy. We had a very raucous manor indeed. Sean tries to keep up as best he can, but the twins are nine and he is only three—the youngest of the lot during that time.

Between you and me, I have no idea what will become of Caroline. Terry has offered to introduce her to naval officers, but she begs off every time. If a letter comes to Matthew from

Kipp and we read it out loud at the table, she excuses herself and leaves the room. I don't think there is any future for her in that direction. Her face may be better—well, she is stunning, isn't she?—but under her skin she is far from well. Mum calls her a bird with a broken wing. Now that she has broken off with Tanner, she could return home, but she shows no inclination to do so. She talks to her mother once a week on the phone but appears to be holding a grudge against her father. I pray with her about it, and she's grateful for that, yet it seems to make no difference in her attitude. I continue to pray for her on my own.

Edward saw Lord Buchanan when Parliament commenced, of course. At first Buchanan refused to greet him. Then he delivered a scathing attack on Father in his first speech of the session and another one on Edward a week later. After that he makes mocking bows to both of them when they meet.

Edward says Buchanan has that American woman on his arm again—Lady Hall, or Lady Kate, as she likes to be called. Edward cannot understand Lady Kate's sweetness. It's in such marked contrast to her partner's harshness. But apparently Lord Buchanan is at his most courteous when he's in her company. No warmth, of course. He is never the hypocrite. He's just cold and correct.

If Caroline is no longer the bait to trap Kipp, will that be Kate's role? Edward says she is quite lovely. I wonder if Kipp will find her attractive? However, when he returns from the Rif it will not be Lady Kate he seeks out. It will be Caroline. I am sure of that. But will she receive him? She's said she won't countless times now. Caroline says Kipp blames her for his wife's death, but we're not sure why he'd do that. Apparently Kipp called Caroline an awful name and said she'd be an unfit mother. I can scarcely believe it, but something happened that set Caroline against him like rock.

One thing we Danforths are united about is praying daily for protection against Lord Buchanan's villainy. He told Edward he still hopes to destroy us. We can only place Christ between ourselves and his darkness. Thank goodness Mother and Father don't know the half of it.

But on to pleasanter things. Terry and Albrecht. What to do? I see Terry two or three times a month, and I enjoy his company very much. Albrecht writes every week, and his letters are beautiful to read. He's so articulate. Cornelia, I wonder if he isn't in love with me? Not infatuated but actually in love? I haven't given him an answer on going on the sabbatical trip with him. I can't decide what to do. I think I'd adore being in his company every day, just as I was in Switzerland. Terry will be on the *Hood* somewhere in the Med during that time. I'd still need to have a chaperone of some sort or Papa and Edward would become positively unstable. It seems ridiculous at my age, but there you are. Who on earth would the chaperone be?

Well, I can't equivocate forever, much as it seems I should like to. Albrecht and the baron are paying a visit on the tenth of September, a Friday, and staying the weekend, which is grand. What answer I can give Albrecht about the sabbatical is a different matter. I must continue to pray, read my Bible, and go to church. Perhaps God's light will shine in with the answer. Albrecht and I have been very close in the past. Perhaps I gave my kisses too freely, but I did think of him as the only man in my life a year ago. Now I must be more careful and discreet. Explaining why to my theologian won't be easy.

One bright spot! Albrecht's book has been translated into English, and he's bringing me a copy! We can use it to set the mood by talking about it and praying together before we do anything else. That, I hope, will help the rest fall into place. Don't you think?

"Here it is! *Voila!* as the French say."

Albrecht handed Catherine a square package. They were standing by a dry fence of fieldstones Skitt and Harrison had erected to the west of the manor of Dover Sky.

"This is exciting!" She ripped at the brown paper and string with her fingers. "Em and Vic always open things so carefully. They try to save the fancy paper Christmas presents are wrapped in. I've never been able to do that." The book finally was in her hands, and she dropped the torn paper and broken string on the grass. "The book jacket is wonderful, Albrecht! Mountains, a sunrise, a cross on a peak…is this Pura?"

"Yes."

"*My Spirit.* What a wonderful title. What is that in German?"

"*Mein Geitz.*"

"And Hitler's is *Mein Kampf,* which translates as *My Struggle.* How are your book sales compared to his?"

"I suppose I sell one to every three of his."

"Isn't that still good?"

"*Ja, ja.* It's just a question of how much we're reaching the German people. And while Hitler's message is covering a lot of ground, so is mine." He opened the book to the third page as she held it. "Look here."

> This book is dedicated to the German people. And to C.F.D.,
> without whom its grace and breadth and depth would not
> have been possible.

Catherine immediately felt heat creeping up from her neck and spreading over her face. "My goodness, Albrecht. I haven't blushed like this since I was sixteen and thought I was in love with one of the Coldstream Guards at Windsor Castle. Why did you do me such an honor? All I did was proofreading duties."

"No, Catherine, you did much more than that. I value you as a friend, and as a thinker, and as a woman with a rich heart."

"You're making my blush worse, Albrecht. Who told you what my middle initial is?"

"Your father. He mentioned you once by calling you Catherine Faith. It's an extraordinary name and utterly who you are, so I've remembered it ever since."

"Thank you. I don't know what else to say. I shall read the book, of course."

"And keep a pen and pad of paper by your hand so you can make note of misspellings and poor grammatical structure, yes? Those can be fixed when the book gets reprinted."

She laughed. "I suppose I shall." She opened the book in the middle and read a paragraph. She looked up at Albrecht. "And what is Herr Hitler doing these days?"

"Not much. Germany is coming along well—the best we've been since the war. He's toned down his rhetoric and likes to portray himself as a moderate. Regardless, his Nazi Party continues to hold very few seats in the government, in the *Reichstag*, and no one appears much interested in him anymore."

"That's good."

Albrecht shrugged and gazed at a horse cropping grass on the other side of the stone fence. "Yet his book is selling, and membership in the Nazi Party is growing by tens of thousands each year. So what is really going on in Germany, hmm? Suppose we encounter economic struggles again. Would he gain in popularity?"

"If he does, you'll just have to write another book to counter his influence, won't you?"

"*Oh, ja.* Just like that you think?"

"Why not? You have the mind for it…and the spirit."

"Ah, Catherine, you have such confidence in me." He placed his hand over one of hers. "Come to the mountains with me. Please. You mean so much to me. I adore you."

"Albrecht, I—I can't just drop everything…"

"I know you have your brother and his wife to welcome back from several years in America. Naturally you must be at Dover Sky for that. And there is that naval officer to see. He will be going south to the Mediterranean in January, yes?"

Her face burned again. "Yes, Terry will be on the *Hood*. I didn't know you knew him."

"I've never met him, but it's no great secret that he's in your life. Catherine, it's not a surprise. How could a rose of such beauty like you go unnoticed year after year? I can't blame him for falling in love with you. I can't blame any man."

"He has never spoken of love or marriage, Albrecht."

"But his love is revealed in his eyes, isn't it?"

She flipped through pages in the book without responding.

"Catherine, I am not a jealous man. Any attention another pays you is just a confirmation in my heart and mind that what I see in you is not based on some wild Teutonic notion of romance. It pleases me to know others understand what I understand and admire about you. I am acknowledging that you will want to bid him a proper farewell when he leaves for his sea duties." He kissed her hand. "Then please do me the honor of coming away with me to Pura and, in the spring, the Rhine."

"What are you proposing?"

"That the baron and I come and get you after your friend has sailed. We will go to Switzerland together and reside in the chalet until Easter. At that time, we will embark by boat for a spring journey down the Rhine. A delightfully slow journey to appreciate the beauty of the country and our time together. When we reach my family home, we can stay there for some time. My parents would like to meet you. And I promise there will be a few surprises along the way—pleasant ones, I assure you. Please say yes."

"It sounds like you plan for us to be gone a long time."

"Until June or July. And Sean must join us, of course. The horses will be watching for him in Pura."

Catherine smiled into his intense eyes and serious face. "It sounds splendid, Albrecht. And Sean would love to join us, not only for the white horses but to go on a long boat ride. He'd love to see ancient castles. Yet you are speaking of being gone six months. I can't conceive of it without a member of my family along as an escort to save us from public scrutiny and scandal. But everyone has lives of their own, and six months is a long time to ask someone to accompany us. That's half of 1927!"

He nodded. "I understand completely. Are you averse to spending the winter at Pura in the company of the baron and me like you did last year? Our servants would be there as well, of course."

"No, I feel quite all right about that. But to extend our time together another three months on some sort of river cruise? No, I feel that is much too much."

"What if your mother were to join us for the journey down the Rhine?"

Catherine stared. "My mother? You're joking. I don't think she'd leave Father. And she loves having Vic and Ben there. And now they have the baby Timothy Mum dotes on, and young Ramsay, of course. She would never agree."

Albrecht brought a letter out of the pocket of his suit jacket and gave it to her. "Read this," he said with a smile.

> My dear Professor Hartmann,
>
> Thank you so much for broaching the subject of the Rhine tour directly to me and not through my daughter Catherine. I have talked things over with Lord Preston and also with my youngest daughter, Victoria. We have all prayed about the matter and are in agreement. I shall join you most gladly. Victoria and her children also accept your kind invitation. We will plan to meet you at Dover Sky the first Monday after Easter.
>
> We look forward to the Rhine journey very much. We will, of course, bring two of our servants to see to our needs and be a nanny to the children. I shall ring up Catherine about the matter.
>
> I do look forward to seeing the baron again and to meeting your mother and father.
>
> You are most kind.
>
> Lady Preston

"I don't know what to say." Catherine read the letter a second time. "Should I be angry that you went behind my back and orchestrated this? Or should I be grateful you cleared up all the messiness that created an obstacle to my joining you?"

"If it's any consolation, it was the baron's idea. He felt it would spare you a great deal of stress and confusion."

"Hmm. Does he tell you what to do, Albrecht?"

"Not at all. But he knows how much I'd hoped to spend time with you. So he suggested I approach the matron of the family herself. I was well aware if she said no that nothing would come of my hopes and plans. Even now with her approval, you are free to say yes or no. I'm well aware of that and accept the risk."

"I see." She handed the letter back to him. "Well, I don't feel any anger whatsoever. If anything I feel relieved. I can sit in the chalet at Pura and look at the mountains if I like. I can go along the Rhine in a boat if I wish. I can say hullo to my sister Libby and goodbye to my friend the naval officer. As my mother wrote, you are too kind."

A smile moved over Albrecht's lips. "So you are saying yes?"

She swatted him on the shoulder with the book. "It's only so I can have the time to read this through from cover to cover and make notes on it."

"And what about the author?"

She tapped *My Spirit* against his cheek. "You may use the months in Switzerland and on the river to introduce me to him again."

Train Station, Port of Dover

Lord Preston slapped his gloves against his pant leg. "The train should be here by now."

Catherine had her arm through his. "My goodness, Dad, it's not due for another five minutes."

"Are you sure we have the date right?"

"Of course. Tuesday, the twelfth of October. Stop fretting."

"I wanted to be in the House today. Lord Buchanan and Labor are up to more mischief."

Lady Preston had his other arm. "The prime minister can handle the situation. So can Edward."

He peered down the track. "Why all this nonsense? 'Meet us at Dover.' Why couldn't they have taken a ship that docked at Liverpool and be done with it? What does Dover have to do with it?"

"They want to be at Dover Sky, Father."

"Whatever for? Why is the whole world moving to Dover Sky? First you, and then Lady Caroline, and then Kipp's son Matthew, and now this. Absurd." He took out his pocket watch and snapped back the silver lid. "Ha!"

"What, Papa?" Catherine giggled. "Two minutes to go, and you can't see the smoke?"

"It's no laughing matter, my dear. We don't even know where they docked. Why all the secrecy? I feel as if we're in the middle of something cooked up by Sir Arthur Conan Doyle."

"I'm Watson then, Dad. You can be Sherlock. And Mum is the landlady—what's her name?"

Lady Preston patted her husband's arm. "There, William. Is that what you were anxious to see, my dear?"

Black smoke smudged the horizon.

"Ah!" Lord Preston snapped open his watch a second time. "Late."

Catherine grinned and hugged his arm. "By what? Thirty seconds?"

"Thirty-five."

"Think of it, Father. We haven't seen them in three years. How exciting to have the train pulling into the station now."

"Yes—if indeed they are on it. I could do with a little less cloak and dagger and a spot more frank and open declaration of the reasons for the odd nature of their return from America."

"Soon all will be made known. I thank God they've come back to us."

A smile played on Lord Preston's lips. "I do thank Him for that too. I do praise Him."

The locomotive slid past and the brakes screeched. White steam tumbled over the platform. Doors of coaches opened and people climbed out. Lord Preston glanced quickly up and down the length of the train.

"Can you see them?" he asked. "Can you see them?"

"No, they're not...There they are!" Catherine pulled free of her father and pointed. "Down near the end."

Lady Preston squinted. "Why, Libby is dressed so...so American—her hat, her jacket, her pearls."

"Oh, Mum, she looks pretty. And Michael is such a handsome sight in the suit and hat he's wearing."

"He looks American as well."

"He *is* American. Come on! I can't wait here for them." Catherine rushed down the platform ahead of her parents and caught Libby in her arms. They hugged and laughed and kissed each other's cheeks. Then Catherine put her arms around Michael. "How marvelous you both look!" she exclaimed. "I can't believe it. You're here in England. It's been ages."

Libby smiled. "If we're marvelous, you must be spectacular. Look at her, Michael!"

He kissed Catherine on the forehead. "She's a real doll, all right. Did you miss us?"

"Did we ever! Ben will be doing handsprings."

"I'm more than ready to help run the airline again." He patted Catherine on the back. "Here's your mum and dad, Libby."

"Ah, Michael! Splendid!" Lord Preston stretched out his hand, and Michael shook it. "How was the voyage? How was the train ride?"

"Fine, William. You're looking very well."

"Thank you! I try to walk every evening when I'm in London."

Lady Preston was hugging Libby. "Your hair is so short, but I must admit it looks just right. My, you've lost weight."

"Hullo, Mum. I guess I've been away from English cooking far too long." She hugged her mother back. "You look younger than when I left."

"Now I know America did something to you, my darling. It's a good thing you're back here to stay."

"Who do we have here?" Lord Preston smiled at a dark-eyed young woman wearing a dark dress who was standing behind Michael and Libby. "Are you with Libby and Michael?"

She curtsied in her dark dress. "I am, sir. My name is Lucy, but everyone calls me Montgomery."

"Ah. And which do you prefer?"

"Montgomery, if you please, my lord."

"Then Montgomery it shall be. And who is this?"

A young Chinese girl in a green dress was holding Montgomery's hand and staring at Lord Preston.

"Father." Libby came and stood behind the young girl, resting her hands gently on her thin shoulders. "This is Jane. She has so looked forward to meeting you and Mum. She's nine."

"All right!" Lord Preston crouched. "Hello, my dear. Welcome to England."

The girl smiled so suddenly and so brightly that Lady Preston exclaimed, "Oh my, how sweet she is! Who is she? Why is she in your company? Where is her family?"

"We are her family, Mum."

"I beg your pardon, dear?"

Michael walked over to take Libby's hand. He stroked Jane's shiny black hair.

"She is Jane Danforth Woodhaven," said Libby. "She is our daughter."

10

January–May, 1927
Plymouth and Devonport, Southern England

"I feel like I'm going to lose you."

"Don't be so dramatic, Terry." Catherine wiped a raindrop off his cheek with her gloved fingers. "We've seen quite a lot of each other, haven't we? And once you're back from the Med, I'm sure we'll see a lot of each other again."

"Are you positive?"

"As sure as I can be right now."

"A boat trip down the Rhine sounds pretty…well…"

"With my mother and sister in tow, along with Victoria's two children. Hardly a recipe for a Hollywood romance."

Fordyce held the large black umbrella closer to her head as the wind gusted and the downpour increased. "A man will find a way to your heart. I know I would in that situation."

"Terry, he's very old world, very German, and a theologian from a prestigious university. I'm not going to be stuck on a boat with Don Juan."

"He cares about you as much as I do, doesn't he?"

"Possibly."

"Then how can you say nothing will happen?"

"Excuse me, sir." A sailor in a peacoat came to attention behind them and saluted. "Your presence aboard is requested. We will be weighing anchor in under an hour."

Fordyce turned, straightened, and returned the salute. "Very well."

The sailor saluted again, paused as Terry returned the salute, and then left.

"I have to go." Fordyce put the umbrella in her hands. "Your driver's waiting."

"Harrison can wait a bit longer. He won't mind."

He tipped up her chin with his finger and thumb. "How lovely you are. May I?"

"Of course, Terry. You needn't ask."

The kiss was soft and careful, as if he were unsure of himself. Suddenly he wrapped his arms around her and pulled her into his chest and kissed her with the strength of the storm that was sweeping over them. She almost let the umbrella go in the wind as she responded by throwing her arms around his neck. The rain struck them both but they continued to kiss.

When Terry broke off the embrace, he turned and strode quickly down the pier to the *Hood*'s gangway. He did not look back.

"God go with you, Terry," Catherine said quietly.

"Lady Catherine?"

She glanced at Harrison. He was holding the door of the Rolls open.

"No, thank you, Harrison. I want to watch the *Hood* sail."

"You can do that from the comfort of the car, m'lady."

"I can't actually."

She stood in the rainfall and waited. Hundreds of men scurried back and forth on the *Hood*'s deck. She could hear names being called and caught distinct phrases as they carried over the water. A half hour went by. An hour. Shivers moved up and down her spine. The thick lines that kept the battleship tethered to the shore were released. More orders echoed across the water, sounding like she was in a valley of mist listening to hunters shout to one another. The gray ship and escort vessels slipped through clouds of fog, engines thrumming and rumbling.

Harrison had the door open for her when she turned away from the ship. "My lady."

"Thank you so much, Harrison. I know it was foolish of me."

"Not at all. I would do as much or more for Holly. I hope he saw you wait."

"I don't know. Perhaps he glanced this way from the bridge."

"I'm sure he did."

There was a blanket in the backseat. She pulled it around herself as she settled in. Harrison leaned back and handed her a thermos.

"What is it, Harrison?" she asked, unscrewing the top.

"Hot coffee, m'lady."

"It couldn't possibly be from the manor. We've been gone for ages."

"I went for a stroll while you and Leftenant Commander Fordyce were chatting. That's good Navy coffee. No rum in it, mind you, but that coffee will warm you up like a shovelful of coals in your stomach."

"Thank you, Harrison." She put the thermos to her lips. "You're an absolute lifesaver."

Dover Sky

"What is she whispering?" Caroline asked.

Libby, Jane, and Caroline were in the parlor visiting. Montgomery, the servant Libby had brought with her from the United States, was attending them.

"She says you're the most beautiful woman she's ever seen." Libby grinned at Caroline. "After her darling mother—me—of course."

Caroline smiled at Jane. "Thank you so much. That is very sweet."

"She means it too. She never says anything for show."

"Jane?" Caroline showed her a large red valentine trimmed in lace. "What do you think of this?"

"It's perfect! I love it, Caroline."

"Shall we make one for your Aunt Holly?"

"Yes, please!"

"What about Bev and Norah and Nancy and Harriet?"

Jane nodded. "I do want to give them something too."

"And the boys?"

Jane grimaced. "Not ones trimmed in lace."

"You're right." Caroline laughed. "Perhaps trimmed in rock. Their valentines will last longer that way."

"Can we send some to Aunt Catherine and Sean in Switzerland?"

"We certainly can," Montgomery replied. "Are you ready to come with me and make a start? I have scissors and glue and plenty of stiff red paper."

Jane jumped up from where she was sitting. "Do you mean you have all of it right now?" She seized Montgomery's hand.

The maid's dark eyes sparkled as she smiled. "I do! Let's go to the craft room."

"Where are Charles and Matthew?"

"In the big playroom with their toy soldiers."

"Can we visit them later?"

"Of course. But valentines first, all right?"

The two of them left the parlor, and Montgomery closed the door firmly behind them.

"She's nine going on nineteen," Caroline commented as she got up and poured herself tea.

"Jane has always been that way as soon as she's comfortable with the people she's with," said Libby.

"Would you like a cup?"

"Yes, thank you."

Caroline handed Libby a cup of tea on a saucer. Steam curled up from the hot liquid. "You know, I really never heard how you and Michael came to adopt Jane."

Libby sipped at her tea. "It was all rather straightforward. Many Chinese families went to the United States to work on the railroads during the 1800s. In this one Chinese family, a son went to the Klondike in Alaska when gold was discovered there. He made an exceptional strike and the family became wealthy. They made their home in San Francisco. In 1919, the Spanish flu wiped out almost everyone in their family. The grandmother and one-year-old Jane were the only ones who survived."

"You were never in San Francisco, were you?"

"Indeed we were. We'd traveled to the West Coast to visit some of Michael's California relatives. That's when we were introduced to the grandmother and Jane. The grandmother was friends with several of Michael's uncles and aunts. Her health had fallen off dramatically that winter, and after we'd visited with her several times she asked us if we would take Jane.

"Michael and I had gotten on very well with the grandmother and Jane from the beginning. We thought it over and prayed and decided to go ahead. Everything was done properly and legally, and Jane was excited to be with us but so tearful of leaving her grandmother. We thought it best to stay on in San Francisco for several months. The four of us grew quite close. The woman became like a mother to Michael and me. And Jane truly became our daughter. There was no question of changing our minds after that, regardless of Jane's race and the difficulty we knew this would present to us in England. Michael and I both very much believed God had brought us all together. The grand old lady passed away last summer. We wept and made her funeral arrangements; it really was a very special goodbye, and then Jane was more than ready to come back to New York with us." She looked at Caroline over the edge of her cup. "I can't bear children, you see. At least not so far, and none of the physicians held out much hope."

"I'm sorry."

Libby shrugged. "Michael and I have coped with it well enough. Jane has been a gift from heaven. The three of us get along as if she'd been born to us."

"How are your parents with this?"

Libby stared into her cup. "Not good at all. A Chinese granddaughter? *Oriental* is the word they use. Of course it affects Jane. She pretends otherwise, but she sees Mum and Dad doting on Matthew and Sean and it hurts her. She so badly wanted another grandmother. There's nothing we can do except love her more than they ignore her. Even your son gets more attention from my parents."

"Libby, I apologize—"

"No, that's not necessary. I don't mean to censure you or Charles.

He has his own row to hoe without a father around, not to mention what you've been through. I want Mum and Dad to bless you, I honestly do. I just wish they would accept Jane." Impulsively, she reached out to take Caroline's hand. "Thank you for your many kindnesses to her. It helps fill in the gap."

"I adore her. And I'm certain Charles is sweet on her even though he'd never admit it."

Libby sank back in her chair as she tapped her fingernails against the teacup. "To be honest, I worry most of all about Matthew. Since his mother died and Kipp is fighting some dreadful guerrilla war in the Rif, the boy doesn't get much parental support. We thought Kipp would come home once the battles were over and the Berbers surrendered, but the rebels who wouldn't lay down their arms scurried deeper into the mountains. I hate the thought of him out there. But Harrison has been grand with young Matthew, I see. And he quite obviously worships you."

Caroline chuckled. "Not so much, but we do get along."

"I was told Christelle specifically asked you take on guardianship of Matthew after her death."

"Who told you that?"

"It was in a letter."

Caroline ran her spoon around the inside of her empty cup. After a few moments of listening to the clicking sound she looked up at Libby. "I don't know how much you've heard. Christelle wanted Kipp and me to marry and raise Matthew and Charles together. She believed we still loved each other. She asked us both to honor her request."

"And this was something you couldn't do?"

"Chris wanted me to let Kipp know I still loved him even while she was alive. I argued against the idea, but she was so insistent. She was already suffering so much from the cancer that I didn't have the heart to say no. I approached Kipp. We began to have a relationship again. Only a few kisses, a few words, a few embraces, no more, Libby, I assure you. But it was quite lovely for both of us. Once Kipp found out about Christelle's health, he changed. I believe he was overcome by guilt. It didn't matter that this was what she wanted and even tried to orchestrate. He felt he'd betrayed her by admitting we still had feelings for each other. So he took it out on me. He treated me as if I had been a seductress. Christelle wanted us to love one another again, but Kipp was having none of it. He didn't want me for Matthew's mother and he didn't want me for his wife because he only wanted Christelle. He didn't want to think about life without her."

Caroline's eyes were glimmering with tears. Libby put down her cup and took both of Caroline's hands in hers. "He was grieving," Libby soothed. "You know he was grieving. People want to blame someone when that happens—you, me, themselves, God."

"Kipp called me a harlot, Libby. And he meant it."

"I'm so sorry." Libby pulled Caroline to her feet and took her in her arms. She felt the heat of her friend's tears against her neck. "That's not Kipp. You've known him for years. You loved him. If you really think about it, you know that wasn't his heart talking."

"But it *was* him talking, Libby. No one has ever made me feel so much like dirt. Not even Tanner. When Kipp writes letters to Matthew, I try to care, but it's too painful to think about him. That's why I always get up and leave when they're read aloud for the family. It's very hard. I loved him for so many years, and that love was a big part of who I was. Now I'm confused. I'd rather not have anyone if I can't have him. Yet if he came through the door now and said he wanted to marry me, I'd probably turn my back on him."

"You wouldn't, Caroline. You'd feel differently about him if he stood before you and said he still cared for you."

Caroline pulled back and pressed her fingers into her cheeks. "No, Libby. I don't want him. I don't want anyone."

"Caroline, don't say that! You're so beautiful, any man would want to be with you. Don't let bitterness overtake you."

"I don't want any man to be with me—not even Kipp. I hate my beauty. I wish I could tear the skin off my face. The beauty everyone talks about just brings me misery. If only I had the courage to use acid or a knife or a broken piece of glass to change what I look like."

"No! Don't talk like that!"

"I would do it, Libby. God forgive me, I really think I would do it."

My dear Libby,

Here at Ashton Park Easter week is almost over. Father and I so meant to get down to you for a visit but, alas, it is not to be. Victoria, the children, and I need to go directly to Dover from London this coming Monday, April 18th, right after Easter Sunday at Jeremy's church. I do hope to see Michael at church for I know he has a small place nearby. I realize he usually spends his weekends with you at Dover Sky but I was given to understand his presence would be required at the airfield on Good Friday and Easter Saturday, so perhaps he'll show up at the Sunday service? In any case, we are meeting Baron von Isenburg in Dover. He is escorting us to the Rhine in Germany. We are so excited! Catherine and Sean should be waiting for us by the time we arrive.

Your father and I are very sorry we won't get a glimpse of you this Easter, but Victoria and I will be sure to return with Catherine to Dover Sky for a get-together in June or July.

Richest blessings in Christ,
Mum

P.S. I hope Matthew and Charles got the chocolate Easter eggs I mailed down last week. They are the special Cadbury ones, and I was sure they'd love them.

Dover Sky

"Is there anything I can get for you, Lady Caroline?"

"Hmm? No, I'm quite all right, Skitt. Thank you. I was thinking of wandering over the estate with my bag of bread crumbs for the geese and swans."

"Does her ladyship think she is up to that?"

"What do you mean?"

"Well, you were feeling faint just an hour ago. You sent all the others off to the May Day celebrations in London without you."

"I know. I'm much improved now. A little exercise and fresh air will do the trick, I'm sure."

"There was talk of Lord Kipp showing up today or tomorrow on furlough, m'lady."

"Or much later in the week. Yes, I know."

"If he comes while you're out on the grounds, should I direct him to you?"

"If that's his wish, Skitt, you may tell him where I'm gone. But I do relish some privacy."

"Of course, Lady Caroline."

Caroline, in a pale-blue dress, made her way towards the pond. Once she was out of sight from anyone in the manor she turned left and disappeared within a grove of willows showered with bright-green leaves. The trees were bent over what Harrison called "a slither of a stream" that emerged from the ground, trickled several hundred yards, and then flowed back under the grass and earth. She sat down, kicked off her shoes, and dipped her toes in the water. After a minute of this, she unbound her hair and dropped the pins in the stream to watch the ripples. She splashed her face until water streamed off her skin and through her hair. Circles of shadow and saucers of sun created a pattern on her cheeks as light fell through the leaves and branches.

All right. It's not as if I'm doing away with myself. Well, I suppose I am in a way. Doing away with this silly, ridiculous beauty called Caroline Scarborough. Charles will still have a mother—a better one, a plain one. No more men will bother me. No Tanners, no Kipps, no lords, no soldiers, no village idiots, no one who might hurt Charles or me. I'll be free of the lies of flattery and betrayal. A different face means a different life.

She brought a knife out of the paper bag. The blade was about six inches long and glittered where the sun struck it. The Kaiser's eagle was stamped into its base near the hilt. Kipp had given it to her as a gift early in the war, and she had never thrown it away. Ten minutes of steady polishing and sharpening had brought out its luster once again.

If only it were so easy for us to bring back the shine we once had.

She ran her thumb over the dagger's edge. It was sharpened on both sides. Blood sprang from her skin. She smiled. *Sharp enough. Fine cuts*

*like threads of silk will do it. You will not want me, Kipp. No one will want
me. I thank God for that.*

There was only the sound of the birds and only the movement of
their wings as they slipped from branch to branch. She touched the
the dagger to her smooth, white cheek but did not press it in. *I must do
this before you come home. When you come, I might weaken. I might love
you once more. I might throw the knife into the stream. You might take
me in your arms and hurt me again…and again. The dagger only hurts
once…just once.*

Heidelberg, the Neckar River, Germany

"Ah, there you are. What do you think of Heidelberg?" Albrecht
asked Catherine.

"My goodness, I feel like I'm in a fairy tale. Are we going to stay here
for a while or go back to the Rhine?"

"We're on the Neckar right now, and it flows quite a bit further.
We'll probably berth here a few days. Mother and Father will want to
visit the Heidelberger Schloss. They always do."

"You make it sound like such a chore."

"I've been inside more times than I can count."

"Everyone will want to go into the castle—the boys especially. I
want to go into the castle too."

"Your wish is my command, my dear Catherine. Though I must say
I look forward to returning to the Rhine and continuing to float those
historic waters. There are plenty more castles to see and a special magic
seems to hang in the air when we're on the water."

She pushed him. "And there is no magic in Heidelberg? I thought
you said the other night there is magic anywhere I am."

He gently put his arms around her waist. "That's true. I forgot for
a minute. And the Heidelberg sun brings out all your color and delicate features."

"My delicate features?" She laughed and then glanced around. "Where is everyone?"

"Forward or below. Hans has laid out baked treats and chocolates in honor of May Day. The children are hovering about the table like hummingbirds, and their mothers and grandmothers are hovering about them like hawks."

"Not this mother."

"Sean is with Lady Preston."

"She'll probably eat more than he does." Catherine smiled up at Albrecht. "Was this your timing? Hans laying out the sweets…you and me alone at the stern of the vessel…Heidelberg Castle drifting slowly into view?"

"What mortal can plan such things? I prefer to think it is just meant to be."

"I see." She fingered a button on his shirt. "The journey has been lovely so far, Albrecht, but far busier and noisier than I expected. Two grandmothers, a grandfather, my sister, her baby, two boys, the baron."

"At night—"

"Even at night there is no peace and quiet. By the time there is, I'm too exhausted to meet you for a *tête-à-tête* under the stars. By day we talk books, history, art, religion, and politics. By night we do the same until I am drooping."

He lifted a hand and ran his thumb over her cheek. "That is why I have brought you here now."

"This peaceful moment won't last. Sean and Mama will come looking for me any minute now, and that will be that for our little interlude by Heidelberg Castle."

"They won't."

"Why won't they?"

"I told Hans I must have at least a half an hour with you. I told Martin too. So there are…how shall I say it? Ah, guards posted to block all paths to the stern. We have twenty-five more minutes."

She continued to toy with the button. "You sound very sure of yourself."

"Sure of myself? No, I feel very hesitant right now. But I am confident of my guards. The children and grandmothers and grandfather shall not get past them."

"Mama can have a temper."

"My men will charm her."

"Charm her? With what?"

"Roses. Coffee. Mints. Whatever pleases her."

"All to what end?"

"Time alone with you, naturally." He put his lips to hers. When she didn't push him away, he kissed her hair and throat and then went back to her lips. This time with more passion.

She responded with a surge of her own and tugged on his hair with her fingers as she kissed him, tugging harder and harder. His arms were around her back with a sudden force that made it difficult for her to catch her breath. But she had no intention of ending the kiss, luxuriating in it as the boat floated over the water.

Finally Albrecht drew back.

"Oh…" she said softly, "I wish you hadn't."

"We have more time. But there is something I want to ask you."

"Ask me? Ask me now? I would rather you brought your lips down to mine again."

"It's the most important thing I have ever asked you."

"Is it?" Her eyes were large and dark and flecked with light. "What are you up to, Albrecht Hartmann?"

Dover Sky

Kipp finally spotted her shoeprints in the mud by the small stream under the willows. She hadn't been at the pond or any of the fieldstone fences and he'd been about to head back to the manor when he thought of the willows.

She loves trees but especially the willows at her family's estate.

There he saw her sitting by the stream.

"Caroline."

She didn't move.

"Caroline. I'm back from Africa. It's been years."

Still she didn't move.

"I'm sorry. It's been more like forever. No letters. No cables. But I need to talk to you alone."

She remained like stone.

"What's happened?"

He ran towards her. She suddenly turned her head and brandished the dagger at him.

"Get back, Kipp. I have to do this. At least four cuts to the face. I just haven't had the nerve."

"Caroline, have you gone mad? Give me that knife!"

He lunged, but she put the dagger to her throat. "I'll do it. I don't care anymore. Life is nothing but a great darkness."

"No, it's not. I want to talk to you. I want to start again."

Her laugh was harsh. "Oh, I knew you'd say that. You don't look like Kipp – you've lost too much weight and your skin is as dark as mud – but you sound just like him. More promises. I'm not interested. And when I'm done with my face you won't be interested either."

"Caroline, please don't. You're so beautiful – "

She laughed again. "My famous beauty. What good has it ever done me? Broken heart after broken heart. You called me a whore."

"I was a fool. I was worse than a fool. God forgive me. Christelle was right."

"Christelle, ah, Christelle, what was she right about?" Caroline put the point of the dagger against her cheek. "You won't love me without a face you can kiss, Kipp Danforth."

"Don't!"

He tried to seize the dagger a second time but she thrust it at her throat again.

"I'll finish myself off, Kipp, I swear it. Stay back."

"All right. Do it. Go ahead, do it. I'll join you." Kipp brought a pocketknife from his pants pocket and flipped it open. He put it to his cheek. "If you can cut your face to ribbons, so can I. I'm to blame for your misery. So if you're going to do four cuts, I'll do eight."

"You won't!"

"I will!"

"Stop it, Kipp!"

"Who do you think I thought about when I flew from the Orkneys to Cape Town? You and Chris. Who did I think about after I crash landed in the Sahara and was half crazy with thirst? You and Chris. All the fighting I've done with the French Foreign Legion in Morocco, all the heat and flies and bullets and killing; who was on my mind hour after hour, day after day? You and Chris."

Caroline saw him press down on the knife. She shrieked and threw herself at Kipp, twisting the pocketknife out of his hand with a fierce burst of strength and flinging it into the trees. He seized her dagger hand and they fell to the ground, rolling over and over in the mud and water, her fingers wrapped tightly around the hilt, his hand bending back her wrist and trying to break her grip. She cried out and slapped him and clawed his eyes but he wrenched at her wrist until she dropped the dagger in the stream.

"That hurt!" she yelled, blue eyes blazing.

"I don't care!" he shouted back.

She went at him again with her nails and tried to pull his hair but his head was so close shaven there was nothing to grasp. Kicking at his legs and biting at his hands, she pushed him against a willow trunk and started beating him with her fists. He caught her hands and threw her into the shallow stream, immediately launching himself at her and pinning her there so that her hair was under water and the current running over her cheeks and eyes. Unable to squirm loose she lifted her head and tried to bite his ear, finally swinging her head so that her heavy wet hair struck him in the face.

"I hate you!" she cried.

"I love you!"

"Shut up, Kipp Danforth!"

"No!"

He began to kiss her cheek, cold water mixing with the taste of her skin.

"Don't touch me!" she screeched.

But he continued to kiss her, his lips finding her eyes that she screwed shut, and her throat that she twisted back and forth to get away from him, and her lips that she sucked in and held tight against her teeth. He let go of her hands and put his arms under her back and lifted her out of the stream, cradling her and kissing her with more and more intensity. She dug her nails into his back and slapped at his neck and shoulders but nothing stopped him. When she opened her mouth to shout something at him his lips were there quickly, pressing against the softness and fullness that had always been part of the great beauty of Caroline Scarborough. Suddenly she laced her arms around his neck as tightly as she could and began to cry as he held her, kissing back with a fire and abandon as desperate as the blows she had rained on him moments before.

"Oh, Kipp, what are we going to do?" she cried.

"Marry me."

"Don't be mad. What sort of proposal is that?"

"It's the best I can do right now."

"Look at us. Thank the good Lord that Harrison went to London today."

"Marry me, Lady Caroline Virginia Scarborough."

"I can't, Kipp. I hate you, you know I hate you, a lovers' quarrel in a creek doesn't change that." They kissed again, their arms around each other. "When do you want to have the wedding?"

"Tonight."

"Oh, Kipp, why wait for tonight?"

Heidelberg, the Neckar River, Germany

Catherine's eyes remained wide. "Now you've got me frightened, Albrecht."

"It's not a matter involving fear." He pushed strands of hair out of her eyes. "Or perhaps it is."

"What are you talking about? Have you decided to join the Nazi Party? Is Herr Hitler waiting to receive us at his castle on the Rhine?"

"Nothing like that! It is much more pleasant a prospect. I want to say I love you. No more than that. *Ich liebe dich.*"

"No more than that? That's a lot, Albrecht."

His hand moved slowly down the side of her face. "There is also the fact that I find you the most beautiful woman alive."

Her hand reached up to grasp his. She brought it to her lips and kissed it. "Thank you. *Danke schön.*"

"And something else."

She smiled. "Well, the arrival at Heidelberg is turning out to be quite a moment in the lives of Albrecht Hartmann and Catherine Danforth Moore."

"It is, isn't it? Let us have many such moments. A lifetime of such moments." He cupped her face in both his hands. "*Catherine, heirate mich bitte.*"

She let out her breath. "I don't think I need a translation. Albrecht, you can't mean it."

"Of course I mean it."

"I'm not ready to—"

"When will you be ready?" he cut in. "You're still young. You can have more children. Build another home—build a castle! How many more years, Catherine? Five? Ten? I love you. Marry me on this boat. Marry me on the Rhine. Marry me when we reach my family's home on the river. But please, can we stop this yes, no, yes, no, back and forth?"

"Albrecht—"

"Marry me. Marry someone who cherishes you. Or marry Leftenant Commander Fordyce. He loves you too, I'm sure. There is no reason for you to keep living alone. I want you to wed Albrecht Hartmann, but if not me, another man who will treasure you and give Sean a family. No more waiting, Catherine. Please, no more putting it off. You are a woman—strong, intelligent, full of compassion, and beautiful. It is time to choose, don't you think?"

"I don't know what to think."

"Of course you do." He kissed her on the lips. "Give yourself a moment, and then tell me yes or no. One or the other. I will celebrate the one and survive the other. But here on the river at Heidelberg, I must know. You have turned all this over in your heart for years. Tell me what you've found. Today. Here. Now. Tell me what you see in your heart and soul, Catherine. Tell me what you feel for me and how strong that feeling is."

11

June, 1927
London airstrip

The silver monoplane circled the airfield, did a victory roll, and came in for a landing. Michael walked out to it while the plane's three propellers were still spinning. Ben jumped down, a large smile spreading across his face.

"Look at her, Mike! Isn't she a beaut? We've got two of them up in Lancashire, and this is the first of your pair I'm delivering."

Michael reached up and ran his hand over the single wing. "The Fokker F. VII B/3M. Three engines—all of them 220 horsepower. Eight passengers. How's she fly?"

"Like a dream. Let's get some petrol into her and you can take her up."

"I'd love that."

"We've given her a name." He patted the letters painted on the engine cowling—*Dover Sky.* "One of ours up north is the *Ashton Park.* Did you get down to Dover Sky last weekend?"

"No, it was too busy here at the London airstrip. But Libby and Jane are doing great."

"I couldn't believe it when you rang me up last month about Kipp and Caroline. I thought that flame had died out years ago."

Michael smiled as he admired the airplane. "I guess it never did.

We came back from May Day celebrations in London, and Lord and Lady Scarborough were already there, along with an Anglican priest. Thank goodness Lord Preston had tagged along with us and traveled down from London! Lady Preston is still in Germany with Vic and Catherine, so she'll be sorry she missed it. Anyway, away we went right there and then to the swan pond. I stood with Kipp, and Libby was Caroline's matron of honor. They honeymooned in France before he returned to the Foreign Legion. Now he's back tangling with Berber guerrillas in the Rif. And Charles and Matthew are now brothers, not just best friends."

"Will Kipp ever come back to our airline, do you think?" asked Ben.

"He can't muster out until sometime in '28. Let's keep our fingers crossed that he comes back in one piece. He told me he misses the flying, especially the races. How are you holding up without Vic and the kids?"

"Pretty good, but I miss them. I do miss them." Ben slapped the fuselage with the heavy pair of leather gloves he'd just pulled off. "Speaking of racing, there's an endurance contest being set up to honor Charles Lindbergh's solo flight across the Atlantic. Wasn't that something? You must be proud, Mike! He's a fellow American."

Michael nodded. "It took a lot of guts. So many others went into the drink or crashed and burned up."

"So that's what this race is—a way to honor what Lindbergh's done. Orkneys to Gibraltar nonstop for the first leg. Second leg is Gibraltar to Freetown, Sierra Leone, nonstop. Then it's straight to Cape Town, South Africa. That's the tough part. Fastest time wins. Race is in August. I'm signed up. Do you think you'll have a go?"

"Crewing with you?"

"That's what I had in mind."

"Won't our girls have a fit?"

Ben put his arm around Michael's shoulders. "I always tell Vic, as another Yank pilot put it, '*There are old pilots, and there are bold pilots, but there are no old, bold pilots.*'"

"I'm sure that gives her a great deal of comfort."

Ben shrugged. "When your time's up, it's up whether you're in the air or on the ground."

Hartmann Castle, the Rhine River, Germany

Dear Libby,

Well, my dear, you had your bit of excitement with Caroline and Kipp up and tying the knot on May Day out of the clear blue, as they say. Mum is so disappointed for not being present at the wedding of her son. But she's gotten her revenge. I expect you got wind of the cable we sent to Dad in London. Imagine our surprise when a week after we received your telegram in Heidelberg we had no sooner docked at Hartmann Castle on the Rhine then Catherine and Albrecht announced their engagement!

Mum was floored, I can tell you. On top of that, Catherine insisted they be married at the castle. Dad couldn't get free of his commitments in time, as you know, so that's how everything worked out, didn't it? Father at Kipp's wedding and mother at Catherine's. You acting as Caroline's matron of honor, I doing my bit as Catherine's. Michael standing for Kipp, and one of Albrecht's brothers standing for him.

The wedding was amazing. Picture a spectacular hall hung with old tapestries that have been cleaned and dusted for the occasion, a ceiling as high as the sky, stained-glass windows like in a cathedral, torches burning in brackets on the stone walls. My goodness, Lib, I thought we'd gone back to 1000 AD in H.G. Wells' Time Machine. And they did the wedding service right through twice—first of all by a Lutheran minister who only spoke German and then in English by an Anglican priest. Heaven knows where they hauled him out from since they only had ten days to prepare.

That's really nothing compared to what our sister was wearing. They had this gown for Catherine that must have belonged to one of Charlemagne's wives or daughters. Do you remember how we were taught about Amaudru, his first child and girl? It was royal purple and scarlet studded with diamonds and rubies. Albrecht looked like a German prince in his outfit.

Honestly, what with its sash and medallions. You can imagine how ecstatic Mum was when the parents admitted they could trace their line back to emperors and empresses.

So despite all the snubbing from the British nobility, Mum and dad have almost got all they wanted now. You're married to a Woodhaven, Kipp is married to a Scarborough. Robbie's married to a Dungarvan and Irish aristocracy, Emma's husband is practically a bishop, and now Catherine's wed into German wealth and a royal bloodline. It's just Edward and I who have spoiled things by wedding commoners.

As if Catherine and Albrecht haven't had pleasure enough bobbing along the Rhine all spring, the pair of them are off honeymooning in Austria. Well, I don't begrudge Cathy that or her fairy-tale marriage. She's had a tough life the past few years. God bless her! I hope she never has to grieve over a lost husband again. I don't know how I'd hold up if I ever lost Ben.

I'll drop a line again soon. I have no idea when we're coming home now.

Love to all, and hugs and kisses to Jane and Michael.
Your Vic

Dover Sky

"You miss him, don't you?"

"Very much, Holly. It seems like all my life I've wanted to be married to the blonde, green-eyed Kipp Danforth. But something always happened to prevent it. Now that we're actually married, I have so much lost ground to make up. I can't bear that he's out in Morocco again with the French Foreign Legion."

Holly was sitting next to Caroline on a swing on the back porch. "Would you really have gone ahead with Lord Buchanan's scheme?"

Caroline glanced at her. "The plan where I was supposed to yell that I was being attacked after I enticed Kipp to my room?"

"Something like that."

"That was why Tanner beat me. It wasn't just because I wouldn't clean the blood off the cane or polish the silver handle. I told him his plan was mad, and I had no intention of trying to destroy a family who cared for me as much as the Danforths did. I confessed all this to Kipp on our honeymoon in France." With a brief laugh, Caroline looked down at her hands. "It seems we spent half our time apologizing to one another for things that have happened over the years."

"I can see your love for him."

"I adore him. He's every dream come true."

"Do you think Tanner still has a plan against the Danforths?"

"Yes, I do."

"Do you have any idea what he intends to do?" asked Holly.

"I don't. For all I know, he means to get back at me as well."

Holly smiled and put her arm around Caroline. "Fear not. We're in this together. We shall fend off his assaults."

"Truthfully, I'd scarcely think of him from one day to the next except for Charles. When I look at my son I can see he's already a brighter soul than his father ever was." She bit her lip. "It's Kipp I worry about. If anything happens to him in that dreadful desert, I shall go to pieces. I know I shall."

"Ah…" Holly took one of Caroline's hands and gripped it. "I may be a lapsed Anglican, but I still know a bit about talking to the Almighty. May I? On your behalf?"

Caroline's smile was timid. "I should like that."

"Hullo?"

Libby looked up from the rosebush she was fertilizing. She saw a tall man in a dark-blue naval uniform. "Yes?"

"I came by to see if Lady Catherine was back from the Continent. She expected me to call. I'm Leftenant Commander Terrence Fordyce." He smiled and jerked a thumb over his shoulder. "I asked your butler, but he wasn't a wealth of information. He sent me 'round back here and told me to speak to Lady Elizabeth Woodhaven."

Libby stared at him for a full second before moving. "Ah, yes." She got to her feet and brushed dirt off her dress. Removing a gardening glove, she extended her hand. "I'm Catherine's sister Elizabeth, but please call me Libby, Leftenant Commander. How do you do?"

He took her hand. "A pleasure. A beautiful day for working on roses."

"It is. I must get this done while I can. My daughter is having a birthday party in a week, and my schedule will be an absolute shambles once I start to organize that in earnest."

"How old will she be?"

"Ten—and she's making sure everyone knows it. It makes her the eldest child among the Danforth brood."

He laughed. "She'll rule, will she? Queen Victoria or Queen Elizabeth?"

"Either one, so long as it's not Bloody Mary." Libby removed her wide-brimmed straw hat. "My husband and I were in America for several years. That's why you and I have never met, but Catherine wrote me about you."

"Did she? Good things, I hope."

"Very good. Have you not heard from her lately?"

"No, nothing at all. I realize she was on a journey along the Rhine and may not have been free to post a note or send a cable."

"Yes." Libby glanced about her. "Will you take a short stroll with me, Leftenant Commander?"

She led him west towards the Knight property and the oak trees. He fell in step beside her.

"Unquestionably, Catherine would have tried to send you a message," Libby began. "But you're quite right. She has been in locations that are out of the way, which would make sending telegrams and letters awkward. As soon as she is able, I know she'll write you. Unfortunately, that could be weeks."

"Is everything all right?"

"Well, it is and it isn't." Libby took in a deep breath. "Really, she should be telling you this, but it can't be helped. And it wouldn't be fair to keep you in the dark. My sister Catherine has married. I believe you know of Albrecht Hartmann, a German theologian? He is now her husband."

Fordyce stopped walking as if he'd been caught and held. "Married! For how long?"

"Just this month."

"I see." He remained motionless. "I admit this is a lot to take in."

"I'm sure it is. I'm so sorry. I know you and Catherine had a marvelous relationship."

Fordyce looked at the oaks in the distance and then the stone fence beyond them. "Married to Hartmann. Well, bless him, the lucky dog." He forced a smile. "Will Lady Catherine be returning to Dover Sky, Lady Elizabeth?"

"Libby," she reminded him. Then she shook her head. "Not to live. They'll be living in Tubingen, where Albrecht lectures at the university. Summers will probably be spent in Switzerland or at Hartmann Castle on the Rhine."

"Switzerland and the Rhine, eh? I can't compete with that on Royal Navy pay." He straightened his hat. "I won't take up anymore of your time. Thank you so much, Libby. I'll be heading back to Devonport."

"Please don't run off. I'd like you to meet my husband and daughter. They're down feeding the swans."

"I don't want to interfere with your Saturday."

"Not at all. Michael has good friends in the United States Navy. He's been aboard several of their battleships, including the *USS Arizona* and the *USS Oklahoma*. He'd love to meet you, and you'd have oodles to talk about. Do stay on for a bit."

"The *Arizona* and *Oklahoma*, you say?" Fordyce grinned and shrugged. "Why not? A chat would soften this morning's news. I can drive away with my head full of information about keels and engines and funnels and guns—at least for a while."

She smiled back at him as she brushed damp strands of ginger hair out of her blue eyes. "That's the spirit! Let's head to the pond. We have two dozen swans with us this week. It's quite something to watch."

"Two dozen!"

"Indeed. Twenty-four down to the youngest cygnet. All under the protection of King George himself."

My dear Terry,

I fear this will get to you too late and you will have heard about my state of affairs from other sources. You may think that out of sight is out of mind regarding you, but that is not so. I asked but there wasn't a telegraph station within a hundred miles of Hartmann Castle. Now that I am in Vienna, there are plenty of them but I simply couldn't send you the news that way. It was too cold. So this letter will have to do even though it will take much longer to reach you in Devonport.

Albrecht and I were married early in June. It was not an easy decision to make, but it was a decision I had to make. I dragged my heels on this matter far too long. I care for you dearly, Terry. You have a great heart and a great soul. I doubt that will make you feel better about things right now. I'm certain news of my marriage will come as a slap to the face. I was not rejecting you; I was just saying yes to Albrecht—if that makes sense.

I will continue to pray for you and your safety on the high seas. I have no idea when we shall see one another again, and perhaps that's just as well. You will be in England and the Mediterranean, and I will be in Germany and Switzerland.

God bless you and all the best to you, my dear Terry.

Catherine

"Is the sailor man in the uniform coming?"

Libby brushed her daughter's gleaming black hair and tied a purple ribbon at the top. "You mean Leftenant Commander Fordyce? I don't think so, honey."

"But we invited him, and he said he might."

"He's quite a few miles from here on his big ship. It's not so easy for him to just pop over."

"Grandfather William is coming down from London, isn't he?"

"Yes."

"And Uncle Jeremy and Aunt Emma? And aren't Uncle Edward and Aunt Char coming too? And all my cousins?"

"Of course! It'll be an absolute mob. And there will be gifts from your relatives in America too. Did you see that huge parcel from Grandpa and Grandma Woodhaven that's on the table on the porch?"

"I did! I'm so excited!"

"Hold still a moment." Libby tied an orange ribbon next to the purple one. "There!"

Jane looked at herself in the oval mirror on the vanity. "Purple dress. Purple stockings. Purple and orange ribbons." She grinned. "I love these colors. What about Grandmother Elizabeth? Is she coming?"

"She's still in Germany with Aunt Vickie and your cousins Ramsay and young Timothy. It's too bad. Grandfather William will have your present, and Uncle Ben is bringing the ones from Aunt Vickie and Ramsay. Here are your purple gloves."

Jane tugged them on, and they went up to her elbows. "Will he really fly in?"

"Yes, he really will. Then he'll be off again after a hug and a kiss and a piece of cake."

"Ooh! I think I could fly without a plane! I'm so happy!"

"Here…" Libby gently arranged an orange silk scarf about her daughter's neck. "Go show yourself to your father. He's hanging balloons on the porch with Skitt and Montgomery."

Jane's smile grew sly. "Monty likes Skitt."

"Why, who told you that?"

"No one." Jane made circles like glasses around her eyes with her fingers. "I can see for myself."

Libby laughed. "Is that right? And how is Skitt dealing with this bit of Dover Sky romance, Lady Jane?"

"Ha! I don't think he knows what to do…except get tongue-tied."

"You look smashing in purple and orange. They're the colors of our coat of arms."

"Indeed." Jane curtsied. "Thank you, m'lady."

Libby straightened and gently pulled the sides of her blue summer dress as she curtsied back. "You're welcome, m'lady." She opened the bedroom door. "Come, let's go downstairs to your father. He'll be bowled over by the beauty of his princess."

"His *enchanted* princess."

"Quite right. His *enchanted princess*."

They heard car doors slam, and Jane ran to the open window.

"Leftenant Commander!" Libby heard her husband call out. "Hey! It's great to see you here!"

"Wouldn't miss it, Michael. Haven't been to a proper birthday party in years."

Jane swung her head around and laughed. "You see, Mama? He *did* come! He *does* like me."

Libby went to the window and put a hand on her daughter's shoulder. "Well, that's not really a surprise, is it? Everyone adores you, Lady Jane."

"He's my knight."

"Your knight? I thought your father was your knight."

"Dad is my father knight. Leftenant Commander Fordyce is my *knight* knight." She stared, suddenly puzzled. "There is something different about him. I thought I had his uniform utterly memorized." She bolted from the room and down the staircase.

"Jane!" Libby called after her. "Slow down!"

She watched from the window as Jane raced out the front door and practically came to attention in front of Terrence Fordyce.

"There's the birthday girl!" Fordyce handed her a present wrapped in purple paper with orange bows. "For the rest of your life you'll always have two numbers in your age. Unless you live to be one hundred, then you'll have three."

Jane took the gift. "Thank you, Leftenant Commander. You remembered about my favorite colors."

"So I did."

"Do you realize your uniform is not the same?"

"It's not? What's different about it?"

"I'm not sure."

Michael walked up and put his arm around Jane. "Honey, I think it's the same uniform Lieutenant Commander Fordyce wore last Saturday."

"It isn't, Dad."

"Everything's exactly the same."

"No."

Fordyce put his hands in his pockets. "Are you sure you're not mistaken, Jane?"

Jane eyed him up and down. Then she pointed at his hands. "Take them out of your pockets."

"Jane," Michael soothed, "calm down. I know it's your big day but—"

Fordyce grinned and removed his hands from his pockets. He turned them toward her, palms outward. "No rabbits, my dear."

Libby smiled as Jane played with his sleeves and then put her knuckles to her mouth. "Oh Jane," she said before chuckling.

"The cuffs are different!" Jane shouted.

"Jane, no yelling!" her father said.

She challenged Fordyce with the intensity of her dark-eyed stare. "They are, aren't they?"

"Jane!" Michael corrected again.

"It's all right." Fordyce held up his hands as if she'd pulled a gun. "Jane's spot on. I have three thick gold stripes on the cuffs instead of the two thick ones with a skinny one in between."

Jane's dark eyes glittered. "What are you now? An admiral?"

"Not quite. A commander. After that comes captain, then commodore, and then admiral."

"Do you get your own battleship?"

"I can have a ship, Jane, but not a battleship."

"Are you getting a ship?"

"Not yet. I am our captain's right-hand man on the *HMS Hood* now. One of them, anyway."

She turned his present over in her slender brown hands. "Does this have to do with the Royal Navy?"

"It does."

"May I open it?"

Michael laughed and shook his head. "Remember the deal, Jane? First everyone arrives. Then we'll play games. Then comes the cake and ice cream. And then—ta da!—you can open the presents."

"But no one's here but old people."

"The kids are coming. And Charlie and Matt are around here somewhere."

"They're off doing something secret with Aunt Holly and Aunt Caroline. It's so boring right now."

"Jane!"

"Can't I open this one while we're waiting? It is my birthday after all. Please, Dad?"

Michael rolled his eyes up. "Just one, but only if *Commander* Fordyce says, '*Aye, aye, skipper.*'"

Fordyce nodded and said, "Go ahead, Jane."

She tore the paper off and then opened the box underneath. She pulled out a naval officer's hat. "It's the same as yours!"

"It is, but smaller. I hope it fits you."

She quickly put the hat on her head. "It's perfect…only a little tight. Thank you so much."

He saluted her. "Happy birthday, Commander."

Jane ruled the day. Not only was she older than her nearest competitors—Jeremy and Emma's ginger-haired and green-eyed Peter and brown-haired, brown-eyed James, neither of whom would turn ten until December—she was also taller than the other children and much faster on her long legs. After the games that included the pinning of the tail on the donkey and a hotly contested croquet match, they consumed cake, lemonade, ice cream, and dozens of pork sausages called bangers that were roasted over a fire.

Jane soon sat surrounded by mounds of wrapping paper and gifts, her commander hat squarely on her head. Uncle Ben had dropped a basket of dolls by parachute, done a victory roll, and then zipped away. Grandfather William had arrived late with German and Swiss dresses shipped from Grandma Elizabeth on the Continent. He also had bags of Swiss chocolate for all and steel swords with blunt edges for the boys. The gifts from America included a large dollhouse that could be plugged in so the rooms lit up and the fireplaces glowed. At bedtime a raid was launched by the boys against Jane's room. It was led by the twins and their seven-year-old brother, Billy. Charles, Matthew, and Owen were eager recruits. All brandished their steel swords from Grandfather William. But Jane had a sword of her own and no fear. A few lightbulbs were lost before order was restored and everyone marched back to their bedrooms. Skitt continued to keep an eye out as he prowled the halls long after the doors were shut.

Michael left Jane's room and entered his through an adjoining door. He closed it and then leaned against it. He let out his breath as he looked at Libby before starting to laugh.

"I think Mary, Queen of Scots, has finally settled."

"I'm glad to hear it. She can be a monster if she doesn't get her sleep."

"I'm pretty sure there's a sword somewhere under her blankets."

"Is there? That's surprising."

Michael stared as her sharp tone registered. "Hey, what's the matter?"

Libby was sitting in her nightgown on the edge of the bed and filing her nails. "I'm just shocked she has a sword of her own. My dad certainly didn't give it to her."

"What do you mean?"

"He had swords for everyone but her. When she asked for one, he said the extras were for Sean and Ramsay and Tim when they come back from Germany."

"So he just brought them for the boys—"

"Only one of the dresses they gave her fit, do you know that? I helped her try them on while the boys were roasting bangers with Harrison."

"I'm sure your mom did the best she could. She wouldn't know Jane's size."

"She knows it all right. Vic cabled me and I cabled her the measurements back weeks ago."

Michael sat next to her on the bed. "Look, she had a terrific day. I'm sure she's forgotten all about the dresses that didn't fit."

Libby examined her nails. "Until next week. Then the tears will come."

"She has that incredible dress from Kipp and Caroline—the one from Morocco. She looks like a sultan's queen in that."

"She does. With her skin color, high cheekbones, and dark eyes and hair she's stunning."

"She'll be all right."

"She won't be all right. She knows my mother and father don't approve of her being our daughter."

"They need time, Lib."

Libby flared. "Time? It will be a year in October. It's precisely the sort of thing that happened when they didn't approve of Victoria and Ben or Edward and Char."

"So they'll come around eventually."

"You don't know that. Mum and Dad went through years of being snubbed by their friends because of Vic and Edward's 'low' marriages. I'm sure neither of them is interested in a repeat of that experience, and certainly not over a little, lost Chinese girl from America."

He rubbed a hand over his face. "I'll talk with them."

She smiled even as she shook her head. "Dear Michael, my American hero." She kissed him on the cheek. "They'll listen politely to their precious son-in-law from the United States. They'll nod. They'll offer you tea or coffee. And a week later…maybe two weeks…nothing will have changed."

"Jane's status doesn't seem to bother anyone else in the family—"

"With the exception of Edward. But then he doesn't approve of Catherine marrying a German, so why should he approve of you and I adopting an *Oriental*?"

"If Jane were among the schoolchildren in London or Liverpool, they would be merciless because she's different."

"And that's why she's not among the schoolchildren in London or Liverpool!" snapped Libby. "That's why we're at Dover Sky and a tutor comes from Dover three days a week. How do I protect my daughter from her British grandparents?"

Michael gripped her hand and put it to his lips. "We love her. She knows that."

"Of course we do."

"And the day will come when your mom and dad will too. I believe that."

"Darling, you believe anything. You're always on the up and up."

"Ever since I met my English nurse during the war."

Her blue eyes lost their fire and softened. "Yes, that's true. Ever since her." She leaned her head against his chest and his arm went around her. "I expect you're right. They'll become proper grandparents one day. I just don't know what it will take."

12

August, 1927
The Orkney Islands, northern Britain

Ben Whitecross peered out of the cockpit at a black and yellow airplane also idling on the runway. It was the same kind of three-engined Fokker he was sitting in. "Von Zeltner again. Doesn't that bloke ever give up?"

Michael Woodhaven leaned over from his seat and looked back past Ben's shoulder. "He probably wonders the same thing about us."

Ben glanced at his brother-in-law's neck. "A bit flashy for an endurance race, don't you think?"

Michael patted the orange silk scarf. "Jane asked me never to take it off, so here it stays. You can always put on sunglasses if it's too bright for you. I'm sure Ramsay had something for your pocket."

"He did." Ben grinned and tugged out a large wooden soldier dressed as a fighter pilot, complete with goggles and a white scarf. "It does look like me, don't you think?"

"With its wooden head? You bet."

They both laughed and returned to checking the dials and gauges.

"Oil looks good." Ben tapped the face of one of the gauges. "Petrol is topped up."

"Well, it won't be if they don't get this show on the road. We've been idling for ten minutes already."

"Looks like something's up."

A tall man in a long trench coat waved his arms. Another man beside him had a blue flag that he was unfurling.

"Right. Here we go. We're fourth in line. The Belgian is first, then the Dutch lad, then Zeltner, and then us. I've got the first leg to the Channel. After that it's your stick."

Michael settled himself into his seat. "We'll go over Dover Sky as we agreed?"

" 'Course we will. Won't cost us any time. The whole crew'll be there except Catherine and Albrecht."

Michael checked the map on his knee. "No reason we can't do a fly-over of Tubingen. It's within the flight path."

"I doubt they'll be on the rooftop watching for us."

Michael shrugged. "I'll do it anyway."

"It'll probably be dark."

He shrugged again.

"Our turn." The man with the blue flag was waving it at them. Ben opened the throttle. "In any case, we can't play cricket with the whole clan. Robbie's still in Palestine, and we'd have to go well out of our way to fly over his head."

"Can't have that. We should visit him after."

Ben grunted. "Could do."

"There's Kipp in Morocco."

"African landfall's Algeria, one country over. Then we land in Sierra Leone for our second leg. We'll not see Kipp anymore than we'll see Robbie."

Michael rustled around in a paper bag at his feet and pulled out a large ham sandwich. With a wink at Ben he bit into it.

"Hey, mate!" Ben protested. "That's for later."

Michael shook his head. "I'm famished."

The Fokker roared into the sky.

Lord Preston paced back and forth in the library at Dover Sky.

"Where are the children?" he suddenly asked Victoria.

She put down her teacup. "With Harrison and Holly, of course."

He glanced over the faces in the room. "What about Caroline?"

"On a stroll with Jane," said Libby who was sitting next to Victoria.

Edward had both arms along the back of a couch he was sprawled in. "Relax, Dad. The BBC will broadcast if there's any news of the race. The planes were all there at Gibraltar."

"Two days ago. No news from Sierra Leone. Africa is the rough spot, Edward. None of them will have enough fuel."

"They've all strapped on extra containers of petrol they can release into the main tank if they need it."

Lady Preston's hands were clasped tightly in her lap. "Do stop this pacing and fretting, William. You're making me anxious. I was quite all right after you and Jeremy prayed an hour ago. Now you follow it up with your lion in the cage restlessness, and now I'm on pins and needles."

"Sorry, my dear. Forgive me." He cocked his head. "What's that?"

Jeremy was sitting next to a radio that was housed in a cathedral-shaped wooden cabinet on four legs. He'd been listening to weather reports and music with the volume turned down. Hearing the broadcaster's voice at the same time as Lord Preston, he turned a knob.

"This is the BBC. We've heard by cable from colleagues at Cape Town Radio," the announcer said.

Outside the library windows that had been opened to let in the summer breeze and the salt air from the sea, a boy shouted, *"I'm a plane! I'm Daddy."*

"Two airplanes have landed. At the time the cable was sent to London from Cape Town, another aircraft was spotted approaching the landing site from the north and west."

"Vrooooom. Vroooooom."

"There are reports of at least one plane going into the sea as it followed the African coastline. Fishing vessels attempted to reach the aircraft before it sank, but they were unsuccessful. It remains unidentified."

"Ramsay! Watch out! You almost ran over your brother!"

"Right, everyone! Round to the back of the manor for oatmeal cookies with chocolate chips! Missus Norah and Missus Bev have baked up dozens!"

"Another telegram from Cape Town Radio has reached us at our studios here in England. The news in it is at least an hour old. A plane has crashed upon arrival at the Cape Town airfield. Cape Town confirms it is one of the four British planes entered in the endurance race in honor of Charles Lindbergh. There are no further details."

"Yaaaaaaay!"

"Hurry! Last one gets the horse's oats!"

"Lord Preston?" Skitt had entered the library.

The family members were hanging on every word the broadcaster spoke. Libby and Victoria held each other's hands. Head down, Lord Preston merely grunted in response to Skitt's summons.

"It's the telephone, m'lord. Do you want to take it in the parlor?"

"Who is it, Skitt?"

"It's the prime minister, m'lord. He says he has important information for you."

ALBRECHT AND CATHERINE

AIRCRASH AT CAPE TOWN LANDING SITE. MICHAEL KILLED. SURGEONS IN CAPE TOWN REMOVED BOTH OF BEN'S LEGS. IT IS STILL TOUCH AND GO WHETHER HE WILL SURVIVE. AT HIS PARENTS' REQUEST MICHAEL'S BODY IS BEING SENT FROM SOUTH AFRICA TO NEW YORK. AS YOU CAN IMAGINE WE ARE QUITE DEVASTATED HERE. VICTORIA AND LIBBY ARE BEARING UP BUT WE ALL COULD USE YOUR PRAYERS. IN PARTICULAR PRAY FOR BEN. WILL SEND ANOTHER TELEGRAM WHEN THERE'S MORE NEWS.

JEREMY

Dover Sky

"I feel old, quite old, my dear." Lord Preston awkwardly patted Libby's hand. "I don't know what else to say."

Libby looked down at her hands in her lap. "I don't suppose any of us have words for some of these things, do we, Father?" She tried to smile. "I could have lost him during the war. We had almost ten years together because he wasn't shot down like his brother. That's something, isn't it?"

"It is, yes."

"You are in agreement that Jane and I travel back to New York to see the gravesite? And attend the special memorial service in September?"

"Of course."

"I don't want to leave Vic's side, but we must go, Father. Mum doesn't seem to understand."

Lord Preston closed his eyes a moment. "It is a great blow. Two years ago Christelle and now this. And Kipp still fighting with the Foreign Legion in Africa. It's too much for Elizabeth."

"I asked Ben, and he said it was the right thing to do."

He patted her hand again. "Never you mind about Ben. We all have our eyes on him. His leg stumps are healing up nicely, and he gets around very well indeed in his wheelchair. The doldrums have passed, and his spirits are much brighter. If he thinks you should go to New York and be with the Woodhavens, then that is what you should do."

"He wrote a lovely card about Michael for Mr. and Mrs. Woodhaven."

"Wonderful. And so have your mother and I. We expressed our condolences by telegram, of course, but a card is so much more personal."

Libby wiped at one of her eyes with a handkerchief. "You have all been very kind." She put the cloth to her nose and blew softly. "I don't know what I'd do without family."

"Times like this remind us why the Lord gives us one another—not to quarrel with but to be nurtured and defended by."

"Please keep Jane in your prayers too."

Lord Preston nodded. "Naturally we do."

"I fear Mum and you still have a problem with her Chinese background."

"Nonsense."

"Michael loved her dearly." Libby put the handkerchief to her nose again.

"We all do, my dear."

"Commander Fordyce has been very nice to her since Michael's death."

"Indeed."

"He always has a gift for her."

Lord Preston was silent.

Her tears came. "I just want Mum and you to see she is as much a Danforth child as Ramsay or Peter or Owen. She so badly needs your love now that her father is gone."

"She has it, my dear. She has it unreservedly."

Dear Libby,

Now that you have been in New York several weeks and it is more than two months since Michael's passing, I pray a good many of your wounds have healed. I do not expect you to be on top of the world, of course. I only hope you see some light at the end of the tunnel.

You know how long your sister Catherine grieved over the loss of her husband, Albert. And Kipp almost threw himself off a cliff when Christelle died. We are still reaping the bitter fruit of his recklessness—a crash landing in the Sahara and enlistment in the French Foreign Legion putting him right back in another war. Terrible. I fret over him every day. Please do not take Catherine's or your brother's route in your sorrow.

Grieve, yes, but not as one without hope. I trust that a year from now you shall see your way clear to engagement with a man as fine as Michael. You are still very young and must look to the next fifty or sixty years of your life.

This brings me to the matter of Jane. I know you and Michael felt it was a good deed while you were in America to adopt her. Indeed, it was a gracious act of Christian charity. But now you must forge a new life for yourself. Surely the Woodhavens will take her in and give her a home? It is one thing for Catherine to hang on to Sean. He really is her son and our blood runs through him. But you cannot move ahead and look for a husband of your station with a girl from the Orient calling herself your daughter and a Danforth. For one thing, it simply isn't so. For another, no Englishman will accept you with Jane at your side. She is a sweetheart, and you have done your best by her. Let the Woodhavens take her in and raise her in remembrance of their son.

You need to begin again with a clean slate. I am certain that within months of it being known your mourning period is over and that you are unattached to Jane, any number of excellent men will be calling at Ashton Park or Dover Sky for you. I am convinced of it.

Forgive me for being forthright. I know you won't like it, but someone must say these things while you are deciding what you will do and where you will live. Your father will not talk about these matters, so it is left up to me. Spend as much time in New York as you need, and then return to England alone. Believe me, such a course of action is the best way to begin again. It is the best route for you to follow.

All my love, my dear Libby. God bless you.

Mother

October, 1927
London hospital

"I could feel a buzzing or tingling in my legs. When I looked down they were both twisted at impossible angles. There was no pain at all. I looked over at Michael, and I could tell he was dead. People worked to yank the canopy back and then reached into the cockpit. Some men hauled out Mike. It was Zeltner who cut away my harness and got his hands under my arms. He and his copilot pulled me free. I was in and out of consciousness over the next few days. They used morphine and heart stimulants to keep me going. By the time I was in the clear, they had already shipped Mike's body to New York City. Once I was strong enough, they started flying me in short hops back to England."

Jeremy sat in the chair by Ben's hospital bed. He was dressed in black clothes with a white clerical collar at his throat. Ben didn't look at him as he spoke, and Jeremy stared at the floor.

"I've tried to put up a bold front, but it's hard, Jeremy. Every day is very hard. They say I won't walk again, that it'll always be a wheelchair for me. They've scratched flying so there's not much to look forward to. I keep wondering how Mike would have stood up to this. Lib says he was an absolute bear when he crashed during the war. Maybe he learned from that and would have been more chipper than I am."

Jeremy cleared his throat without looking up. "You don't know that. He may have been much worse having gone through this twice."

Ben, sitting up in the bed with a pillow behind his back, kept on talking as if Jeremy hadn't spoken. The sun was going down, and the room was darkening but neither moved a hand to turn on the bedside lamp. "Mum and Dad have no idea I'm feeling this way. Neither do Vic and the boys. It's bad enough losing Michael. They don't need me moaning and groaning and adding to the gloom. So whenever I see them I play 'the man.'"

"Surely you can be honest with Victoria."

"I can't. She said she's reminded of losing our first baby, and that she feels wretched when she sees me without my legs. *I thank God every day you haven't lost heart,* she said. So I've got to soldier on. I need *your* help for that."

"What can I do to help?"

"Just what you're doing. Listening. Giving me a few upbeat words now and then. Saying a few prayers. Since you lost your right arm and hand while fighting in France back in 1914, I know you understand some of what I'm going through. That helps too, along with the other things."

"I'll come over from the church as often as you like, Ben. Once or twice a day if you want."

"I won't be here forever. What's the date today?"

Jeremy looked up. "Wednesday, the twelfth of October."

Ben glanced at him. "They've taken plaster casts of my stumps now that they've shrunk down. They'll start fitting metal legs with cushions and straps in about a week. I'm going to make myself walk, Jeremy."

"You'll do it."

"And once I get the hang of walking, I'm going to fly again."

Jeremy nodded, his eyes strong and dark behind his glasses. "Right. You will."

"I need you to put the backbone in me."

"Believe me, Ben, you've got plenty of it."

"I need more. They'll adjust the legs until the fit is just right, give me some walking lessons, and then after that I'm on my own. They want me close enough so I can drop in if there's a problem. I plan to take up residence at Dover Sky."

"Just you?"

"No. I'll bring Vic and the boys down. They'll have Charles and Matthew to play with, not to mention Jane. She can be their big sister."

Jeremy sat up in the chair and took off his glasses. "That will be fine. Emma and I would love to bring Peter, James, and Billy to Dover Sky once a week. Overnights on a Friday would be best. We'd head back on Saturday afternoons so I can be ready for church on Sunday." He pushed the right temple and earpiece of his glasses under his wooden hand so the lenses were upright. Then he polished them with a white cloth from his pocket. "Ben, I take it you're not aware Libby and Jane won't be returning to Dover Sky? They'll be wintering in Germany with Albrecht and Catherine."

"What?"

"They are heading straight there from New York. I gather she's supposed to be in Tubingen by the end of the month."

"But why isn't she returning to England? My Ramsay loves Jane. He finds her quite the tomboy."

Jeremy smiled. "My lads feel the same way. Though Jane plays the princess well when it strikes her fancy. In any case, Lady Preston wrote a letter to Libby in New York City telling her to have done and leave Jane with the Woodhavens. Something about starting afresh without being encumbered by Jane now that Michael is gone."

"You're joking."

"I'm afraid not. You can imagine how well that went over. Libby's heartbroken. She loves Jane, and Jane is a strong link to the life she had with Michael. Lib dashed off a letter in reply, certainly not the kind Lady Preston wanted to get. Now there's a great row going on between the pair of them. Catherine invited Libby to Germany, and Lib accepted straight off. Now it appears Jane will be big sister to Catherine's son, Sean, instead of your boys and mine. She'll have a friend in Baron von Isenburg's daughter, Eva, too. The von Isenburg girl is twelve, so they're close enough in age."

"I can't believe what you're telling me. It never rains but it pours."

Jeremy finished cleaning his glasses, put them back on his face, and returned the cloth to his pocket. "All the more reason we'd be happy to come to Dover Sky once a week. We'll work on keeping the family together rather than permitting these squabbles to break us apart. And for you and I to stick together and get you back on your feet and up among the clouds and swallows."

"I'll make it, Jeremy—with your help and God's. What I can't control is what's going to happen next. This family gets bad news in bunches. It'd be a deathblow, wouldn't it, if Kipp came back from Morocco in a pine box or Robbie got a bullet in the back in Palestine?"

"Let's not believe in deathblows," Jeremy said.

13

March–June, 1928
Jerusalem

> I was glad when they said unto me, Let us go into the house of the LORD.
> Our feet shall stand within thy gates, O Jerusalem.
> Jerusalem is builded as a city that is compact together:
> Whither the tribes go up, the tribes of the LORD, unto the testimony of Israel, to give thanks unto the name of the LORD.
> For there are set thrones of judgment, the thrones of the house of David.
> Pray for the peace of Jerusalem: they shall prosper that love thee.
> Peace be within thy walls, and prosperity within thy palaces.
> For my brethren and companions' sakes, I will now say, Peace be within thee.
> Because of the house of the LORD our God I will seek thy good.

"Thank you." Robbie leaned back, loosened his uniform collar, and closed his eyes. "I need to hear that every day of my life."

"Shall I read it a second time?" asked Shannon.

"Can't hurt."

She read Psalm 122 again from the Bible on her lap.

Robbie and Shannon were sitting together on a terrace that overlooked the Old City of Jerusalem. For miles the green tops of palm trees stirred in the warm breeze. Walls and buildings made of large square stones the color of honey sprawled between the palms. Directly in front of them was the Dome of the Rock, its gold roof flaming in the afternoon sun. Below them men and women in various types of robes crowded the streets. As Shannon read, voice after voice called out in Hebrew or Arabic as donkeys brayed while the harnesses on their necks and shoulders jingled from the attached small silver bells.

"Your voice is sweeter than those shouts," Robbie said, opening his eyes and looking at Shannon.

"Only because I'm not selling anything. If I were, then the Dublin fishmonger in me would come out soon enough."

"Do you think so?" Robbie ran a finger over both sides of his dark moustache. "You look splendid. How are you feeling?"

"As splendid as I look, kind sir." She placed a hand over the roundness of her stomach. "I think it's time you wrote your mother and father."

"Well—"

"Come! I am almost four months along. Doctor Schultz says I am as healthy as a horse—a Connemara horse at that."

"Still I worry."

She closed the Bible and smiled at him. "My silly British soldier. What happened to me happened so many years ago. Yes, back then they were worried about a miscarriage. Not anymore."

"You were badly hurt."

She reached across the space between them and ran a hand down the side of his face. "I was. Now I'm healed. And the man who beat me so badly is dead and gone. Write your mother and father. Heaven knows they could use some good news."

"Very well."

She pinched his cheek gently. "That's not the only thing that's worrying you, is it? What happened today?"

"What happens every day. This time it was a group from the Grand

Mufti. They are concerned that the Jews are planning to take over the Temple Mount. You know, where the Dome of the Rock is. They fear they'll rebuild a temple like Solomon's."

"What do you think?"

"Really, I can't see it. But every now and then one of the Jewish leaders spouts off about a Jewish nation that extends from Dan to Beersheba and about erecting a new temple on Mount Moriah—the site of the Dome of the Rock. And then the Muslims get agitated, and their mullahs whip them into a frenzy. There's bound to be trouble."

"So did you talk to any of the Jewish leaders about this?"

Robbie stared at the Dome of the Rock. "Of course. But what can they do? They can't control every Jew in Palestine anymore than the Grand Mufti can control every Muslim. I'm constantly getting reports of imams ranting about wiping out all the Jews in Jerusalem, and not only Jerusalem, but the entire length and breadth of Palestine. So the Jews smuggle in more guns to defend themselves. And the Muslims smuggle in more guns to defend themselves. I only have a hundred British soldiers, Shan. I can't stop a war. If they want another Belfast, I expect they are going to get it."

"Surely things aren't as bad as all that, love. We have many Muslim and Jewish friends, and we all get along well together at our dinner parties."

Robbie drummed his fingers on the arm of his chair. "Yes, because we're all moderates, aren't we? But moderates never run revolutions or uprisings. And when the day of trouble comes, they are swept away by the fanatics and hotheads who will murder anyone or blow up anything for their great cause. Moderates never kill like fanatics do. That's why they never last, and the position they take for peace and goodwill vanishes with them."

Shannon took his hand. "So what's your next step?"

He sighed. "Just housekeeping chores. I've asked the Jewish leadership to remember the ruling in '25 that forbids the use of chairs and benches and prayer screens at the Western Wall of the Second Temple where the Jews gather to pray.

"The Muslims are anxious that nothing be left there on a permanent basis. They're afraid it will become the start of a synagogue, and a synagogue will be followed by a full-blown temple going up."

Shannon laughed. "That sounds rather ridiculous."

"Yes, well, what sounds ridiculous in another country or up here on our terrace makes complete sense on the streets of Jerusalem. And it usually ends up with someone getting beaten or shot."

Tubingen, Germany

Catherine stood by the window with the letter in her hand. "The big news is that Shannon is five months along now."

"What!" Libby turned away from her bedroom mirror. "Five months? That's wonderful! But why are we only hearing about it now?"

"I don't know. She's due in September."

Libby waited another moment before going back to applying her lipstick. "Boy or girl? Do they say?"

"They don't say."

"What's your guess?"

"Heaven knows we have enough boys to populate a private school in Oxfordshire. I say we need a girl to be a proper cousin to Jane."

"That's sweet, but Jane will be in university by the time this little one is six."

"No matter. They can catch up to each other when they're in their twenties and thirties."

"Maybe." Libby gazed into the mirror and puckered her lips. "We need to send Shannon a card."

"We do." Catherine picked up another letter. "Ben is coming along better than hoped, Vic says. He's gotten the hang of those artificial legs and can move about on his own pretty well, though he still uses a cane."

Libby stepped back from the vanity and slipped her arms through the sleeves of a long, blue woolen coat. "That's marvelous. It really is."

"Jeremy and Emma swing by every Friday night. The children have a grand muck up together, Vic and Em and Caroline have a terrific chat, and Jeremy closets himself with Ben. No one knows what those two go on about since they've never been that close."

Libby wrapped a dark-blue scarf about her neck. "Mmm."

"Oh dear. Papa's lost the dogs."

"No."

"Gladstone in January and Wellington at the beginning of March. What a shame. Vic says he's absolutely devastated."

Libby came to the window and peered over her sister's shoulder at the letter. "I feel so bad for him. He loved them so much. Well, we all did. Does the baron know?"

"I doubt it. Unless someone wrote him or cabled him separately."

"He gave Papa those German shepherds."

Catherine nodded. "I remember." She kept reading, her lips moving.

Libby craned her neck. "What's the rest of it about?"

"Little things." Catherine paused. "She mentions a letter from Kipp. He's well. Sent Matt and Charles a couple of Foreign Legion caps in the mail. Y'know—with those flappy things at the back. Caroline's stuffed the sweatbands with newspaper, and the boys are marching up and down the estate with wooden rifles Harrison carved for them."

"No. Before that."

"Nothing, I told you."

Libby's eyes snapped to indigo blue. "I can read, thank you. I didn't know Dad and Mom were having a big row over me."

"I tried to spare you the news. Why carry that around in your head?"

Libby took the letter from her sister. "It actually does help to know he's taken my side. No, I'm not happy about them having a long drawn-out fight. But yes, it is nice to know one of them thinks enough of Jane to fight for her." She kept reading. "Ben is determined to fly again. You skipped that part too."

"Look, you told me all this reminded you of how you helped Michael get back on his feet and back in the air after his crash during the war. I didn't see the point of making the comparison even sharper."

"I'm a big girl, Cathy, I can handle it. I cried myself dry in America."

"Mum! What's taking you so long?" Jane stepped through the doorway, her arm linked through another girl's. "The sun is going to go behind a bunch of clouds. You said we could shop in the old part of Tubingen before we go to Switzerland this weekend." She half sang, "It's a beautiful day in May…"

Libby handed the letter back to her sister. "If Uncle Albrecht has finished all his marking and all his student interviews, we can go."

"The students are gone, Mum. The streets are empty. There's never been a better time to go to the shops."

"Yes, I'm ready then." Libby put a hat on her head and looked in the mirror. She smiled at the reflection of Jane and her friend. "Good afternoon, Eva. You look exceptional."

Eva was the same height as Jane. She had dark skin similar to Jane's. Eva's flaxen hair was separated into two braids that framed her face, and her blue eyes shone like suns out of dusky cheeks. She grinned. "Thank you, Mrs. Woodhaven." She glanced down at her black coat and black leather boots. "Papa said he would spoil me because I did so well at school this spring." She pouted, her lower lip pushing out from her mouth. "But I cannot come up to Pura with him for another four weeks."

"We shall have your rooms perfectly ready for you and the baron and be counting the days," Catherine announced.

Jane bounced up and down on the balls of her feet. "Montgomery is waiting at the front door, Mama."

"Good. So we're all ready to walk by the riverfront and those colorful old houses?"

"More than ready."

"Downstairs to Montgomery then." Jane and Eva were gone in a flash, giggling as they raced down the steps to the front door.

"Girls!" Libby called after them, "A herd of wild elephants couldn't make more noise than the pair of you!" She glanced at Catherine. "We'll be back in a few hours but not in time for tea."

Catherine nodded. "Don't rush. You've never enjoyed the city without the mob of university students. You'll have Eva here in time to attend mass with the baron? At St. Joannes Evangelist?"

"Of course. I promised Jane and I would join them."

"That's splendid." Catherine held up an envelope. "There is a letter for you when you find the time."

Libby stopped in the doorway. "For me? Not for both of us?"

"Certainly not for both of us."

"Who's it from?"

"A secret admirer, I believe."

Libby came back into her room. "What rot. I'll be ready for a man in my life when the clock strikes midnight for 1941." She took the envelope from her sister's hand and read the return address. "I don't know anyone in the Royal Navy. Oh!" Her cheeks flamed immediately. "It's not what you think it is."

"Isn't it? And what do I think it is?"

"Terry. Terry Fordyce. He quite adores Jane. And the feeling is mutual. Even Michael remarked on how the two of them hit it off from the first."

"So why isn't the letter addressed to Jane?" Catherine asked.

"Why, he—he naturally…she being so young…he obviously thought it best to correspond with her through her mother so there would be no hint of any sort of impropriety."

"Impropriety? She's a child." Catherine folded her arms over her chest. "Why don't you open it and read the first page aloud?"

Libby's face reddened. "Why would you ask such a thing?"

"I don't really care to hear the first page, Lib. I just want you to be honest with me. You know very well to whom Terry is writing. My guess is this isn't the first letter you've received from Terry Fordyce, is it?"

"No."

"But you didn't think to mention it to me?"

Libby's temper flared and her blue eyes suddenly sparked with color and heat. "Well, why would I? The two of you used to be…well, an item, as the columnists would say. I didn't want you to get the impression I was going around with him behind your back."

"Is that what you're doing?"

"We're friends, that's all. Just friends. How on earth could I go behind your back with him anyway? You're married to Albrecht, and you haven't seen Terry in a year and a half. You're not interested in him anymore, right? He's out of your life. I don't need your permission to post him letters or receive them from him."

"I am married—happily married. But Terry was and is very dear to me. It could have been him in my life. You know that."

"I do. That's why I haven't talked about the letters."

"I wouldn't want him coming for a visit, Lib."

"He's not going to come for a visit. He just got back from the Med on the eighth of May."

"How do you know?"

Libby licked her lips and kept her eyes on Catherine's. "He sent a telegram the other day."

"I see."

Libby suddenly thrust the envelope at her sister. "Go ahead, read it then."

"I won't."

"You want to know what he's saying to me? You think you still own him?"

"I don't think that."

"Of course you do. You may be married to Albrecht, but you still think of Terry as your property. Is that just in case things don't work out with Albrecht?"

Catherine's face stiffened like granite. "How dare you."

"Terry and I are friends, no more. I have no intention of taking him out of Jane's life just because you can't let go. And if he should want to visit one day, why can't he?"

"It would be very awkward. I don't want him here."

"Then if he comes you can throw me out. Throw Jane and me out into the street. We'll find lodgings somewhere else in Tubingen. Or we could head for Stuttgart or Heidelberg...even take the train east for Munich and be out of your life completely. Father will see us properly set up."

"I don't want you out of my life."

"Then you will have to let me have my own friends, including males...even old men friends of yours."

Catherine's face was pale. The light in the window whitened as the sun moved into a cloudbank. "I don't know if I can do it, Libby. I think it's too much to ask of me."

Libby stared before she whispered, "You still love him."

Dover Sky

Edward smacked his fist into the palm of his hand.

"It was a scurrilous attack directed at me and my alleged pro-German sympathies."

His father looked up from his newspaper. "Labor attacks the government for what it considers our pro-French stance. Lord Buchanan would have found a way to go after you even if your sister hadn't married Professor Hartmann. Besides, Hartmann is well respected at our universities. You must ignore Buchanan."

Edward paced back and forth in the parlor. "How can I ignore him? Did you catch his snide remark about my ties to the Orient and the Boxer Rebellion in Peking in 1901? About the massacre of missionaries and Chinese Christians?"

"I did."

"First he lays Germany and its problems at my feet because of Catherine's marriage to Hartmann. Then he smears me with the Boxer Rebellion because Libby is rearing an Oriental girl as her own. My own family is working against me."

"For heaven's sakes, Edward." Lady Preston set her cup in the saucer in her hand. "Your father and I come to Dover Sky for the summer to get away from politics. Must you go on and on?"

"There will be an election next year, Mother. Suppose I lose my seat due to the antics of my sisters?"

"You are not going to lose your seat. What that vagabond from the Hebrides has to say is of no consequence, especially when it comes to matters of the family. We will decide what is right and wrong among us. The voters will respect that. Catherine has married a prince—there is no other word for Albrecht. And we have absolutely nothing to be ashamed of in terms of her conduct."

Lord Preston was back to reading his newspaper. "In any case, the German economy is doing very well indeed."

"And the Chinese economy? How well is it doing?"

Lady Preston's eyes flamed. "If anyone is going to take Libby to task for her choices, it will be your father and me. Not you, Edward, and certainly not the Labor Party. I am not in agreement with what Libby has done. I pray she may still change her mind, but the poor girl has been through more than her share of tragedy and grief. Imagine losing her husband in a plane crash!"

"I know, Mother."

Lady Preston lifted the teacup to her mouth, her face still cut by lines and wrinkles of rage simmering just under her skin. "Your father and I are having our own row about Libby and Jane. We don't see eye to eye on this issue, but I will say that Jane is a beautiful girl who deserves every opportunity to develop into a lady. I simply hope it happens somewhere else and with a different family—preferably American."

The pop of a cricket bat striking a ball came through the open window. Edward bent and looked out, keeping his hands in the pockets of his striped trousers. "Ben's just made a hit. Ramsay is running for him."

Lady Preston's sharp lines smoothed and rounded into a full smile. "Ben is exceptional. All week I've watched him when he didn't think anyone was about. Working on climbing stairs. Walking on the grass and falling a dozen times. I understand it's much more difficult than getting about on concrete walkways. But he climbs to his feet and carries on no matter what. I could see the sweat on his face. And how it must hurt! He went back to London twice in the past fortnight, Victoria tells me, to get his artificial limbs adjusted. He never quits, does he? A good lesson for our family. And for you, Edward."

"Yes, yes, all for England, tallyho, Mum."

She glared at him over the rim of her cup before changing the subject. "How is Charlotte feeling?"

Edward finally smiled. "She's a great beauty, isn't she? Three months along and such color in her eyes and cheeks. I've fallen head over heels with her all over again." He glanced out the window again. "She's chatting with Victoria, Emma, and Holly. Ben's still at the bat. Harrison's bowling. Owen's doing very well for himself fielding." He let out a lungful of air and nodded. "Quite right, Mum. The fight must go on. Our family's worth fighting for, isn't it? And our country, of course."

"I should hope so, dear." She set her cup and saucer on the white wicker table beside her. "That's more like the Danforth spirit."

Lord Preston glanced up from his newspaper again. "I'd like to take *Pluck* out to blue water tomorrow morning. Are you game?"

Edward scooped a handful of cashews from a glass dish. "I'd like that, Dad. Can I bring Owen?"

"By all means. Short rations and weak grog, but I hope the salt air and enemy action will make up for it."

Edward popped a large cashew into his mouth. "I'm absolutely certain it will."

Jeremy and Ben stood under the willow trees in the dusk. The lights of Dover Sky could not be seen from where they stood.

"One of the stumps had shrunk a bit more. They had to make some changes in London."

"How do your legs feel now?"

"Never better. I can't say I'm pain-free, but it's much improved from a few months ago."

Jeremy smiled. "You've made a lot of progress."

"I'm doing it for Vic, Ramsay, and Tim. But I'm doing it for Michael as well."

"I understand that."

"So it's time for the next big step, Jeremy. I've got to go up."

Jeremy squatted by the thin stream of water and took up some pebbles with his left hand. "When?"

"This summer." Ben gazed west through the willows at the last line of red light where field and sky met. "Look, I've got to do it on the day we crashed in August. Not before and not after. In one of our Fokkers. I have to be ready on that day."

Jeremy tossed the pebbles in his palm. "How will Victoria feel about it? Or your mum and dad?"

"They're bound not to like it. They'll be superstitious about the date and say I'm tempting fate. But you don't believe that, do you, Jeremy? You're a Christian minister. God's bigger than our doubts and fears, isn't He?"

Jeremy kept tossing the pebbles.

Ben glanced at him. "Or are we prisoners of fate?"

Jeremy shook his head. "Not in Christ." He dropped the pebbles and stood up, brushing off his pants. "You have a destiny that's in God's hands. We all do. So how do we go about getting you up?"

"It's mostly hand movements. I just need a few run-throughs with the rudder while I'm on the ground because that's what is operated with my feet. The chaps we have managing the airline are going to drop in with one of the Fokkers on that day. Then they'll take it back to London because we have a lot of business these days."

"Will that be enough time for you to get a feel for the controls?"

"More than enough. I'm thinking it will be far easier for me to fly than to walk or run."

"All right."

"Jeremy, will you go up with me? I need a copilot."

Jeremy looked at him in surprise. "I've never flown. Why are you asking me? Get one of your flying chaps to crew with you."

"You've helped me get this far. I want you up with me. Nothing's going to go wrong. My hands are steady as rocks. All I need is to walk through the basics with you in case I need your help with the stick. I want Jeremy Sweet up there with me." Ben grinned. "You're my good luck charm."

Jeremy smiled. "An Anglican good luck charm? What happens when they take the Fokkers away? How do you keep up your flying skills then?"

"Our SPAD S.XXs have been mothballed. They're bringing in one of those as well and leaving it here at Dover Sky. I'll keep flying with it." He paused. "So what do you say, Jeremy? Will you go up with me? Will you fly?"

Jeremy nodded. "I will, Ben. Why not?"

The English Channel, near the Port of Dover

"What do you think, Owen? How d'ya like it?"

"I love the sea, Grandpa. Dad says he misses being a sailor on a battle cruiser."

"Does he indeed?"

Edward laughed and wrapped a line tightly around a cleat on the mast. "I don't like going into the drink. I like it best when I'm on top of the waves and not underneath them."

Owen smiled and closed his eyes as spray broke over *Pluck*'s bow. "I like the wind and the water, Dad."

"I see that. I expect you're a bit of a sea dog. Likely in your blood. What say, Father? Didn't we have seamen on Mum's side as well as the Danforth side?"

Lord Preston, in a dark-blue peacoat like the ones Owen and Edward had on, had both hands on the spokes of the wooden wheel and an eye on the mainsail as he steered. "We did. Sailed with Drake and Nelson—officers, privateers, explorers."

"Who, Grandpa?"

"Too many to mention. Your grandmother is a Cornwall, and they have as many sea dogs as the Danforths."

The yacht slit through the Channel waters and chop, the waves like cold iron, the sky a mix of gray and blue and white, gulls turning in wide circles above their sail. The boat was trimmed in navy blue, burgundy, and white like the Union Jack that flapped at its stern.

"You must tell me one story." Owen tugged on a line slick with salt water. "I am your crew."

Lord Preston barked a short laugh. "Indeed you are. I have one tale then. I can tell you more when we're ashore. This is from your grandmother's side, mind. A Cornwall. A midshipman. Perhaps five years older than you are now. On board a British frigate right in this Channel.

Got into a fight with a French warship with more guns. After a lot of smoke and flame and noise, Cornwall's ship only had two working cannon, while the French had more than a dozen still in play. So what to do, Owen? Two guns, powder and shot running low, the Frenchmen bearing down on you. Do you turn tail and head for England or strike your colors and go to a French prison?"

Owen puzzled this out. His blue eyes were so much like his mother's as they remained motionless even as his dark-red hair, just like his father's, was whipped about by the wind. "I wouldn't want to do either, Grandpa."

"Ha! Duck your heads. Coming about." The boom swung across the boat, and Edward and Owen stooped. "Spoken true like our brave Cornwall midshipman. Sheet her home, if you please, Master Edward." Edward sprang to secure the line for the mainsail. "They surprised the French, Master Owen, by coming right on and ramming them, bowsprit to bowsprit. The French cannon were useless to inflict harm. Then they boarded her, screaming like devils, cutlasses slicing the air, pistols flashing, and after ten minutes they had her! Indeed, sir, they had her. They kept a prize crew on board, and sailed both side by side back to an English port. Might have even been Dover. In the great hall at Dover Sky you will see a painting of this very thing. When we are back and have our tea and jam I shall point it out to you."

Owen's cheeks were red and his eyes bright as wind and wave lashed them. "You must tell me another, Grandpa."

"On shore in the officers' mess. But I have a grand sea poem for you. Fragments of it, mind you, bits and pieces, windblown spume and hard hurled sea spray, but extraordinary for all of that. Now this poem must be memorized, Master Owen, word for word. Are you ready?"

"I am, sir."

"Very well then. *Ulysses* by Alfred Lord Tennyson."

Lord Preston began to recite as *Pluck* continued to press ahead through the sea.

> *I cannot rest from travel: I will drink*
> *Life to the lees: all times I have enjoyed*

Greatly, have suffered greatly, both with those
That loved me, and alone; on shore, and when
Through scudding drifts the rainy Hyades
Vexed the dim sea: I am become a name;
For always roaming with a hungry heart
Much have I seen and known; cities of men
And manners, climates, councils, governments,
Myself not least, but honored of them all;
And drunk delight of battle with my peers,
Far on the ringing plains of windy Troy.

There lies the port; the vessel puffs her sail:
There gloom the dark broad seas. My mariners,
Souls that have toiled, and wrought, and thought
with me—That ever with a frolic welcome took
The thunder and the sunshine, and opposed
Free hearts, free foreheads—you and I are old;
Old age hath yet his honor and his toil;
Death closes all: but something ere the end,
Some work of noble note, may yet be done,
Not unbecoming men that strove with Gods.
The lights begin to twinkle from the rocks:
The long day wanes: the slow moon climbs: the deep
Moans round with many voices. Come, my friends,
'Tis not too late to seek a newer world.

Push off, and sitting well in order smite
The sounding furrows; for my purpose holds
To sail beyond the sunset, and the baths
Of all the western stars, until I die.
It may be that the gulfs will wash us down:
It may be we shall touch the Happy Isles,
And see the great Achilles, whom we knew
Though much is taken, much abides; and though
We are not now that strength which in old days

Moved earth and heaven; that which we are, we are;
One equal temper of heroic hearts,
Made weak by time and fate, but strong in will
To strive, to seek, to find, and not to yield.

"Hurrah!" Owen clapped his hands. "That is my poem! To strive, to seek, to find, and not to yield! I shall never yield! But what is wind-blown spume, Grandfather?"

"The thick white foam that gets in your hair and eyes like dande-lion fluff. Will you have it memorized for me by the time we sail again, Master Owen?"

"I shall. Will you tell it to me again?"

"Over tea and jam, sir, over tea and jam."

Edward smiled as a large wave broke over the length of the yacht, soaking them all. "I think you told me the very same poem at the very same age. Only it wasn't on a boat."

Lord Preston gazed up at the set of the sail. "It was on the Liver-pool docks."

Dear Caroline,

The heat can just about drive you crazy out here. Heat and hate. It takes me places I don't want to go in my thoughts. Should I have married you after the war instead of Chris? Why couldn't I understand how much I cared for you? How was it possible for me to love both of you at the same time? The long stretches of inaction are as murderous as the fighting with my head spinning around like this. But I pray, I think of how sweet a person you are, I remember how much we both loved Chris, I think of Matthew and Charles and I know how lucky I am…how blessed.

In case you wonder where that picture is of you on our wed-ding night, the one where you're indoors by the candles at

Dover Sky with the biggest smile I've ever seen on anyone, well, it's here in Morocco with me. I look at it all the time. It's a bit curled from being in my pocket, and I suppose faded by the sun, but it's still you—the most beautiful woman in the world, a beauty that never ended with what I saw but carried over to what I always knew about you within and without.

I miss you very much.

Kipp

My love,

Please don't keep going back to the past. Yes, there was a lot of pain and confusion. But you loved a lot too. And now you are loving me with all your heart. I know that. We also have two sons we adore. And me, well, I have loved you since I first saw you at that Christmas ball at our estate when I was sixteen. Nothing has changed since then no matter what I've said or how I've acted or how disappointed I've been. God blessed me with a family and a friend I loved named Chris, who sees us from heaven and who wanted us to love each other and be together for the rest of our lives. Oh, Kipp, we have lived such an exceptional story! Look at what's happening for us. I wouldn't want to change anything because if I did I might change what we're experiencing right now.

I'm waiting for you. Come back to me, Kipp Danforth. Our honeymoon was too short. We need another as soon as you return to Dover Sky. The boys can come too. We have to go somewhere and just be the two of us and sometimes the four of us. I look forward to that very much.

I am so in love with you!

Caroline

Dover Sky

Victoria lay beside her husband in the dark, turning things over and over in her mind. Finally, unable to drop off, she placed a hand on his shoulder.

"Darling?" she said softly.

"Mmm?"

"Are you asleep?"

"Mmm."

"I just want you to know because I don't think I've ever said it in so many words, that I think you are amazing."

Ben opened his eyes and lifted his head. "What?"

"You crashed and lost one of your best friends. The doctors removed both of your legs below the knee. But you didn't give up. You're walking. Most importantly, you didn't give up on your wife or your children."

"My wife and children? How could I?" He sat up. "Were you afraid of that?"

"Yes."

"It hasn't been easy, Vic—"

"I know that."

"But it never entered my head to abandon you or the boys. Not once did I dwell on that."

"Do I have Jeremy to thank for that?"

"Partly."

"I need a hug, love."

He gathered her into his arms.

She reached down and touched one of his stumps. "This doesn't matter, you know," she whispered.

"Shh."

"It doesn't, Ben. You're more of a man than most of those walking about on their own two legs. You're magnificent, honestly."

"You shall give me a swollen head, and then I'll have problems with that part of me too."

She played over his chin and lips with her fingers. "Tim and Ram are so proud of their father. Are you aware of how much they love you?"

"I think the world of them. I'm glad they feel the same way."

"Ramsay asked if there was another war if you would enlist and fight. I said no, that you couldn't fly in the military again. Then he asked if you might not fight on the ground like Uncle Kipp is doing. I said probably not. He wept, Ben, how he wept. I held him but I couldn't comfort him."

Ben said nothing for a moment. "You know, don't you?"

"I do know."

"How?"

"A woman's intuition. Comparing notes with Emma. Jeremy didn't let anything out of the bucket, if that's what you're thinking."

"I have to do it, Vic. I love flying. It's a bigger part of me than my limbs were. I can't let it go. And I owe it to Mike. I do. He fought back and flew again after his crash and his brother was killed. Well, Mike was my brother too, wasn't he? So I owe him the same. I've got to go up. I've asked Jeremy to go with me."

"Jeremy? He's never flown a plane in his life. Why can't you go up with someone who can take the controls if something goes wrong?"

He stroked her hair. "Nothing will go wrong."

"How can you say that?"

"Look, it's easier for me to fly than to walk. Almost everything I do up there is with my hands. The rudder's the only thing I work with my feet. I will practice on the ground with that until I'm confident my metal feet know their place. Vic, climbing stairs is more difficult than manipulating a rudder. And I'll show Jeremy how to do that just in case I need help."

"But why Jeremy?"

"Because his words helped me get this far—along with everyone else's, of course. Yes, along with your words and prayers too. But I took my darkness to him, unloaded it on him, and he bore it."

"Is that the only reason?"

He ran his hand over her back, up and down, up and down.

"Perhaps it's because he lost his arm in a war so he understands what I've been going through and what still lies ahead. I want us both up there on the anniversary of the crash."

She dug her fingers into his arm. "The anniversary? Ben, what on earth are you thinking?"

"I'm not going to be ruled by fear, Vic. I simply won't. God is bigger than the finger of fate, isn't He?"

"Ben—"

"Isn't He?" He kissed the top of her head and her soft auburn hair. "I'm going to change a day of darkness into a day of light. I'm going to take a day of mourning and make it a day of celebration. I have to, Vic. And God will help me."

"My lord?"

Lord Preston swished his razor in the basin of water in his bedroom. "Yes, what is it, Skitt?"

"I thought you might wish to come downstairs, m'lord."

Lord Preston stroked away foam on his cheek with the razor. "I'm in my robe. Why should I want to go downstairs right now?"

"There is something you should see."

"Can't it wait?"

Yips suddenly sounded through the window.

"What is that?" He rushed to the window. Three puppies were romping about on the grass with Harrison. Baron von Isenburg stood watching and leaning on a cane. Lord Preston ran to the door and threw it open. Skitt stood there in his butler suit.

"Why on earth didn't you tell me, Skitt?"

"I did, m'lord."

"Next time it's a dog, shout, '*Dog! Dog!*' And then I shall respond far more appropriately."

"Very good, sir."

Lord Preston rushed down the staircase, lather flying from his face as he tightened the belt about his maroon robe. "Elizabeth! Elizabeth!"

She popped her head out of a doorway just as he reached the front door. "Whatever is the matter, William?"

"Dogs! The baron is here with dogs!"

"The baron? He's supposed to be in Switzerland with Catherine and Libby!"

Lord Preston swung open the front door and let it bang against a wooden holder for canes and umbrellas. Running down the steps to the lawn, he became an instant attraction for the puppies.

The pups, one black, one brown, and one brown-and-black—tumbled towards him, their tails thrashing.

"Gerard, what is this? What is this?" Lord Preston went to both knees and the puppies scrambled all over him, licking his face and hands until he laughed. "Praise God, what is going on? Where are you going with these rascals? Why are you here?"

"These are Belgian shepherds, Vilhelm. The black one is the Groenendael kind, the brown one a Malinois—you see it has a short-haired coat while the other two are longer haired—and the brown-and-black one is a Tervuren. I have named her Poppy since the breeder is in Flanders, and there is that famous poem from the war about that area. Indeed, I've given the black male that very name—Flanders. His coat reminds me of the long fields of dark soil. It is up to you to name the Malinois."

"I?"

"The puppies are home, Vilhelm. That is to say, wherever you hang your hat is their home."

"Impossible."

The baron lifted his cane. "I saw your family to the Hartmann Castle on the Rhine, and then I came back as quickly as I could through Belgium to the coast. My chauffeur drove, and I watered and fed and pampered the beasts." He lowered his cane and watched his friend play with the puppies. "Once I heard you had lost Gladstone and Wellington, I set the wheels in motion. I know the breeder well, and these will be extraordinary dogs. I expect them to be with you at least until 1945. I have also had them blessed."

"No."

"Yes! By a priest in Ypres. I hope they will in turn bless you, my friend."

The black puppy had his face right in Lord Preston's and was washing the statesman thoroughly.

"They shall, Gerard. I have no doubt of it."

July–December, 1928
Dover Sky

"Who was that at the door, Skitt?" Lady Preston asked.

"It's a cable, m'lady." He brought it into the library and presented it to her on a silver tray as she sat with her tea in the library.

"A silver tray, is it, Skitt?" she asked as she put her teacup in the saucer and set both on the small table next to her.

He smiled.

She picked up the envelope. "It's from Germany, I expect."

"Paris, m'lady."

"Paris? What on earth?" She examined the envelope more closely. "It's addressed to Lady Caroline Danforth. Why have you brought it to me?"

Skitt's smile was gone. "It bears a government stamp, ma'am."

"It bears a—" Lady Preston's face whitened. "Oh no! Dear God, please, no." She bowed her head and closed her eyes. "Pray, give me a moment. Fetch Lord Preston."

"Yes, m'lady."

Lord Preston was at her side within ten minutes. "I was running the puppies about with Harrison. We must keep them away from the pond and the swans."

Elizabeth was slumped in her chair, her face drawn and looking ten years older.

"What in heaven's name is wrong?" He saw the cable in her hand. "Bad news? Where from?"

"France."

"France…" His mind raced. "No…not Kipp!"

"Of course Kipp. What other member of the family rushed off across the Channel to enlist in the French Foreign Legion?"

"May I see it?"

She lifted her hand, and he took the envelope.

"Why haven't you opened it?"

She put a hand over her eyes. "It's addressed to Caroline. Even if it wasn't, I really don't think I could, William. I can't bear more bad news. Can you imagine what this will do to Caroline if it's what we think it is?"

Lord Preston turned the envelope over in his hand. "It's not addressed to us so I don't feel comfortable opening it."

"Would you feel more comfortable giving it to Caroline without reading it first so we are unprepared to help her cope?"

He tapped it against his pant leg. "There is a teakettle in the front parlor. I shall steam it open."

She pushed herself wearily out of the chair and followed him. The kettle was plugged in and once the water came to a boil, he held the envelope over the spout. "Thank goodness it is not a whistling kettle," he said.

Lady Preston watched him from the wicker chair she'd sat in. "A small mercy God has granted us, yes."

"There we are." He unplugged the kettle and the cloud of vapor vanished. Peeling back the seal carefully, he brought out the telegram. He waited a moment. "Lord, help us." He glanced at the words. "The cable is in French."

Lady Preston made a fist and gasped. "Of course. And I don't know French and you don't know French. I do know the word 'mort' means dead. Can you see it there?"

"I don't know what I can see or can't see. Holly!" he called as he noticed his sister walking past the doorway. "Holly, how is your French?" he asked when she stepped inside the room.

"*Magnifique.* I learned a great deal from Christelle."

"Are you able to make sense of this?"

Holly, dressed in trousers and a coat, took the cable. "I was just about to go over the grounds with Harrison," she said, noticing her brother looking at her clothes. She scanned the telegram.

Lord and Lady Preston stared as they waited impatiently.

Holly frowned in concentration. "Ah…"

"What is it?" demanded Lady Preston. "Is he dead? Is Kipp killed?"

Holly looked up. "Not at all. He's been wounded. He was treated in Paris and is being honorably discharged from the French Foreign Legion. *La libération honorable.*"

"Discharged?" Lady Preston's face and eyes took on color as she smiled.

Holly smiled back and handed the cable to her. "He's coming home, Elizabeth."

Caroline saw Kipp from a distance when he returned, stepping out of a cab, right arm in a sling, the puppies and children running up to the car. He was taller and thinner than she remembered and his skin was much darker than May of 1927 when they had married. Matthew, who was six, threw his arms around his father's neck as Kipp scooped him up with his good arm. Her son Charles, seven, stood off to one side, stiff and awkward, smiling, but not sure what to do. Kipp put Matthew down and offered Charles his hand. Charles shook it. Kipp patted him on the shoulder and said something she couldn't hear that made her son laugh. A warmth went through her.

He was a man absolutely without fear. I think he's the only man I have ever met who was incapable of fear.

She remembered reading the words in a newspaper. The American pilot Eddie Rickenbacker had said it about Canadian ace Billy Bishop but it had made her think of Kipp from the beginning, even after they broke up. His blond hair blazed in the morning sunlight as he spoke with Ramsay and Owen and knelt to pet the Belgian Shepherds.

So finally you have let your beautiful hair grow back.

His mother came quickly across the lawn from her white rose bush by the front porch, tugging off her gardening gloves, and Kipp put an arm around her and hugged her with enough force to knock the broad-brimmed straw hat from her head. She put her fingers to her mouth and laughed as Kipp kissed her on both cheeks, French style. Lord Preston hurried out the front door with Skitt and Norah.

Caroline smiled to herself. *It is all right for you to have him now. I know he wishes to greet you. But he wants me most of all. After he is done at the manor house he will find me. And then it will just be the two of us.*

She was standing in a cluster of red poppies that had sprung up a hundred yards north of the house and to the east of the pond. Walking slowly, hearing voices calling out to Kipp as Harrison and Holly came up from the stables, she headed away from the manor and towards the northern end of the property. The poppies streamed ahead of her to an old dry stone fence spattered with orange lichen that separated Dover Sky from the McPhail acreage. She trailed her fingers over blossoms that began to show pink, white, and orange as well as scarlet among the tall blades of green grass.

Did Harrison do this? Or Holly? I'm sure they didn't just sprout here on their own.

She followed the stone fence to the west, getting farther and farther from Kipp and the house. The McPhail fields were overgrown but pleasant enough despite that, bending and rippling in the July breezes like long hair. Without thinking about what she was doing, Caroline took off her sun hat and shook her hair loose from its pins so that it fell over her shoulders and back and began to move with the breezes like the tall grass.

"Caroline Virginia Scarborough."

She looked up in surprise at a figure standing in a copse of young oak trees by the fence.

The man put a finger to his lips. "Shh. Don't say a word."

He emerged from the shadows in his sport coat and pants, arm in a khaki sling. "They think I'm freshening up in my room, you see. I slipped out the back door."

She opened her mouth to reply but his hand went over her lips gently. "No. No words. The first thing I want from those perfect lips is a kiss. And a long one at that." He put his arm around her. "It's like water to me. And I've been in a desert, you know."

She tried to respond again, her lips moving against the palm of his hand, but he shook his head. "Really. There's nothing to say."

Her eyes softened to a pale blue.

"Do you know my hand over your lovely mouth has the effect of a Moroccan veil covering the lower half of your face? It accentuates the blue in your eyes and the bright gold of your eyebrows. As if there's nothing else in the whole wide world." The corners of her eyes moved. "Do you know, I think you're smiling at me beneath that veil."

Her lips kissed his palm.

"Ah, thank you, but I shall need a great deal more than that if I'm to survive."

She kissed his palm a second time.

"I'm grateful. But it isn't quite what's needed." He put his head by hers and whispered in her ear. "Most beautiful woman in the Empire and the world, your dress and your eyes and the sky over your head are exactly the same color right now. Did you know that?" He closed his eyes, taking in the scent of her blonde hair and skin. "Most beautiful woman in the Empire and the world, if I remove the veil, do you promise not to speak?"

Her eyes softened to a lighter blue so that they looked as if they were the color of clear air.

"I'll take that as a yes."

He removed his hand. Gazing down at her face he entwined his darkly tanned fingers in long strands of her thick hair. Her eyes were still and unmoving and fixed completely on his. He took in as much of her beauty as he could without doing anything more than twine her hair around his fingers and feel her warmth against his chest and breathe in the smell of the perfume at her throat and shoulders. Then he closed his eyes and put his lips to hers, slowly and almost awkwardly as if he had never kissed her before, then adding more energy and force until he heard the air leave her body and felt her fingers dig into his arms and move higher and higher to finally grip his back with all the strength she had. She refused to let go or lighten her hold, drawing him farther and farther from England and Dover Sky to a place that was all Caroline Scarborough and her sapphire eyes and golden hair, all her cloud white skin and poppy red lips.

Dover Sky

"What did you do? Sell tickets to the event?"

"I did. There's a grand prize."

"And what is that then?"

"A free hop over the Ditch to Holland—with you at the controls."

"Terrific prize!" Then Jeremy looked sourly at the control panel of the Fokker, a three-engine aircraft. "I'd like to win it myself."

"Maybe you will." Ben continued to taxi the plane over the grass airstrip while working the rudder with his metal feet. "I think I have the hang of this."

"We could crack up, and you're as chipper as a lark."

Jeremy stared through the glass at the people standing shoulder to shoulder nearby. Everyone in the family except Catherine and Libby were watching. All the servants were out, along with dozens of neighbors.

"I don't see any other way of doing this except with a bit of levity." Ben glanced at Jeremy's white face. "Our roles have reversed over the past few weeks, haven't they? You were always on the positive side of things and telling me to take everything on. You prayed with me. Read the Bible with me. Now I'm walking, and today we're in a plane. And you're the one who looks like he's a fog bank."

Jeremy's smile was thin. "And you're the sunshine?"

"We're going to be fine." Ben grinned. "Can't help myself, Jeremy. I love being in an airplane again. Love the feel of it, love the smell of the cockpit and the leather gear, love the throb of the engine. I thank God I'm here. I can't do the stark and stoic look today, mate. Sorry." He turned the plane around and headed east, keeping tabs on the red windsock. "You're one of the reasons I'm in the plane at all a year to the day after the crash at Cape Town. That's why you're along for the ride. My crazy way of honoring you."

Jeremy stared straight ahead. "It felt like an honor a fortnight ago. Now I feel like I've been asked to take over a coronation at Westminster Abbey without a shred of advice from the Archbishop of Canterbury."

"I *have* given you advice. Showed you how to work the stick and watch the gauges. In fact, the only thing that really can go wrong is my feet not being able to handle the rudder. In that case, you just do the dance with your feet like I tell you to do. I'm not going to keel over and pass out, Jeremy. Heart and lungs are fine. Stop fretting. It's going to be the kind of day that redeems the day everyone remembers so far as a tragedy." Ben laughed and shook his head. "Can't believe I'm about to fly again. It's marvelous." He opened up the throttle and the engine roared. "Enough fooling around. I'm more than ready. Whisper a prayer, my good vicar. We're up and away to where angels soar."

"I wish you wouldn't put it that way."

The Fokker streaked along the grass. Victoria clamped her hands onto both her sons, and Emma put her knuckles to her mouth. The aircraft lifted smoothly and gained height rapidly, soon disappearing to the south over the Channel.

Kipp kept a pair of Zeiss binoculars trained on it until the plane was a black dot. "Well, at least they're up and away safely," he said.

No one else spoke. Even the children were silent, picking up on the nervousness of the adults. Harrison had the three shepherds on leashes, and they were quiet as well, sitting on their haunches, tongues out, sensing the mood, and waiting for a different moment to arrive. Six or seven minutes went by before the plane's engines could be heard again, this time coming from the direction of Dover. Kipp raised his binoculars to his eyes and laughed.

"What do you find amusing?" snapped his father.

"Jeremy's at the stick, and he's doing very well for himself—for an Anglican cleric, I must say."

"What!" Emma reached for the binoculars. "I don't believe it."

"Go ahead. Take a look. You can see right into the cockpit."

Victoria's dark-green eyes were on Kipp. "Is Ben all right? What's happened? Why is Jeremy flying the plane?"

Kipp smiled and put his hands in his pockets. "No doubt Ben is sitting up straight and tall and grinning ear to ear."

"I can see Jeremy!" Emma shouted holding the binoculars to her face. "It is him! Why, he's doing splendidly!"

The Fokker howled over their heads. Lord Preston clapped a hand to his straw hat to hold it on. "Good heavens, sir!" he yelled. "Slow down! You're a man of the cloth!"

Kipp took the glasses from Emma. "Right. They're coming in. Jeremy is leaning back with his eyes shut so Ben's back at the helm. This is the tricky part. Let's see how he does with the landing. After all—"

"Do stop, Kipp. Please." Victoria was staring at the Fokker as if she could make it land perfectly by force of sheer will. "I'm trying to pray."

The Fokker touched down, bounced once, and then all the wheels met the grass together.

"A three-point landing!" Kipp chuckled. "Marvelous."

A number of people clapped.

"Well, sis?" Kipp looked at Victoria. "God or Ben's skill?"

Victoria was standing with her eyes closed and her hands still clamped tightly on Ramsay and Tim. "The two should never be far apart, Kipp Danforth, should they?"

Hartmann Castle, the Rhine River, Germany

Libby found her sister high up on one of the Hartmann Castle's battlements, wind blowing her dark hair straight back.

"How on earth did you get through that door?" Libby asked. "It's been locked tight ever since we arrived."

Catherine was leaning with her arms folded on the parapet and taking in the view of the Rhine River Valley. "To keep the children out. All of the turrets are locked up, but I have the key."

Libby stood beside her. "It's breathtaking."

"I agree. I never tire of it. I don't know which I prefer—Pura or the Rhine."

"Fortunately you don't have to choose. You can have both."

Catherine nodded. "I can."

"The summer's almost spent, and we've never returned to the conversation we had in Tubingen, Cath."

Catherine didn't reply immediately. She kept looking out over the valley. "Maybe there's a good reason," she finally said.

"What's the good reason?"

"I love Albrecht."

"I know you love Albrecht."

"So there's nothing more to discuss."

Libby folded her arms on the parapet next to Catherine. "So you don't mind if Terry pops over for a visit?"

Catherine's jaw tightened. "I wish you wouldn't do that."

"Do what?"

"Start fights."

"If you love Albrecht and don't have a problem with Terry—"

"I love Albrecht, and there is no problem with Terry."

"Except you love Terry too."

Catherine's face darkened. "I don't. I can't."

"Oh Cath. *Don't. Can't.* What do they do to help you when you have feelings that frighten you?"

Catherine put a hand to her face. "Please don't bring this up. I honestly don't have answers for you."

Libby watched a rolling swarm of blackbirds swirl past the top of the castle. "Soon it will be autumn." She leaned over and kissed her sister's head. The wind was blowing Libby's ginger hair and Catherine's dark hair about their faces. "If the day ever comes when I want to see Terry, I will not bring him to Tubingen, Pura, or to this castle on the Rhine."

Catherine didn't respond. After a moment she lifted one of her hands off the parapet and grasped Libby's shoulder.

"And if a day ever comes when there is much more emotion between

Terry and me," Libby went on, "well, that day is far, far away. Michael still has my heart. But should life happen again with another man, and if that man is Terry, we will not live within a thousand miles of you, my dear. I would not wish to see you in turmoil and pain over things you can't control or understand."

Catherine whispered, "I wouldn't want that—wouldn't want you so far away. Please. There's conflict between Mum and you, and Mum and Dad, and Edward is in his high-and-mighty snit because I married a German and you adopted a girl from a Chinese family. No more rifts."

"You've been hurt enough in your life, Catherine. I don't need to add to it."

Catherine turned her head and touched her other hand to her sister's cheek. "You said once you were a big girl. So am I. We've both lost so much. I've tried to make a new start. You deserve a chance too. How can I stand in the way of something like that?"

"Just so you understand Terry and I are talking—only talking. There's no hand of God in this, Cathy. No touch of the divine driving us forward."

Catherine smiled crookedly. "You don't know that."

DEAR MUM AND DAD

WE HAVE A BABY GIRL AS BEAUTIFUL AS SHANNON AND AS BIG AS HER FATHER. NINE POUNDS FOUR OUNCES. BORN ON 3 OF SEPTEMBER. MOTHER DOING FINE BUT IT WAS A LONG DELIVERY. WE HAD TO COAX OUR GIRL OUT. JANE FINALLY HAS A FEMALE COUSIN. WE'VE NAMED HER PATRICIA CLAIRE. SHE REALLY IS LOVELY. WE HOPE TO HAVE FURLOUGH NEXT YEAR SO WE CAN BRING HER TO ENGLAND TO SEE YOU. GOD BLESS AND THANK THE FAMILY FOR THEIR PRAYERS.

ROBBIE

Old City, Jerusalem

Robbie nudged the toe of his boot against the shattered panel of wood. "Tell me what you saw, Sergeant."

They both looked as nurses and doctors helped wounded men and women into ambulances. Above the massive stones of the Western Wall, hundreds of Muslim worshipers gazed down from the Dome of the Rock at the splintered wood and wounded bodies and listened to the cries of pain. British soldiers and police were everywhere.

"Sir." The sergeant had a strong Scottish accent. "The worshipers here at the Wall—the Jews—they had brought some chairs for the sick and the elderly, which they've done before. But they also brought a prayer screen covered in a kind of cloth—this is it here at your feet—so's men and women could pray together; the screen separating one group from the other."

"Who took exception to this?"

"Well, sir, the sheikhs did so far as I could see. I know they were warning the Jerusalem commissioner who was visiting up on the Rock there. He came and told the rabbi to take the screen down. I overheard that part of it word for word. The rabbi asked if they could leave it up until the prayer service was over. The commissioner, Mr. Keith-Roach, he said that would be fine."

"So did they take it down?"

"They understood from the commissioner they could finish their prayers first. Ten minutes later a great shouting starts: 'Death! Death! Kill the Jews! Strike down the Jewish dogs!'"

"Who was doing that?"

"Muslims on the Rock and others in the streets here."

"Then what?"

"The prayers were over, but the rabbi didn't take the screen down immediately. Not sure why. He was tending to other matters, talking with the people who had been praying at the Wall, and so forth. Suddenly the shouting became like screams—bloodcurdling screams—and the commissioner sent in ten or twelve armed men to get ahold of the prayer screen."

"Armed? Are you sure?"

"Armed, sir."

"Did the Jews have any weapons?"

"None. They were just ordinary folk."

Robbie squinted into the light over the Dome of the Rock. "I take it the Jews tried to protect their prayer screen?"

"Aye, sir. It was a sacred object, like."

"Of course."

"They fought back, wouldn't let the men Keith-Roach sent in to take it. So heads were broken. The prayer screen, as you can see for yourself, was torn apart."

"Was anyone shot?"

The sergeant shook his head. "I thank the good Lord, no."

Robbie put his hands behind his back. "Very good. I'm grateful for your report. Keep the peace here as best you can."

The sergeant saluted. "Yes, sir."

Robbie returned the salute and bent to pick up a fragment of the screen that measured four or five inches across. Several Hebrew letters were carved into the wood. He ran his thumb over them. He stood up and put the broken piece of the prayer screen in the chest pocket of his uniform.

Dear Catherine,

Here I am writing you from Jerusalem, sis. It seems the family is divided between England, Germany, and the Holy Land these days. How are you getting on there in your new life? What does Sean think of it all? A five-year-old like him must be overjoyed at seeing the castle in Tubingen every day and watching custodians polish suits of armor to a gleam. Of course, he's seen the old castle at Ashton Park, but he was very young when you left there to take up residence at Dover Sky. He can't remember much of Ashton, I'm sure.

I want to ask after Libby, as well. Please send her my regards and Shannon's. I pray things work out between Mum and her, and I'm glad you've given Jane and Libby a place to stay until then. How do the two of them like Germany? How are their language lessons coming along? "Sprechen Sie Deutsch?" is all I know.

Shannon and Patricia are doing so well. I wish I could say the same about Jerusalem. Things are not so holy in the Holy City. Back in September we had a bad incident at the Western Wall where the Jews pray. Then in October the Grand Mufti, Haj Amin al Husseini, made matters worse by ordering new construction near the Western Wall. He purposely had mules laden with building supplies led through the area while the Jews were praying. The drivers made every effort to ensure the mules dropped their excrement right at the Western Wall. Filthy water was thrown on the Jews as well. Can you imagine how the Muslims would react if that were done to them at the Dome of the Rock?

Now we even have a Muslim holy man, a muezzin, doing the call to prayer just a few steps from the Western Wall precisely when the Jews themselves are praying. I doubt you've ever heard an Islamic call to prayer. It is loud and long and stark, a plaintive cry that carries over every other sound. Quite understandably, the Jews are upset at all this.

The Jerusalem commissioner has his hands full. So do we. There are not many of us soldiers. We're just a token force really—the British Palestine police also have all they can handle. How well the police will handle the unrest I don't know. They certainly overreacted when the Jews set up a simple prayer screen at the Wall back in September. By last count over 1200 of the police officers are Muslim Arabs. Less than 500 are Christian Arabs, and only about 320 are Jews. I don't know how evenhanded the justice they mete out is bound to be in 1929.

Listen to me prattle on. A month from Christmas and what sort of good cheer am I bringing you? My purpose in writing is to tell you we had Patricia Claire baptized Roman Catholic shortly after her birth. This was Shannon's wish, and I felt no inclination to say nay. After all I was ready to be baptized a Catholic when I was stationed in Ireland years ago. So were you before you and Albrecht patched things up.

Do you ever give a thought to picking up where you left off? I suppose not. Albrecht is Lutheran. I understand the baron is a practicing Catholic, though I doubt that will have any bearing whatsoever on your situation. Well, I wanted to share the news about my baby's baptism with you because I felt you'd be interested and sympathetic. I'm quite happy about it, but please not a word to Mum and Dad right now! I think that might really drive them 'round the bend.

We'll certainly send you and Libby and Sean and Jane a few Christmas cards from Jerusalem. I might even get a chance to get down and pick something up from Bethlehem. Some camels and a nativity scene carved out of olive wood perhaps? It's a lovely wood, and I'm sure the children would love the donkeys, shepherds, magi, and all the other figures that go into the Christmas story. Even sophisticated eleven-year-old Jane might like setting it up.

That's all for now. Must get this off in the post. Love to all. God bless you in every way during the remaining weeks of 1928.

Cheers,
Robbie

Christmas Eve
Tubingen, Germany

"Catherine?"

"Yes, Albrecht?"

"What do you think of this sentence?" he asked as he came into the library, reading glasses on and hair askew, holding a sheaf of papers covered with typing:

As the Christmas tree was removed from the realm of pagan ritual by Martin Luther and redeemed and made whole to honor the love of God we find in Jesus Christ, so the German heart must also be released from any vestiges of a Nordic pagan past, and be redeemed and made new in Christ, so that a true and spiritual Germany may emerge from our confusion once again.

She closed the book she was leafing through and smiled. "It is a long sentence, love."

"I know but—"

"Nevertheless, I like what you say and how you bring things together. How will it sound in German?"

His head was down as he reread the sentence to himself. She watched for a moment—the movement of his lips, the shape of his fingers on the sheets of paper, the tangle of his light brown hair, the slender strength of his body. Light and warmth moved swiftly through her as if she'd drank hot tea. She stood up and took the pages from his hands.

"It is Christmas Eve, Albrecht. We have that lovely fir tree from Bavaria downstairs."

He stared at her. "Yes, of course. But I—"

"Time to put away pens and thinking caps. Time to celebrate the love of God in Jesus Christ you like to write about."

"Another half hour." He half-smiled. "It may seem to you that I am obsessive, but we want this essay published to coincide with New Year's Day. Hitler has been yammering about an economic crisis to try to draw attention back to his political ideas. We cannot ignore him. Membership in the Nazi Party continues to grow."

"But he still has hardly any seats in the *Reichstag*, correct?"

"That can change with one election. A bad year for Germany, and his party could go from fourteen to fifty or sixty seats overnight. Do you know how many stormtroopers he's recruited—those thugs of his in brown shirts? We estimate at least 400,000. That's almost half a million, Catherine! And the Treaty of Versailles restricts the German army to only 100,000 troops. Hitler could take over the government with a snap of his fingers."

"He won't, Albrecht. You know he won't. Hitler's smart enough to understand he needs far more than half-a-million brutes to govern Germany. He needs the German people behind him. He doesn't have that. He'll never have that."

"You don't know that for sure. History turns like a weather vane in the wind. One moment east, the next moment north."

"Albrecht—"

"Just a half hour."

"Your half hours are hours and your hours are days." She ran her hands over the sweater on his chest. "I have many confusions about many things, but one thing I have been successful at sorting out is that whatever else I feel, I know I feel great love and affection for you."

"Do you?"

She removed his glasses and placed them on a table. "I do." She gently put her lips to his. "No more academics. Or rather, if you must be theological, live out your theology in your marriage. Right now. Right here. The house is empty for a few hours…"

"Catherine—"

"Begin with a kiss. Don't you find a kiss pleasant?"

"Naturally."

"Especially mine?"

"Only yours."

"Ah…" She continued to kiss him. "I've found the year difficult in many ways, Albrecht, not least of all because of Mother's unkindness towards Libby's daughter and Edward's hostility towards our relationship. Often I didn't know what to think or do about anything. But when I look at you and I hear the students singing carols outside our house for their favorite professor—"

"Come, you exaggerate."

"I realize whatever else may not be settled in my life, I know you are my favorite professor too."

"Catherine—"

"Albrecht, tomorrow is Christmas. Show me I mean something to you."

He didn't speak again. He framed her face in both of his hands even though his fingertips were smeared with ink from replacing typewriter ribbon. He put his lips against her eyebrows, her eyes, her cheeks, and finally her mouth. She slipped her arms over his back, and her fingers found their way to his soft brown hair.

"I understand so little from one moment to the next," she said in a quiet voice. "But I understand this."

15

March–August, 1929
St. Andrew's Cross Church

Ben peered closely at the stained-glass window depicting Jesus speaking with the centurion. "When was this one made?"

"The 1700s. Early on, I believe, in the history of St. Andrew's Cross Church." Jeremy, in his clerical robes and a white collar at his throat, stood behind Ben. "Kipp took a great interest in this particular window as well when he was here for the baptism of Edward's newborn."

"Yes. Sorry I missed that. Colm Alexander Danforth. Handsome baby?"

Jeremy smiled. "With his great shock of black hair and brilliant blue eyes he takes after his mother certainly."

"And now Caroline's with child, hmm?"

"She is. The baby's due in the fall."

"I've been flying too much. Vic says I'm trying to prove something." He walked away from the window and sat in a pew. "We're back to Ashton Park. I'll take up the reins in the north, and Kipp will handle the airline in the south. He'll be doing much the same thing Michael did, dodging back and forth between the airfield and Dover Sky."

Jeremy sat next to him. "That's what you wanted to chat about?"

"No, no, actually not. I wanted to thank you again for helping me get back on my feet and up in the clouds. It's been a great thing…a great blessing."

"And I got to fly and see you return to your natural element. It was a great blessing for me too."

"Speaking of natural elements. Well, I was wondering what, ah, what you would think of me…taking holy orders."

Jeremy's eyes opened wide behind his glasses. "What did you say, Ben?"

"Not in the Church of England. That's beyond me, and my background is Methodist—the Wesleys, you know. Even when I was a stable boy I fancied having a pulpit and saying the good words."

Jeremy couldn't think of a response.

"It's always been in my head to go to Africa—to see the jungles and the animals—rhinos and lions and giraffes. I used to think of combining the two—Africa and being a missionary. And now, well, I could fly, couldn't I? I could be a missionary pilot or something like that?"

"Have you talked with Victoria about this?"

"No, not yet. She'd think I was off to prove myself on a grand scale. I wouldn't act on any of this for another year. But then I'd want to step down from the airline and start to train with the Methodist Church, with an eye to heading to British East Africa and lending a hand in matters of the spirit and everything else."

"You've never mentioned any of this before, Ben. There hasn't even been a hint."

Ben shrugged. "I've brought it up now and again, but life swept me up in its rough-and-ready current like it does everyone. I had no intention of going to France during the war, but there I was. Had no idea of flying a plane, and one day there I was up in the clouds. Didn't know I'd win the Victoria Cross or marry William and Elizabeth Danforth's youngest daughter or have children with her, but that's how it turned out. Back of my mind I held onto the Methodist Church and Africa and missionary service even though I couldn't see how it might come together."

Jeremy raised his eyebrows and blew out a mouthful of air. "I see."

"I know you're Church of England, and I expect you don't approve of my being a Methodist minister, but—"

Jeremy waved a hand. "This is not 1780, Ben. I know many fine Methodist clerics. That doesn't matter to me one bit. I'm just a bit taken aback by everything you've said. It's like standing on the beach at Brighton and suddenly getting slammed by a monstrous ocean wave."

"You don't think I'm suited?"

"I don't think that at all. You're a fine man. I'm just trying to take it all in. Look, I can't say it's right or it's wrong. It's your life, and it's your decision to make. But you are going to have to bring Victoria in on this—and the sooner the better."

Ben glanced away. "I know, I know. But I don't want her thinking I just came up with this off the top of my head so I could show the world what a man with two tin legs was capable of. The dream's been a part of me for a long time."

"Explain that to her."

Ben looked up at the arched ceiling of stone. "Perhaps in the spring."

"It won't get easier."

"Not with Victoria Anne Danforth it won't, right enough."

Jeremy rubbed his hand over his mouth. "But there's something more important. Is this just an idea you've been carrying around since you were a lad? Or do you feel a call?"

"A call?"

"Do you...do you think God is part of this? That He's speaking to you about becoming a minister?"

Ben folded his arms over his chest. "And what would that sound like?"

"I really can't describe it."

"This happened to you?"

"It did, yes."

"The impression has always been with me. Since I was a schoolboy. It's never left me alone. Always nagging, always pestering, always tugging at my sleeve and grabbing me by the arm—even when I flew during the war and even when I did all the air races. It's got a grip on me like a fever. Or like a dog with its teeth sunk into my leg."

Jeremy's smile grew.

Ben looked at him. "No music. No angels in white. No pleasant warmth tingling through my body. Just this constant at me, at me, at me. I don't suppose that sounds at all like God, does it?"

Jeremy laughed. "Actually, it sounds a good deal like Him."

Dear Cornelia, my diary,

April fool's! I thought I was coming along quite nicely as far as love and marriage were concerned. I adore Albrecht, I absolutely do. And after those chats with Libby last year I thought I'd gotten this whole issue of her having a relationship with Terry Fordyce off my chest. Now she's off to Cartagena, Spain, where the Royal Navy ships have berthed for two weeks. He cabled her, she thought about it for five seconds, and then she went downtown and sent back a telegram accepting his invitation. Jane remains here with Albrecht, Sean, and me. She's pouting quite a bit. I think our almost-twelve-year-old has a bit of a thing for Commander Fordyce.

I have no wish to rush off to Spain, and I have no desire to see Terry. I'm looking forward to traveling to Pura with Albrecht very much, and that's only six weeks away. But I must confess I still don't like the idea of Libby spending time with Terry. She continues to tell me it's no more than friendship, but what woman takes a train hundreds of miles to see a man for two or three days simply for the purpose of developing a friendship? Why not wait a bit until his ship is back in English waters in May or June?

Of course she wants to see him as soon as possible. Of course she has every right to see him. But this man was once very precious to me. I don't know if what I'm feeling is jealousy or possessiveness or what. I can only say it is very hard to think of her spending hours in his company—dining with him, making him laugh, enjoying his gallantries. I don't wish to be with him, but I don't wish for her to be with him either.

I pray all these confusing and conflicting feelings I have will be gone when I wake up. I pray that Terry will become no more than any other man out there floating around on the sea in a boat.

Danforth flat, Port of Dover

Charlotte watched as her husband smacked his fist into his palm over and over in the front parlor of their Dover flat. "Lost! And now Labor holds the reins of the greatest nation on earth in its grip! The greatest nation and the greatest empire!"

"You and your father have retained your seats. That's something."

"So did Tanner Buchanan."

"Still, you won reelection, and we all know it was a difficult campaign. I'm very proud of you, persevering right through the swamp and heat of May and June."

"We may still be MPs, Char, but we have no power."

Charlotte leaned forward on the couch. "I spoke with your father at some length, Edward. Yes, Labor has more seats in the House—but barely. And they didn't win the popular vote. They don't have a clear majority. The day will come when they will need to cross the aisle. Ramsay MacDonald is prime minister for a year or two, but eventually there will be a hung Parliament. At that point, if MacDonald wants to form a government capable of passing legislation, he must patch together some sort of national coalition. That's how your father put it."

Edward threw himself into an armchair. "I have no desire to be on the same side of the aisle as Tanner Buchanan."

She smiled, reached over, and rubbed his shoulder and back. "Love, if you wish the Conservative Party to continue to exert a positive influence on British politics, I doubt you'll have much choice. Of course you could sit on the Opposition benches and glare at Lord Buchanan from there, perhaps shake your fist at him now and then, and even occasionally pitch a wadded ball of paper at his head."

"They'd escort me from the chamber *tout de suite* for that."

"But how exciting. You might actually bop him between the eyes. Then he'd challenge you to a duel of honor and you'd run him through. No more evil Lord Tanner. Triumph! His last words? '*Why, I am justly killed by mine own treachery.*'"

Edward laughed. "Here I am, tired and flustered by it all and yet how is it possible that my Pendle Hill beauty can still make merry with me?"

She took his hand and curled her strong fingers tightly around it. "After ten years of marriage too."

"Well, you look ten years younger, Charlotte Squire, not ten years older. Are you sure we're not traveling backwards in time on H.G. Wells' invention?"

She tugged his arm over to her and kissed his hand while keeping her dark-blue eyes focused on him. "What if we were? Would you still have me? Still marry me in that great heap of rocks and battlements in Scotland?"

"I'd do it a hundred times over—a thousand times over."

"Prove it, Lord Edward Danforth, MP."

"Prove it?"

"Take me to our room, hold me in your arms, and tell me in exactly a thousand different ways how and why you still love me." She stood up, and still holding his hand dragged him to his feet.

"You're joking! Colm will be up and wailing in two hours. You need what little bit of sleep you can get."

She pulled him across the room. "Yes, well, that's what nannies and warm bottles are for. Do put some effort into it, Edward. I feel like I'm trying to heave anchor on that great new battleship they just put into service."

"The one named after old Admiral Rodney? How I'd love to sail on her. Sixteen-inch guns!"

"There, we got some life out of you with that. Come along. You can do it. Only two or three more sea miles, and you can snuggle up to your new berth. Rule Britannia, Lord Edward. Britannia rule the waves."

He grinned as she yanked him into their room and shut the door.

"You're as mad as a hatter," he said.

Old City, Jerusalem

"Death to the Jews!"

"Strike for Allah! Strike!"

Thousands of men boiled from the Dome of the Rock into the streets.

"Right!" snapped Robbie. "Leftenant Kirke!"

"Sir."

"They're bent on murder this time. Go after them with your platoon. Work with the police. Arrest the leaders."

"Yes, sir."

"Leftenant Skilling!"

"Sir."

"Follow him with your men."

"Yes, sir. What if—what if the mob won't let us arrest their leaders, sir?"

Robbie's eyes were like rock. "Fire weapons to warn them. If they're killing Jews or they assault your troops, direct your fire as seems most appropriate."

Robbie turned to the British soldiers still at attention behind him, their eyes fixed on the Western Wall. "Leftenants Stark and Kettle!"

"Sir!" the two officers responded in unison.

"Take a pair of armored cars. I shall be in another. Follow me. Bring your platoons. We are heading to the Mea Shearim neighborhood."

"Yes, sir!"

Robbie leaped into an armored car. The engine roared and the car shot forward. The driver threaded it swiftly through the narrow and crooked streets of the Old City. Eventually the convoy and troops were forced to a standstill as hundreds of men in robes called Thawbs jammed the roads and lanes. Robbie saw a Jewish man and his wife hauled from their house and stabbed to death. He unholstered his

Webley revolver and fired two shots into the air. The mob shrank back, shouting. Jumping to the ground, Robbie pointed his pistol at the killers who glared back at him in a mixture of fear and rage, deep and dark frown lines crisscrossing their faces. The rest of the soldiers joined him.

"Corporal Reynolds. Sergeant Ward."

"Major Danforth?"

"Sir."

"Arrest these three men on a charge of murder. Chain them and put them in one of the armored cars."

"Yes, sir."

The tallest of the three Arabs sneered, bent down and wiped the blood from his knife on the dress of the woman he'd stabbed, and spat at Robbie. "British pig. You and your Balfour Declaration. This is holy war, a *jihad*. Beware."

"There were Jews living here thousands of years before Mohammed was born. And they shall continue to live here side by side with their Arab neighbors. Drop your knife."

"In fifty years there will be no Jews in Jerusalem or within a thousand miles of Palestine."

"They are 'people of the Book' according to the Qur'an. They are to be accorded tolerance, respect, and liberty under Islamic law. Have you forgotten the Prophet's words?"

The man spat again.

Robbie thumbed the hammer back on his revolver. "Are you ready to die for breaking sharia law?"

"You would not do it."

The mob around Robbie, the armored cars, and the other British soldiers seethed as people shrieked, "Death to the Jews! Kill the Jewish dogs!"

"They are 'people of the Book'!" Robbie shouted above the clamor. "Do not defile your faith! Obey the Prophet and return to your homes!"

"The Mufti has blessed us!"

Robbie thrust the revolver at the three men. "Corporal Reynolds! Sergeant Ward! Do your duty!"

"Sir!" The corporal and sergeant stepped forward with manacles. The crowd reacted by throwing stones and sticks at the soldiers.

Robbie swung his pistol quickly over to the men in the mob who were closest to him. "Are you ready to die violating the words of the Qur'an? Are you ready to die defying the words of Mohammed?"

A man lunged at him with a sword. Robbie shot him in the shoulder, and he collapsed with a scream. Then Robbie shot the man next to him in the foot. The mob fell back, cursing and breaking apart as men fled into alleys and arched doorways. Robbie aimed his pistol back on the three killers, including the tall Arab who had spoken before.

"Drop the knife or I will shoot. All three of you—drop your knives. If you do not, I will open fire."

The tallest man's eyes remained full of black fire but he laid his knife down on the body of the dead woman. So did the other two. The sergeant and corporal rushed up with the chains.

"You will regret this, British!" the tall man said between clenched teeth as the manacles went on his wrists with a loud snap of iron.

Robbie glanced at the window of the house the Arabs had dragged the man and woman from. A small girl with dark curls and round brown eyes gazed at him. He thought of his daughter's eyes and face.

"I doubt it," he replied.

Dover Sky

"Dad! I think you'd better come in the house and listen to this."

"Yes, what is it, Edward? I'm rather busy here." Lord Preston was covered in soap and water as he and his grandchildren washed the year-old Belgian shepherds on the lawn amidst loud squeals and shouts. "We've decided on a name for the brown one instead of calling him Shepherd all the time. Now he must learn to answer to Charlemagne. Isn't that a grand name? Doesn't it suit him?"

"Dad, it's the BBC," Edward said, leaning out the window. "They're announcing a second day of riots in Jerusalem and Palestine."

Lord Preston hesitated as he was about to run a brush over the squirming Flanders' long, black coat. "A second day? Why, we've heard nothing about it." Covered in water, he ran up the steps of the manor and through the front door. The radio was playing in the library. Charlotte was walking up and down in front of the stacks of books, eight-month-old Colm Alexander in her arms. Edward stood near the radio with his hands in his pockets and head down.

> We continue to receive cables and signals from the Old City and outlying areas of Palestine. Fatalities have mounted since the unrest broke out into open violence yesterday, August twenty-third. Mobs of Arabs are assaulting Jews in their neighborhoods and homes in Jerusalem. There have also been attacks in Hebron. Dozens of Jews have been killed, the pharmacy in a medical clinic destroyed, and a synagogue desecrated and set ablaze. There are reliable reports of massacres on an unprecedented scale. We shall continue to provide updates as they become available.

"Dear God!" Lord Preston stood perfectly still as the water ran off his clothing and spread across the polished hardwood floor. "We must pray now! Skitt?"

Skitt was right behind him. "My lord?"

"Pray, fetch Lady Preston and other members of the family. Have them gather here." He looked at Edward. "Please get the prime minister on the phone."

"MacDonald? Why he's Labor, Father. He won't talk to you."

"Of course he'll talk to me. He'll need you and me if he hopes to form a national coalition government in a year or two and stay in power. More to the point, we've never had cross words. Ring him, please."

"All right."

Lord Preston's shoulders sagged after Edward left the room. Charlotte moved quickly to his side and put a hand on his arm.

"Da, are you all right?"

"Just overwhelmed, my dear. How quickly we move from happiness to fear." He leaned over and kissed her infant's forehead between his wide, blue eyes. "But God is great."

Old City, Jerusalem

"Get back!" Robbie grabbed a Tommy gun from inside the hatch of the armored car and fired a burst over the heads of the men in the mob. When they failed to react, he sprayed bullets at their feet so that stone chips sprang into the air. Shaking their fists, they retreated.

"Death to the Jews!"

"Kill the dogs!"

"Strike the infidels! Praise Allah!"

The mob surged toward the Jewish shops and houses once again. Robbie, who had only had two hours of sleep in the armored car the night before, saw dead children lying in their own blood in the road. This was the third or fourth time he'd witnessed that atrocity since they'd arrived on the scene. A flame of anger shot through him. "Leftenant Kettle!" he barked.

"Sir?"

"Your men will fire a volley over their heads. If they fail to fall back, aim low and shoot the men in front."

"Sir."

Chunks of wood and rocks bounced off the armored cars. The sudden blast of rifle fire made the Arabs in the back of the mob scatter, but the leaders still pushed towards the Jewish homes, trampling the bodies of the murdered boys.

Robbie aimed the Tommy gun at a heavily bearded man holding two swords whose white Thawb was streaked with blood. "Get out of here! *Yella, yella!* Hurry up."

The man continued to edge past the armored car.

"Leftenant Kettle! Fire at their feet!"

The officer shouted the command, and British rifles blazed. The leaders cringed, suddenly shouted, began to chant, and ran past the armored car—three or four dozen of them, the heavily bearded man in front. Robbie vaulted from his armored car and chased them as they swarmed a house. They broke the door and windows and seized two women by their hair.

Robbie struck several men with the stock of the Thompson submachine gun, knocking them to the pavement. The bearded man swiped at him with a sword, and Robbie rammed the barrel of the Tommy gun straight into his face, crushing his nose. He fired two rounds into another man's leg and another two into the shoulder of a man who was beating one of the women.

"Kettle! Arrest them! Every one of the devils you can lay your hands on. Knock them flat if they won't hold still for the manacles!"

"Sir!" The officer turned to his platoon. "Men, seize the Arabs directly in front of you. Stick your gun barrel in their guts if necessary. March each man off to the side and chain him up. If your man won't go with you voluntarily, give him a rifle butt to the head to wake him up. These are murderers, lads. No kid gloves now. He takes the chains or you flatten him. D'ya hear me?"

As the soldiers sprang forward, the Arabs fled. Several of the privates made rugby tackles and brought their men down. Others chased rioters into back alleys and along empty streets where families cowered behind locked doors. Robbie kicked the bearded man in the ribs as he tried to get up and brandished one of his swords. Robbie placed his boot on the back of the Arab's head and pressed down with his body weight to keep the man in place. He glanced at the two women who had been assaulted.

"Go to a neighbor's house," he ordered. "Bar the door. If you have any weapons, don't hesitate to use them."

"We have nothing," one of them said.

"You have axes to chop wood, don't you? Knives to slice bread and meat? Use those if you must."

"Are—are you going to leave us alone, sir?"

"No. A section of my men will stay to guard this street—ten or twelve men. You won't be left unprotected. I have to go to other neighborhoods to see what is happening. There is rioting everywhere. Where are your men?"

One woman's face looked as white as snow and ice. "Dead," she responded. "They were killed at the synagogue."

Robbie tugged a knife from his boot and tossed it to the woman, sheath and all. "Keep that by your side. If you have to protect yourself and your children, remember Deborah and remember Jael. Bear in mind how Jael slew Sisera, the enemy general, by driving a tent stake through his head. If you have to do the same, do it. A child's life is worth a thousand of these murderers' lives."

"*Toda raba.* Thank you."

"How old are you?"

"Eighteen."

"That's young to be married."

She shrugged. "Not among us. In any case, I am one of the daughters—not a wife."

"I see. Do not lose the knife."

"I will not."

"What is your name?"

"Michal."

"Like the wife of King David."

She offered him a fragment of a smile. "One of them."

"A fiery one, if I recall."

"With good reason, sir."

"Yes. Well, put that spirit to use if men try to slay you and your household." He pointed at the knife. "I shall be back for it."

"I will keep it in my hand until you return."

"That's an excellent place."

Robbie bent down and dragged the bearded man to his feet. The Arab growled through fingers dark with his own blood as he held his nose. Robbie manacled him and then shoved him roughly towards the armored car. Looking back over his shoulder at Michal, he said, "I will not cease to pray for you...and your people."

She bowed her head briefly in thanks.

Dover Sky

Lord Preston paced his study while Edward and Kipp watched. "A week of killing, rapes, mutilations, and desecrations. Hundreds of people killed, and hundreds of arrests. Still no word from Robbie! The prime minister assures me there have been no reports of British fatalities. I thank God for that, but what of the others? Mostly women and children—unarmed, defenseless, posing no more threat to the Arabs than a cloud in the sky. Attacks totally unprovoked as far as the reports Mr. MacDonald has read. The viciousness utterly without cause except hatred. Exceptional hate—where does it come from? How does it live in people's breasts, in people who were made in the image of God, the people who were sons of Ishmael?"

Kipp and Edward kept their eyes on him but didn't reply. They noticed their father's face was haggard and gray, his white hair uncombed.

Lord Preston paused in his pacing to look at a painting of Jesus in the Garden of Gethsemane. "Well, the worst is over I'm told. The prime minister assured me he would ring us with information on Robbie the moment he hears anything. So we shall wait on that and trust God." He looked at his sons. "What would I tell the families of the murdered if I were there? What would I say to them of the ways of the world and the ways of God? How might I possibly bring them a morsel of comfort? What words could someone use that could make any difference at all?"

Safed, Palestine

The colonel slipped into the back of the car next to Robbie. He tugged off his leather gloves and stared straight ahead. "How long have you been sitting here, Danforth?" he asked.

"Ten minutes, sir."

"Saw all you could stomach of Safed and Hebron?"

"Yes, sir."

"Yet you were in Ireland, weren't you?"

"Even at its worst, Ireland was never like this, sir. There I didn't walk into houses and find twenty or thirty men, women, and children murdered in cold blood. I didn't find young girls raped and tortured and stabbed to death. I didn't walk into orphanages and see the horrors I saw here in Safed."

"No. I expect not." He sighed with a low groan. "At least some Arabs hid Jewish neighbors in their homes."

"Yes, sir. I take some measure of hope for the future in that."

"Do you? I wish I could be as sanguine as you."

Robbie shook his head. "I don't feel sanguine, sir. It's one straw to grasp on to, that's all. Not much."

"What does your crystal ball tell you?"

"My crystal ball? I wish I could say I see one nation of Arab Christians and Arab Muslims living side by side with religious Jews and socialist Jews, forming a kind of coalition government just as we would do back in Britain, sir. But massacres like these—pogroms, really—just ensure the Zionists will argue other Jews into the desire to establish a totally Jewish state. Muslims will hate them for it, so the fighting will carry on regardless of the peace that moderates and well-wishers dream of."

"Why not form two separate nations, Danforth?"

"That would be like Ireland and England, sir. Never the best of friends."

"Well, I shall continue to hope for some sort of miracle." He glanced at Robbie. "You're right. You are not as sanguine as you first appear." He patted the back of the seat in front of him. "Corporal. Let's leave this place and get back to Jerusalem."

The driver started the engine of the car. "Very good, sir." The vehicle stirred up dust as it headed off. Army lorries full of troops and police followed them.

"Nevertheless, I should like your full report on my desk in two days, Danforth. Sanguine or not."

"I will have it for you, Colonel."

MUM AND DAD

WE ARE ALL RIGHT HERE. SHANNON AND THE BABY ARE DOING FINE. I WAS NOT INJURED DURING THE RIOTING. WILL WRITE A LETTER IN A FORTNIGHT. AS YOU CAN IMAGINE THINGS ARE PRETTY HECTIC HERE IN THE AFTERMATH. PRAY FOR THE PEACE OF JERUSALEM.

OUR LOVE

ROBBIE SHANNON AND PATRICIA CLAIRE

Jerusalem

In summary:

As far as we can ascertain, between the dates of August 23rd and August 29th, 133 Jews were killed and some 300 injured. During the same period, 115 or 116 Arabs were killed and more than 230 injured.

The Jews were killed and wounded by Arab rioters for the most part, though there is evidence some were victims of British gunfire. The majority of Arabs were killed and wounded by soldiers of the British Army and officers of the British Palestine Police Force who were trying to halt the massacres. A small number of Arabs were killed by Jews defending themselves or retaliating for Arab assaults. In the worst case, an Imam and six others were slain. For the most part, Jews neither attacked rioters nor defended themselves.

Casualties occurred in Jerusalem, Hebron, Safed, Motza, Kfar Uria, and Tel Aviv.

124 Arabs have been charged with murder, 50 with attempted murder, 250 with arson and looting, and almost 300 with less serious offences.

70 Jews have been charged with murder, 40 with attempted murder, 31 with arson and looting, and 21 with less serious offences.

Jews and Arabs—Arab Muslims in particular—have become more firmly entrenched in their positions as a result of the riots. Jewish proponents of an all-Jewish nation now dominate the political landscape. By the same token, Muslims who desire an all-Arab or even all-Muslim Palestine under sharia law hold sway among their population.

Recommendations:

The British military garrison must be reinforced in 1930. One hundred soldiers is not a sufficient complement to deal with the tensions in this region.

Talks between Jewish and Arab leaders must continue, mediated by British officials.

The British military and police in Palestine and the British Government in Westminster must brace themselves for increased hostilities between Arabs and Jews over the next decade. Nothing will appease Zionists except a fully Jewish state. Nothing will appease Muslims except a fully Muslim Palestine.

The Grand Mufti bears watching. He could have quelled the rioting before it began, but it appeared to me he was whipping the Arabs into a frenzy against the Jews at the Dome of the Rock. He does not have the best interests of Great Britain at heart and certainly not the best interests of those among us who desire an amicable solution to the Jewish–Arab problem.

"*Shalom, Michal.*"

"*Shalom...*major."

"You may call me by my Christian name please, Michal. I'm Robert, but you can use Robbie if you wish."

She stood in the doorway and smiled, her eyes and hair dark. "I prefer Robert." She handed the knife in its sheath to him. "You have come for this."

Robbie took the knife. "This and to see how you are."

"Frightened like the other Jews here. Hoping it will not happen again, but knowing it will. Trusting the British will protect us, and realizing we must also protect ourselves."

He pulled the knife from its sheath. "You used it?"

She dropped her eyes. "I tried to clean it well."

"What happened?"

"That night a man came through the back window. Your soldiers didn't see him. He put a hand over my mouth and tried to force himself on me. I put the knife into his back. His finger jerked the trigger on his pistol several times. Your men rushed through the door, knocking it down. They saw what had happened. A corporal ordered the man's body be carried away and placed in the street far from my house."

"He didn't report the incident."

She kept her eyes on the ground. "He said I acted in self-defense, and he did not want me charged with murder."

"You would have been exonerated."

"The corporal wasn't sure."

Robbie looked at her a few moments. "So in the end you were like Jael."

"In the end I was a frightened Jewish woman grabbing whatever came first to her hand."

He tossed the knife in his palm and then slipped it into its brown leather sheath. He handed it back to her. "Good Sheffield steel, that. You'd better hang on to it. You might need it again."

"I hope not."

"Hope but be prepared to defend yourself against those who have different hopes."

She lifted her eyes to his and took the knife. "Thank you, major."

"Robert."

"Yes, Robert. *Toda raba.*"

Robbie touched his fingers to his officer's hat. "Perhaps I will see you again, Michal."

"Perhaps."

She watched him climb into his armored car. He remained standing in the hatch as it drove away. She followed him with her eyes as the vehicle negotiated the street between vendors selling kosher meat, vegetables, and baked sweets. It slowed down, sped up, slowed down, sped up according to traffic. He looked back once and they saw each other.

16

"Now Hitler has what he wanted—economic chaos!"

"Please calm down, Albrecht."

"Calm down? Let me explain the situation." After moving a stack of books, Albrecht sat next to Catherine on the couch in his study. "So long as our economy was doing well, Hitler had no real power to attract the German people. I was alarmed by the number of his storm-troopers and the fact that Nazi Party membership kept growing, but I was comforted that he wasn't drawing in the majority of the population. Germany was at work, and our money was good. However, a great part of this was due to massive loans from the United States that helped us get back on our feet. The money was used to subsidize various employment schemes and businesses and to shore up our currency, not to mention shore up the government."

He paused to remove his reading glasses and run a hand through his hair.

Catherine waited.

"Now with the stock market crash in America in October, everything has changed drastically. Fortunes have been lost, wealth has vanished overnight, millionaires are throwing themselves out of windows in New York City because they are suddenly penniless. And because they are paupers, America is in danger of becoming a pauper too. So with this financial crisis, America is already making sounds we don't want to hear in Germany—that they are short on cash, that they need to deal with the economic disaster in their own country, that they need to recall their international loans. Yes, every single loan. They are going to take them back."

"Has this actually happened yet?"

"My sources tell me the tremors are certainly being felt in Berlin. It's not noticeable to you or me at this point, but employment is being affected and the Deutschmark is losing ground rapidly. It will be quite obvious in 1930. In any case, the workingman who has lost his job or had his wages cut already sees it. The financiers and capitalists who are taking it on the chin see it. And what do you think they are saying on the street, in the beer halls, in the private clubs, in the business meetings? That if Hitler was smart enough to predict this economic collapse in 1928, then maybe he is smart enough to fix it in 1929 and 1930."

Catherine felt an uncomfortable coldness in her body, and she clasped her hands together. "I see."

Albrecht gazed out the study window at the slow spinning fall of snowflakes. "Hitler is already making more speeches, already saying democracy doesn't work—certainly not for Germany. That the Fatherland has always done well with a strong man at the helm, like Charlemagne or Bismarck...like himself. He and his henchmen are trying to manipulate the situation and have him appointed chancellor over the nation. So far he hasn't succeeded in budging von Hindenburg on the matter. The day may come when our elderly statesman and president has no choice but to bow to Hitler's demands. If the economic situation worsens and the Nazi Party continues to grow, and if Hitler wins more seats in the *Reichstag*, well, von Hindenburg will be backed into a corner."

"Your views do not cheer the soul, Albrecht. I hope you exaggerate the threat facing Germany."

"If it faces Germany, it faces Europe as well." Albrecht squeezed her shoulder. "I shall be late for dinner. Do not wait for me. The Brotherhood of the Oak are meeting in half an hour in a small room in a museum."

"The Brotherhood? You have not met for years."

He stood up and took his suit coat off the back of a chair. "That tells you others share my rosy outlook."

"That suit coat is badly wrinkled. Let me iron it for you."

"No time. It is just men with cigars and pipes and fear in their eyes, Catherine. Believe me, they will not be looking at my coat and its wrinkles."

"No? Exactly what do these men look for from you?"

"Fight." He wrapped his red scarf about his neck. "They look for the German fighting spirit. Hitler and his brownshirts, with their swastikas and their fists, have it. The Brotherhood look for it in those who have a different vision for Germany and a totally different heart. And they hope to God they can find it."

Dover Sky

Lord Preston jingled coins in his pants pocket as he held the phone to his ear and patiently repeated his words. "No, Longbottom. No shipyard worker in Liverpool or Belfast will be asked to pick up and go home, ending his employment with us."

"But, my lord, the economic crisis in America has touched us all. You are losing profits. If you wish to ensure a fairly high cash flow despite international circumstances, you must trim expenditures."

"Out of the question. The pound has already lost buying power for my workers."

"And for you."

"Nevertheless, we shall weather the storm without putting anyone out of work. The most I will agree to is a ten percent wage cut across the board for office workers as well as those on the docks. They must be told this is to ensure Danforth Shipyards and Shipping continues to stay in business so they can keep their jobs. We've taken the same steps at the textile mills in Preston. Baxter and I tried to ease the sting of this by initiating the provision of hot lunches for employees. This will keep more food on the table at home. I should like you to set up the same sort of thing in Liverpool and Belfast."

"Such an arrangement cannot be brought about cheaply, my lord."

"I know that."

"Some will see it as charity and refuse it."

Lord Preston jingled the loose change in his pocket again. "I can do nothing about that, Longbottom. They will have to look to themselves and to God as far as that is concerned. The hot meals will be available for all employees of Danforth Shipyards and Shipping if the workers wish to enjoy them and bring some relief to their economic hardships. Have you seen what the price for a loaf of bread is now? Heaven knows the farmer and the miller feel the pinch as well as the grocer, but still it is outrageous. My people in my companies must keep their wages at home and take care of their sons and daughters."

"Very good, my lord. I see your mind is set."

"It is indeed." Lord Preston smiled as he watched Caroline walk past the parlor door with a baby wrapped in white blankets in her arms. His voice changed completely. "Ah, Longbottom, if only you were down Dover way this weekend. My son Kipp—you remember Kipp the pilot—Kipp and his lovely wife, Lord and Lady Scarborough's daughter Caroline, have had themselves a child—a girl as beautiful as a sunrise, I swear it. Well, you know how we grandfathers are. I shall send a photograph up to you."

"Pray convey my best wishes, my lord. That is marvelous news. May I ask after your granddaughter's name?"

"Cecilia. Cecila Printemp. A bit of poetry in that, eh?"

"It's wonderful, my lord. Isn't 'printemp' French for spring?"

"It is. There is a story behind that. My son's first wife, Christelle, was from France, you will recall…"

"Of course."

"Well, she was great friends with Caroline. Before her death, she asked if my son and Caroline might not marry and create a family. It took a while, but that is precisely what came about, and it has turned out splendidly."

"Ah."

"Cecilia has the fairest hair and the bluest eyes I've ever seen, Longbottom. The black-and-white photographs don't do her justice, really not, I say. Someone should go about looking into manufacturing color film."

"I believe there are projects afoot, my lord, even in these hard times, in Europe and in the United States. Should I look into an investment on your behalf?"

"Do that, yes! Do that. It may be shares can be had at a reasonable price at this time in the development. Certainly color photography is something I would like a hand in bringing to the world. Even if it is only to help grandfathers show off the God-given beauty of their grandchildren."

"Not a small thing, surely."

"Indeed not! Most certainly not."

My dearest Catherine,

Your father and I congratulate you and Albrecht on your announcement. A child is due to arrive! What a fine way to cheer up a dreary February of rain and clouds. How God has blessed us with grandchildren of late—Patricia Claire to Robbie and Shannon in Jerusalem in September in '28, Colm Alexander to Edward and Charlotte in January of '29, beautiful Cecilia to Kipp and Caroline just this past October, and now you tell us we are to have yet another grandchild in August 1930! A grand way to start the decade off.

I haven't been to Germany since that tour of the Rhine several summers ago when you and Albrecht wed at Hartmann Castle much to everyone's surprise and delight. It is time for another visit, especially now that you are with child. I shall certainly not wait until August. I want to see you as soon as possible. It has been far too long. Naturally I look forward to seeing Sean Albert. He's seven years old this Easter, imagine that! And I look forward to seeing dear Libby as well. It really has been ages.

Father cannot come. He and Edward are both on the Opposition benches now and challenging the Labor government for every inch of ground. Lord Buchanan baits them without mercy. What a to-do whenever Edward and that man lock horns. How long the present situation shall last is anyone's guess, but for now the two Danforths are sequestered at Westminster and sharing their flat in London. It does make me smile to think of that—as if they were a pair of bachelors.

I shall arrive at Tubingen by rail just before Easter then. Skitt will accompany me. Yes, Skitt. Old Harrison can play the butler and see to Dover Sky's needs. A maid from Ashton Park will come too. Do you remember Margaret? I hope I shall not put you out too much, but it is past time I saw the Teutonic side of the family (as your father calls you all).

God bless. I am counting the days.

Mum

Tubingen, Germany

"Ah! There you all are!" Lady Preston smiled as brightly as she could as she took first Catherine and then Libby into her arms on the platform at the train station. "My girls! How I have missed you!"

"And we you, Mother," said Catherine, hugging her back.

"You are coming along quite nicely, I see," Elizabeth said, looking at Catherine's bulging abdomen.

Catherine rubbed her hand over her stomach. "I am. Plenty of kicks too."

"Wonderful."

"Hullo, Skitt," said Catherine. "It's been a few years, hasn't it?"

He bowed his head as he held Lady Preston's luggage. "You look well, m'lady."

"Thank you. Do you remember Jane's maid, Montgomery?"

A short slender woman with flashing black eyes dressed in a long, dark coat smiled at him. "Hullo, Skitt. How have things been at Dover Sky?"

"Never a dull moment, Lucy."

"Please. No one uses that name. I like it when people call me Montgomery. I think it sounds very distinguished."

"Montgomery it is then. This is Margaret, maid to Lady Preston."

Montgomery extended her hand to the orange-haired young woman. "How do you do, Margaret?"

Margaret took the hand. "Very well, thanks, Miss Montgomery. It's a pleasure to meet you."

Lady Preston spotted Sean standing back a ways looking a bit awkward in his dark suit and tie. "Sean Albert Hartmann! How handsome you are! Come, give your grandmother from England a hug and a kiss, my dear!" Sean smiled and came forward, dutifully putting his arms around Lady Preston.

"*Willkommen,*" he greeted.

"Why, thank you. *Danke schön,* isn't it?" She hugged him again. "You are getting so tall. What are they feeding you?"

"Schnitzel." He grinned. "And beer."

"Beer? I should hope not!" She looked over his shoulder at two tall girls. "And who do we have here?"

Jane stepped up and kissed Lady Preston on the cheek. "Hullo, Grandmother. It's so nice to see you again. I hope your journey was pleasant."

"Thank you." Lady Preston put a hand on each of Jane's shoulders and pecked her on the cheek. "Except for the waves in the Channel, everything was splendid. Who is this beautiful girl with you?"

"Grandmother Elizabeth, this is my very good friend, Eva."

"Eva. Such a lovely name."

"She is Baron von Isenburg's daughter, Grandmother."

"The baron's? Of course! Eva, your father is an old and dear friend of the family. Come, let me give you a hug." Eva dutifully let the older woman put her arms around her. Lady Preston held the girl at arm's length after the hug and gazed at her. "Eva von Isenburg. How tall and straight you are—as straight as your father. And how becoming your blonde hair and blue eyes are."

"Thank you."

"I must take you shopping. There are so many things I should like to buy the daughter of Baron von Isenburg." She glanced at Jane. "And you too. I must take the pair of you Easter shopping tomorrow or the day after. What do you say to that?"

Jane smiled. "I'd like that, Grandmother Elizabeth."

Eva nodded. "Jane and I know the best shops, Lady Preston. It would be a delight."

"Oh no, no Lady Preston, Eva. Grandmother Elizabeth will do for you as well. All right?"

Eva bowed her head. Even under the dark tone of her skin everyone could see the blush spreading over her face. "As you wish. It is an honor."

"I'm sorry, Libby."

"For what?"

"She doesn't mean anything by it. Mum is just set in her ways."

"Is that what it is? Suppose she had snubbed Sean like that? Would you still be so forgiving?"

Catherine sighed and placed her hands on Libby's shoulders from behind. "Perhaps not."

Libby bit on her thumbnail and looked down through the window in her bedroom to the street rippling with cars and trucks and wagons. "Oh, Eva, how beautiful you are! Oh, Eva, how tall and straight you are! Oh, Eva, how I'd love to take you Easter shopping. Oh, Eva, you must call me Grandmother Elizabeth."

"I know."

"The old bat."

"Hush."

"I wish she would turn around and go back to England. I'd pay for the cab to the train station out of my own pocket."

"I think she's settling in for several weeks, Lib. She loves being with the baron."

"And with your husband, the German prince."

"Shh."

"And with your son, and with the baron's daughter, and even with Montgomery, Jane's maid, for heaven's sake. But Jane? Ah, well…Jane, you can come shopping with Eva and I…if you wish, Jane."

"Bear up as best you can. Everyone else treats Jane like gold. The baron is everything Mum is not when it comes to your daughter. He's with Jane constantly. Mum is in and out of our lives like the wind from the Channel."

"Jane feels the rejection keenly."

"I know she does, and I'm sorry. But Mum's only a small part of our family tree. Just a branch, really."

Libby continued to bite at her thumbnail. "Just a grandmother."

"Perhaps we should have Mr. and Mrs. Woodhaven over here. Extend an invitation."

Libby shrugged. "They're wonderful people, but they can't hop over to Germany on a ship in half a day like Mum can. They'd visit once, have their long ocean voyage, and disappear again for a few years. Jane is thirteen this June, Catherine. She needs a grandmother now. A real one."

Catherine rubbed her sister's back. "Perhaps the baron can have a talk with Mum."

"He wrote her once about Jane. She claimed she treated all her grandchildren the same and adored Jane. She told him I had the problem, not her."

"I see. Well, I'll pray with you, if that helps."

"Certainly, it helps. For a few minutes. Then it's back to the real world."

"Lib—"

"Honestly, Catherine, I have prayed up and down and all around. Mum's still the same year after year. She considers Eva von Isenburg more family than her own granddaughter. She bent over backwards on the marriages of her children and even felt she bent too far. Now she refuses to bend an inch regarding a granddaughter just because she has Oriental blood in her veins. And that is that. Not even God can budge her. I've done everything but wear a hair shirt and lie on a bed of nails to get His help. If you want to pray with me, go ahead, but it's not going to change anything. I'm stuck with Lady High-and-Mighty Preston as a grandmother for my child."

Libby suddenly turned to face her sister, tears coursing down her cheeks, her blue eyes shot through with fire. "And if I want to marry Commander Terrence Fordyce, I'm going to marry him. If you don't like it you can lump it. I'm tired of going through all this turmoil alone."

Lady Preston stepped out of the hat boutique and linked an arm through Eva's. "The yellow hat with the small blue flowers was absolutely perfect for you. It brings out the colors in your eyes and your hair."

"Thank you, Grandmother Elizabeth. It is, yes, a lovely hat but so expensive. You are spending too much on me."

"Nonsense. It's Easter. We celebrate Jesus Christ's resurrection." She glanced at Jane, who was walking by her side but a few steps back as they headed down the crowded sidewalk. "Don't you agree, Jane?"

"Certainly, Grandmother."

"You mustn't fret. We've found the right dresses for Eva and the perfect hat, and we will soon do the same for you."

"It's all right. I just like being with you and Eva."

"Trust me, Jane. The right dress is in a window somewhere. If not today then tomorrow."

"Oh!" Eva tugged Lady Preston towards the shops. "Now we are seeing these young men in Tubingen. Give them plenty of room, Grandmother, please. They are always spoiling for a fight."

"Who do you mean, dear?"

"The men with the brown shirts and armbands. Don't stare at them. Just look in the shop windows." Eva looked at Jane. "Get out of their path, Jane. Come and look at this toy train running through the Alps. Hurry!"

But the six young men were already upon them, taking up half the sidewalk as they strode through the crowds. People stepped into the street to avoid them. One brownshirt spotted Jane as she moved away.

"Look at this!" he called to his friends. "Can you believe it? One of these creatures is on our sidewalk!"

The other five men glared at Jane.

"A China dog is not fit to stand where we stand!"

"What are you doing desecrating German soil, China dog?"

"Get out of our country! Germany is for Germans only!"

"*Ja, ja,* Germany is for purebloods only! No filth bloods, no mongrel bloods!"

One of the men grabbed Jane by the arm and swung her into a lamppost. There was a loud crack as Jane hit her head. She cried out, and the same young man punched her in the stomach. "Shut up, China dog!"

Another brownshirt seized Jane's long, dark hair and pulled until in her pain she struck out at him. She screamed, and he laughed and jerked so hard blood sprang out along her hairline.

"What are you doing! What are you doing!" Lady Preston ran towards Jane and the six men, pushing them aside and slapping at their arms. "Let her go! Do you hear me? Let her go!"

They laughed and shoved Lady Preston back against the building.

One of them sneered at Eva. "Hey, little beauty, tell your mother to stay out of this or we'll use her skull for an ashtray."

Eva's eyes were dark-blue slits. "You really are pigs."

His face darkened. "Be careful or we will smack you into a wall and ruin your pretty face."

Lady Preston struck out at them with her hands and shopping bags. "Get away from Jane! Leave her alone!"

The one with his fingers twisted in Jane's hair gave her another sharp yank and Jane fell to her knees.

"Please stop! Please stop," Jane cried through her sobs.

"Police!" Lady Preston threw herself at the one who had Jane by the hair. She pummeled him with her fists, not caring when the shopping bags ripped open and the contents spilled onto the cement. "Someone help! Help!"

The young man shoved her so hard she fell. "Get out of here, you mad woman! No one is going to help you! No one helps a China dog!" He kicked Jane in the ribs. "All we do with China dogs is kill them!"

"No vermin allowed in our cities!" another one yelled.

"Purify Germany!"

Lady Preston didn't understand German, but when two other men in brown shirts and swastika armbands joined the first six and began kicking Jane, she hurled herself over Jane's body so that the toes of the black boots cracked into her sides. "Help us! Help us!" she cried in English. "Someone help us!"

None of the bystanders made a move to help. Most just walked on, heads down. Some hung back, faces set like stone as they watched. When Eva realized no one in the crowd was going to act, she ran at the eight Nazi youth, shrieking curses in German, pounding them with her fists, and tearing at their faces with her fingernails. Blood streaked their cheeks and foreheads. Flying into a rage, they slapped her as hard as they could, threw her to the sidewalk next to Lady Preston and Jane, and kicked all three women as savagely as possible.

Lady Preston wrapped her arms tightly over Jane's head as the blows rained down. "My baby, my poor baby! Oh Jesus, help us! Help us, Jesus!" She reached out a hand to Eva. "Come here, girl. Come here, my poor girl! God, help us! God, God, please help us!"

Suddenly police whistles blew and officers charged the eight Nazis. Fists smacked into heads and police clubs crunched against legs and arms. Bystanders finally jumped in and beat the Nazis with their walking sticks, umbrellas, and rolled-up newspapers. The brownshirts fled, holding their arms and putting hands to the cuts on their faces, shaking their fists and vowing revenge as they ran down the street and into an alley.

Lady Preston was weeping. "Jane, my dear. Oh, my poor child. There is so much blood. Say something to me—anything. Please open your mouth and talk. Eva, look at me. Are you going to be all right? Oh God, help us!" Lady Preston focused on the Germans standing around them. "Please help us! We need a doctor and a nurse. These are my granddaughters, and I need help getting them to a hospital. Please have pity and help us."

Albrecht and the baron stood stone-faced and stiff as they waited for the doctor to open the door and come out of the hospital room where Lady Preston, Jane, and Eva had been taken. Catherine and Libby were in the room with the patients, doctor, and nurses. The sound of a grandfather clock in the waiting room was loud. Montgomery sat on a couch against the wall. She was leaning forward, and dried streaks of tears crisscrossed her handsome face. Margaret sat next to her staring into space. Skitt stood beside the couch, his face a thundercloud. Sean sat several feet away in a chair. He stared straight ahead, barely taking in the framed picture of the Black Forest.

Finally Libby and Catherine came out of the examination room, followed by the doctor—a young man with coal-black hair and a small, coal-black moustache.

"Baron von Isenburg, the staff at the hospital cared for the women very well. I only needed to adjust a few of the bandages." The doctor nodded at Skitt and Montgomery. "I would like to speak with the family privately in my office. Will you two sit with the women and keep an eye on things? All three are heavily sedated and shouldn't wake till morning."

Montgomery shot to her feet. "Of course, doctor."

"If you spot any fresh bleeding, call a nurse right away."

"We will," promised Skitt.

The doctor led the others downstairs, Sean trailing the procession, his face the color of ashes. The doctor ushered everyone into his office. Once they were seated by the fireplace, the doctor paced and told them what the physicians at the hospital had already told them. All three had cracked ribs. In Lady Preston's case, the injuries were more serious due to her age. Time and rest would heal their wounds. Jane had unfortunately lost some of her hair because it had been pulled out by the roots.

"As for the wounds inside…time and prayer and the love of family must help with that. I caution that you will have to be patient.

MURRAY PURA

Recovery could take a long time. Please avoid any of these Nazi brutes in the future even if you must cross the street. Don't go near any of their street rallies, not out of curiosity, not out of anger, not for any reason whatsoever. These brownshirts will not go away any time soon. If you must take young Jane out in public, consider having her wear a veil. You might consider getting her out of Germany. Another such attack would be extremely destructive to her spirit. Today the police and a handful of people helped out. Another day no one may help." He stared at the baron and at Albrecht. "Such is Germany in 1930."

Early the next morning, Catherine and Libby arrived to sit with the patients. They sent Skitt and Montgomery away to rest. The two sisters sat side by side facing the beds. The curtains were drawn, but a thin slit let a few rays of pale white light into the room. The beds were close together, and sometime during the night Lady Preston and Jane had linked hands. Both were sound asleep but their grip held.

Libby wiped her eyes with the back of her hand. Catherine squeezed her arm. "They will get better," Catherine whispered. "In a few weeks they'll be up and about and getting on with their lives. You'll see."

"It's not that. I don't understand the ways of the world, and I'm like Father in that I certainly don't understand the ways of God. I never thought the Nazis would be the ones who brought Mother and Jane together."

July–November, 1930
Hartmann Castle, the Rhine River, Germany

Dear Cornelia, my diary,

We are at Hartmann Castle on the Rhine. We left Germany for Switzerland as soon as Mum and the girls were on their feet. We stayed in Pura through May and June and then came here.

Mum is still with us, along with Skitt and Margaret, Jane's maid Montgomery, Eva and the baron, my Sean and my Albrecht. Mum wants Jane and Eva to go to England to live. This is being debated right now, though no longer with Libby present. She's at Dover Sky visiting with Terry under the watchful eyes of Holly and Harrison and Caroline and Kipp.

First things first. Mum and Jane and Eva are all right—but not really all right. Their bodies are healed for the most part and their spirits seem strong. But Mum will not return to Tubingen, and Jane is hesitant about going back as well. It's impossible to keep the German news from them. We may be on the Rhine, but we are not on the moon. We are all aware that the economy remains in rough shape and that Herr Hitler and the Nazis are taking full advantage of the bleak situation. Just the other day two boats drifted past heading south, hours apart, each with large red-and-black swastika flags flying from their sterns. Any thought that the Nazis are a passing phase is dashed. Clearly some Germans are looking to them to bring the country into a golden age of prosperity and success.

The great blessing has been how Mum and Jane have come together because of the attack by the brownshirts. No more talk of Jane being adopted or not being of English blood and all that rot. Mum says she is a Danforth through and through. Jane cries when she talks about how Mum fought to protect her, putting her body over Jane's and absorbing the blows. The two are inseparable now. It does the heart good to see. You can imagine the happiness this has brought Libby.

So now my feelings about Libby and Terry. I can truthfully say the street incident with Mum and the girls and the Nazis shook me awake. If God means Terry to be part of the family, who am I to stand in His way or, indeed, in the way of my sister's happiness? Jane could have been beaten to death, and Libby would have been left with no one. Any lingering feelings I may or may not have for Terry Fordyce simply have to be locked in a steamer trunk and stored away in the attic. My sister comes first. If she marries my navy man, God bless her, and may she have a new start on a life that is filled with love and miracles. In any case, they wouldn't be making their home in Germany—not with Terry being an officer on the *Hood*. So I shan't see him unless I go to the wedding. I find I am quite strong enough to do that now—if they get to that place—and I look forward to it. No wedding has been announced—not even an engagement—but if I were betting on the horses, I would be betting on Libby and Terry.

Finally I must mention my pregnancy. It is much easier than Sean's was, but I don't think that necessarily means it's a girl. I crave strudel, so whoever is coming into the world has a very strong sweet tooth. I intend to give birth in this lovely old castle, which has Albrecht on needles and pins. He has a doctor and midwife standing by. And, as I reminded my German prince, it is not so many years ago that most babies were born in the home, not in hospitals. We'll be fine. These castles represent some of the best of the German spirit, and I want a child crying its first cry and taking its first breath in one of them. That is my fairy tale.

Jerusalem

"How is your Arabic coming along?" the man asked.

Robbie poured his friend some sweet strong coffee. The windows in his office were shuttered against the bright Jerusalem sun. "*Jayed.*"

"Glad to hear it." The slender man in the white Thawb and keffiyeh lifted the small cup of coffee to his mouth. "You have made it exactly the way I like it, major. Just the right amount of sweet; just the right amount of bitter."

"It sounds like you're talking about Palestine, Azad."

The Arab laughed. "I suppose I am." He set the cup down. "Did you attend the hangings on the seventeenth of June?"

"Yes."

"Did the three men die well?"

"They died, Azad."

"Only Arabs were executed."

"Many other Arabs and Jews received life sentences. The three who were hung were convicted of multiple murders and mutilations."

Azad picked up his cup again and sipped. "It won't matter. The Palestine Arab Congress will twist it to suit themselves. So will the Zionists."

Robbie drank from his own small cup of coffee. "Let's talk about your writing. What sort of novel are you working on?"

"Two friends in Jerusalem. One Jewish, the other from an Arab family that has moved into the city from a village. The story is tragic."

"I'm just working my way through your first novel with an Arabic–English dictionary by my side. There is a good deal of *joy* in that book."

"I wrote it fifteen years ago, Robert."

"I've read portions of it to my wife. You know how the Irish are about literature. They believe they created it. She quite likes your prose, even in my rough and ready English translation."

Azad bowed his head briefly. "Convey my thanks."

"We must have you over for dinner."

"I should like that. Please, let us do it sooner rather than later."

"Why? Is something about to happen?"

"Something is always about to happen, Robert. My fear is that eventually too many things will happen. The British will leave, Jews and Arabs will be at each others' throats, and we will have half a dozen countries in this region at war with each other. Arab Christians in one place; Arab Muslims in another; Orthodox Jews in Safed and Jerusalem; Jews who no longer believe in God in Tel Aviv and Haifa."

Robbie leaned over the table between them and poured more coffee into Azad's cup. "Where will you be?"

"England. Where else does a nonpracticing Muslim run to?" He wrapped both hands around his small cup of fresh coffee. "But the believers will come there too eventually and find me. So then I will flee to America or Canada."

"I suppose if we miss the dinner date here we can always make arrangements at my family's estate at Ashton Park."

Azad smiled. "If there is a great deal of green, I will come."

"Lancashire is as green as a *keffiyeh* full of emeralds."

"Count on me then." Azad drank from his cup. "You opened fire on Arabs during the riots. You testified against a number of them at their trials."

"Azad—"

He held up one dark hand. "It is true you arrested several Jews as well. One was attempting to burn down a mosque. Your testimony put several Jews behind bars. They should have been hung for what they did."

"Several Arabs as well as Jews had their death sentences commuted to life imprisonment."

"I do not say this to incriminate you in any way. Those on both sides who still choose to see clearly understand you are fair and evenhanded.

But others only see what they do not like. You will be surprised to learn I don't come to warn you of what the Arabs might do but the Jews."

"What do you mean? No one has attacked British troops or officers. Not Jews, not Muslims."

Azad took a biscuit from the tray next to the coffee. "You spoke with members of the Hope Simpson Royal Commission this past year, didn't you?"

Robbie nodded. "I was ordered to cooperate. I spoke with the Members of Parliament who drafted the Shaw Report as well."

"Do you know Sir John Hope Simpson?"

"Yes. He's a friend of the family in England."

"I understand the report will be presented this fall. There are rumors about what is in it. The rumors have the Palestine Arab Congress singing praise to Allah and Jews gnashing their teeth. Hope Simpson will recommend Jewish immigration be restricted."

"The Shaw Report was made public in March. It said the same thing."

"So Hope Simpson will push the line that much harder."

Robbie was quiet a moment. "How reliable are your sources?"

"Very. The reason Hope Simpson will give is that there is not enough farmland to support the influx."

"Nonsense. The Jews have planted eucalyptus trees to drain swamps. They've irrigated desert no one wanted. They've taken the worst land Arabs have sold them and raised crops."

"I grew up in this region. Many Arabs living here now did not. They are immigrants just as a large number of the Jews are immigrants. From what I understand the report does not go into great detail about Arab immigration." Azad spread his hands. "Hope Simpson had to give some rationale. That is what he chose—insufficient arable land. If true, Zionists will never accept such a proposal. Should your prime minister, Ramsay MacDonald, implement it, British officers will be targeted. So I ask you to be careful, my friend. Vary your driving routes. See there is security keeping an eye on your home. Perhaps MacDonald's hold on power is too weak for him to act on the report. Or perhaps he will find the support he needs close at hand."

"Or perhaps your sources are inaccurate. Perhaps Hope Simpson will not recommend a hard line on Jewish immigration. Perhaps Westminster will pay no attention to either Shaw or him." Robbie smiled. "Or perhaps you exaggerate the threat to the British army and myself."

Azad sipped at his bittersweet coffee. "Perhaps."

Ashton Park

At the dinner table, Lord Preston was cutting into his mutton when Ben cleared his throat. The older man glanced up and cocked a white eyebrow as he chewed and swallowed. "Mmm? What's on your mind?"

"I was wondering if you were heading to Dover Sky for the summer, sir? Or are you remaining here at Ashton Park?"

"I will go down. But first I'm waiting to hear from Lady Preston on the birth of Catherine's child. Once I have that cable in my hand, I'm on my way to Germany and the Hartmann Castle on the Rhine. I have never seen it, and I very much want to take Catherine's son or daughter into my arms among those crenellations and merlons. I must say I am looking forward to a trip abroad."

"Will Elizabeth be returning with you?"

"She'd better be!" Lady Grace darted a glance at Ben. She held her soup spoon firmly. "She's been in that dreadful country since Easter and all because of a Chinese girl!"

"Thank you, Mother." Lord Preston wiped the corners of his mouth with a white napkin as Tavy hovered over him with a silver coffeepot. "The Chinese girl is our granddaughter, and Catherine is happily married to a German professor of theology."

"You're making all that up." Lady Grace's attention returned to her soup, eying it suspiciously. "Tavy, did you exchange my soup bowl for this one?"

"No, ma'arm."

"Because I had more soup than this."

"Shall I ladle a bit more into your bowl, Lady Grace?"

"No, thank you, Tavy. You will not. Having my own soup returned to me will be sufficient, if you please."

"Very good." Tavy brought a fresh bowl of soup curling with steam from his cart and placed it before her. He removed the bowl. "There you are, m'lady."

"Ah." She half-glared and half-smiled at him. "Now that wasn't so hard, was it?"

"What's that?" Sir Arthur looked up from his plate on the other side of the table.

"Someone took my soup. I have it back now. All's well."

"Grace, it's the same soup, year in, year out. What bowl it's in hardly matters."

"It matters a great deal who has been sipping at my soup. I want my own bowl, untouched, unspooned, thank you."

Sir Arthur sawed away with knife and fork. "The cook tests the soup by putting it to her lips. That's what you're eating, and you've been eating it since 1909."

Lord Preston laughed. "Ben, you're going to get lost in the shuffle. Speak up, my boy, before there's another incident with soup or dumplings or mutton."

"The mutton is fine." Lady Grace's voice was rimmed with frost. "I'll trouble you to mind your manners and keep to your own plate, William."

"Sir!" Ben blurted. "William, I have intentions of going into the ministry. I've talked it over with Victoria, and she's in agreement."

"Ministry? What?" Lord Preston put down his fork. "Ben Whitecross an Anglican priest like Jeremy here?"

"Not exactly Anglican—"

"Please, my boy, enough. I much prefer to hear 'father' from you."

"Yes, of course. It's just that this is something of an announcement I want to make."

"Not Anglican? What then? Baptist? Presbyterian?"

"Methodist, Father."

Both of Lord Preston's eyebrows shot upward. "Do you say so? You mean like John and Charles Wesley? Like circuit riders on the American frontier? Count von Zinzendorf and the Moravians?"

"Yes, sir."

"What's this about, eh?" Sir Arthur looked back and forth between Ben, William, and Jeremy, who was sitting at the table next to Emma. "Not another air race?"

"The Wesleyans, Sir Arthur," Jeremy said, still working on his soup. "Ben is thinking of being ordained with them after a period of training."

Sir Arthur narrowed his eyes at Jeremy from behind his glasses. "And what will you do, sir?"

"I?"

"Are you thinking of becoming a Wesleyan as well? Is this going to be a family thing?"

"Not at all. I'm content in the Church of England."

"'Amazing Grace' is a fine hymn, very fine."

"Yes, well, that's by John Newton, Sir Arthur, an Anglican."

"O for a Thousand Tongues to Sing; Love Divine, All Loves Excelling; Christ the Lord Is Risen Today."

"Quite right, Sir Arthur." Jeremy smiled and laid down his soup spoon.

Tavy whisked spoon and empty bowl away.

Jeremy continued. "We use those hymns by Charles Wesley all the time at our church in London."

Emma folded her hands under her chin. "I adore 'Hark! The Herald Angels Sing.' Charles Wesley wrote those words too."

Lord Preston nodded at Emma and then looked at Ben. "What about the airline, young man?"

"Kipp is buying me out for my share of the partnership. With Michael and I both gone from the picture, he'll become the head of the business. I expect he will hire more managers."

"But you've always loved flying."

"Part of the plan is that I will keep one of our old SPAD S.XXs. It's quite lovely to fly, Father."

Lord Preston smiled at the use of the term. "Thank you. And you feel a call to preach the gospel?"

"Yes, sir."

"You wish for a Methodist church or are you content to be a lay preacher?"

"I should like a church to pastor. Victoria shares with me a certain enthusiasm for missionary work in Africa, so perhaps we'll wind up there in due course."

"Africa? The Dark Continent?"

"There have been Methodist missionaries going there for generations."

Victoria put a hand on Ben's. "I was shocked when he first raised the subject with me, Father. But when I thought back, I did remember he used to talk about the Methodist Church before he left for the war. So it's been in his head and heart even before flying."

"Has it?" Lord Preston caught Ramsay's eye. "What does the eight-year-old think, hmm?"

Ramsay's somber face suddenly brightened with his smile. "I should like to see lions and gazelle and wildebeest, Grandfather William."

"Ha! And what about Timothy?"

The five-year-old with his mother's auburn hair and green eyes didn't smile at all. He looked at his grandfather with a serious face. "I should like to see giraffes and elephants and God in Africa."

Lord Preston chuckled. "And so you shall. Undoubtedly, so you shall." He turned back to Ben. "Sounds like the Lord's hand is on your entire family, Ben." He went back to his mutton. "Capital."

"Shall I reheat that in the oven, m'lord?" Tavy asked, now standing at William's shoulder. "Or bring you a fresh portion piping hot?"

"Hmm? Not at all. I don't mind cold mutton." He glanced up from his plate a moment. "Well, well, Jeremy, did Ben bring you up here to play the role of *HMS Rodney* to Ben's *HMS Hood*? Are you the big guns meant to ensure the First Sea Lord's opinion is properly swayed to support his endeavor?"

Jeremy sipped his water. "Ben and I have talked about this, naturally.

He sought out my advice as a clergyman. Ben is a fine man, but I wondered if he truly was, um, *cut out* to be a man of the cloth. Just like most in the family, I saw him as a dashing pilot and, after the accident, as a man who simply wouldn't quit. I ought to have expected God had his hand on Ben's life for him to come so far and surmount so many obstacles."

"So the two of you have discussed this?" asked Lord Preston.

"Yes."

"And prayed together?"

"Indeed we have."

"So you are in support of his desire to train as a Methodist minister? You see the Divine spark in him?"

"I do. I most certainly do. I am sure God is in this, Father."

Lord Preston pushed himself back from the table and walked around the table to Ben.

Ben slowly got to his feet.

Lord Preston wrapped his arms around the younger man. "My boy, I praise God. I am overjoyed! Elizabeth will be as filled with rejoicing as I am. Have you said anything to the servants here at Ashton Park? Anything at all to our good Baptist, Mrs. Longstaff?"

"No, sir."

"Well, that is something we must announce when they bring us our cobbler and ice cream, eh? But first let me offer up a prayer for you. This is a great thing—an extraordinary moment. We must go to God with it and thank Him. Don't you agree, Reverend Whitecross?"

"Why, of course, sir. But I'm no reverend yet. Far from it."

Lord Preston kept his arm around Ben's shoulders. "Man looks on the outward appearance, but God looks on the heart."

Hartmann Castle, the Rhine River, Germany

The mist rose up like a grey ship from the Rhine and moored itself over Hartmann Castle. Lord Preston walked around an inner courtyard with his new granddaughter in his arms, his daughter Catherine at his side in a cloak and hood. They spoke quietly with each other and laughed just as quietly. After half an hour, the sun had still not won out over the haze. While he conversed with his daughter, Lord Preston found his mind drifting away to Danforth Castle and the age of chivalry that had touched both England and Germany with a strong but gracious hand. He looked at the babe in his arms, then he kissed the sleeping child's forehead and murmured, "Angelika."

"Ah. There you two are."

Catherine put a finger to her lips as her husband approached. "Shh. She's sleeping."

He smiled and looked at the baby in Lord Preston's arms. "That's because she was up all night singing."

"Oh…" Catherine stifled a laugh. "Is that what you call her screeches?"

"I have heard far worse from choirs, believe me." He turned to Lord Preston. "Lord Preston, after much discussion, Jane and Eva have decided to weather the storm for now by returning to Tubingen. Next week Jane will meet with her tutor and Eva will return to school. It's true the Nazi presence is not great there, and they feel the incident at Easter was one that will not be repeated."

Lord Preston's features grew rigid. "I pray not."

"Libby will remain in Germany with her daughter. In addition, Lady Preston wishes to linger till the New Year, another month or so, if you have no objections. She is welcome to remain with us as long as she likes."

"Elizabeth must have found something wonderful in the German air, to want to stay that long. Well, I have Ben and Victoria and their children at Ashton Park, so I shall not get too lonely. I suppose you will have a grand celebration at Christmas, Albrecht?"

"With our new baby girl? Of course! You can count on us having an especially large tree in the great hall."

"You mean to enjoy the holiday here?"

"Yes. The area is magical, especially if we are blessed with a fall of snow."

"I should like to see that some year." Lord Preston gently handed the infant to Catherine. "What news of the election?"

Albrecht's face lost its new-father glow. "I just received the paper. With the stock market crash last year and the economic downturn, the Nazi Party and its goblins, including Goebbels and Himmler, have picked up momentum. I feared this. They have one hundred and seven seats now. A day ago they only had fourteen. This makes them the second largest party in Germany."

"I'm very sorry to hear it. You still think Jane will be safe?"

"I would not take her to Munich or Berlin. It's my hope that if financial conditions improve over the next twenty-four months we will see Herr Hitler and his cronies fade into oblivion once again."

"Hmm." Lord Preston gazed up at rooks that had flown into the courtyard and found several window ledges to perch on. "I hope you're right. The Labor government of Ramsay MacDonald will be forced to make unpopular cost-cutting measures this Parliament. And it seems clear from what I've read in the papers from New York and Toronto that the United States and Canada are heading into a serious depression."

Albrecht put his hands behind his back. "My sense of it is that the German people mistrust Hitler and his brownshirts. He may have won more seats this election, and he may be straining at the leash to gain the presidency or chancellorship of the nation, but he will not get either. People see what happens in the streets and at political rallies when his Nazis are present. They represent absolutely the worst side of the German character."

Lord Preston nodded and put a hand on his son-in-law's shoulder. "Nor can Britain ever let down its guard. Bullies and fascists lurk in the corners of every democracy. Only good men like yourself keep them at bay." He suddenly smiled. "You should write another book."

"That very thing was raised by the Brotherhood last week. Frankly I didn't think they would go forward on the idea, but Bruno Dressler rang this morning and said they very much want me to begin working on a first draft for publication in the spring or summer."

Catherine laughed as she cradled Angelika. "That's marvelous, Albrecht!"

"Indeed." Lord Preston shook Albrecht's hand. "What will be the theme? How shall it differ from your other book released to offset Hitler's propaganda?"

"They wish me to challenge Hitler directly, as if he and I were engaged in a public debate at the university. Toe to toe and blow for blow, so to speak."

"That sounds fairly aggressive and combative, but perhaps that's the very approach needed. Have they suggested a title for this work?"

Albrecht nodded. "They wish to play off the success of Hitler's title and raise sales as well as eyebrows. His, as you know, is called *Mein Kampf,* which means 'My Struggle.' Mine is to be entitled *Mein Krieg,* which means 'My War.'"

Parliament, Westminster, London

"Danforth. Fancy meeting you here. You're so far away on the benches in the House I thought you'd fallen into the Thames." Buchanan strode across the empty foyer in the Parliament buildings, silver-headed walking stick in hand. "Waiting for Daddy, are you?"

Edward kept his hands clasped behind his back. "Stanley Baldwin, actually."

"Baldwin? Old Has-Been Baldwin? You've hitched your cart to the wrong star, Danforth."

"Do you think so? Your minority government will fall soon enough, Buchanan. And when it does, Baldwin will be first man in the kingdom once again."

Buchanan lifted his thick eyebrows and curled his lip. "The Conservative Party is finished as a political force. So are you and your father. What will you do when Dover finally tosses you out on your ear? Sell pencils to the reporters on Fleet Street?"

Edward turned his back on Buchanan and gazed through a window at the November rain coming down in long, gray streaks. "Run for Ayrshire South, of course. That would be the easiest plum for me to pick from the Labor tree. They have a slacker as MP, no mistake about that."

"Insult for insult, blow for blow, eh?" Buchanan's voice was low. Edward half expected to get cracked over the head by the walking stick. "I'm far from finished with your lot, Danforth. Everything continues to fall into place. Hold fast to what you have. Soon enough you'll not even have that left."

Edward grunted. "You won't live to see the day, Buchanan." He turned his head slowly and their eyes locked. "Believe me, you won't."

18

December, 1930–May, 1931
Christmas Eve, Tubingen, Germany

> *Stille Nacht, heilige Nacht!*
> *Alles schläft, einsam wacht*
> *Nur das traute, hochheilige Paar.*
> *Holder Knabe im lockigen Haar,*
> *Schlaf in himmlischer Ruh,*
> *Schlaf in himmlischer Ruh.*
>
> *Stille Nacht, heilige Nacht!*
> *Gottes Sohn, o wie lacht*
> *Lieb aus deinem göttlichen Mund,*
> *Da uns schlägt die rettende Stund,*
> *Christ, in deiner Geburt,*
> *Christ, in deiner Geburt.*

The baron bent and poked the logs in the fireplace. "Sean, will you get me some more wood from the basket?"

"*Ja, Opa.*"

"Now we must have a song from Britain, Elizabeth…and then America, Jane. But Elizabeth first; she must begin it."

"Me?" Lady Preston laughed, her fingers fluttering to her mouth and face. "Don't be ridiculous, Gerard. Catherine and Libby can do that far better than I can."

"They will have their turns."

"Oh heavens."

"Mum," Catherine said as she rocked Angelika in her lap, "you have a lovely voice." Angelika was mesmerized by the firelight.

"Victoria has the voice, my dear."

"Where do you think she got it from?"

Libby jumped in. "Oh come, Mother. You'd think he'd asked you to sing *The Messiah*." Libby got up from her chair and plopped down next to Lady Preston on the couch. "I'll help you. I have the perfect song. I'll start but you have to come in."

"Of course, my dear."

"You all have to come in, all right?" She raised her eyebrows at Jane and Eva. "All right?"

Jane smiled. "Yes, Mum. We'll raise the roof."

"*Ach,* don't do that." Albrecht was mixing hot apple cider in a pot by the fire. "It's snowing."

Libby started singing an old French carol, and soon the other women joined in:

> The holly and the ivy,
> Now both are full well grown.
> Of all the trees that are in the wood,
> The holly bears the crown
>
> Oh, the rising of the sun,
> The running of the deer.
> The playing of the merry organ,
> Sweet singing in the choir.
>
> The holly bears a blossom
> As white as lily flower;
> And Mary bore sweet Jesus Christ
> To be our sweet Savior.
>
> Oh, the rising of the sun,
> The running of the deer.

The playing of the merry organ,
Sweet singing in the choir.

The holly bears a berry
As red as any blood;
And Mary bore sweet Jesus Christ
To do poor sinners good.

Oh, the rising of the sun,
The running of the deer.
The playing of the merry organ,
Sweet singing in the choir.

The holly bears a prickle
As sharp as any thorn;
And Mary bore sweet Jesus Christ
On Christmas Day in the morn.

Oh, the rising of the sun,
The running of the deer.
The playing of the merry organ,
Sweet singing in the choir.

The holly bears a bark
As bitter as any gall;
And Mary bore sweet Jesus Christ
For to redeem us all.

Oh, the rising of the sun,
The running of the deer.
The playing of the merry organ,
Sweet singing in the choir.

The holly and the ivy,
When they are both full grown,

Of all the trees that are in the wood,
The holly bears the crown.

The rising of the sun
And the running of the deer,
The playing of the merry organ,
Sweet singing in the choir.

Montgomery and Skitt stood just outside the alcove in the great hall where the family had settled in with cider to sing carols and open presents.

"Well, they won't be needing us for a while," Montgomery said in a low voice. "Come on, I want to show you something."

"What if they ask for something?"

"They have German staff who are always at their beck and call and come at a quick march as if trying to show us up." She seized his hand in her strong grip. "Come on!" She led him down a stone hall that still held centuries-old iron brackets for torches. Dropping his hand, she used both of hers to tug on the handle of a huge oak door. "They made 'em this thick to hold up against arrows and axe blows and fire."

"Do you need a hand?" Skitt put his hands next to hers and pulled. "Oh! It's stuck."

"It'll open. It always does."

"How many times have you been here?"

"Enough." She glanced at his face. "And all alone, don't worry."

"I wasn't worried."

The door finally gave with a long moan. A gust of cold air spinning with snowflakes blew over them.

"What does this open to?" asked Skitt.

"A turret." Montgomery went outside, hugging herself with her arms. "Brrr. It's nippy but the view is worth it."

"What you can see of it. It's dark as pitch."

"The lights of the village are far below. Look."

Skitt had his hands in his pockets and his shoulders drawn up around his ears. "Lovely," he said.

"Don't tease."

"I'm not. I like the sheer drop of thousands of feet. You think I'd land near the sweets shop?"

She punched him in the arm. "Running off on me?"

"Never."

She opened her fist and ran her hand up and down the sleeve of his butler jacket. "I shall miss you, Skitt. I feel I got to know you better here than I did in England. Especially after we nursed Lady Preston and young Jane together."

He smiled. His eyes were used to the darkness now so he could make out her petite features clearly. He brushed a cluster of snowflakes off her maid's cap.

"It strikes me that you haven't seen much snow, have you?" she asked, still moving her fingers up and down his arm.

"Not much, no. I did see a snowfall once when I was a boy. It was in the Welsh mountains."

"It snows all winter in New York State."

"Is that still home?" He brushed at her cap again. His fingers strayed and touched the dark hair pinned up underneath.

"Home's wherever Jane winds up. Dover Sky. The Rhine. Perhaps Ashton Park one day."

Now his fingers touched her cheek. "It's snowing all over you."

"Have you ever caught snowflakes on the tip of your tongue, Skitt?" she asked.

"I confess I haven't."

"You should try."

"I'd rather try this." He kept his hand on her face as he bent slightly and kissed her softly on the lips.

"Oh how I shall miss you when Lady Elizabeth returns to England, my lovely Skitt. I pray Libby, Jane, and I will visit England this summer. I'll do everything in my power to convince her she ought to marry Commander Terry and move us back across the Channel lock, stock, and barrel."

"That's a good plan. You could stir up the Nazis as well. That might help your plans along."

"Those gangsters! I prefer a wedding between Commander Fordyce and Lady Libby be the reason for our move."

He put his lips against her neck and shoulder. "I would prefer a wedding too."

"Now, my dear Jane, I have a special gift for you."

"But it's not Christmas morning yet, Grandmother Elizabeth."

"We won't tell the others, will we? Jesus was born on Christmas Eve, wasn't He? So that is a wonderful time to give someone a gift."

"Unless He was born at two or three. Then that really would be Christmas morning."

Lady Preston laughed. "You and your wit. Please shut the door, Jane."

Jane got up from the bed where she'd been sitting next to her grandmother. The air current caused the candle that lit the room to flutter. The girl closed the door, and when she turned to come back Lady Preston was holding up a necklace of rubies that flamed brilliantly in the candlelight. Jane stopped and put a hand to her mouth.

"Merry Christmas, my dear!"

"Grandmother! Not for me?"

"Yes, for you. And this as well." She patted a hand on a red dress folded up by her side. "Both came from the Far East long ago. You know what the Far East is known as today?"

"China and Japan and—"

"The necklace and dress are from China and fairly traded, I must say, by my great-great-grandfather Welcome Cornwall. He was a great seaman, Jane. Twice he circumnavigated the globe. He was an extraordinary man. We have one of his ship logs and three of his diaries."

"I should like to read those."

"I thought you might, and so you shall when you come to Ashton Park, which I pray will be soon." She set down the necklace and lifted up the dress. It gleamed in the candlelight. "Pure silk. Come. You must try it on. I want you to wear it with the necklace Christmas morning in the great hall."

"I can't, Grandmother Elizabeth."

"Nonsense! Of course you can. You will be fourteen this coming year, but you already look like a lady. You are so tall and perfectly proportioned. You will turn all the men's heads when you come of age. Why, you already do. Don't think I haven't noticed."

Jane could feel a blush rising from her neck. "Grandmother, that's not true."

"Of course it's true. You will soon grow into the kind of exceptional beauty men paid a king's ransom to woo and wed in the days of the great dynasties. Emperors would have courted you with pearls and gold. Now, alas, you shall have to settle for Germans and Englishmen. Hopefully a dashing one!"

Jane giggled. "You're such a storyteller. I should like very much to wed a naval officer like Terry Fordyce."

"I don't blame you one bit. He cuts a fine figure. Hopefully your mother will grasp the fact and make him her husband—the sooner the better."

"I think he's very close to asking for her hand."

Lady Preston's mouth formed a perfect circle. "Oh? And what will your mother say?"

"Yes, yes, a thousand times yes."

"Are you sure?"

"I am."

"Well, praise God if we have a wedding to look forward to. But now here we are prattling on, and it's past midnight. Come, off with the old and on with the new." She shook the dress so that it seemingly burst into fire in the flickering light.

Jane quickly removed her outer clothing and slipped on the sleeveless dress. It held to her figure perfectly.

"Ah, my beautiful child." Lady Preston gazed at Jane and sighed. "With your long, dark hair and lovely legs and face—well, there are no words adequate for your beauty. You're stunning, my dear. What a grand way to celebrate the birth of our Savior. You look royal! I wish your grandfather were here to see you." She stood up and placed the necklace of rubies around Jane's neck. "I saved this for my first granddaughter, and that's you, I'm happy to say. It will ride on your throat just above the neckline of the dress. Oh, you look like a queen! These are from Burma, or so the good Captain Cornwall recorded in his diary. The rubies are of the finest hues of scarlet and vermilion." She kissed Jane on the cheek. "Walk about the room and let me look at you."

Crimson and gold rippled up and down the silk as Jane moved about the room shyly. Lady Preston clasped her hands together at her chest and nodded her head. Finally Jane stopped in front of a large, freestanding, oval mirror rimmed in dark wood.

"I—I scarcely recognize myself." Jane's eyes were dark and wide. "I look so much older."

"You do. You do indeed. And tomorrow you shall have black high-heeled shoes, and we shall arrange your hair by sweeping it back and add a red poinsettia. I purchased long red gloves for you to wear. We shall add some eye shadow and mascara too. You must meet me here at seven, and we'll make you the toast of Hartmann Castle!"

Jane turned from the mirror. "I am very happy, Grandmother Elizabeth. You should not love me so much."

"Yes, dear, I should. This much and more, so much more."

DEAR LIBBY

YOU WILL NOT WANT TO HEAR HOW WARM A MARCH DAY IS ON THE SOUTH COAST OF SPAIN SO I SHALL NOT TELL YOU. INSTEAD I WILL SAY HOW MUCH I ADORE YOU AND THAT I LOVE YOU WITH ALL MY HEART. AND SOMETHING ELSE. YES I KNOW THIS OUGHT TO BE DONE IN PERSON AT A FINE RESTAURANT OR BY A LOVELY SEASCAPE BUT I CAN'T WAIT FOR MAY! I AM LOOKING AT WHITE CLOUDS OVER A BLUE SEA WITH WHITE BIRDS IN A BLUE SKY AND I AM THINKING OF THE ASTONISHING BEAUTY OF THOSE BLUE EYES GOD GIFTED YOU WITH—AND GIFTED ME WITH FOR I AM FREE TO GAZE INTO THEM AS A SAILOR GAZES INTO THE VAST IMPENETRABLE DEEP.

MY DEAR LIBBY I WANT TO MARRY YOU. I WANT YOU TO BE MY BRIDE. I WANT TO LIVE WITH YOU FOREVER AND A DAY. YES I AM ASKING YOU BY TELEGRAM! I MEAN IT WITH ALL MY HEART. PERHAPS BY ASKING YOU IN MARCH IT MEANS WE CAN BE MARRIED THIS SUMMER AS SOON AS I STEP OFF THE SHIP IN GOOD OLD ENGLAND. LIBBY I LOVE YOU! I LOVE YOU! PLEASE SAY YES YES YES!

YOUR GALAHAD

TERRY

GALAHAD

YOU ARE ABSOLUTELY MAD BUT YOU'RE RIGHT. I'D LOVE TO MARRY YOU AS SOON AS YOU SET FOOT ON SHORE. WE CAN EVEN BE WED ON THE GANGWAY OR ON THE DECK IF YOU'D LIKE. OR RIGHT IN THE WATER WITH WAVES BURSTING OVER OUR HEADS. I DON'T CARE. THE IMPORTANT THING IS TO DO IT. I SHALL MAKE ALL ARRANGEMENTS. SEE YOU IN MAY MY LOVE.

YOUR LIBBY

OH AND THE ANSWER IS YES YES YES!

Plymouth and Devonport, Southern England

The *Hood* docked in May, and Libby was there to welcome Terry home. She waited by the car with Skitt and Jane for two hours as they watched sailors scramble over the huge deck securing the battleship. Finally Terry walked down the gangway in uniform, a sailor behind him toting a seabag over his shoulder.

"I've missed you!" Libby cried as she threw her arms around him. "Look at your tan! I'm jealous."

"You look wonderful. A woman like you doesn't need a tan. Besides, ginger-haired women burn and peel."

"Not this ginger. Our honeymoon is still on, isn't it?"

He laughed and stroked her cheek. "As long as the wedding's still on."

"Oh, it's on all right. I can hardly wait to get away with you to the Mediterranean and take in some very hot sun."

"Mum!" Jane was at Libby's side, pulling on her dress. "Are you the only one who gets hugged?"

Terry wrapped his arms around the young woman dressed in a red coat and hat. "How tall you are now. And how lovely you are. You must grow a foot every month."

"I will be fourteen next month. I have to keep growing to keep ahead of the Sweet boys. They're holy terrors."

"Are you still one up on them?"

"I am." Jane smiled up into Terry's face. "You're almost as dark as me."

"But not as pretty."

"Thank goodness. I want a father, not a flower." She dropped her eyes and played with the brass buttons on his uniform. "I know the wedding's not till next week, but can I—may I—call you Dad now?"

He put his fingers under her chin and tilted her head. "I'd love that."

"Really?"

"Yes, really. Let's start right away. How is my daughter today?"

Jane's smile opened up her face. "She's fine, Dad. She's very fine indeed."

They hugged again. Looking on and thinking of Michael and then the death of Jane's birth father, Libby's eyes glittered with tears she brushed at with her fingers. *Thank You, God. Thank You for this miracle. Thank You, my God.*

Dover Sky

Lord Preston put his glasses on his nose to read the list in his hand. "The photographer arrives the morning of the wedding. We must get the family pictures taken after the ceremony. And special baby pictures—Catherine with Angelika and Shannon with Patricia Claire."

Lady Preston was at a table nearby with a pen and a pad of paper. "For heaven's sakes, William. Patricia is hardly a baby—why, she's almost three."

"How big can she have gotten?"

"You'll find out soon enough. Aren't you and Harrison picking them up at the pier in Dover?"

"Yes, yes, after lunch." He glanced over his glasses at his wife. "What are you jotting down?"

"These are meal suggestions for Mrs. Longstaff. She and Norah have matters quite in hand, but I didn't see Harrison's Cock-a-Leekie soup here or your Welsh rarebit on the menu."

"But the pheasant—we have the pheasant? There are hundreds of guests coming."

"We have dozens of pheasants. Not to worry, Dear. Stick with your own list, please."

Lord Preston removed his glasses and placed them in his coat pocket. "I must see how my aviation room is coming along. Ben and Victoria are flying down with the children before supper."

Lady Preston scribbled on her pad. "Oh you and your aviation room. By all means, look in on it, William. There's nothing more pressing than that."

The day of the wedding began with a May shower, but by noon the sun was shining. The ceremony was held down near the pond, the swans keeping their distance and paddling about in the middle of the water. Kipp and Caroline's daughter, Cecilia, who would be two in October, and Robbie and Shannon's daughter, Patricia, who would turn three in September and was quite noticeably not an infant anymore, were the flower girls. Jeremy and Emma's twins, Peter and James, both thirteen, their younger brother, Billy, ten, along with Caroline's son, Charles, aged nine, Kipp's son, Matthew, aged eight, Ben and Victoria's son, Ramsay, also eight, and Edward and Charlotte's

Owen, who was eight too, were chosen to usher the lords and ladies and other guests to the chairs arranged neatly on the lawn by Harrison and Skitt. Jane held the rings on a red-velvet cushion by the outdoor altar where Reverend Jeremy Sweet, St. Andrew's Cross, Church of England, London, assisted by Ben Whitecross, Methodist Chapel, Lime Street, Liverpool, brought Commander Terrence Fordyce and Libby Danforth Woodhaven into holy wedlock before God and people on the late Queen Victoria's birthday.

After the ceremony, the photographer was trying to arrange the large Danforth family on the grass for family photographs but the children kept bolting and chasing each other across the large expanse and the adults kept edging towards tables groaning with soups, meats, and greens placed amid crystal bowls filled with crimson punch.

"Now Ben and Kipp, you are the fliers in the family. You see what we've done with this room here? There are so many sea paintings at Dover Sky, I decided it was time to balance out the equation."

Oil paintings and watercolors of aircraft covered the walls. In some, the planes were lined up on the ground or warming up for takeoff. In most, they were in the air darting through clouds, flying over the whitecaps of the Channel, or navigating above the patchwork quilt of the Kent countryside. Four or five were paintings of war with Sopwith Camels pitted against Fokker triplanes, SPADs looping and rolling in aerial combat with Fokker D.VIIs. Kipp examined one of a Sopwith Camel taking on the red triplane of Baron von Richthofen.

"Is this supposed to be the Red Baron and Roy Brown going at it on April 21, 1918?" he asked as he bent down to peer at the brass plate on the frame. "Well, he's got the planes and the weather right, but from what I understand, the two never went at it head-on. The baron was after one of Brown's chums, so Brown dived on him from behind and cut loose with his guns. The baron carried on for a few more miles and crashed behind our lines stone dead." Kipp straightened and grinned as he glanced about the room. "But it's marvelous, Dad!

Really quite something. I'll make this my official headquarters when I'm home for the weekend. I'll do all my airline paperwork in here." He walked behind an oxblood leather armchair and tapped a watercolor that showed Sopwith Camels with the morning damp rising off their wings like steam. "That brings back memories, eh, Ben?"

Ben nodded. "It does. Whoever painted that one had to have been there."

"He was." Lord Preston stood with his hands behind his back. "Whenever possible I employed veterans who had an eye for detail and knew pilots' movements and moments."

"It's brilliant." Ben was taken by the portrait of an officer standing by an SE5a. "I love this one. Is that Ball?"

Lord Preston smiled. "I'm so glad you're pleased. It is Ball, yes."

Kipp dropped into the oxblood armchair. "A welcome respite from that madness on the lawn. I wish someone would fetch us some cold drinks."

Lord Preston pressed a buzzer by the door. "There's bound to be someone indoors. Let's see who shows up."

"You'll have to do something for Robbie now, Dad," Kipp said. "You do know that, don't you?"

"What do you mean?"

"The great hall has sea paintings for the likes of Edward and Terry. Now Ben and I have this aviation room. But what about Robbie? He's British Army. What are you going to do about that?"

"Hmm, it will take some time to plan, won't it? You're right, of course. Absolutely right. There should be a room with its feet firmly planted on the ground."

"How long's Robbie's furlough?"

"Six months."

"Then he has plenty of time to help you with it. Waterloo, Agincourt, Crecy, the Somme—a proper mud-and-blood room."

Lord Preston hummed as he glanced about at the airplane paintings. "Do you know, I was thinking, we don't quite have it right any longer. With our song 'Rule Britannia,' I mean. 'Rule Britannia, Britannia rule the waves, Britons never shall be slaves.' There is something else we must rule if we're to keep our heads above water, so to speak. The air—am I right?"

Ben slowly lowered himself into an armchair like Kipp was sitting in. "I think you have it, sir. Enemies don't require boats to cross the Channel now."

"Exactly, so I thought of this." He hummed again. "Tell me what you think."

> Rule Britannia, we rule the skies and waves.
> Britons never, never, never shall be slaves.

Lord Preston laughed. "My voice is not what it used to be."
Kipp and Ben clapped.
"That's excellent, Dad," said Kipp. "It really works."
Ben was grinning. "Well done."
"Do you think so?" Lord Preston smiled and admired an oil painting of a Nieuport 17 dropping into a dive. "Now if we can only convince the BBC to give it some airtime, hmm?"

"Cath?"
Catherine glanced up from the cradle Angelika was sleeping in. "Cheers, Lib. I'm just settling her down for a nap, otherwise she'll be a German–English bear this evening. How are you holding up with all this madness? Where's the groom?"

"Terry's off with Jane and Eva and the boys. They're on a march around the whole estate."

"That will take forever and a day. No worries though. It'll all be over tonight, and Terry can whisk you away to the Med."

"He can't actually. He's due to sail tomorrow with Dad and a crew of eight or ten."

"Eight or ten? My goodness! Does he fancy he's back on the *Hood*?"

Libby smiled down at nine-month-old Angelika as she slept, hands curled in a pink blanket. "He finds he can't say no to Jane or the older boys, including Sean. Your son was a bit put out not having been included in the ceremony—"

"Oh Sean's fine. He wouldn't have liked ushering old ladies to their seats anyway."

"Well, be that as it may, he's skipper of the *Pluck* at the crack of dawn tomorrow. He gets the wheel for two hours."

"He doesn't!"

Libby sat on the new swing that had been placed on the front porch. "They'll make a sailor out of your boy yet."

"His father was around the Belfast docks all his life, so I suppose Sean comes by it honestly." Catherine sat next to her sister and made the swing glide back and forth. "Are you never going to have a honeymoon? Marches and sailing and fireworks tonight and that's it?"

"Terry promises me the moon by the weekend."

"The moon by the weekend? Any woman should find the patience in her to wait for that, Lib. Imagine! The moon, you lucky girl." She moved the swing faster. "I want you to know I'm happy for you. No cheek, I really am. I'm madly in love with Albrecht, and that's where my heart wants to stay. There's no point in denying a certain fondness for our dashing naval officer, so I'm glad you've brought him into the family. It's so nice to have him on board. He'll do us all good. Terry always brings out the best in everyone, especially the children." Catherine's eyes glimmered. She smiled and gave Libby a quick kiss on the cheek. "You and I have both lost husbands. But I looked at the crew today with the children racing over the fields, and I feel I've recovered at long last. We're one happy family. I truly feel that. God bless you, sis. God bless your marriage."

Libby leaned her head against Catherine and put her arms around her.

Skitt closed the door and made a show of dusting his hands off. "That's that then. Lord Preston said I am free to turn in. He intends to be up with the baron quite a bit longer. I've given the old German a bottle of brandy and a decent supply of cigars. For all I know, they'll be at it all night."

Montgomery took his hand. "Good heavens. What on earth are they going on about?"

"German politics."

"Ah."

"We both know what a nasty topic that can be."

Montgomery nodded. "We do. But it brought us together, didn't it? I remember how I loved you as you tended Jane and Lady Preston with me day after day. Not many men can do that, you know—be strong and be sweet."

"Is that what I am?"

She pressed his hand to her lips. "Yes."

"Fancy a walk to the pond?"

"I'd love that."

They headed out the door and down over the lawn under the May stars, holding hands. Skitt was in his black-and-white butler uniform, and Montgomery was in her black-and-white maid outfit and cap. She laughed but quickly covered her mouth with her hand.

Skitt smiled at her. "What's that?"

"I'm just thinking about you and your ponding."

"My ponding? What?"

"Sitting all night in the rushes with your cricket bat and flask."

"Oh that. Well, it's over and done with. Haven't made my blind in the reeds for years."

"You were still at it when I arrived here from America."

"There was still poaching going on then. It stopped, so Harrison and I finally gave up on the summer vigils."

She giggled with her hand over her mouth again. "Did you ever whack anyone with your bat?"

"Mosquitoes and gnats and midges, that's about all."

"And the swans have been all right since you stopped lurking?"

"Yes, Monty. They've been all right. God save the king's swans."

The moon was at half as the swans, white and starlike, floated silently, heads tucked back under their wings.

"Dreaming," whispered Montgomery as she watched them drift. "Just dreaming. Them and me."

"Am I to ask about your dreams?"

"My dreams are you, love. My dreams are all you."

"It's absolutely brilliant." Terry swung the door back and forth. "I mean, who would have thought?"

Libby sat up in bed, smiling, her arms wrapped about her knees. "None of us children, I can tell you that. And we were up and down all these hallways on rainy days. To us it was just a locked door. We picked it once and got in, and it was like a horrid old closet heaped with ratty coats and mothballs. The smell was wretched. We couldn't stand it, so we never went back. If only we'd thought to pick the lock hidden behind the coats and swung the second door open. And then got through the third door into this room here. My goodness, what a triumph that would have been! All these oils of great ladies and grand dukes to stare at. Sabers hanging on the wall to take down and swing through the air. Daggers to play with. That suit of armor in the corner there—what a mess we would have made. And we'd probably have taken off a few fingers or heads with the swords. It doesn't bear thinking about on my wedding night." She stretched out a hand. "Come to bed, love. There are better things for you to do tonight than open and close a secret door over and over again."

"It's a marvel of engineering. We're quite safe here from the whole brood. Even the evil twins Peter and James."

"We are, so let's make the best of it. Remember that you're shipping out early in the morning on the good ship *Pluck*. They'll storm this room with pikestaffs and maces if you're not at the front door at five."

"And in full uniform too."

"What?" Libby laughed. "Who on earth asked you to do that?"

"Who do you think? She'll have the commander's uniform on I had tailored for her, so she insisted we be look-alikes tomorrow."

"The things you get yourself into over *our* girl." She patted the quilt. "Come along now. Or is the brave naval officer afraid?"

"I am a bit, you know." Terry came over and sat on the edge of the bed. "Mum always told me to watch out for ginger-haired women."

"Well, it's too late now. You're stuck with one."

"Sounds ominous."

"Oh, it is—very much so." She took his chin in her hand. "I love you, Commander."

The baron opened the window wider to let more of the smoke out of the room. Then he promptly lit another cigar and took another sip of brandy.

"You believe he has the support of the upper classes?" asked Lord Preston, putting down his tea.

The baron nodded and blew out a stream of white-and-gray smoke. "And the middle class too, which is more worrisome. He promises one thing to one group and promises something else to another. Hitler keeps hammering away at the failure of democracy and pointing to the successes of strong monarchs and emperors in Germany's past. He holds up the need for another Bismarck. He makes remarks about the success of Benito Mussolini in Rome. People are listening as the economy and employment continue to decline into a pit no one seems able to pull us out of. It's the same in America, in Britain, and in the whole of Europe."

"Yes, I'm afraid some draconian measures will be coming down from the Labor government. I can't fault them, but it will not go over well. Even in Parliament's corridors and foyers I hear mutterings about the need for a strong man to lead us and implement strong measures. I suppose there are fascist groups everywhere these days, not just in Spain, Italy, and Germany." Lord Preston poured himself another cup. Steam curled up like smoke from the match the baron had just blown out. "But now, Gerard, what about the military? Isn't Herr Hitler afraid of them just a bit?"

"Not at all. As I've mentioned, his personal army—his brown-shirts—number close to half a million now. The Treaty of Versailles restricts Germany to 100,000 soldiers, and Hitler's forces could overwhelm them in a matter of hours. But that's a moot point because the army is on his side for the most part. If he gains control of the government, the soldiers will simply fall into step with the Nazi Party. To them Hitler is like another Blucher, the victor of Waterloo along with your Wellington. *Ran wie Blucher*—charge like Blucher, they say. They already see Herr Hitler's aggressiveness in that light. Germans admire courage from the top."

"Is it courage?"

"Certainly he has that along with his fanaticism. And the state of the world's economy is slowly bringing him to power."

"What does the Brotherhood of the Oak intend to do?"

The baron shrugged. "You're one of us, Vilhelm. What do you intend?"

"Our navy is strong. Should Hitler take over, we could keep him blockaded on the water."

"Hopefully it won't come to that." The baron gazed at his friend through the cigar smoke. "What about the air? How is England fixed there?"

"We're not on a war footing. The RAF is not much to speak of these days. Neither is the army. Everything is reduced and restricted. No one expects trouble. Everyone is watching the pound and the shilling. Few care about Berlin. Germany is considered a broken reed."

"That could change overnight with one election. Hitler would tear up the Treaty of Versailles. That much is clear from his rants. He would rearm Germany. You know that."

"I do, and a few others see it too. But we aren't listened to." Lord Preston tapped his teaspoon on the rim of his cup. "What do the Germans and Austrians of the Brotherhood plan to do?"

The baron kept his eyes on Lord Preston. "If the economic depression continues to play into Hitler's hands and he gains more and more ground, our only option would be to stop him before he forms a government."

"How would you do that?"

"Assassination."

Lord Preston set the spoon down sharply. "Assassination? Are you mad, Gerard? It was the assassination of the Archduke that set off the Great War."

"There would be unrest in the aftermath, certainly. The Nazis would run amok for a few days. Blood would be spilled. But it would be limited and over quickly. Ultimately the Nazis would be headless and wither on the vine." The baron turned to look at the darkness through the window. "Better a week or two of civil war than two or three years of war in Europe."

Lord Preston stared at his friend's back then reached for the small bottle of brandy and poured a capful into his tea. "I shall pray, Gerard. Ask for guidance and wisdom. I know we're dealing with serious matters. I know sometimes great risks must be borne. But I'm not comfortable being an assassin. I'm not comfortable with overcoming darkness by using more darkness."

The baron continued to gaze out the window. "The Lord has placed us in such a world where the choices available to us fall far short of heaven. The dark choices are often the only way to regain light."

"I pray not," replied Lord Preston.

19

August–October, 1931
London

"Right, then." Edward paced the flat he shared with his father in London. "Now that Ramsay MacDonald has resigned, we can have a proper election and get the Conservatives back in power."

His father sat in a chair sipping tea. "Labor is split over the budget and Ramsay has stepped down, that much is true. But the prevailing mood amongst Conservative and Liberal MPs is to get MacDonald back in the prime minister's chair right away at the helm of a National Government."

"What?"

"The economic crisis worldwide is simply too serious to put party before country, my boy. An election we must have, yes, but with a national coalition vying for votes against Labor, not all the parties split up into their usual bits and pieces. So when we go back to the House in a few minutes, it is Stanley Baldwin's wish that we support MacDonald as head of a National Government."

"What about Lloyd George and the Liberals? They hold the balance of power."

"They do now. If the British people back a National Government in this time of crisis, which I believe they will, I doubt the Liberals shall keep that hold."

"It's a mess," Edward fumed. "I look at where Germany is headed, and now we have a golden opportunity to do the same. But you're saying we want to put that deadweight Ramsay back in the prime minister's chair."

"And where is Germany heading that we should be following after it?"

"A moratorium on democracy. You're right, it is an unprecedented financial crisis and must be met with unprecedented measures. But not dead men like Ramsay leading the dead men of a National Government. No, Father, we must thrust democracy aside for the time being."

"I beg your pardon?"

"Have the election, yes. But place Baldwin back at the helm of a Tory majority. Give him sweeping powers. No more elections for ten years. Strong trade ties with Italy and Germany. High tariffs for trade with those not part of the Commonwealth or the Empire. Cut relations with the League of Nations. Build up our navy and army and air force. Make our ships the size we want them to be. Put the British laborer to work on tanks and fighter planes and battle cruisers. Our economy will be revived in half a year, and Great Britain will be back to work and happy."

Lord Preston set down his cup. "A moratorium on democratic government Englishmen have fought and died for since the Magna Carta? How do you propose to get the support for that even if we're facing a financial crisis?"

"We need a strong man now, Dad. We need a monarch or we won't weather the storm. This democratic pattern of voting and revoting every few years is rubbish. We put a good man in and we keep him there until everything is sorted out."

"What if it takes decades?"

"So be it."

"Who put all this into your head?"

Edward smacked a fist into his hand. "It is going to work for Germany, and Germany has been in a far greater hole than we've been. It must work for us."

"The elimination of democracy will work for Germany? You would replace the free vote of the people with a dictatorship?"

"The baron was adamant about this back in May, and he was right."

Lord Preston's face sharpened. "Baron von Isenburg promoted this line of thinking? I don't believe it."

"The strong man, the clearheaded man, the man with unprecedented powers wielding them wisely and ably without the nagging hindrance of opposition parties or debate or national elections is the man best able to steer his country out of economic chaos. Freedom to act decisively. That is the thing, Father. Liberty to act in order to bring this nation the very liberty it requires and deserves."

"Whether the baron was goading you to get a reaction, I don't know. But if you wish to have a future with the Conservative Party, you must support Mr. Baldwin's wishes for a National Government with Ramsay MacDonald at its head and put away this rubbish about a moratorium on democracy."

Edward went back to pacing. "We do what we need to do and win a National Government with a majority of Conservative seats. Then we oust Ramsay, replace him with Baldwin, and vote in necessary and extraordinary powers for the government that give him—and us—a free hand to do what needs to be done to put Britain back on her feet strong, free, and unrestrained."

Lord Preston stood up and straightened his suit jacket with a strong pull from both his hands. "It's time to return to the House and support Ramsay MacDonald's return to the office of prime minister."

"By all means. It's what we do after winning the election that counts."

Lord Preston nodded. "Indeed it is."

"Elizabeth?"

"Ah, William. It's a very good connection. How did you get on with your speech in Liverpool?"

"We have mutiny at Invergordon in Scotland."

"Mutiny! Not on the *Hood*?"

"Yes, on the *Hood* and many other vessels as well. It is a black thing. I gather there were rumblings for days, but it got under way in earnest on the fifteenth of September—yesterday—and is still going today. Turn on the BBC this evening, and they will tell you what they're permitted to broadcast about the events."

"Why haven't the Royal Marines on board the ships put it down?"

"The Marines have joined the mutiny."

"Oh no!"

There was a rustling of paper at Lord Preston's end. "There is no mention of officers joining the mutiny. Indeed, they've done their best to get the sailors to return to their duties."

"Libby will be frantic down at Dover Sky."

"I have no word on Terry."

"I shall call her. Robbie and Shannon are with her. And Caroline."

"Well, don't panic her. There are no reports of violence. No shots fired. No beatings. No one hurt. No officers assaulted."

"Of course I won't panic her. The minute you hear anything else, please ring me."

"I shall. I have another election rally tomorrow. How is Edward's campaign getting on, do you know?"

"Charlotte reports he's on top of the world and prophesying Baldwin's return to power."

"He's saying that? When will the boy learn to keep his mouth shut? If Baldwin or Ramsay MacDonald get wind of it, they'll throw him out of the party."

"Please, William."

"It's true, Elizabeth. They will skin him alive."

"All right, Dear, that's quite enough. Go back to your speechwriting. I shall call Libby up straightaway."

Dover Sky

Robbie tugged a white-faced Libby into the library where Kipp was adjusting the dials on the large, wooden radio set. "I'm telling you, the news is good, Lib."

"You're only saying that."

"I'm not. The BBC is saying that."

"They only tell us what the Royal Navy permits. Heaven knows what they're holding back. They always held back casualty reports during war. Remember how they covered up the losses at Jutland?"

"It's 1931 now, Lib, not 1916. Listen."

> The *Hood* has sailed from Invergordon as ordered. All mutinous activities appear to have ceased on board the flagship. No casualties have occurred. This is true of all the other ships as well. After two days of unrest and disobedience, we have no record of fatalities or serious injuries. All ships have followed the *Hood* out of port as ordered. All ships are away. The mutiny has ended without resort to force.

"There you have it."

"I admit it does sound hopeful, Robbie. But I shall feel better when I get a cable from Terry. Certainly he would have gotten one away before they sailed."

"I should think so. And I shall stay up with you until it arrives, dear girl."

"That's not necessary, but thank you."

"I'm on six-month leave, remember? I have nothing better to do but to pester you until the courier arrives at the door. Kipp can't wait up because he has an airline to run."

Kipp smiled as he stood by the radio. "That's the truth."

"Shannon can't because she has to be available for Patricia Claire when she wakes at five or six."

"Available?" Shannon raised a golden eyebrow. "Is that what I'll be?"

"You will. And Caroline has her hands full with little Cecilia."

Caroline laughed. "Indeed I do. No stretch there."

Robbie bowed. "So you see, Lady Libby, there is only myself, but I shall be sufficient to keep you awake and alert until the good news comes to the door. We shall play checkers."

"I detest checkers."

"Chess then. Chess and we'll snack on coffee and biscuits."

Libby made a face at him.

"Chocolate biscuits." He mussed her hair and she slapped his hand. "Lib Danforth, lady or no lady, could never resist milk chocolate digestives."

"I'm no lady."

"We can discuss that until three or four in the morning."

She wrinkled up her mouth. "How happy that makes me."

The cable arrived at two thirty-seven. Robbie had put Libby in check for the third move in a row. Libby was at the door first, followed by Robbie, who tipped the courier and then read the cable out loud over her shoulder.

> DEAREST LIB
>
> YOU WILL HAVE HEARD THE NEWS. THIS WAS MY FIRST CHANCE TO DASH OFF A NOTE. WE WEIGH ANCHOR IN TWO HOURS. THE LADS HAVE RETURNED TO THEIR DUTIES. THERE WILL BE CONSEQUENCES BUT AT LEAST NO ONE WAS HURT AND THE NAVY AND ARMY DID NOT SEND IN TROOPS. I WILL SEE YOU AND JANE VERY SOON INDEED. ALL MY LOVE.
>
> TERRY

"Such good news!" Libby turned and slung her arms about Robbie's neck. She kissed him on the cheek.

"It is. And it means I can go to bed now. I'm tuckered."

"I'm not. I ate too much. One more game of chess?"

He laughed and groaned. "You lost all the others."

"I won't lose this one. I'm sharp now. I always do well at chess when I've had welcome news. Isn't it the same for you, Robbie?"

"It's not. I simply sleep better."

"Capital! Then I shall beat you up one side and down the other."
She put her arm through his. "Come on. I feel like a stick of dynamite."

"Well, blow up quickly then and be done with it so I can go to my
pillow as soon as possible."

Election Night, 1931

"Dad? Is that you?" Edward held the phone to one ear and put his
finger in the other as people cheered and shouted behind him.

"It is. Congratulations, my boy. Another October election, another
Guy Fawkes on the horizon, and once again you've come out on top."

Edward laughed. "I have indeed. So have you. So have we all. Imagine, Baldwin has four hundred and seventy seats and Labor only forty-
six. It's a miracle! Really it is! And that villain Buchanan is out. We have
James Orr MacAndrew in Ayrshire South now—our own man."

"It's a great blessing. But now, my boy, you must keep your opinions
to yourself. Ramsay MacDonald will continue on as prime minister—"

"Surely not, Father!" blurted Edward. "We have all the seats! Baldwin should lead the government!"

"Nevertheless, MacDonald will carry on. Mr. Baldwin and the
party think it best in these troubled times. And you must think so
too, Edward, and voice your support so that everyone can hear. Recall
what happened when MacDonald agreed to head up a National Government of all parties—Labor threw him out permanently. If you are
perceived as being an opponent of the National Government the Conservative Party helped bring into being, Mr. Baldwin will have you
ousted in like fashion. Stick with your party, Edward. You can do much
good there and eventually be rewarded for your loyalty."

"How rewarded? I've been in office seven years and haven't been
offered a cabinet position."

"Your time will come, dear boy. Persist and your time will come. My
best to lovely Charlotte and my two wonderful grandsons. Tell Owen

to keep *Sea-Fever* fresh in his mind. We will get another sail in before Guy Fawkes. I shall drop down to Dover Sky on the weekend. Tell Colm I'll see him soon."

"Yes, I'll tell them, Dad."

"Good night, my boy. Once more, congratulations. Keep what I've said before you at all times."

"I will, sir. Thank you. Love to Mum."

London

> Danforth,
>
> Let us put our differences aside and talk. You see what is happening in the government and the country. Believe it or not, you and I share a number of the same concerns. Come to Tollers tomorrow afternoon at three. Ask for Edmund Henson's private room and give out your name as Jack Thistle. Do not fail to arrive at the appointed time. It will be to our mutual benefit and certainly offer you an opportunity for political advancement.
>
> Buchanan

Edward entered the crowded Tollers, but he didn't recognize any of the men at the tables amidst the haze of pipe smoke. He shook his umbrella so that water drops spattered the carpet just inside the door. He folded it shut and removed his silk top hat.

"May I assist you, sir?" A uniformed waiter asked and then smiled. "I'm afraid all the tables are occupied."

"I'm here to see Edmund Henson."

"Your name?"

"Tell him Jack Thistle has arrived."

"One moment."

The waiter vanished into the back. Edward stood by the door staring straight ahead. The waiter returned quickly.

"This way, sir."

Edward followed him down a short hallway that had doors on either side. They came to the last one. The waiter knocked, opened the door, and stepped aside. Edward went into the room and immediately saw Buchanan seated at a wooden table smoking a white, long-stemmed pipe.

"Danforth." Buchanan removed the pipe stem from his mouth. "Good of you to come."

The waiter closed the door.

"What the devil are you playing at?" snapped Edward. "Why all the cloak and dagger?"

"Gently, Danforth. We need to be discreet." He indicated a man Edward hadn't noticed seated at the far end of the table. "I presume you've met Sir Oswald Mosley, the Sixth Baronet?"

Edward briefly inclined his head. "Sir Mosley. I didn't expect to see you here with Lord Buchanan."

The slender man with a dark moustache and flashing black eyes smiled. "Why not? He and I both admire Mussolini and Hitler and their ideological inclinations. As do you."

"As do I, sir?"

"Death to the communists. No trade with Moscow. A strong man at the top rather than the weak and slow action...or rather inaction... of the democratic process. High tariffs to protect British manufacturing from international trade. Nationalization of our major industries. A solid and innovative network of public works to reduce unemployment. A strong army, navy, and air force." Mosley patted a sheaf of papers in front of him. "All of your thoughts are on paper. In addition, a person may track the development of your thoughts by means of your speeches that are recorded in *Hansard.* Like many other good people in Europe, you are a fascist, Lord Danforth."

Edward took a chair opposite Buchanan. "I've never called myself that."

"The left would make it a dirty word, but the fascist movement has worked wonders in Italy and Rome. In time it will work wonders in Madrid and Spain, as well as Berlin and Germany. Soon enough it will change London and Britain if true Englishmen like yourself join our cause."

"Your party was wiped out in the election, Sir Mosley. You lost your seat in Smethwick."

"A temporary setback. I plan to spend time with the fascist leaders in Rome and Berlin to sharpen my strategies and tactics. They began in the streets and won the people to their side. So shall we."

Edward placed his top hat on the table. "Herr Hitler may have the second largest party in Germany, Sir Mosley, but he is far from winning the German people to his side."

"Do you doubt he will go further, Lord Danforth?"

Edward drummed his fingers on the arm of his chair. "I shall be kicked out of the Conservative Party if I consider this, let alone have to deal with what my father will say."

"Let us not rush things. We meet in private for now. In a year or two, once the time is ripe, we come forward. My plan is to unite all the fascist groups in Britain to make one formidable force. Until then, we do what we do out of the public eye." Mosley nodded at Edward. "I see a cabinet position for you, Lord Danforth. And for you too, Lord Buchanan." His dark eyes remained on Edward. "Can we bury the hatchet?"

Edward glanced at Buchanan. "How is it you have summoned me to this meeting when you know the bad blood that exists between us?"

Buchanan shrugged. "I'm willing to abide by a truce until the nation is back on its feet again."

"But you were with Labor, the lovers of communism and socialism."

"I had no other choice, Danforth. I couldn't join the Conservative Party because you and your father were in it. The one party that most actively opposes your own is Labor, so it wasn't a difficult decision to make."

"Labor's policies are utterly at odds with the agenda Sir Mosley proposes."

"I'm out of Labor now, Danforth, so all of these issues you raise are moot. I can now show my true colors and not kowtow to the Labor line in order to strike out at the Danforth clan."

"And what will keep you from striking out at us if I join forces with Sir Mosley and you?"

"I will," Mosley stated, his voice having the ring of iron on iron. "There can be absolutely no infighting. We must provide a united front against our foes if we are to pull Great Britain out of this economic depression. Is that clear, Lord Buchanan?"

Buchanan inclined his head. "Very much so."

"Lord Danforth?"

Edward nodded. "I will abide by the truce, Sir Mosley. I will abide by the truce for king and country so long as Lord Buchanan stays true to his word."

Buchanan grunted. "No fear of that, Danforth."

20

April, 1932–January, 1933
Lime Street Chapel, Liverpool

Ben Whitecross looked over the congregation in the small room. The place was packed. Officials and bishops from the Methodist Church in England sat in the front row. His wife and two sons were right behind them, seated next to Lord and Lady Preston. At the back, with all their children, sat Jeremy and Emma and Kipp and Caroline. People Ben had been caring for the entire two years he'd been at Lime Street Chapel were watching him closely, eyes fixed on his face and the small movements of his hands. He turned a page of the large Bible that lay open on the pulpit in front of him.

"I suppose I have an adventurous spirit," Ben said. "God uses that. He certainly used it in the life of the apostle Paul. Paul wanted to go everywhere with the gospel, including Europe, Spain, and Asia. My text today is from his words in his second letter to the Corinthians: '*To preach the gospel in the regions beyond you, and not to boast in another man's line of things made ready to our hand.*' I've loved being among you here. The Lord has fulfilled a dream I kept hidden for years—to minister to people in His name. Up until now, I've worked with horses and flown airplanes and been blessed with marriage and children. I could successfully argue that my entire life has been a blessing. Coming to the pulpit was one way of thanking God. Going to East Africa, to Kenya specifically, is another. Christians have been serving there for a century, but many places remain untouched. Many live and die and pass into eternity without hearing about the God of love and His Son, Jesus Christ. So that's where I need to go. Regions beyond that need someone to preach, to pray, and to fly in medical supplies and Bibles. With the gracious support of the Methodist Missionary Society, your tithes and offerings, and the help of my family and our own resources, I'm on my way to Kenya in a fortnight. My wife and children will join me at the end of the year once I have everything prepared. I praise God for the opportunity to take His light and His love to the African people. It will be the grandest adventure of what has already been a very grand life."

The Methodist officials got up and gathered around Ben. They prayed over him.

Lord Preston nudged his daughter Victoria. "Isn't this something, my dear?" he whispered. "Who would have guessed it? Ben Whitecross VC a missionary to Africa. You must be very proud. One accomplishment follows another accomplishment in his life. And they said he would never walk again after that airplane crash. But no, one adventure comes swiftly on the heels of another with him."

Victoria stared straight ahead at the bishop who had placed his hands on her husband's bowed head. "Ben Whitecross's adventures will be the death of me, Father," she replied without whispering or keeping her voice low.

Tubingen, Germany

"Baron?" Catherine opened the door and smiled. "What brings you to the house on such a fine summer day? I thought you'd be out on a long nature hike with Eva."

"She's on some sort of outing with a few of her friends." The baron's face was etched in sharp lines and tense. "I must see Albrecht right away. Is he at home?"

"Of course. Is everything all right?"

"The election results are official. Herr Hitler won two hundred and thirty seats. He now has the largest party in the government."

"Oh no!" She stepped aside. "Please go directly to his study."

"*Danke.* I apologize, Catherine."

"For Hitler? It is certainly not your fault, Baron. Please come in. Albrecht will want to discuss this news with you."

The baron found him behind his desk, hair uncombed, a day's growth of beard showing on his face. Papers and books were stacked higher than his head.

Albrecht looked up from the pad he was writing on. "Ah, Gerard. What brings you here? You know, you were right after all. We should have fled to Pura or the Rhine instead of remaining in Tubingen for July and August. What was I thinking? All because of this new book the publishers are hounding me for after the success of *Mein Krieg* and *Mein Geist*—"

The baron interrupted him. "Have you listened to the news?"

"The news? No, I haven't had the time. I've been chained to this desk since six this morning."

"The votes have been officially counted."

Albrecht took off his reading glasses. "What has happened?"

"The Nazis now have the greatest number of seats in the *Reichstag.*"

"Impossible!"

"Hitler's star is rising. Now he is demanding that von Hindenburg make him chancellor."

"Will von Hindenburg do it?"

"Today? No. He detests Hitler. Next week, next month? Who knows?"

"We must act."

The baron took a seat and removed his hat, a fedora with a feather in its band. "A meeting has been called for this evening at Schultz's home. We've already set a number of things in motion. It remains to determine the right place and time. There will be several target shooters in place at whatever outdoor location is selected. A grenade will also be thrown, possibly two. However we don't want any bystanders injured or killed. Only Nazi Party members."

"Perhaps Goebbels or Himmler can be eliminated at the same time."

"If those sycophants are standing close to him, yes."

Albrecht lifted a piece of paper on his desk and glanced over it. "I do not do this lightly, Gerard. I am just now writing a chapter on following in the footsteps of the Prince of Peace."

"Yet our Lord also drove the merchants out of the Jewish temple with a whip."

"Yes, but He killed no one."

"Do you wish to halt the assassination attempt?"

"God forgive me, I do not. And I will have to answer to Him for my decision. But what else can be done? The more powerful Hitler gets, the more danger he puts Germany in. When is the meeting?"

"In an hour."

Albrecht stood up and tugged on the gray blazer that hung on the back of his chair. "We should leave now."

The baron also got up. He locked the door with the twist of the latch.

Albrecht frowned. "What are you doing? An hour is not a great deal of time to get to Schultz's villa out in the country."

"We're not going there. The Brotherhood is betrayed."

Albrecht stared at him as if he'd been punched in the stomach. "Betrayed?"

"Yes, betrayed. Hitler's brownshirts are going to surround Schultz's villa and burn it to the ground. Whoever escapes will be beaten to death."

"How do you know this?"

"I have betrayed them. Wegner and I betrayed them."

"*You*?" Albrecht moved towards the door. "Don't spout nonsense, Gerard. If what you say is true, we must phone Schultz and the others immediately."

The baron thrust a hand against Albrecht's chest. "There will be no phone calls. Sit down."

"Are you mad? How else can we reach them in time?"

"We aren't going to reach them in time. That was the deal I struck with Wegner and Ernst Rohm, the leader of the *Sturm Abteilung*. The stormtroopers get the Brotherhood, I join the Nazi Party, and you and your wife and children stay alive."

"What?" Albrecht's face lost its blood. "I have not agreed to any such terms. Let me by."

"No."

The two men struggled, and Albrecht quickly pinned the older man to the wall. The baron quit struggling, and Albrecht stepped back and turned to unlock the door.

The baron struck him from behind with the butt of a luger pistol he'd pulled from his pocket. Albrecht fell to the floor, and the baron pointed the gun at him. "Stay there. Do not attempt to get up. Your wife and children are at risk, man. Think of them. It is open warfare on the streets between the Nazis and the communists. Scores have been killed. Do you think anyone will care about you or me or a dozen more at Schultz's home?"

With blood running down the side of his head, Albrecht glared up at the baron. "How could you do this? You of all people?"

"Survival. Mine, Eva's, yours, Catherine's, Sean's, Angelika's. Wegner was an infiltrator from the beginning. Once talk turned to actual plans for assassination, he told me in confidence that the brownshirts had marked all of us for execution. Because of my prominence as a member of the upper class, I was permitted to renounce my affiliation with the Brotherhood and swear allegiance to Adolph Hitler. I did that with the understanding that you and your family would be under my protection and not be harmed. You will not go to the villa to die tonight with the others."

"Eva will hate you for this."

"She already knows. Once I explained I was joining the elite of the Nazi Party and not the brownshirts she was in agreement. In fact, she has joined the League of German Girls, the young women part of the Hitler youth. That is where she is today...out of harm's way."

Albrecht sprang for the gun, but the baron struck him on the head with it again. The professor fell back against the desk before dropping to the floor.

"Enough of your heroics, Albrecht. Do I have to kill you to save your life and your family?" The baron could see that Albrecht was almost unconscious. Setting down his pistol on a chair by the door, he quickly removed his suit jacket, shirt, and dress pants. Underneath he wore black pants and a brown shirt with a red swastika armband, along with a black tie and black strap that ran across his chest from right shoulder to left hip. "This is in case Rohm forgets about the bargain. I am one of Himmler's SS, you see. Untouchable, really." He picked up the Luger again. "We'll remain here until I receive the phone call that the villa is gone and the Brotherhood finished with."

"How can you talk that way about our comrades?" groaned Albrecht.

"They were fools mostly, weren't they? Do you seriously think they could have pulled off the assassination? And even if they had, would that have helped Germany or hindered it? The time for killing Hitler was five years ago. Now he is our future. There is no one else who has his vision. What I am helping you do is imminently practical, Albrecht. We shall have to do away with your books, however. I am sorry for that. There were many good and patriotic chapters."

"Lord Preston will be furious with you."

"I expect he will. But he has the luxury of living across the Channel. You and I must make the best of things here. Support Hitler, that is the route to take. And we are taking it."

"Do you seriously believe Catherine will support this?"

"If she wants you and her children to live, yes. You know what the brownshirts are like, Albrecht. Wild dogs. They will catch you on the street and slaughter you all."

"Not the children."

"Oh yes, certainly the children."

"Even tonight...what you're allowing at the villa...there will be a storm of protests."

"There won't be. Right now large communist cells are being eliminated in Munich and Berlin. The villa will be one small part of the news tomorrow morning. More communists will be killed tonight than the tiny band in the Brotherhood. No, the greater slaughter will get the greater attention. Few will care about what happened to men who were planning to overthrow the government with bombs and bullets. Yes, that is the story that will be given out, my friend."

"Don't call me that. Don't ever call me that again."

"As you wish, but you have a poor way of thanking someone who kept you from being burned alive and your family shot."

"They would not have dared kill Catherine and my children."

"Certainly Rohm would have dared. Hitler already considers you an enemy because of your books."

"You are everything I have written against that is wrong with our country. You are the bad German who will lead us into more misery."

For the first time anger cut across the baron's face. "If there are bad Germans, you can lay the blame at the feet of the British and the French. The Treaty of Versailles was without grace or magnanimity to a fallen foe. It not only spawned Hitler but our need for Hitler. If worse comes to worse in Europe because of Hitler, the blood is on the hands of those who threw the German people in the dirt and ground them down under their heels."

There was a soft knocking at the door and then it opened. Catherine stuck her head through the opening. "Baron?"

"Yes, Catherine?"

"I'm sorry to interrupt your talk with Albrecht, but there was a phone call for you. The gentleman only wished to leave a message."

"Ah, yes. What was it?"

"*Deutschland uber alles.* That's all he said. Does that mean anything to you? He was a bit of an odd duck."

"Thank you, Catherine. I agree the man who called is indeed a strange one. But his message makes perfect sense."

"All right. We'll see you two in a bit." She closed the door.

The baron kept his hidden pistol on Albrecht and nodded. "The Brotherhood of the Oak no longer exists."

"I suppose it gives a man like you pleasure to say that."

"It gives me no pleasure at all, Albrecht. It was something that had to be done if Germany is to experience a resurrection."

Dover Sky

The motorcycle came to a stop and the rider climbed off.

"I'm looking for Lord Preston."

Lord Preston was sitting in the shade by the manor and brushing his three Belgian shepherds. "I'm Lord Preston, young man. Do you have a cable for me?"

"Yes, m'lord. It came to us marked highest priority so I was sent up from Dover at once."

"I see." Lord Preston got to his feet and took the telegram from the courier.

Lady Preston sat upright on the porch swing. "Is it from Jerusalem? Another baby, I hope."

"It's from Germany, my dear." Lord Preston gave the courier a five-pound note. "Thank you very much indeed." He watched the courier turn and leave before opening the telegram as the motorcycle roared off.

Lady Preston watched him battle the urge to ball the note in his fist once he'd finished.

"What is wrong, William? Is Catherine all right? Is it the baby?"

"Nothing is all right now. Nothing."

"Please tell me what the cable says."

He slowly turned to face her and read it aloud:

LORD PRESTON

THE BARON HAS BETRAYED US. HE PERMITTED STORMTROOPERS TO MURDER THE BROTHER-HOOD OF THE OAK WHEN THEY MET LAST WEEK. IN ADDITION HE HAS JOINED THE NAZI PARTY AND IS NOW A HIGH-RANKING OFFICER WITHIN HIMMLER'S SS.

MY FAMILY AND I ARE NOT IN DANGER AS LONG AS I FOLLOW THE NAZI PARTY LINE. FUTURE BOOKS I WRITE CAN ONLY DISCUSS THEOL-OGY PROPER NOT THEOLOGY AND POLITICS AND CERTAINLY NOT THEOLOGY AND HITLER.

I MUST WATCH WHAT I TEACH AT THE UNIVER-
SITY IN THE FALL. ALL THIS AND ADOLPH HITLER
IS NOT EVEN IN FULL POWER. THERE ARE GRIM
DAYS AHEAD FOR GERMANY. THE BARON CLAIMS
HE IS OUR PROTECTOR AND SAYS THAT IS WHY
NONE OF US WERE HARMED BY THE BROWN-
SHIRTS. HE SAYS WEGNER WAS A NAZI PLANT IN
THE BROTHERHOOD. WE HAVE SEVERED RELA-
TIONS WITH THE BARON AND HIS DAUGHTER.
EVA HAS JOINED THE NAZI YOUTH. I AM SORRY I
CANNOT SEND YOU BETTER NEWS.

ALBRECHT

Lady Preston left her husband and walked into the manor. Passing
Skitt, she asked if he'd seen Jane.

"I believe she's feeding the swans with Lady Caroline and Lady
Holly," Skitt responded. "Do you wish to speak with her?"

"I do."

"I shall go down to the pond at once."

"Send one of the footmen, Skitt."

He left through the front doors as if she hadn't spoken. Lady Preston shook her head and carried on up the staircase to her room. Sitting
at her reading desk, she pulled a large scrapbook towards her that she'd
been working on. The first page had fine gold script across its black surface: *Libby's marriage to Commander Terrence Fordyce, May 24, 1931.* She
lingered over the black-and-white photographs that followed, especially the ones of the baron posing with her and her husband, ones of
Eva linking arms with Jane. For a moment she felt she should remove
the pictures. She went to another set of photographs instead.

The gold script read, *Robbie and Shannon off to Palestine again with
Patricia Claire in October. I long for the day Robbie will be based in
England.* There were photographs of Robbie and Shannon and their
daughter at the dock, and others of the three of them walking up the
gangway, looking back at the camera. Several showed them standing
on the deck and waving.

"Too far away," murmured Lady Preston. "You three in Jerusalem. Catherine and Albrecht and Sean and Angelika in Germany. All of you too far away. All of you in danger."

She put a hand to her face and closed her eyes a moment. She prayed. Then she looked back at the scrapbook and turned pages until she found the picture she wanted. It took up an entire page and was mounted sideways. Tugging it away from the corners that held it in place, she glanced at the families standing on the lawn shoulder to shoulder: Caroline with Cecilia in her arms, Kipp beside her, arm around her waist, Matthew and Charles standing in front of them; Edward and Charlotte to their left, Owen sitting with two-year-old Colm in his lap on the grass; Emma and Jeremy with the twins, Peter and James, and their young son Billy; Victoria, Ben's arm around her shoulders, Ramsay and Timothy standing at attention and not smiling like everyone else; Catherine and Albrecht holding hands, Sean gripping his mother's other hand, Albrecht cradling Angelika in his free arm; Libby and Terry with Jane standing between the two of them, beaming, their hands resting on her shoulders; Robbie and Shannon and Patricia Claire at the end of the row, each of their faces darker than anyone else's, including Terry's. Behind all of them stood William and herself, as well as Harrison and Holly. At her husband's feet, unseen by the camera lens, were the three Belgian shepherds—Flanders, Poppy, and Charlemagne. Turning over the photograph she saw her handwriting in India ink: *All together in one spot at the same time. Miraculous.*

"I hope this happens again soon," she said out loud. "I don't know how, but soon, Lord."

"Grandmum?" Jane stood in the doorway, flushed from running in the summer heat. "Skitt said you wanted to see me and that it was important."

Lady Preston nodded and smiled. "Indeed, I do wish to speak with you, and yes, it is a matter of some importance, my dear. Please sit down in that chair there."

Jane took her seat. "Is something wrong? What did I do?"

"You didn't do anything, my dear Jane. Set your mind at ease about that."

"Then why do you have such a serious look on your face?"

"Because I have serious news to tell you. We just received a telegram from Germany."

"Oh…is the baby all right?"

"The baby is fine. It is something else. I want to say first of all that I am sorry, so very sorry, but you may not correspond with Eva von Isenburg anymore."

"Skitt, may I see you for a moment, please?"

Skitt had just stepped into the manor, humming under his breath, an engagement ring from a pawnshop in Dover in his pocket. Thoughts of meeting Montgomery that night by the pond and what he would say to her dominated his thoughts. He slipped into the small room Holly used as an office and smiled.

"How may I help you, m'lady?" he asked.

"Well, you're quite chipper, aren't you? I suppose a day off agrees with most of us. Please have a seat."

Still smiling, Skitt hitched up his pant legs and placed himself in a chair. "So what's this about then?"

Holly appeared reluctant to begin, glancing at a ledger open on the desk in front of her and tapping a yellow pencil against her teeth. Finally she turned to face the butler.

"We've had an amazing run at Dover Sky, Skitt. Almost ten years we've been using it as a year-round home for members of the Danforth family, and you've been butler for all of them. You've done an extraordinary job."

"Thank you, m'lady. It's hard to believe a decade has gone by."

"Near to it. An astonishing set of years. Marriages, births, the children growing like weeds. I'm sorry to tell you it must now come to an end."

"What's that?"

Holly met his gaze without enthusiasm. She turned the pencil around and around in her fingers. "Lord Kipp has purchased a home in London. He's had enough of only seeing Caroline and the children on weekends. We can't blame him, can we? It so happens Lord Edward has done the same. I imagine sharing a flat with his father whenever Parliament was in session finally wore thin. Both of them bought places within a few blocks of each other and of Jeremy and Emma, so they'll have a bit of a village going on amongst themselves."

"I see."

"It's much the same story for Commander Fordyce and Libby. He's weary of driving from Plymouth and Devonport whenever he has shore leave. He'd much prefer to have his wife and daughter closer to hand. It's true there are the four months he's in the Med each winter, but the rest of the time he's in British waters and would dearly love to be able to pop in and see his loved ones whenever the opportunity presents itself. He's in the process of securing a house near homeport. He wants Libby and Jane moved in by the time he returns from winter maneuvers in May. Montgomery, naturally, will move with them."

"Of course."

Holly half-smiled. "All of this is months away so far as Commander Fordyce and Libby are concerned. It's only September, and Libby and Jane shall be remaining here for the winter. However at Easter they will move into their new house. Once they're gone, any reason for Dover Sky to remain open year 'round is gone. Harrison and I will be returning to Ashton Park at summer's end next year, as will the rest of the staff. Tavy is senior butler at the Lancashire estate. We'd like to keep you on, but I'm afraid the only position available would be senior footman."

"Footman?"

Holly's face reddened. "I'm so sorry, Skitt. Both Harrison and Todd Turpin will be handling grounds at Ashton Park, so there's no opening there, I'm afraid."

"What about groundskeeper here at Dover Sky?"

"Ah, well, Fairburn is returning."

"What? Fairburn?"

"His services are no longer required at the estate where he was employed in France. He applied to return here to his former duties at Dover Sky some time ago, and naturally Lord Preston could not refuse."

Skitt stared at her. "Where does that leave me, Lady Holly?"

"You are a valued family servant, Skitt. We wish to see you employed here through the fall of 1933. Once the families have left and Lord and Lady Preston have completed their summer holiday, you will be released from your duties. Harrison and I shall remain until Fairburn arrives. If you don't wish to take up a position as senior footman at Ashton Park, perhaps you might wish to serve as assistant chauffeur or in some other capacity."

"Assistant? I expect I might find that a bit difficult, Lady Holly, after having been my own man for so long, so to speak."

"I well understand that, Skitt. If you wish to move on to another family, no one will think the worse of you for it. The Danforths will provide excellent references and assist you in finding suitable employment. Good butlers are worth their weight in gold. It would not be long before we found you another family."

Skitt cleared his throat. "Thank you, but there is the matter of Montgomery. We have reached an understanding, you see."

"Have you?"

"Well, I hope we have. I expect I shall find out soon enough. Has she been told about her move to Plymouth and Devonport in the spring, do you know?"

"I believe Libby spoke with her this morning."

"This morning?"

"Yes. Libby was at a loss to explain why Montgomery seemed down at the mouth with the news. What you've just told me makes her reaction perfectly understandable. I'm so sorry, Skitt, but there's no reason to keep Dover Sky open after Easter."

Skitt's mood hadn't improved by the time he made his way to the pond to wait for Montgomery. The moon was a thin slit cut by a silver blade, the stars like the small diamond in his pocket that he had half a mind to toss in the water. The September night was as soft as cashmere, yet his mind was jagged with ruined plans and a bleak future. When he saw Montgomery approaching silently over the lawn, he tried in vain to put a smile on his face and hold it. She took his hands and gazed up at him.

"You look absolutely shattered, love," she said. "It's good to see that."

"It's good?"

"I should have felt devastated to come down here and find you dancing a jig what with the news. I felt horrible this morning after Libby spoke to me. She was puzzled for I'm no better at hiding my emotions than you are. I told her it had nothing to do with her or Jane or the Commander. Honestly, I adore them. Don't be angry, but I had to let the cat out of the bag a bit. I said you and I had come to an understanding, and it would be difficult to have you at one place and me at another. Was it wrong of me to tell her that?"

Skitt let the air out of his lungs and shook his head. "Not at all. I did much the same thing. It changed nothing. I got her sympathy and little else. The Commander's household is too small to require the services of a butler."

"I shall go with you, Skitt, wherever you have a mind to go. I shall. Cheer up. We're not going to be separated."

"You can't let Libby down. They count on you to help them with Jane. She needs you. She'll be a young lady soon enough."

"There are plenty of English maids who can fit the bill."

"*Fit the bill?*" Skitt laughed. "You act and speak so much like one of us it takes a quaint expression like that to come along and remind me you're American. I love you dearly, Montgomery, but you can't let Libby and Jane down. You really can't. You might feel all right about it for a day or two, but then you'd think of Jane's tears and fall apart."

"I wouldn't, you know."

"You would, you know. Imagine if we got a letter saying Jane was having a rough go and was down in the dumps and they couldn't bring her out of it? Don't tell me you wouldn't feel it like a dagger to the heart. That's the sort of woman you are. It's one of the reasons you're a treasure. You can't abandon the Fordyces and trail after me to heaven knows where. It won't work."

She wrapped her arms around him. "Then what are we going to do? I might not be able to live without Jane, but I can't live without you either."

"I don't know. I swear I don't."

"What's in your pocket?"

"What d'you mean?"

"You keep playing with something. You won't even put your arms around me."

Skitt took his right hand out of his pocket and embraced her. "There. Will that do?"

"I'm not a chore, surely."

"I'm distracted by the day's events. Even Fairburn, the former groundskeeper who quit and worked for another family, warrants more attention than I do. They've rehired him as groundskeeper here."

"He doesn't warrant my attention!" She kissed Skitt on the lips and darted her hand into his pocket. They wrestled briefly, but she pulled away and ran off towards the water. She opened her hand, and the moonlight glinted off the ring. "Oh!"

Skitt watched her. "It's not much."

"Not much? It's adorable. I utterly love it." She smiled at him. "Who's it for? Norah Cole?"

"Don't be mad. You know who it's for. But what's the point?"

"What's the point?"

"We can't do anything about it. You shall go to Plymouth, and I shall wind up in northern Scotland or Wales or the Isle of Man, for all I know. I might as well be on the moon and you on Neptune."

"We'll work it out, my love."

"How?"

She came back to him and put the ring in his hand. "I don't care about *how* right now. I just want to receive my ring properly, that's all. If it is to be my ring."

"Of course it's your ring. There's no one I love half so much as you. But it's such a small thing...all I could afford."

"It's a great thing. I want to wear it with all my heart."

"Very well." Skitt turned the ring over in his hand and watched the wink of light hit the diamond. "I'm at a loss for words, really."

"Come on, Skitt. You can go on about rugby scores till everyone's asleep in their ale."

"Rugby scores are easy. It's just numbers. A beautiful woman is something else again."

"Well, that's a good start. Carry on."

Skitt put his hands behind his back. "I've asked for some help."

Montgomery looked around quickly. "From whom? Not Harrison."

"From William."

"What! Lord Preston?"

"I have it here." Skitt unfolded a piece of paper. "Shall I go ahead?"

"Yes, yes, go ahead. I'm going to die if we keep up this dance."

Skitt squinted and read the words slowly as one of the swans, waking up, flapped its wings.

> Let me not to the marriage of true minds
> Admit impediments. Love is not love
> Which alters when it alteration finds
> Or bends with the remover to remove
> O, no! It is an ever-fixed mark
> That looks on tempests and is never shaken
> It is the star to every wandering bark
> Whose worth's unknown, although his height be taken
> Love's not Time's fool, though rosy lips and cheeks
> Within his bending sickle's compass come
> Love alters not with his brief hours and weeks
> But bears it out even to the edge of doom
>
> If this be error and upon me proved
> I never writ, nor no man ever loved.

Montgomery smiled. "Wonderful. Your voice is perfect. And you did write it out, after all."

"So I did." Skitt brought the ring out from behind his back. "Your eyes flash just like it flashes, you know."

"Do they?"

"Black jewels. I've been fascinated by them ever since I first saw you years ago when you came to Dover Sky with Michael and Libby and Jane."

"Really?"

"They dazzled me. I used to have a fancy for Lady Catherine y'know. But not after I had a look at you."

"I'm astonished and flattered. But was it just the eyes that brought you to me, Skitt?"

"You know it wasn't. You have a beauty like a starry night, yes. But a spirit just as brilliant."

"Ah, now that's sweetly said. As good as anything from your friend William Shakespeare."

"I don't have anything else to add. Will you marry me, Montgomery?"

"You know I will."

She held out her hand, and he slipped the ring over her finger. It was loose.

"Arrr," he growled. "It doesn't fit proper."

She twined her arms around his neck. "There are ways to fix that."

"I don't want you fat. I love you exactly the way you are."

"I have no intention of getting fat." She ran her lips over his. "Enough talk. We're to be married. Let's kiss to that for the rest of the night."

Gloom descended on Skitt once again. "What good is all this, Montgomery? We can't do anything about it. How can we be married if we can't even live together?"

"You must pick up the habit from the Danforths. They seem to be very good at that sort of thing. The husband's in the one place and the wife's in the other. Like Ben in Africa and Victoria here. Or Kipp in Jerusalem and Caroline pining away for him at Dover Sky."

"I don't want to be good at that sort of thing. I want you in my arms every night."

"And I want to be there. Now no more of this." She began to plant short, sharp, fiery kisses on his lips and cheeks. "We shall be happy, you and I. Something will work out, my lovely man."

"I don't see how." But Skitt closed his eyes and responded to the sparks landing rapidly on his face and mouth with pleasant stings.

Terry showed up at Dover Sky the day before Guy Fawkes with bags of sweets and strings of firecrackers for everyone at the estate. As far as children went, with Caroline and Kipp living in London, only Jane remained, who at fifteen thought of herself as a woman, not a girl. Nevertheless, she grabbed candy and firecrackers with a squeal, popping the first in her mouth till her cheeks bulged and tossing the others all about her as they exploded overhead and in the grass.

"Skitt!" Terry called as the butler stood on the front porch of the manor. "Harrison is busy with pruning. Will you give me a hand with the effigy?"

He and Skitt, a rough tweed coat over his black and white uniform, stuffed large pants and a large gray coat with straw, filling both sleeves, as well as a tall hat that bulged to reveal a head with button eyes and a button mouth. Keeping Guy Fawkes upright with a long wooden pole they ran through his back and up to his neck, they placed him in the middle of a large mound of brush that Harrison had been collecting all week as he cleaned up hedges and groves and thickets.

"Do you think it needs anything else, Skitt?" Terry asked.

"Well, Commander, perhaps if we could find logs and some thicker limbs the bonfire would burn a great deal longer."

"Good idea. Let's fetch a barrow and see what we can find."

As Skitt pushed the barrow along, twice having to take it back from the naval officer dressed in corduroy pants and coat and shirt, Terry clapped a hand to his shoulder. "Libby tells me you're engaged."

"Yes, sir."

"That's wonderful news. Congratulations."

"Thank you very much, Commander."

"Now that you're settled on Montgomery and I'm settled on Libby, perhaps we can let the Catherine business go the way of the wind. What do you think, Skitt?"

Skitt's face quickly turned scarlet. "Lady Catherine was a young man's fancy and folly, sir."

"And I was the unwelcome rival."

More blood filled Skitt's cheeks and he kept his head down, pushing the barrow ahead with renewed vigor.

"I don't mind, Skitt. Lady Catherine is a fine woman. But I'm head over heels with Libby's ginger-blonde hair and ocean-blue eyes, just as I expect you can't get enough of Montgomery's shining black locks or flashing dark eyes."

Skitt couldn't keep himself from smiling. "Aye, there you have it, sir."

"I have a proposal for you. Once we're living close to the Royal Navy docks, I shall be entertaining considerably. Captains, commanders, leftenant commanders, commodores, even the odd admiral. There will be some busy seasons when I'm ashore. Too much for Libby to handle on her own, and Montgomery will have her hands full with Jane turning sixteen and seventeen and, eventually, twenty-one, Lord help us. What do you say? Is butlering that sort of crew something that piques your interest at all?"

"What, sir?"

"Do you want to work for me, Skitt? I could use you, and heaven knows I trust you with the lives of everyone in my family. You can think it over if you'd like, but I'll be shipping out in a couple of months and it would be nice to know how you feel about it one way or the other before the *Hood* weighs anchor after New Year's Day."

"Think it over?"

"Certainly. We're not going to be one of the large Danforth estates you're used to serving, but you'll still have a lot to look after, not to mention—"

Skitt dropped the barrow handles and seized the commander's hand, forgetting for a moment where he was and who he was. "With all my heart! With all my heart, sir. Montgomery and I shall be married and serve your family together with pride and distinction. It's a brilliant plan if you don't mind me saying so, sir. Absolutely brilliant."

Terry laughed and pumped his hand. "Why, then, the bargain is sealed...sealed and done. You're a Royal Navy butler come Easter, Skitt. A butler in the tradition of those who served Nelson and Rodney and Jellicoe, though I am a minnow compared to those leviathans. You shall have an outfit suited to your station—dark-navy trimmed with deep burgundy all set off by the crisp white of your shirt. How does that sound?"

"Capital, sir, capital! May I leave you for a moment? Only for a moment, mind. I must run and tell Montgomery. She is just on a walk with your daughter along the northern boundary of the estate. I must catch them up. I must tell her what's happened."

"By all means, go, man. Faint heart never won fair lady. Run as if your life depended upon it."

"I will do, sir. Thank you. Bless you!"

Terry saluted as Skitt vaulted the barrow and raced for the stone fence to the north of them. "England expects every man to do his duty!" he called after him.

British East Africa, Kenya

"May I open my eyes now, Ben? Honestly, we're not youngsters in the stables anymore playing our silly games."

"Just a moment. I have to position you just so. There. All right, Lady Victoria, you may take a good look."

She opened her eyes to a tall mountain peak rising out of the jungle and grasslands white with snow at its summit. She put her knuckles to her mouth.

"My heavens, Ben! How high is that?"

"More than 19,000 feet—almost four miles."

"It's magnificent. I never expected something like this. And what are those beasts moving across the fields? Not giraffe?"

"What other creature has such a long neck?"

"I'm amazed. Utterly shocked and amazed. Have the boys seen this yet?"

"Not at all. They've been with the bishop—Stevenson. He's introducing them to some of the African children. I wanted us to look at Mount Kilimanjaro together."

"Kilimanjaro. What a beautiful name. What does it mean?"

"I've heard so many stories about that: mountain of caverns, mountain of whiteness, mountain of greatness. I prefer mountain of greatness."

"Of course you would."

He put his arm around her. "Though calling it mountain of whiteness ties in with the name Whitecross much better."

"Can it be climbed?"

"It can. One day we shall do it. For now it's good to gaze at it and to think of God and give thanks."

She leaned into him and took his hand. "Only you would do this. Only you would bring me here. I didn't want to come to Africa even though I acted as if I did. I didn't want another 'Ben Whitecross and God' adventure that involved airplanes and skies and dangers known and unknown. But now I'm so grateful. This is a spot of extraordinary beauty. And truth be known, I feel much safer here than I did back in Europe and England."

"Really? Why do you say that?"

"That Hitler fellow taking over as chancellor of Germany. Dad's in a flap about it and his old friend Baron von Isenburg joining the Nazi Party. Mum is terrified and wants Catherine and Albrecht to get out of Germany with Sean and Angelika before something happens."

"What's going to happen?"

"I don't know, really, but everyone is expecting something to blow up. I hate all the rumors and gossip. Nasty memories of when I was young and the Great War started: you disappearing to the Western Front, Folkestone being bombed, and Mr. Seabrooke getting killed. I feel much safer here among the lions and gorillas and snakes actually."

Ben laughed. "I'm glad to hear it. I must thank Herr Hitler for his part in making Kenya so amenable to you. Half my battle's won because he's created such a threatening environment in Europe."

"Don't joke, Ben Whitecross. The Europe situation leaves me with an ugly feeling."

He kissed the top of her head. "Don't worry, Vic. Nothing in the world is going to happen. Europe and Germany and Britain will sort themselves out like they always do. We already had our world war and no one wants another. So while the great leaders of the great nations huff and puff and move pieces about on the checkerboard, you'll be here serving God and gazing at Kilimanjaro every morning and evening. Think of the sunrises and sunsets on that peak. Think of how it will bless Ramsay and Tim to live in a magical world with magical beasts far from the English rains and fogs."

She smiled. "When you put it that way it fills me with peace. I never thought Africa could do that."

21

May, 1933
Germany

Ten-year-old Sean Hartmann locked his fingers around Albrecht's hand. "I don't feel comfortable with you going to Berlin, Papa. I feel like Herr Hitler is watching you whenever you set foot out of Tubingen."

"I am not so important, son. No one is wasting time putting binoculars on me, I assure you. But I promise to watch what I say at the university. There will be no politics, no rants, no roars."

"You roar like a lion at the dinner table."

"The dinner table is a German man's pulpit, podium, and lecture hall. But there the roaring stays. What I do at the table, I will not do at the university. Don't fret. Instead pray and, of course, while I'm away you must take care of your mother and baby sister. Especially your sister. She is almost three and gets into everything. And she wanders off! Angelika will go out the door and walk all the way to Berlin to see the tigers at the zoo if you let her."

Sean laughed. "I won't let her, Papa. I'll watch her like a hawk."

"That's my knight. What color is your horse today?"

"Still dapple gray."

"A good color. Ride well. Make sure the sword is large enough. Nothing less than a two-handed broadsword will do."

"That's what I have. Don't be afraid for your family, Papa."

A cable arrived for Albrecht as he kissed Catherine and Angelika goodbye. He placed it in his coat pocket and pulled it out to read as the cab darted in and out of traffic on its way to the train station.

> ALBRECHT
>
> WHETHER YOU READ THIS OR NOT ONCE YOU SEE IT IS FROM ME I DO NOT KNOW. I IMPLORE YOU TO BE CAREFUL ABOUT WHAT YOU SAY AT HUMBOLDT UNIVERSITY. BERLIN IS BERLIN AND NOW THAT HITLER HAS COMPLETE POWER ARRESTS AND DEPORTATIONS OCCUR DAILY. THIS INCLUDES ACADEMICS SUCH AS YOURSELF. THEY KNOW WHO YOU ARE. THE GESTAPO WILL MOST CERTAINLY ATTEND EACH OF YOUR GUEST LECTURES. DO NOT GIVE THEM ANY EXCUSE TO REPORT YOU. THINK OF YOUR WIFE AND CHIL-DREN. STAY WITH TOPICS LIKE THE ATTRIBUTES OF GOD AND THE VIRTUES OF THE CHRISTIAN LIFE.
>
> WHETHER YOU BELIEVE IT OR NOT I REMAIN YOUR FRIEND AND GUARDIAN. HEIL HITLER.
>
> GERARD

On the train to Berlin, Albrecht opened a newspaper that summed up and praised the events of the twenty-third of March, the day the *Reichstag* passed the Enabling Act. It gave Hitler and his Nazi Party broad, sweeping powers. "All for the good," the paper crowed. "Look at how well off the nation is six weeks after the fact."

"So Goebbels, minister of propaganda," murmured Albrecht so other passengers couldn't hear him, "tell me why dictatorship is better than democracy."

The article didn't immediately weigh in on why a strong man at the top was the best form of government. Instead it printed parts of

Hitler's speech on the day the Act was passed and he became absolute ruler of Germany:

> By its decision to carry out the political and moral cleansing of our public life, the Government is creating and securing the conditions for a really deep and inner religious life. The advantages for the individual that may be derived from compromises with atheistic organizations do not compare in any way with the consequences that are visible in the destruction of our common religious and ethical values.
>
> My Government will treat all other denominations with objective and impartial justice. It cannot, however, tolerate allowing membership of a certain denomination or of a certain race being used as a release from all common legal obligations, or as a blank check for behavior that is difficult to punish, or for the toleration of crimes.
>
> My Government will be concerned for the sincere cooperation between Church and State.
>
> My struggle against materialistic ideology and for the erection of a true people's community serves as much the interests of the German nation as of our Christian faith.
>
> The national Government, seeing in Christianity the unshakable foundation of the moral and ethical life of our people, attaches utmost importance to the cultivation and maintenance of the friendliest relations with the Holy See.
>
> The rights of the churches will not be curtailed; their position in relation to the State will not be changed.

Why, Herr Hitler, Albrecht thought as he folded the newspaper and put it away, *"you have become a theologian."* He watched the trees and fields and towns slide past. *We must meet and write a book together on the German Jesus. What would he look like, I wonder? Would he wear a swastika or a cross?*

Humboldt University, Berlin

Albrecht always liked walking up to Humboldt University by cross-
ing the large plaza to its front and taking in the stately buildings and
columns and statues. But something had changed. He'd expected to
see the Nazi flags with the swastika draped over government buildings
around Berlin. He didn't expect to see them flying from flagstaffs on
the university campus. Nor did he expect to see students wearing swastika armbands or faculty members giving one another the stiff-armed
Nazi salute. With a tightness in his stomach, he made his way to the
office of the head of the Faculty of Theology.

"Dr. Mueller," Albrecht said as he bowed his head and offered his
hand, "it is good to see you again."

"Ah, Professor Hartmann." The large man, a head taller than
Albrecht and twice as heavy, pushed himself away from his desk and
rose to grip Albrecht's hand. "I'm glad you arrived safely. How are you?"

"I'm very well, Herr Doktor. How is your wife?"

"Splendid. I trust your wife and children are in good health?"

"They are, thank you." Albrecht set down his briefcase and unwound
the red scarf from his neck. "I was surprised to see the university had
become so...politicized."

"Hmm? Oh, you mean the flags. There is a cultural event tonight.
Goebbels is giving a talk as well. The student body is quite excited
about it. So is the faculty, truth be told."

"But these are Nazis, Dr. Mueller. They are not in support of free
thought or free speech."

"They are our legal government, professor."

"Why the armbands? Why the Nazi salute?"

Dr. Mueller smiled. "You have been around students long enough
to know how quickly they jump on bandwagons and rally around
causes."

"And their teachers?"

"The salute is Roman in origin. Jacques-Louis David's *Oath of the
Horatii* inspired it, I suppose, based on what he knew of Ancient Rome.
No doubt that is why the Italians are so comfortable with it."

"Excuse me, Herr Doktor, but few faculty members should be comfortable with that salute. Many of them have read Hitler's *Mein Kampf.* You have read it. You told me when it came out that it was the worst thought the German mind could produce."

Dr. Mueller's face grew rigid. "I never said that."

"I have it in a letter."

"Then I ask you to destroy that letter. I was in error when I wrote it."

"Dr. Mueller—"

"Professor Hartmann, the Nazi Party is our legal government. Adolph Hitler is our greatly esteemed leader. There will be cultural events at universities across the nation tonight that are inspired by good Nazi ideology and theology. I trust you will linger long enough after your evening lecture to take part in ours. Now, let me escort you to the lecture hall where you will be giving your first talk at the top of the hour. Heil, Hitler!"

"Hitler is a high school dropout, Herr Doktor. He has always despised deeper thought and intellectuals. And his stormtroopers are even worse. How many of them have had a university education? They scorn us."

"Heil, Hitler!"

Albrecht retorted, "Hail, Caesar!"

"What!"

Albrecht hesitated and then responded in full. "Hail, Caesar, we who are about to die salute you."

Mueller's eyes almost spat fire.

Albrecht smiled. "Merely an academic exercise, Herr Doktor. *Ave Caesar, morituri te salutamus.* Weren't you just talking to me about Ancient Rome?"

Mueller brushed past Albrecht on his way to the door and into the corridor. He marched ahead of his guest to the lecture hall. When they arrived, Mueller took Albrecht's arm. Dozens of students were already seated and waiting. Two men in black leather coats sat at the back.

"You see the police are here, Albrecht. The *Gestapo*," Mueller warned in a low voice nodding slightly toward the back row of seats. "Be careful what you say, professor, or you will find yourself arrested and taken somewhere far away. We've already lost several members of our teaching staff. Play the Nazi game, and you will weather the storm. If you remain ramrod straight and self-righteous, the winds of change will surely break you. I shall meet you for supper. Heil, Hitler."

"Jewish professors, Herr Doktor? Jewish colleagues? Are they the ones the Nazis have purged from among you?"

"Heil, Hitler."

"Friends like Mandelbaum in chemistry and Goldstein in physics? And you let them? You did nothing?"

"I say again, 'Heil, Hitler.'"

Albrecht could not resist. "Hail, Mary."

Mueller stared at him in shock.

Albrecht continued. "*Hail Mary, full of grace, the Lord is with thee. Blessed art thou among women and blessed is the fruit of thy womb, Jesus. Holy Mary, Mother of God, pray for us sinners now and at the hour of our death.*"

Mueller snapped his head away. "We will skip the formal meal with the faculty. You can see yourself out after your last lecture this evening. Don't expect any visits from the other professors. Associating with you puts us all at risk." He turned and walked quickly from the room.

A spirit rose in Albrecht he refused to quell. He greeted the students as he arranged his notes at the podium by saying, "You know, I am going to change my lecture altogether. I have a sudden inspiration to forgo my scheduled talk on the historical Jesus and to examine the "Mary Prayer," which I'm sure you are all well acquainted with. '*Ave Maria, gratia plena, Dominus tecum. Benedicta tu in mulieribus, et benedictus fructus ventris tui, Iesus. Sancta Maria, Mater Dei, ora pro nobis peccatoribus, nunc, et in hora mortis nostrae. Amen.*'"

He spoke for an hour, took the numerous questions that came his way, bowed when the students applauded, and remained at the podium for the next lecture as the first group of students left and a new class made their way in. He looked toward the back and noticed the police hadn't moved. Both were still in their seats. The dark-haired one was scribbling rapidly in a black notebook.

His second lecture was on Paul's letters to the Corinthians, and

Albrecht emphasized the chapter on love. The third lecture Albrecht had entitled "The True Cross," and it centered on the sacrifice of Jesus at Calvary. At the end of the lecture, he compared the broken cross of the swastika with the unbroken cross of Christ. By the time he gave his final talk, it was dark. He lectured on one line from the gospel of John: "He then having received the sop went out immediately. And it was night."

The police left when the last few students finished speaking with Albrecht. They didn't look his way or say a word.

The dining hall was deserted and there wasn't much left to purchase when Albrecht arrived, but he was able to get a hot bowl of cabbage soup, a large portion of rye bread, and a wedge of hard cheese, along with a cup of coffee. Shouts and singing filtered into the hall from outside, and he asked a waiter what was happening.

"A cultural event, sir," the waiter responded. "You would be most welcome to join in, I'm sure."

Albrecht finished his meal and went out to the plaza. The first thing he saw was a bonfire in the middle of the large, open space. It was surrounded by thousands of students and stormtroopers singing Nazi marching songs. He spotted Mueller tugging a cartload of books from the direction of the library, laughing with two *Gestapo* who were helping him—the same men who had taken notes at the lectures. Albrecht thought they were going to set up a display in the plaza. To his horror, once the men reached the bonfire, students grabbed the books and hurled them into the flames. Mueller and the police officers helped them.

"You heard Reich Minister Goebbels!" Mueller shouted. "No to decadence and moral corruption! Yes to decency and morality in family and state!"

The students cheered and then began to chant. Albrecht saw a large microphone from a radio station being adjusted so listeners at home could hear the chant clearly. Trucks pulled up with cargoes of books that the students and professors took up by the armload and threw into the heart of the fire.

"Destroy the un-German spirit!"

"Cleanse the nation! Cleanse the universities! Cleanse our blood!"
Singing erupted again.

> We will continue to march,
> Even if everything shatters;
> Because today Germany hears us,
> And tomorrow, the whole World.

> And the elders may chide,
> So just let them scream and cry,
> And if the World decides to fight us,
> We will still be the victors.

> They don't want to understand this song,
> They think of slavery and war.
> Meanwhile our acres ripen,
> Flag of freedom, fly!

> We will continue to march,
> Even if everything shatters;
> Freedom arose in Germany,
> And tomorrow the world belongs to it.

No sooner had one song finished before professors and students
and stormtroopers began to thunder out another.

> Germany awake from your nightmare!
> Give Jews no place in your Empire!
> We will fight for your resurgence!
> Aryan blood shall never perish!

> All these hypocrites we throw them out!
> Judea leave our German house!
> If the native soil is clean and pure
> We united and happy will be!

To the swastika, devoted are we!
Hail our Leader, Hail Hitler to thee!

Students rushed by Albrecht loaded down with books. He grabbed one of them and shouted, "What are you doing? Think of what is happening here! This is a great university! Do not tear it down in one night!" Volumes spilled from the youth's arms. Albrecht saw the names *Helen Keller, Albert Einstein,* and *Victor Hugo* on the spines.

The youth cursed and punched Albrecht in the face so hard he staggered backwards, clutching his briefcase. Then the student knelt, scooped up the books, and ran towards the fire.

"I will deal with this!" seethed Albrecht. He headed towards the blaze. "Before God, I will stop this!"

A young woman dressed completely in black seized his hand. "Do not fight them, Professor Hartmann. They are wild enough to throw you into the flames along with the books."

He tried to shake his hand free, but she held it with a grip like iron.

"What are you doing?" Albrecht raged. "Let go of me! I do not fear them!"

"You should fear them. They are many, and you are but one."

He looked at her gray eyes, blonde hair, and tense face. "I can make them listen."

"No, you can't. Not unless you are Goebbels or Himmler or Adolph Hitler himself. You have family, don't you? A wife and children? Do you want them all to be picked up by the *Gestapo?* They have already done it to other teachers here in Berlin—and not all of them were Jews."

She released his hand. He could still feel the pressure from her strong fingers.

"Write us another book instead," she told him. "You will have to publish and distribute it in secret, but it will eventually find its way into all corners of Germany. People will read it. Fight the Nazis that way… and the professors who have forgotten what they represent."

"Who are you?"

"My name is Stefanie Brecht. Write the book for me, if for no one else."

She vanished into the dark. He couldn't tell which way she'd gone. He turned back to the fire. His mind much calmer, he walked towards the sheets of flame. Thousands were singing the Nazi songs now. The plaza was full.

"*Our Father which art in heaven,*" he prayed under his breath. The winds of the fire sent pages whirling into the night, along with ashes and sparks. One after another flew over Albrecht's head or landed at his feet. He stopped and picked up several. He recognized names of American writers such as John Dos Passos, F. Scott Fitzgerald, and Ernest Hemingway, along with British writers Rudyard Kipling, D.H. Lawrence, and H.G. Wells. There were German writers too—Erich Maria Remarque and his novel *All Quiet on the Western Front*, Bertolt Brecht and his *Threepenny Opera*, and the Austrian psychoanalyst Alfred Adler's *Understanding Human Nature*. A page from Tolstoy's *War and Peace* lay across his shoe.

The man next to Albrecht bent down for a sheet curled from the heat, muttering that he had his hands on a piece of Franz Kafka rubbish. Albrecht made a sudden decision to get away from the plaza. He kept his head down as he passed some SS officers whose eyes glittered like fire stones. A number of charred papers were scattered over a hedge, speared by the sharp points of the pruned branches. He plucked several free that were stuck together and glanced at them as he made his way through the crowds and off the campus.

"Heinrich Heine's play *Almansor*," he said out loud. Reading over the pages one after another in the streaks and flares of light, he dropped each on the pavement once he was finished. Near the bottom of the last page his eyes caught a phrase he went over twice. Three SS men hurried past him towards the bonfire, coming from the direction of a bookstore that had all its windows shattered. The men's arms were crammed with books. Albrecht's quick glimpse revealed that several of the volumes were titled *Mein Geist*. Albrecht saw a photograph of his face on the back cover of one and quickly looked away. He placed the charred sheet from Heine's 1821 play into his coat pocket. The words he'd noticed ran through his mind like a line of fire as he made his way through traffic and across roadways, getting further and further from the red-and-black flames:

"*Das war ein Vorspiel nur, dort wo man Bücher verbrennt, verbrennt man auch am Ende Menschen.*"

He wanted to remember to tell Catherine about this so he mentally translated the words, "*That was only the beginning. Where they burn books, in the end they will burn people.*"

22

July, 1933
The English Channel, near the Port of Dover

> *Push off, and sitting well in order smite*
> *The sounding furrows; for my purpose holds*
> *To sail beyond the sunset, and the baths*
> *Of all the western stars, until I die.*
> *It may be that the gulfs will wash us down:*
> *It may be we shall touch the Happy Isles,*
> *And see the great Achilles, whom we knew*
> *Though much is taken, much abides; and though*
> *We are not now that strength which in old days*
> *Moved earth and heaven; that which we are, we are;*
> *One equal temper of heroic hearts,*
> *Made weak by time and fate, but strong in will*
> *To strive, to seek, to find, and not to yield.*

"Capital! You still remember it!"

"I remember all of Ulysses by Tennyson, Grandfather. But I have another surprise for you."

Lord Preston put his hand on Owen's shoulder as the eleven-year-old steered the yacht. "Steady there, steady. You have a surprise, do you? And what is that?"

"Are you ready for it?"

"'The sun is shining, the ship is heeling to port and responsive to the helmsman, fair stood the wind for France. Fire away.'"

Owen's red hair blew straight back, dark with wet where sea spray had struck. Owen kept his blue eyes focused straight ahead as he recited a different poem:

> *Whither, O splendid ship, thy white sails crowding,*
> *Leaning across the bosom of the urgent West,*
> *That fearest nor sea rising, nor sky clouding,*
> *Whither away, fair rover, and what thy quest?*
> *Ah! soon, when Winter has all our vales opprest,*
> *When skies are cold and misty, and hail is hurling,*
> *Wilt thou glide on the blue Pacific, or rest*
> *In a summer haven asleep, thy white sails furling?*

Lord Preston laughed. "Aha! Well done, Commander! I don't think I know the piece, but it's full of salt water and sails, isn't it? Who wrote the poem? How did you come by it?"

"Dad gave it me. It's called 'A Passer-By' and a dead man named Robert Bridges wrote it."

"Dead, was he? Well, he did remarkably well for a dead man."

"There's more to it, but I haven't memorized all of it yet. Except for the ending."

"Let's hear it then. If it's a good ending that is, one full of hope and promise."

"It is a good ending, Grandpapa. Look at those gulls swoop!"

"There's a school close to the surface. Carry on, Commander."

> *And yet, O splendid ship, unhail'd and nameless,*
> *I know not if, aiming a fancy, I rightly divine*
> *That thou hast a purpose joyful, a courage blameless,*
> *Thy port assured in a happier land than mine.*
> *But for all I have given thee, beauty enough is thine,*
> *As thou, aslant with trim tackle and shrouding,*
> *From the proud nostril curve of a prow's line*
> *In the offing scatterest foam, thy white sails crowding.*

"Extraordinary! "*A purpose joyful, a courage blameless, thy port assured in a happier land than mine.*" Let us hope he is right, Owen, and the ship he sees has all that. Let us hope you and I and *Pluck* have it. Let us pray our whole family has it!"

"Aye, aye, sir."

Lord Preston looked out over the whitecaps in the Channel as the yacht cut through the hard-blue of the water. The poem Owen had recited, especially the last lines, made him think of his far-flung family. He wondered about their courage, their joys, and their situations in the places where they'd settled and called home.

He had an image of Robbie and Shannon sitting with their daughter under a grove of palm trees in Jerusalem. Robbie was in his uniform, Shannon in a pale-yellow summer dress, Patricia Claire in shorts and a light, white cotton shirt. Patricia was playing in the dust. Around the three of them stood great stones of the great city thousands of years old. Almost as old, he sometimes thought, as civilization. And the dust that whirled in the hot winds seemed as old as the human race itself.

Another image came but this time of Victoria. Victoria and Ben with zebra running nearby because of lions. And there were Ramsay and Tim, growing tall and dark under the African sun, watching the zebra and the lions, their eyes keen and sharp and clear. Young Tim pointing beyond to the fine line of the horizon, where sky and earth touched at an edge slim as a thread of gold. The elephants were moving slowly there, tall, majestic, silhouetted against the long brightness.

Catherine and Sean and Angelika at the castle on the Rhine and at the chateau in Pura, Switzerland, were next. They were far from the turmoil in Germany, from the marches at night and the burning torches, Albrecht joining his family in the mountains, red scarf about his neck, papers under his arm, pen in hand. He was writing, writing, with Catherine reading each page and tracing each line of script with her finger.

Libby and Jane at the Channel, like he and Owen were, watching the mighty *Hood* steam in and out of port, gulls streaming over its wake. Terry was on the deck at attention and smiling as his family waved. Their lives were solid and sure and impenetrable, strong as dawn over the Atlantic, ribbed with steel like a battle cruiser's hull slipping over the long, grey depths.

Dover Sky stood basically empty but for a few summer days. Ashton Park was empty but for Elizabeth, Holly, Harrison, and himself. Jeremy and Emma in London with their twins Peter and James and their little brother Billy at play in streets and alleys and on patches of grass. Edward and Charlotte a block away, with Owen and Colm running with their cousins—not under palm trees or African skies or the ramparts of German castles, but in the shadow of Big Ben and the Tower of London and Buckingham Palace, still free, still unharmed. Kipp and Caroline with them all, and their children Matthew, Charles, and Cecilia growing as tall and straight as any of the others, books and schools and pencils and the rumble and rattle of cars and lorries and motorcycles, roadways teeming with traffic and people, sunlight coming through cracks between the high buildings of stone and brick finding them, lighting on them, blessing them.

"We have come this far, I thank God," Lord Preston murmured as a wave split in two over the bow. "We have come this far, and we are still together. We have lost some but not all, praise God. Not all. The Lord has granted us a future. I see it just there like I see the coastline of France."

"What did you say, Grandfather?" asked Owen. "Do you want me to come about?"

"Just indulging in a little of my own poetry, Commander. No, carry on to Calais. We'll sup with French fishermen this evening."

"Are we really going all the way to Calais?"

"It is only twenty-five miles…but perhaps not. Your grandmother would have a fit if we didn't return in time for high tea. Still, carry on! We won't come about just yet."

"Do you have a poem for me, Grandfather?"

Lord Preston thrust his hands in the pockets of his peacoat and whistled between his teeth, drawing the flying clouds and blown spume into him along with his breath and all the colors of the sea. "I do! It's from the Bible—Psalm 19. Mind the wheel and take these words to heart, my sailor."

"I shall, Grandpapa."

*The heavens declare the glory of God; and the firmament
        showeth his handiwork.*

*Day unto day uttereth speech, and night unto night
        showeth knowledge.*

*There is no speech nor language, where their voice is not
        heard.*

*Their line is gone out through all the earth, and their words
        to the end of the world. In them hath he set a taberna-
        cle for the sun,*

*Which is as a bridegroom coming out of his chamber, and
        rejoiceth as a strong man to run a race.*

*His going forth is from the end of the heaven, and his cir-
        cuit unto the ends of it: and there is nothing hid from
        the heat thereof.*

*The law of the LORD is perfect, converting the soul: the testi-
        mony of the LORD is sure, making wise the simple.*

*The statutes of the LORD are right, rejoicing the heart: the
        commandment of the LORD is pure, enlightening the
        eyes.*

*The fear of the LORD is clean, enduring for ever: the judg-
        ments of the LORD are true and righteous altogether.*

*More to be desired are they than gold, yea, than much fine
        gold: sweeter also than honey and the honeycomb.*

*Moreover by them is thy servant warned: and in keeping of
        them there is great reward.*

*Who can understand his errors? cleanse thou me from secret
        faults.*

*Keep back thy servant also from presumptuous sins; let
        them not have dominion over me: then shall I be
        upright, and I shall be innocent from the great trans-
        gression.*

*Let the words of my mouth, and the meditation of my heart,
        be acceptable in thy sight, O LORD, my strength, and
        my redeemer.*

If you enjoyed *Beneath the Dover Sky*, watch for
Book 3 in the Danforths of Lancashire:

LONDON DAWN

Coming January 1, 2014

ABOUT THE AUTHOR

 **Murray Pura** earned his Master of
Divinity degree from Acadia University in Wolfville, Nova Scotia,
and his ThM degree in theology
and interdisciplinary studies from
Regent College in Vancouver,
British Columbia. For more than
25 years, in addition to his writing,
he's pastored churches in Nova
Scotia, British Columbia, and
Alberta. His writings have been
shortlisted for the Dartmouth Book Award, the John Spencer Hill Literary Award, the Paraclete Fiction Award, and
Toronto's Kobzar Literary Award. Murray pastors and
writes in southern Alberta near the Rocky Mountains. He
and his wife, Linda, have a son and a daughter.

Visit Murray's website at
www.MurrayPura.com

For more information about Murray Pura
or other Harvest House books, visit
www.HarvestHousePublishers.com

The Wings of Morning

Lovers of Amish fiction will quickly sign on as fans of award-winning author Murray Pura as they keep turning the pages of this exciting historical romance set in 1917 during World War I.

Jude Whetstone and Lyyndaya Kurtz, whose families are converts to the Amish faith, are slowly falling in love. Jude has also fallen in love with that new-fangled invention, the aeroplane. The Amish communities have rejected the telephone and have forbidden motorcar ownership but not yet electricity or aeroplanes.

Though exempt from military service on religious grounds, Jude is manipulated by unscrupulous army officers into enlisting in order to protect several Amish men. No one in the community understands Jude's sudden enlistment and so he is shunned. Lyyndaya's despair deepens at the reports that Jude has been shot down in France. In her grief, she turns to nursing Spanish flu victims in Philadelphia. After many months of caring for stricken soldiers, Lyyndaya is stunned when an emaciated Jude turns up in her ward.

Lyyndaya's joy at receiving him back from the dead is quickly diminished when the Amish leadership insist the shunning remain in force. How then can they marry without the blessing of their families? Will happiness elude them forever?

The Face of Heaven

In April 1861, Lyndel Keim discovers two runaway slaves in her family's barn. When the men are captured, Lyndel and her young Amish beau, Nathaniel King, find themselves at odds with their pacifist Amish colony.

Nathaniel enlists in what will become the famous Iron Brigade of the Union Army. Lyndel enters the fray as a Brigade nurse on the battlefield, sticking close to Nathaniel as they both witness the horrors of war—including the battles at Chancellorsville, Fredericksburg, and Antietam. Despite the pair's heroic sacrifices, the Amish only see that Lyndel and Nathaniel have become part of the war effort, and both are banished.

A severe battle wound at Gettysburg threatens Nathaniel's life. Lyndel must call upon her faith in God to endure the savage conflict and face its painful aftermath, not knowing if Nathaniel is alive or dead. Will the momentous battle change her life forever, just as it will change the course of the war and the history of her country?

Whispers of a New Dawn

The year is 1941 and Jude and Lyyndy, with their adult daughter, Rebecca, are summoned to far-off, exotic Honolulu where Rebecca, a flyer like her father, meets a likeable young pilot. The two enjoy a friendship that seems to be turning into something more serious.....until Sunday, December 7, 1941 dawns on the Hawaiian Islands. Readers who love the simplicity of the Amish, a good romance, and a dramatic historical setting are in for a treat with *Whispers of a New Dawn*.